César
and Augusta

By the same author

Fiction

ALL THE SAME SHADOWS
THE GUILT MERCHANTS
THE GIRL IN MELANIE KLEIN
ARTICLES OF FAITH
THE GENOA FERRY
ONE.   INTERIOR.   DAY

Biography

SIR DONALD WOLFIT C.B.E.
His life and work in the unfashionable theatre

Screenplay (and introduction)

ONE DAY IN THE LIFE OF IVAN DENISOVICH

To Graham & Joanna
with much love

César
and Augusta

RONALD HARWOOD

[signature]

March 1978

SECKER & WARBURG
LONDON

First published in England 1978 by
Martin Secker & Warburg Limited
54 Poland Street, London W1V 3DF

Copyright © Ronald Harwood 1978

SBN: 436 19119 9

Printed in Great Britain by
Richard Clay (The Chaucer Press) Limited
Bungay, Suffolk

for Natasha

because this is a love story

La vie est un songe ... nous veillons dormants et veillants dormans.

Life is a dream ... we waking sleep and sleeping wake.

Essais, II, xii
Michel Eyquem de Montaigne

THREE LETTERS

'What an admirable teacher of composition he was!'

Vincent d'Indy

FROM CAMILLE SAINT-SAENS TO
AUGUSTA HOLMES:

168 rue du Faubourg Saint-Honoré
Paris 1er
2nd February 1875

Astarte!

My *song* was booed not you and if the composer does not mind why should the singer? No, I am not that insensitive. I understand that it was more awful for you having to stand there and receive the whistles and catcalls and hisses. I am concerned, because I know how impulsive you are, that your desire 'to change your *entire* life' is somehow prompted by that one bad experience to which I unwittingly contributed. Divine girl, you are a divine singer and you must, will sing again. But I accept your assurance to me after the concert that you are determined. I promised to help, and help I shall.

I have thought about your problem. You said to me so passionately – and how beautiful you are when you are passionate – you said: 'I want to be a composer, a *serious* composer.' By that I suppose you mean you want to be *taken* seriously. Very well. Then you must study, study, study. You have talent. You need discipline (not your strongest point), and knowledge. Both may be acquired. My advice, therefore, is to go to a teacher who understands composition and can impart his understanding at the highest level. So, if you are in earnest, and really do want to be 'a serious composer', then there is only one man I can confidently recommend: César Franck.

Do you know about him? I think you may have met him at a Société concert or at one of my Monday evenings and I know he is not the most dazzling man to meet, to put it mildly. He is Organist at Sainte-Clothilde (and a fine organist, too, second only, in my opinion, to me) and is Professor of Organ at the Conser-

3

vatoire where he is not a huge success, again to put it mildly. He is fifty-three or -four, a failure as a composer (awful sanctimonious religious works, *awful*) but, and it is an enormous but, he is a first-class teacher of composition and takes on a few private pupils who treat him like a saint. (That sweet soul Duparc is his student and that austere bigot d'Indy, whose mouth waters every time he looks at you, is another.) Franck is, in fact, a very eccentric fellow who seems much older than his years. I find him very comic: you can see him walking from one end of Paris to the other, dressed in the fashion of thirty years ago, chattering away to himself. Socially, he's a terrible bore but a dear bore if you know what I mean. (On my Monday evenings he always sits with Maman and the two get along famously.) All this apart, he is able to impart his knowledge, an unusual gift in one who has failed in a creative art.

As to what tactics you should employ, I suggest you write to him, nothing extravagant, Augusta dear, just a simple straightforward letter enclosing an example of your work. Use my name. If he gives you an interview *do not* wear one of your 'plungers'. Dress like a nun. Wear the highest neckline in your wardrobe. Do nothing to shock him. He leads a very quiet, respectable life and is a person of stern moral character. So is his wife. You will not succeed if you flirt with him as you do with everyone else. Of course, he may not want a young woman in his class at all, and from what I've written you may decide you do not want to be quite as serious a composer as all that. If such is the case we will think again.

Oh, Astarte, let us meet soon. Let us go again to the forest of Fontainebleau as we did before the war. Let us be together. Alone.

You know my feelings,

Camille

P.S. Like you, Maman was very upset by the boos. She fainted, but is now fully recovered thanks to Romain who has been an angel.

C

FROM AUGUSTA HOLMES TO CESAR FRANCK:

11 rue Mansart
Paris
February 1875

Dear Monsieur Franck,

On the advice of many friends whose opinions I value, I am sending you herewith three of my most recent compositions in the hope that you will find them promising enough to consider me as a member of your private composition class.

I am twenty-three years old and French born despite my name; as far as musical composition is concerned I am self-taught. I have, for the most part, followed the profession of singer and in that capacity have been engaged several times by the Société Nationale de Musique. As a matter of fact, we have met at the Société's concerts and at one of Camille Saint-Saëns' Monday evenings, but I have no doubt you will not remember me. I want, most of all, to pursue a *serious* musical career.

Yours sincerely,
Augusta Holmes

FROM CESAR FRANCK TO AUGUSTA HOLMES:

95 boulevard Saint-Michel
3rd March 1875

Dear Mademoiselle Holmes,
    Thank you for your letter and for sending me the three pieces which I return herewith. I remember you well. You are a dramatic soprano.
    Your music is very picturesque. The songs have a distinctly operatic – one might even say heroic – flavour, and perhaps your vocation lies in a theatrical direction. Your compositions are, in my opinion, superior to those of the Vicomtesse de Grandval, the only other lady composer whose work I have had the opportunity of hearing.
    My composition class is full at the moment and I do not see a likelihood of a vacancy in the near future.

Yours sincerely,
C. Franck

PART ONE

'We were all a little in love with her. Not one of us wouldn't have wanted to make her his wife.'

Camille Saint-Saëns

Before rising he lay in the dark with his eyes closed; he did not need to open them to know it was five o'clock and time for his waking game: could he feel the dawn, smell the chill, taste the damp? But what could he hear? To his sorrow, silence. He murmured aloud, Thank you O Lord for giving me life this day, and repeated the prayer in the language of childhood: *Gott ich danke Dir*. He knew he must hurry, but did not move, did not throw off the bedclothes, reach out to light the candle, flounder for slippers and gown. He did not move. He thought: blessed are the meek for they shall inherit the earth – tenor or baritone? Down the passage he heard the maid trying to lay his tray quietly – nothing so loud as the overcareful clatter of one cup on one saucer. He thought: I must hurry.

Like a patient nervously awaiting anaesthetic he screwed tight his eyes as though to help shut out all terrors, but the terrors were all within and the darkness intensified them. The world outside meant little to him; he lived on an interior plane scarred with shadows and the shadows, like all shadows, were black and silent. Beyond the darkness of his own making, through the window which he kept open in all weathers, there was rain or snow or wind – he could not tell which, and did not care – the sound of his own breathing, the maid now filling the copper kettle like a horse urinating, a creaking floorboard – was the Actress turning in her sleep? – but inside: silence, in his head, silence, a rush of silence, an empty cave of wind, the flapping of butterfly wings, a massive crushing silence. And always in these minutes of summoning energy to embark on the mechanical motions of life, he understood in a painfully simple way that he had unknowingly brought the silence upon himself, a separation of thought and feeling, of mind and soul. Yet, he did not despair. He rose each day in the hope that there would be sound again, sound to split his skull. He thought: rejoice and be exceeding glad; for great is your reward in heaven.

9

He was fifty-three years old and it was late. He knew he must hurry. For the moment, he was doomed to listen to emptiness.

Rising, performing his daily act of faith, his hopefulness was rewarded then: in swinging his legs off the bed, feeling the floor beneath his feet, sitting upright, placing his hands beneath his buttocks for warmth, a sound came, a great swelling, not the organ, not violins, not brass, but sound, pure, perfect, yet a muslin shroud, dead in the moment of birth. Always at rising: a sound that refused to be captured, an accompaniment to the stirring of his senses, so brief, so transient, so triumphant and sensuous, so unlike any sound he had ever heard or imagined that he questioned each dawn reality itself. Then, the awful recession, the diminuendo, the passing again into silence.

He drew aside the bedroom curtain an inch and peered out like an inquisitive neighbour. In the light of his candle he saw his own reflection, the window panes obscured by harp-strings of rain, and the silhouettes of the two poplars in the small square garden at the rear of the apartment building. The sky was black. In the bathroom he prepared to shave, splashing cold water over his face, soaping his upper lip and chin – his cheeks, to well below the jaw line were covered by sideburns, pre-commune, wiry, grey almost white. The quarter struck as he cut himself above his Adam's apple and he smiled benignly at the gout of blood, thinking, well, at least there's proof of life, proof he had blood in his veins; perhaps this would be a day to remember.

His face echoed the silence: peaceful, calm, untroubled; a round and unremarkable face, the bushy sideburns adding to its width; eyebrows bushy, too, the eyes timid, almost hidden; nose prominent, chin receding, mouth sensual, expression seraphic. He did not like his face, believing he looked like an unreliable clerk. Wiping off the soap, he winced at his own reflection, pursing his lips as though a discord had been struck. 'E flat,' he said aloud, 'E flat,' and turned to find his clothes neatly laid on the bentwood chair with rotting cane seat and scratched varnish. His trousers were too short, his frock-coat too long, his velvet cravat worn and shiny. Dressed, he decided he not only looked like a clerk, but also was a clerk, a recorder, a notator, nothing, nobody, no one. Next door the bed creaked. The Actress was awake. The bell tinkled. 'E natural,' he said. A discord certainly.

'Who are you?' he asked, entering his studio.

'I'm Arlette, monsieur. I'm new,' the maid answered, looking up startled, placing the coffee tray on his work table at right-angles to the piano. 'Madame is awake.'

'Yes, I know,' he said, pleased to come upon someone unexpected, and thanking God that his eyebrows hid his eyes: the maid's breasts were huge, her dress too low for decency and domestic service. Bending over, in the simple act of depositing his tray on the green baize, her breasts looked as if they would fill his coffee cup, overflow, spill like thick cream on to the tray. He asked God's forgiveness: blessed are the poor in spirit.

'Will there be anything else, monsieur?'

'Nothing. Thank you,' except I'd like to squeeze and kiss your breasts, if I may. Would you mind? How sweet you are, how kind. He bit his lip and cursed his inability to control his imaginings; he cursed himself for being prey to these obsessions. Why, why did he become so obsessed? Breasts were the worst, but by no means all: a sensual mouth, an ankle indelicately revealed, a heady perfume, rich, quiet laughter, even the measured removal of a glove from a lily-white hand could plunge him into wild, remorseless fantasies. Buxom women on the omnibus, a slender student at the Conservatoire and, more than once, God help him, two pious members of his choir in Sainte-Clothilde took possession of his mind. For a day, two days at most, thoughts of these creatures would plague him. He would sit cross-legged. He would confess to a priest. The danger would pass. But to have one of these obsessions in the house, a maid – the idea was intolerable.

Even as he sat he had already decided to tell the Actress she must get rid of this new girl, Arlette – but what would he say? That her breasts disturbed him? That it would take him ten minutes to compose himself before he was able to compose his music? The Actress would play the angry tigress, tell Georges, and then mother and son would go on and on and on, humble, humiliate and enslave him. Future imperfect: as if they needed the excuse of Arlette's breasts to torture him.

Arlette said, 'Are you sure you won't have a fire this morning, monsieur?'

A kindly girl. He would have to say she was clumsy. 'Quite sure. Thank you,' he said.

'No fire?'

He did not feel the cold: such ice within needed the heat of the sun. Or Arlette's breasts. All was not dead. 'No. No fire.'

'Breakfast at half-past seven, then, monsieur?'

'In two hours, yes, thank you, precisely, always at half-past seven.' He could say she was talkative. E natural again, a flurry of demi-semi-quavers. 'Madame wants you,' he said.

Alone, staring forlorn at the blank music staves before him, he sipped the hot, black coffee thick as ink, and, as always at this moment before lifting his pen, he allowed the memory of Claire to intrude, a memory he had clung to, or which had clung to him, for almost thirty years, as though to evoke her and to create were somehow mysteriously related.

The memory, like all else in his life, was repetitive. The image which forever sprung into his mind was isolated, petrified, a composite scene remembered among countless others forgotten or suppressed, but there Claire was at the piano, he beside her, a touching of hands, fingering corrected, her voice an excited whisper, 'But you're engaged, Cousin César-Auguste, to Cousine Félicité,' a cheek of embarrassed crimson, the licking of dry lips, hands crossing, the little fingers adjacent on the B flat, Andante, Haydn, *Il maestro e lo scolare*, the fifth variation, tears, 'Oh, I love you, César-Auguste, I do love you.' And he felt a familiar, welcome stab of pain and of warmth. Each morning of his life, for the past thirty years, he recalled her frightened confession, knew that nothing had come of it except the agony of their separation, accounted himself guilty of cowardice, smiled crookedly with regret and shuddered at the realisation that no one else, not his mother or his father, not his wife or his children, no one but Claire had ever said to him those words, I love you.

He lifted his pen, dipped it in the ink, heard unaccountably his father's voice crying, 'Swine!' and reflected that even the dead tormented him. He tried to warm his hands around the cup that had held Arlette's breasts, delayed another five minutes before turning to the pages on the table, to Christ's Sermon on the Mount.

Six years before he had begun and was now struggling with

12

the Fifth Beatitude: *Blessed are the merciful: for they shall obtain mercy*. Had he taken so long, he wondered, because he dared not confront the Sixth? *Blessed are the pure in heart: for they shall see God?* He opened the manuscript to the last completed page, read what he had written the previous morning and was neither pleased nor disappointed. The process he was about to engage was mechanical: his pen crawled along the lines, dotting and crossing, but he was strangely absent from the music he wrote, as though he had set up an algebraic formula, shape and tone dictating a natural, imperative solution. He did not dare interfere with the method, afraid that the silence he heard upon waking would infect even this mundane, technical habit. He imagined the music, the orchestra, the choir, the voice of Christ, yet did not feel it, as though he confronted not a living being but an ectoplasm. Such music he could write endlessly, knowing it expressed his mind not his heart: that distance again, that separation. Could not art and life be conjoined? *Pardon your brethren*, sang the voice of the Saviour. He paused a moment, dipped the pen, examined the nib as though there he might find revelations, and considered this Christ of his making: pietistic, sentimental, sanctimonious, over-righteous. Yet, knowing this, try as he might, he could not change the image. Why, he wondered, had he nailed himself to a ginger-bread cross? He could remember, in his youth, a Christ within him of such savagery, a barbaric, marauding compassionate Christ, black-haired, wild-eyed, clothed in a loin cloth holding out His pierced hands for all to see the dripping blood. What strident, uncompromising chords of pain and joy that Christ had sounded, but no more, as if He, too, had been struck dumb.

The pen ran dry; again, he dipped it in the ink and continued to write, giving voice to the Christ he questioned, knowing that some would call the music glorious, beautiful, pure, clouds pierced by sunshine, but longing all the while to hear again that lost strain which had grown and died the instant he placed his bare, calloused feet on the wooden floor.

For the two hours he laboured, he was conscious of every second passing. He had known a time when it had been different, when to begin work and to end were lost in the same moment, when the act of creation smashed time, rendered hours meaningless.

13

Two hours have passed, three, four – had they? had they? It seemed as if he had only just begun. But not now; now, the seconds hobbled. Why? What had happened, he wondered?

When had the change taken place? The day he had walked out on his father? Surely not: never had he felt so free, so impudent, so powerful. Every man needs at least one act of rebellion, and every artist many. No; the withering process had been slower. When he married, perhaps? Perhaps. He had exchanged one tyranny for another. Must he rebel again? He shivered; he knew he no longer had the strength or the courage for such an act, for, all the qualities and resources needed to alter his present state required blind faith in the possibility of creation, and that he no longer possessed. He was condemned, he believed, to carpentry.

Was the Actress listening now, was she at the door, at the keyhole, listening? He turned to the piano, struck chords, fingered the theme he hoped would be understood as Charity, as though the act of giving was sad and sorrowful and somehow unresolved: the B natural left you wondering whether there was more to give. Was she there suffering her disappointment, hoping for something jauntier and jollier, hoping for Offenbach or Meyerbeer instead of this mystical nonsense? He played the theme again. She won't like that, he thought. Charity was not her most outstanding virtue.

'What was that theme?' Félicité asked.

They sat at their round dining-table, a diameter apart, she in a tent of velvet and lace, wearing a mob-cap to hide her unbrushed hair; taller than her husband, thinner, sharp, châtelaine eyes, long, thin, prying nose, fidgety hands, blue veined. 'César, I asked you what the theme was?'

César dipped his croissant into the coffee, tilted his chin to catch the drops and stuffed the delicious pastry heavy with butter and jam into his mouth. 'Charity,' he said, chewing.

'Charity? It sounded unfinished.'

'No, I don't think I can do more to it.'

'It's not what I call tuneful.'

'It's not meant to be. It's meant to express the act of giving.'

'But the act of giving isn't incomplete. If you give something it's over and done with. It doesn't hang in the air. You should *think* more about these things, Franck. Discuss them with Georges.

Now, he has *real* intelligence, an immense intellect. The theme should have a proper ending. You ask Georges. I'm sure he'll agree with me.'

Georges was clever, he had to admit; a penalty to have a son cleverer than the father. César's thoughts flew to his younger son, Germain, altogether softer and gentler, who used, as a little boy, to play truant from school but was always to be found on the platforms of the Gare Saint-Lazare or the Gare du Nord, watching the comings and goings of trains; he was far away now, diligent in the department of bridges and footpaths, still a devoted servant of the French Railways. César missed him and, in giving way carelessly to longing, memories he hoped to censor plagued him, despairing memories of Marie-Joseph and Paul dead, between them four years of life. Even after a quarter of a century, he loved his lost children deeply, as though their frailty had demanded compensation. His grief had been so overwhelming, it ran the risk of turning to injustice towards the living: those who remained were not so good by nature, not so bright in mind as those he had lost. Perhaps the silence had begun then.

Félicité said, 'What was all that rumbling in the bass?'

Rumbling, how dare she. 'That's meant to be a hubbub,' he said.

'A what?'

'The chorus. They're rebellious. Mad for vengeance.' He took another croissant, tore it apart.

'Why are they mad for vengeance?'

'Because Our Lord has turned away His face.'

'And that's made them rebellious, has it?' She burped loudly, then, angered, looking at him as though he had been the offender.

'Very rebellious,' he said, spreading the jam thickly.

'You must speak to Georges about that, too. I'm not sure it sounds absolutely right.'

'I want to give the impression of crime and violence in the world,' he said.

'But you know nothing about crime and violence. I believe that's what's wrong with it. You imagine too much and know too little. Bring it out of yourself, Franck, bring it *out*. Let there be *drama*, a good deal of *drama*.' She rang the bell, F sharp in the dining room. 'Allegory is a very difficult business,' she said.

The Beatitudes are not allegorical, he wanted to say. A piece of croissant fell into the coffee cup and he fished it out with a spoon. Arlette entered to clear the table. He glanced sideways at her: she was carrying her breasts on the empty tray like an offering. 'Would monsieur like more coffee?' she asked.

'No, no, no, no, no, no,' he mumbled a dozen times or more, 'no, no, no, no, no, no, no, no.'

'It appears monsieur doesn't want more coffee,' the Actress said in her actress voice. 'You may tidy up.'

When the table had been cleared of plates and breasts, César said, 'A silly girl.'

'Who?'

'The maid.'

'Silly?'

'Talkative.'

'She'll learn.'

Tell her to dress in a more seemly fashion. Tell her not to squeeze her tits into my coffee cup. 'I expect so,' he said, resigned to unworthy thoughts, staring at his pale, distorted reflection in the polished walnut table on which Félicité now drummed impatiently with her bony fingers. She was not yet finished with him.

'This theme,' she said, 'this – Charity. I hope and trust, Franck, that it is not to be cyclic.'

Oh God, but life is cyclic, isn't it? Themes like thoughts and action repeat themselves over and over again. Everything is cyclic. Life isn't written in three movements, allegro, adagio, presto, with three separate themes. Life is continuous and repetitive; the themes, the patterns recur. Look at us, for God's sake. *We* are cyclic, the same theme infecting youth, middle-age and, no doubt, senility. 'I haven't decided yet.'

'I advise strongly against it,' she said. 'The public want to be entertained as well as educated. You must sugar the pill. Give them as many themes as possible, Franck. Pretty themes. The public don't want to listen to the same old thing repeated, unless, of course, it's an aria in an opera they may want to hear again for its beauty. Avoid this cyclic nonsense.' He slid back his chair, about to rise. She said, 'And the dedication? Have you decided on the dedication yet?'

Her question conjured up a petrified collage from the past: he remembered clenching his fist and banging in fury piano keys to make insouciant discords. Alone, in a room in his future father-in-law's house, César in torment, trapped: engaged to Félicité, loving Claire. And she him. Claire loved him. The door opened. Félicité's father, the actor Desmousseaux, a delightful kind man, capable, they said, of success in any profession except, unfortunately, the one he had embraced, asking, All well, César-Auguste? What was that noise? All that banging? Are you all right? Then, then César knew now he should have said, I love Claire, adore her, I cannot marry your daughter, I want to marry your niece, Claire Féréol, release me from this pain. The tableau was replaced by another: a copy of his song *The Angel and the Child*, dedicated, 'To Mlle F. Desmousseaux, in pleasant memories'. And scoring out the words to write, 'For Claire'. How else could he declare his love? How else was he to express the purity and innocence and depth of his feeling? Had he cried I love you from the rooftops of Paris he could not have been more explicit. And had Claire been intrigued or flattered or alarmed to find a song in her hands with her name replacing Félicité's? And the other songs, *Robin Grey* and *Le Sylphe*, 'To my cousin Claire' and even 'To My Dear Cousin Claire', signed CSRGSTFRNCK? Had she understood? No. But Félicité had understood.

'Have you decided on the dedication yet?' she asked again, drumming her fingers faster, horses galloping.

Oh, Claire: everything I write is for you. He said, 'If it's worthy, my dear, it will be yours,' grasping, avaricious bitch, God forgive me.

The drumming ceased. Wearily, she said, 'Will you ever be finished?'

'With what?'

'*The Beatitudes*, of course.'

'Ah yes, it's a slow process, isn't it?'

'And even when they're done, what will be the reward?'

'The beauty of the music, I hope.'

'You're an innocent,' she said, looking away.

'And God's grace, perhaps.'

'You're naïve.'

'I'm late,' he said.

'Don't forget Georges is coming for lunch. You're to be back at one o'clock sharp.'

'Yes, my dear.'

'And don't forget tonight.'

'Tonight?'

'Monday,' she said solemnly.

'Monday?'

'Camille!' she cried, full voice, patience stretched to breaking-point.

'Oh yes, Camille. Monday evening. I'm not sure I want to go.'

'You will go. You never know who'll be there. And if you see anyone from the Opéra, be nice. It costs nothing to be nice. Let it be known that you are considering writing an opera –'

'But I'm not –'

'– that you would like their opinion, their help. Flatter them. They love flattery and it costs nothing.'

'I never know anyone at Camille's,' they're all so smart, so fashionable, so clever and cultivated, what do they want with an obscure church organist?

'Simply go up to people and speak to them. Introduce yourself. Work into the conversation what you've done, who you are –'

Who am I?

'– tell them your name. Everyone knows you're Organ Professor at the Conservatoire, they respect that. Use your position. There's no need to be timid, Franck –'

But I am timid –

'– no need to mumble and stammer. If you think you're important, they'll think you're important. And, remember, if they ask what you're working on, say it's an opera –'

No one ever asks, they know I've run dry –

'– and don't mention *The Beatitudes*. It puts people off, all that saintliness.'

'Yes, my dear.'

'And Franck.'

'Yes, my dear?'

'Don't forget your umbrella.'

'No,' I never forget my umbrella.

'I mean don't forget to *use* it. There's no point in carrying an umbrella over your arm and getting soaked.'

'No, of course not, no, no, no.' He hurried to the door.

'And Franck.'

'My dear?'

'Don't hurry. You always arrive everywhere too early.'

Stepping out of the apartment door into the small garden, he wondered whether the conversation had taken place or whether he had only imagined it: perhaps they had sat in silence.

2

Paris glistened. The boulevard Saint-Michel glistened. César emerged from the front door of his ground-floor apartment into the small garden where the two leafless poplars offered no shelter from the incessant, chill drizzle. The garden was at the rear of the large, white building; César trotted down the path at the side, into the gravelled forecourt, passed through the open wrought-iron gates out into the boulevard. He turned his face to the sky, rather as northerners do to catch the sun, and smiled; soon, his face also glistened. Then, taking hold of himself, he turned right, and set off at a fast pace down the broad avenue lined with plane trees which made more marked the downward slope to the Place Saint-Michel and the bridge across the Seine.

He loved Paris as only a foreigner can love a city he'd dreamed of living in since childhood. Provincial Liège was a light year away. César never failed to sense the excitement of the great metropolis as he began each morning his walk down the boulevard. Paris was, he'd been told by the well-travelled, a small city, a village, close-packed, its energy concentrated, so he spaced the lessons he had to give to allow himself time to walk from one end to the other, occasionally resorting as though defeated to an omnibus, but walking mostly, more than walking, running. He loved the bustle, especially at this moment of setting off, becoming part of an immense awakening when he was seized with a feverish longing for motion, a desire to go faster, faster. The shops were open, the workmen in their blue smocks had marched from the outskirts and been swallowed up; the last of the working women – florists, dressmakers, milliners, cleaners – chattered and giggled, late for work. The office workers, blowing for warmth into cupped hands or chewing one-sou rolls, followed on; young men, tight-suited, tired and sleepless, yawned on their way to catch up the older, wiser, conscientious ones. This was the city, the capital he had wanted to conquer and still wanted to conquer, wanted somehow to belong to these lives that scurried down the boulevard, wanted to belong to the tumble-down buildings with their tiled roofs, and to the great town-houses and hôtels, to the glorious domes and bridges, to the churches and the theatres and libraries and concert halls and to the cafés and to the broad, humming boulevards and avenues. But foreigners never quite belong; he hurried on in hope.

Opposite the Luxembourg Gardens César met the postman. They exchanged their usual warm greeting. César, being a man who lived in expectation of change, looked to the postman as a benign messenger of the gods, but this man, whose name César did not know but with whom he had conversed each morning for ten years, was no Mercury: burly, plodding, bass-baritone, with a luxurious two-pronged beard that reached below the collar of his overcoat and covered the top brass button.

'Don't you think, monsieur, you should put your umbrella up?' the postman said.

'But yes, of course, yes, of course I should,' César said.

'You're soaked already.'

'Am I?'

'Drizzle's somehow more wetting than rain.'

'Yes, I expect it is.'

'Here, let me help you.' The postman rested his heavy bag on the wet pavement, took the umbrella and opened it. 'There you are.'

'How kind, how very kind. Anything for me?' César asked like a child expecting a present.

The postman smiled indulgently, a special smile reserved for the infirm and the insane. 'Now you don't want to read your letters out here in the rain, do you?'

'If you held the umbrella–'

Resigned, the postman reached in his bag and found the letters for No. 95. 'You really ought to let me deliver to the house, you know. You'll be doing me out of a job.'

How many times had the postman said that, César wondered? In rain, in snow, in sunshine and in wind. The postman took the umbrella and held it over the pair of them. A cart sped by, spattering their trousers. 'I don't do this for all my customers,' the postman said.

'I know, I know and I'm very grateful,' and we've said that a good few times, too.

'Anything interesting this morning, monsieur?'

Bills, circulars, and a large envelope addressed in a thick, strident hand. 'Do you mind if I open this?' César asked.

'Why not, it's for you,' the postman replied patiently, taking out his pipe and sucking on it.

César tore open the envelope and slid out a music manuscript, a score, a song, the setting of a psalm, 114, 'When Israel went out of Egypt, the house of Jacob from a people of strange language.' A wave of disappointment washed over him: there would be no change today. And the music too, disappointed him. Holy, holy, holy, César thought: why won't they leave me alone? How do they find me? Composer unknown: Hermann Zenta. Wagnerian, César feared, with a name like that, definitely Wagnerian. Heavy brass, he guessed, and a letter:

Maître!

They tell me you are the best teacher in Paris, perhaps in Europe. I wish to be your pupil. I shall be diligent. Enclosed is my setting of the psalm *In exitu*. Since I have not yet arranged for myself accommodation in Paris, there is nowhere you can write to me. Have no fear. I shall contact you.

I am, dear maître,
Your would-be disciple
Hermann Zenta.

Raindrops caught the corner of the page. César said, 'Yes, a Wagnerian, I fear.'

'A what?' the postman asked.

'The word "disciple": that's the clue. Only a Wagnerian would use a word like that.'

The postman squinted at the envelope. 'It's a Paris postmark,' he said.

'Is it? Is it? There you are. An infection.'

The postman took back the letters and the larger envelope, continuing the ritual. 'Shall I push them through the box just the same?' he asked.

'Please do.'

'Don't forget your umbrella.'

'Oh, thank you.'

'And don't walk too fast. You'll slip.'

'I have to hurry.' César always said that; now, the postman's turn.

'I never hurry. A good steady pace, that's what you learn in this job. Nice and steady, you get there just the same.'

'The brass must be used sparingly,' César said.

'I'll remember.'

'Not too much brass,' he added after a moment, but the postman had already disappeared through the large wooden doors of No. 63.

'Maître!'

On the Pont Saint-Michel, Emmanuel Chabrier called to him. The two huddled together under the single umbrella. 'You look well,' Chabrier said, cheek to cheek.

'Do I, my boy? You don't look too bad either.' César loved Chabrier: fat and jolly, young and scurrilous, irreverent and ebullient; not a bad amateur pianist though he thumped too hard, but his compositions had a certain tone. César said, 'This is the first time I've seen you at this hour of the morning for more than – how long? Six months? A year?'

'No, maître. Three weeks. I've only been away three weeks.'

'Have you? Been away? I thought you worked at the Ministry of the Interior.'

'I do.'

'Well, how can you get away? Government officials can't just go away, can they?'

'Maître, I'm a clerk not a government official. I told my

22

superior my mother was ill in Auvergne. He's a very understanding man.'

'I am sorry. How is she?'

'She's dead. She's been dead for six years. I told my superior a lie.'

'Oh, I see, a lie! I see.'

Chabrier began to whistle tunelessly. César glanced at him out of the corner of his eye: he was up to something, César knew by his expression, like a mischievous cherub. Chabrier continued to whistle – slyly, César thought – and César, as was his custom when conversation seemed to have floundered, smiled and knit his eyebrows feverishly as though they were keeping time to an orchestra that took everything too fast. Then, too casually Chabrier said, 'I've been to Bayreuth –'

César's eyebrows were stilled, the smile erased. 'I must be on my way,' he said.

'Wait a moment, maître, let me tell you –'

'I don't wish to know –'

'I met him –'

'Met him, did you, well, I suppose if you insist on going to Bayreuth –'

'Shook his hand –'

'Shook his hand, did you, well, of course, if you met him –'

'Maître, keep the umbrella still. I'm getting wet. We talked –'

'I must be off.'

'Let me tell you what he's up to –'

'I don't wish to know what he's up to!'

'I'm sorry, I didn't mean to upset you, maître –'

'Poison!'

'What?'

'Nothing.'

'I thought you said poison.'

'I did.'

Like dancers uncertain whether the music had finished, they hesitated. César watched Chabrier to see if he could detect a wicked twinkle in the man's eye. He knew and enjoyed Chabrier's games.

'Before you go, maître –' Chabrier began.

'Yes, but quickly, quickly, I'm late –'

23

'All right, I'll walk with you.' But César did not move, so nor did Chabrier. The fat man asked, 'Have you been to the Opéra recently, maître?'

'No.'

'Why not come backstage with me one night this week?'

'Backstage? Me? Backstage at the Opéra? Me?'

'One of the corps de ballet is Spanish. Juanita is her name. Thighs of thistledown.'

'Please! Have some respect!'

'We could ask her to find a friend for you, maître. We could take them out to dinner. No one would know.'

'Will you please hold your tongue! You know I disapprove of such conversation,' César said, noting that Chabrier smiled and understood why: César's cheeks had flushed, his lips quivered, the pulse in his forehead beat twelve–eight.

'Thighs, maître, and the dearest little bum which twitches when she walks.' Chabrier demonstrated, taking a few steps, feet turned out, waddling like a haughty duck, then resumed the shelter. 'And the other night when she bent to tie her shoes, her bodice fell away just enough for me to see her exquisite little titties –'

'You must stop! I am Professor of Organ at the Conservatoire!'

But Chabrier continued with exaggerated intimacy. 'And for a ballerina she's not badly endowed. Usually they're as flat as table-tops, but that's because of the exercises they do. I always tell them what they need is regular massage. That's where we pianists really come into our own. Well, what do you say? Shall we watch an opera from the wings? Juanita's her name. From Andalusia.'

César did not respond, but observed the raindrops slipping off the umbrella on to the pavement. At last he said, 'Terrible about Bizet. Only thirty-six. And so sudden. Well, I have to hurry. Remember me to your mother. I hope she's up and about soon.' And when César turned his back on Chabrier he allowed himself to smile: venery and Wagner, so very predictable, the fat man's favourite subjects. But then, César remembered and called, 'Emmanuel! Emmanuel!'

Chabrier came bustling back.

'Tell me, my boy, have you ever heard of a composer called Zenta?'

24

'Zenta?' Chabrier repeated in an awed whisper. '*Hermann Zenta?*'

'You know him?'

'Don't you, maître?'

'Never heard of him until this morning. Had a letter from him.'

'You had a letter from Hermann Zenta?'

'I've just told you –'

'Is – is Hermann Zenta here in Paris?' He pronounced the name with solemn respect.

'Evidently.'

'May I ask, maître, why he wrote to you?'

'He wants to join my composition class.'

'Zenta wants to join your composition class?'

César was irritated by Chabrier's astonishment. 'Yes,' he said tetchily, 'that's what I said.'

'Well, I'm amazed.'

'Why?'

'That Zenta should feel the need for lessons.' He shook his head, baffled.

'We are talking about the same Hermann Zenta, aren't we?' César said. 'Heavy chords in the brass.'

'There's only one Hermann Zenta.'

'Well, I've never heard of him,' César said.

'Never heard of Hermann Zenta?'

'Emmanuel, will you please stop repeating everything I say!'

'I'm sorry, maître, it's just that Zenta, I mean, well, Zenta!'

'I don't move in your exalted circles,' César said icily. 'I don't go round shaking hands with people in Bayreuth.'

'Even so, maître, Hermann Zenta. You'll accept him, of course.'

'I haven't decided yet. I've only glanced at one piece, a psalm, I haven't yet met the man. How old is he?'

'I'm not certain, early twenties, I should say.'

'You've met him?'

'No, not actually met him, but I've seen him about.' Chabrier fixed César with a deep, intense stare. 'Maître, I consider Zenta the most audacious, talented, original young composer in Europe.'

'Well, I shall certainly give the boy serious consideration, though

25

I must say my first impression does not coincide exactly with your opinion.'

'No?'

'No. Audacious and original are not words I would use.'

'What, then?'

'Poison,' César said, turned abruptly and walked away, setting off on his zig-zag course half across the city towards the Conservatoire of Music in the rue Bergère, and while he trotted along, still holding his umbrella aloft long after the drizzle had ceased, he thought with affection of Chabrier, liked him despite his unreliable musical opinions. César would make up his own mind about Zenta, although he might seek advice from Duparc who had a good nose for real talent; not d'Indy. D'Indy was too high-minded, too severe, too narrow to spot gifts unless they echoed his own. But César took pleasure in Chabrier's company for other than professional reasons: Chabrier was the only one to treat him like a human being and not like a holy statue. What had he done, César wondered, to inspire such reverence in others? He believed himself not to be austere or saintly, yet, even to his face, some had said goodness shone from him. If only they knew, if only they knew how rooted to the ground he was, how earthbound. People were blind; and deaf. They thought his music holy, inspired, ethereal: they hadn't the wit or the ear to discern that he had not given entirely of himself, had not surrendered to his talent, had not acknowledged the complexity of his own nature, and inexplicably could not. What, César wondered, if he were to shout in the street his secret that he, a composer, hears nothing but silence, that he cannot harmonise soul and mind, cannot bring his life into his art, or his art into his life, what would they see if he confessed he suffered pain because of it? Put him away, they would cry, we have a lunatic in our midst! And yet, he reflected glancing at the passers-by, and at the faces in café windows pressed at the glass watching him, every one of them, he supposed, had within them their own silence of one kind or another; who was he to complain? Alas.

Passing the church of Saint-Eustache reminded him that sins must be forgiven: he confessed Arlette's breasts to an elderly curé, but not the obsessive memories of Claire. He confessed, however, his encouragement of Chabrier's conversation and caused some confusion: the old priest, a counter-tenor with phlegm, said, 'You sound too old to be a ballet dancer,' absolved him all the same and gave him penance. Such, César reflected sadly, were the amercements for an unlived life. More or less refreshed, he passed through the fine Renaissance portals into the rue du Jour and hurried on, coming at last into a deafening cacophony of sound, a score of instruments tuning, the thundering of pianos, swooping clarinets, desperate sopranos aiming for the heights, trumpets careering, an orchestra of Babel. He had arrived in the courtyard of the Paris Conservatoire, and, but for him, the courtyard was empty.

3

César entered the organ room to find Victor-the-pumper alone and, in no time at all, he became aware that something suspicious was going on. At first, he tried to allay his disquiet by telling himself that the happenings were none of his concern but he quickly realised that the contrary was true: a mystery was being spun, like a web, and he was the fly.

To begin with, Victor-the-pumper was shutting the door to the walk-in cupboard where the music was stored and as César came into the room, turned round sharply, leaned heavily against the cupboard door and, panting a little, growled, 'You're even earlier than normal.' And César was convinced he heard movement from inside the cupboard.

Now, César had known Victor-the-pumper for about forty years. He was old and bent but with powerful arms like a blacksmith. He wore a faded, stained blue smock down to his ankles and a black beret pulled at a rakish angle to cover one ear. A maize-paper cigarette drooped from the centre of his lips. His hands were gnarled. He had pumped the organ throughout the long reign of François Benoist, César's predecessor; some said he had been a promising organist himself until arthritis had prematurely crippled his hands but there was no way of knowing for certain; taciturn and gruff, he talked little and never about himself. And that was what made his behaviour this day doubly suspicious. Ordinarily, César could expect to find the old man seated on the low stool near the console, staring at the floorspace between his boots, and on César's arrival he would not look up, but grunt a greeting. Yet, here he was, caught like a guilty husband in a cheap, boulevard farce, his back to the cupboard door.

César said, 'Am I not permitted to arrive in my own classroom when I like?'

Victor looked everywhere but at César. 'You're always early,' he said, 'but never as early as this.'

'I beg your pardon,' César said, trying to sound affronted, but he was not good at sarcasm and seemed instead polite.

'That's all right,' Victor said.

César glanced round the room. 'No students yet?' A delicate but expressive shrug of Victor's shoulders confirmed the obvious. 'Ah well, we'll wait. Any minute now and they'll come trooping in.' César was aware that Victor was watching him closely but pretending not to.

Victor said, 'You should close your umbrella. It's bad luck, an open umbrella indoors.'

César shut the umbrella, then removed his top hat and overcoat and when he turned was startled to find Victor now standing beside him. 'I'll hang them up for you,' he said. César was dumbfounded. In all his years at the Conservatoire, both as student and more recently as teacher, he had never known Victor-the-pumper do a favour for anyone, not even for Benoist whom he claimed to reverence. Meekly, César allowed his things to be taken for him, closely watched the old man cross to the walk-in cupboard, open the door and step inside out of sight. Was there a whisper then, or was Victor wheezing? The old man soon reappeared and returned César's puzzled stare with a dash of defiance. Then, he trundled over to his stool, picked it up, placed it to one side of the cupboard door and sat as though on guard, hunched, watchful.

César said. 'Victor, what's going on?'

'Typical.'

'What?'

'I do you a kindness and hang up your clothes for you, but do I hear thank you? I do not.'

28

'Thank you,' César said, 'but what's going on?'

'What's going on?' the old man repeated, breathing like the organ-pump, 'what's going on? I'll tell you what's going on. We're waiting for lazy good-for-nothing students to come and have a class, though what they learn here, well, I don't know, and that's what's going on.'

César said, 'What's in the cupboard, Victor?' trying to sound stern.

'A dead body. I murdered a woman last night in the rue Poissonière, cut her up into small bits, wrapped the bits in newspaper and I'm hiding them in the cupboard. There, it's out, I've confessed. I must say I've never heard anything like it. I do you a kindness and all I get is questions, questions, questions. I tell you this, Maître Benoist never asked questions.'

César decided to let the matter drop, but he was uneasy. For someone who longed for inner change, the smallest disturbance in the outside world produced in César disproportionate alarm. He stood for a moment perplexed in the centre of the room. As in the courtyard, the confusion of sounds could be heard here, too, but now filtered through the crumbling walls, the paint peeling, the plaster bare. The building was small, neglected and overcrowded; there was a smell of decay in the air, a feeling that modernity was wholly absent giving a sensation of a time long since vanished. The Conservatoire had not changed at all since César's student days: he loved the place then; he loved it now. Normally, he would count on being at ease here but Victor's strange behaviour upset him. What or who was the old man hiding in the cupboard? Drink, perhaps? A woman? Stolen property? What? And without warning, for the first time since adolescence, a name and the face of a boy sprang into César's mind with frightening clarity: Josquin at the window, smiling. César shuddered; the memory vanished. Why think of Josquin now, César wondered, why such a vile memory triggered by the sight of Victor sitting beside the cupboard, a squat guardian – but of what? César shook his head, refusing to allow the past to take hold. Claire, Claire, he said to himself, screwing up his eyes and tightly clenching his teeth, Claire, Claire. He concentrated hard on the present, heard from the room next door Massenet's voice teaching the composition class, noticed that outside it had begun again to rain.

Victor said, 'Well, aren't we going to play the organ today?'

'There are no students yet,' César said softly.

'Massenet's got students. The youngsters like Massenet. The students liked Benoist, too.'

César was about to reprimand the man for impertinence but decided against it. He turned, shuffled to the organ-console and sat on the bench, his back to the instrument, and faced the room, empty but for Victor huddled on his stool close to the floor in the far corner. All around was the noise of musical labour; outside the rain beat a gentle tattoo on the window panes. César became conscious of a pulse in his forehead and massaged the spot rhythmically. Why had Josquin, after all these years, come into his mind? A kind of panic set in, an eddy of thought which was a mechanism to obliterate thought. A picture of Gemmenich, the village near Liège where he was born, appeared and he calmed himself by marvelling at the distance he had travelled from provincial Belgium to the very heart of French musical life, here in the Paris Conservatoire. The self-satisfaction did not last for long: he remembered that he was not first choice for the post, and that the Director, Ambroise Thomas had, in the end, appointed him reluctantly. The word was that Saint-Saëns was first offered the job but turned it down because he was too busy, recommending César as a tolerable alternative. César accepted at once, though he would have preferred to teach composition. But a professorship, albeit of the organ, while not satisfying even remotely his deeper longings, bestowed on him a certain respectability, an illusion of belonging, a sense of security. They paid him 2000 francs a year; he was called Maître; he could look forward to the Legion of Honour, third or fourth class.

'The lesson should've started five minutes ago.' Victor grumbled.

César glanced at his pocket-watch. 'Two minutes ago,' he said.

'Are we just going to sit here all day? Why don't you begin to play? That usually brings one or two in.'

'They'll be along,' César said.

'You should never have put your classes at the same time as Massenet.'

César rose and went towards the door that led to the corridor. Victor, alarmed, said, 'Where are you going?'

César did not answer. In the passage, he stood outside Massenet's door and listened for a moment to a theme being picked out on the piano – is that what Massenet teaches? Chopsticks? He opened the door and looked in. A dozen young faces – easily distracted, César thought – swung round to look at him: eyes bright, expectant, amused, as though to confirm that they regarded the Organ Professor as an elderly buffoon, a clown whose every antic was calculated to produce laughter.

Massenet, receding temples, bumpy nose, heavy, untidy moustache, the look of a pale, literary man, tried to appear displeased but could not entirely conceal his amusement. 'I am giving a lesson, maître,' he said patiently.

'Ah, forgive me, maître,' César said.

A pause; one of the students sniggered.

Massenet said, 'So, what can I do for you?'

'Are there any strays within?' César asked.

'Strays?'

'For my organ class.'

Massenet looked at his pupils; none moved.

César said, 'No strays?'

Massenet shrugged helplessly. César understood, nodded and withdrew, shutting the door. The explosion of mocking laughter was predictable. He returned to his own room and said to Victor, 'I'll play now,' and resumed his seat at the organ.

Victor said, 'I won't be a moment,' and hobbled quickly towards the door.

'Where are you going?' César asked in amazement.

Victor stopped and glowered at him. 'I have to piss,' he said and went out, closing the door. César was baffled and, in that moment of being left alone, was tempted to go to the cupboard and investigate, but almost immediately Victor returned. César said, 'That didn't take you long.' The old man made no response, he proceeded to the back of the console and began to pump.

Eyes closed, César placed his hands almost gingerly on the keys, shuffled his feet to find the appropriate pedals, as though he were

31

searching for an air like the Pied Piper's to lure students to his class, conjure them into his presence. A marked and mystical transformation took place when César improvised on the organ. His face, his whole demeanour altered: gone was the ordinariness; a bleak, craggy concentration took its place. On Sundays, in Sainte-Clothilde, at the great instrument built by Aristide Cavaillé-Coll, there was a similar metamorphosis which produced an extra-ordinary outpouring of music. And even here, in the barren class-room, he brought forth magical sounds and combinations, as though another played who thought no more of silence or of separation. Through the keys, the stops and the pedals he was somehow able to express all his longing and aspiration. To César, his improvisa-tions on the organ wakened the unexpected, created surprise and wonder, as if an enchanted, flowering oasis bloomed in a desert and was afterwards fated to vanish once and for all. The music he made, invented then and there, could not be written down and would not be produced in any other way but through his hands on the keys, his musical mind floating freely. Pure, harmonious noise rather than precise music; stained-glass in which the shapes and figures were barely discernible. There was no expression here of self, but of a luxuriant landscape through which inexplicably, he was a familiar traveller. This very journey was to him a source of hope and he would say to himself, so long as I can do this, all is not lost. For almost fifteen minutes he improvised, technical mastery at one with deft and inspired invention.

Once he opened his eyes and in the small looking glass above the stops had the partial view of the figure of a student standing, listening. All César could see of him were the folds of his velvet cloak, a pair of trousered legs, and well polished shoes, but even so he had the impression of one immersed in the music. Was he the only one, César wondered? Perhaps there were others he could not see. And so he commented on his own playing – 'Modulation, do you understand? We get nothing if we don't modulate. Oh dear! That's awful, I don't like that! Ah now, better, better, you see what a little modulation does for you? Now that's very nice indeed,' – until he felt he had explored the map of his making, knew where the harmonic path led and followed it triumphantly to its conclusion. The last note sounded and died away. Victor ceased to pump. César turned from the console to face the class. There was no one there.

César said, 'Victor, did you not see a student while I was playing?' but Victor was already at the door and without a word left the room. Alone, César had the unpleasant, eerie feeling he was being watched. He wanted to get out of the room as quickly as possible. How could he be mistaken, he asked himself? He was certain he had seen someone or part of someone. But now the room was empty. The day had started badly, he reflected, with Arlette's breasts, and Josquin had come uninvited into his mind, and why had Victor sat like a sentinel by the cupboard? Small things, he supposed, to anyone else, but to him, unnerving, a source of anxiety.

He rose, remembered that his hat, coat and umbrella were in the cupboard and, half-afraid of what he might find in there, crossed to the door and cautiously opened it. The cupboard too was empty. He put on his coat, hooked his umbrella over his arm, and only when he took up his hat did he notice the pale green card stuck like a price-tag in the hat band. On it was printed the letter Z. Gazing at the card, turning it this way and that – could it be an N perhaps? – César hurried from the room, down the stairs, into the courtyard where students were now milling about on their way to the next lesson. César, troubled, was oblivious to their sniggers and snide whispers – 'Are there any strays within?' someone said in a heavy German accent to laughter, and another: 'Excuse me, maître, is it true that too much modulation makes you blind?'

As one struggling for air, César picked his way through the groups of students until he was stopped by a tall, thin young man called Rousseau, pimply, with a servile manner. 'Good day, maître,' he said, 'I thought you played beautifully this morning, but –'

'Ah!' César said with enormous relief. 'It was you then?'

'Me?'

'Listening.'

'Yes, oh yes,' Rousseau said.

'And you were wearing a cloak?'

'A cloak, no, that wan't me –'

'Why didn't you stay? I had some interesting points to make.'

33

'But, maître, I wasn't wearing a cloak.'

'You weren't? But I saw you, my dear boy –'

'How could you, maître? I wasn't there.'

'But you said you were.'

'No, maître –'

'You did!'

'No maître, I said I was listening. I wanted to come in but the notice on the door –'

'Notice? What notice, what door?'

'The notice on your door, maître.'

'I don't know what you're talking about –'

'It said, "No class today, please keep out".'

'What did?'

'The notice on your door.'

'But I never put a notice on my door.'

'It was there, maître, I promise you. I saw Victor pin it up myself. And then afterwards I realised you must be giving a private lesson when the young man came out.'

'What young man?'

'He was wearing a cloak, maître. It must have been him you saw.'

'Did you know him?'

'No, maître, not me. Ask the concierge.'

César took Rousseau's advice. He poked his head round the door of the small entrance lodge. 'Hortense,' César said, 'was there a visitor for me today.'

'Yes, maître,' she sang.

'Did he give a name?'

'Yes.'

'What was it?'

'Foreign, I think.'

'Don't you remember?'

'I wrote it down, I write everything down, it's the regulations, maître, now where is my little book? ah, yes, here, let me see, yes, here we are, maître, Zenta, H. Zenta, foreign, I told you –'

César froze. He looked at the card in his hand. Z.

4

Félicité Franck and her elder son, Georges, sat in the salon next door to the dining room awaiting César's return from the Conservatoire. Georges sniffed the cooking smells wafting in from the kitchen and looked at his watch. He said, 'If he doesn't come in ten minutes, may we eat, maman?'

'Your father is always too early except when he lunches with us.'

'Sometimes I think he's quite off his rocker.'

'*You* don't have to live with him.'

Georges picked his nose. 'Awful,' he said with a little shake of his head. From the ashtray he took up his cigar, puffed, and flicked the ash on the carpet. Although only twenty-seven, there was something about him already middle-aged. He frowned a good deal which gave the impression he was forever struggling with imponderable thoughts. He looked more like his mother: long, thin nose, high cheekbones; he had grown a moustache to hide his father's sensual mouth. His manner was sombre; he did everything slowly, like an undertaker. Twice a week he visited his parents, always arriving early enough to spend first half an hour alone with his mother. He lounged in a well-upholstered leather armchair, legs stretched before him, listening to Félicité complain about César, confess that he would never be anything more than an obscure organist, an indifferent composer, a shabby nonentity. To all accusations, Georges nodded agreement, for between them existed a bond, stronger than the ordinary ties of mother and son, a bond forged, in her case by experience, in his by an objective temperament, and the bond was the contempt they openly expressed for César, not only for what they believed to be his failure as a husband and father, but also for his failure as a composer. They used the latter to punish him for the former. They blamed him for all their own shortcomings. Both had expected more of him.

Félicité loved Georges more than anyone on earth. She forgave him his pomposity, his selfishness, his parsimony, his laziness, because he allied himself with her against their common enemy. But she had no exaggerated hopes about his future, while her hopes for César, and vicariously for herself, were more exact and detailed, founded more closely on reality and therefore, with enough effort she believed, just capable of fulfilment. True, there were vague aspirations too, greed for a richer texture to life, an insatiable need to be compensated for disappointment, a desire for a worldly opiate to deaden the pain of loss but all these longings could be assuaged if only César would do what she commanded and write an *opera*.

She had always been ambitious for him. César-Auguste: what imperial echoes those names produced, what fanfares of blazing trumpets, processions in triumph, laurel wreaths dipped in gold: hail César-Auguste, all hail. And what had he become? A ridiculous, outlandish clerk of works, splashing in puddles, who talked and smiled to himself. Yet, she had never ceased to nurse a hope for an imperial future: when she day-dreamed she saw herself always in a box at the Opéra, the Empress Eugénie-Félicité-Caroline, white plumes in her hair, diamonds at her neck, inclining her head with royal hauteur to the accompaniment of music that somehow she could imagine but which her husband failed dismally to compose.

Lying on the chaise-longue, gazing out through the rain-streaked window, she was given to sighing, sad little moans, painful intimations of sadness trapped in her heart. As a girl, not even in her darkest moments had she ever contemplated a life so bleak, so empty or so meaningless. If not for her darling Georges there would be nothing at all, nothing but silence and her longings, the persistent ache which was always with her. She said 'He gets worse, you know. Days go by and he doesn't say a word to me.' She sighed.

'He's still on *The Beatitudes* I suppose?'

'Of course. He'll never finish them. He doesn't intend to. He'll still be writing them on the day he dies.'

'What one is he on? Fourth, Fifth? I can never remember.'

'Oh, don't ask me, he never tells me anything.'

'Be grateful for small mercies,' Georges said.

'Sometimes I think the silence will drive me mad. Well, of course, it's not exactly silence. I have to endure the noise he makes when he eats. One would think that a poor, harmless croissant could be devoured pianissimo. Not by your father. He manages to make the enterprise sound like a German band under water.'

Both smiled, sickly, knowing smiles. Georges said, 'The trouble

36

with father is that he lacks – he lacks –' He hesitated, searched for the word, then smoothed his moustache with a crooked forefinger, lost in his analysis of César's deficiencies.

'Lacks what?' Félicité asked with a troubled frown. 'Lacks what?' Georges' opinion was eagerly sought.

'Culture,' Georges said with some finality. 'General culture. He is too narrow, too confined. He needs to take an interest in the world. He cares nothing about the other arts. Pictures bore him. Books blind him. The theatre –'

'Oh don't mention the theatre,' she said passionately. 'My father, who was a wonderful actor, always said César lived too much on the inner plane. He needed to see, to hear, to be exposed to the universe –'

'Precisely –'

'We tried as a family to jolt him out of his nervousness. We had the privilege of free admission to theatres, Georges, to the Opéra, to the Opéra-Comique, to the Comédie-Française. We took him everywhere. And he *slept* through everything. Especially the love scenes.' Tears sprang into her eyes. Georges, embarrassed by emotion, gazed into the fire. Félicité said, 'I should have been warned when he slept through the love scenes.'

Georges murmured, 'You weren't to know.'

As though images of the past were projected on the windows awash with heavy rain, Félicité stared at the glass seeing César, César-Auguste they called him then, when her mother first brought him into the house as music-master. He is of impeccable character, her mother said, a character quite as admirable as his musical gifts. He was only two years older than Félicité, but she remembered how shy he was, how timid, what difficulty he had in saying anything directly. He stammered and stuttered, left sentences unfinished, looked from under his brows and blushed in a way that even she, a young and innocent girl, never did. But when he sat at the piano, at a slight angle to the keys, his face and entire being were transformed as though a magic spell had been cast. Almost always his eyes were half-open, sightless, convincing the listener that he was entranced. Our famous music master, her mother called him, the young woman's oracle. Her father liked him, too, but thought he needed broadening out. Mother said that musicians

37

do not have to be well-read like actors. Music was their language which set them apart from other men.

'Can't we eat now, maman?' Georges asked.

'We'd better wait,' she said. Her tears had run their course but not the rain.

'I'm starving,' he said.

Félicité did not hear, she was reliving a source of sadness, a beguiling pastime to one who clung to unhappiness as though it offered security. She heard her mother's voice as clearly as if the woman were in the room: 'We must help him to do something about his dreadful, inhuman father,' and, although Félicité knew that old Monsieur Franck was a vile, vulgar, ruthless man and beastly to his son, she instinctively resisted her family's desire to rescue César-Auguste from his clutches. But her mother when determined was not to be stopped. No matter that César-Auguste was old Franck's principle source of income; no matter that he believed the boy to be another Mozart, and from the age of three drove his son for twenty years, worked him like a drudge, concerts, recitals, compositions, pressing him to earn more and more money, issuing ridiculous and untrue stories to the press, inflating reputation so that others could too easily burst the bubble with their incredulity; none of this mattered. Her mother and father were determined to rescue him. And César-Auguste welcomed their aid, wanted to be part of the Desmousseaux household. I love coming here, he said. Your p-parents are s-so un-un-under-understanding. And Félicité's one ambition was to please him. She was bowed down with perpetual fear in case she made the smallest finger-slip in her lessons which would cause him to tap his foot with impatience. Her lessons rarely went without tears; her father nicknamed her his musical Niobe. Looking back, she acknowledged that she doted on her piano teacher.

The maid, Arlette, entered the room. 'Madame,' she said, 'it's one o'clock. Shall I serve luncheon?'

'No, we'll wait a little longer,' Félicité said, her thoughts far away. She wanted to carry her memories to some conclusion, convinced there were some things of importance still to be remembered.

Georges, watching Arlette bob and go, said, 'New?' but received no answer.

The early afternoon sky suddenly lightened perceptibly; the poplars and the houses beyond them at the end of the little back garden which had been cowled in a gauze of mist and unending rain, were again visible. The coals glowed; the flames billowed like a theatre curtain about to rise and Félicité saw in the flames the face of César-Auguste's father, a skull with a vicious mouth and the eyes of a cadaver. The son was his slave, terrified, driven, cringing, needing all the support Félicité and her family could provide in order to help him make the break from the tyrant. She remembered the conspiracy of whispers, and how exciting it was to devise a secret plan that would effect César-Auguste's escape, enable him to live with the Desmousseaux so that he could work at his music in peace, compose, play, teach, do whatever he liked without having to account for his time to his dreaded father. In those anxious days before he fled from his parents' home, César-Auguste and Félicité were drawn closer together and she would sit in the room while he worked, listening as his improvisations took form, and he would ask with a look what she thought, did she approve. Not once did he speak of personal matters although she knew he longed to; not once did he say or do anything the slightest degree improper: it was as if his feelings were engaoled by an inability to speak of them; as if because he was gifted he had to be punished by isolation from a normal childhood world, and thus never learn the tricks of intimacy, the ability to engage one's feelings with another. And Félicité understood the paradox: music made his life possible and impossible. She could remember feeling his pain, seeing him want to unburden himself but knowing he was unable to. His whole being was stricken by it. Theirs was the strangest courtship: no words, looks avoided, an over-careful physical distance kept between them.

She remembered the song now, remembered him pressing the manuscript into her hands. Ignore the w-words, he said, l-listen to the m-music. *The Angel and the Child* it was called, and it was his declaration of love, expressive of his innocence, purity and ardour. And the dedication: 'To Mademoiselle F. Desmousseaux in pleasant memories'. In pleasant memories – of what? Of hours spent in each other's company, undemanding, yet so loving and giving of each other.

Movement beyond the dripping poplars caught her eye: an old woman, a chestnut-seller, pushed her barrow and took shelter under the tiled portico of the corner house beyond, warmed her hands at the brazier as though she were working mystical passes over a cauldron or, Félicité thought, like an aged Penelope weaving her eternal shroud – it was a shroud, wasn't it? Georges had closed his eyes, his jaw sagged a little as he snored gently. The clock struck the quarter. The chestnut-seller took sheets of newspaper and ripped them in half, laying the halves in a neat pile in readiness to set off again in search of customers. One after the other she expertly tore the sheets.

His father tore up the song in rage, destroyed all the copies one by one. Love, marriage, what César-Auguste wanted, the father was determined to prevent. No one must interfere with his son's career as a virtuoso pianist. How would the old swine survive without his little bread-winner? But his mother, thank God, was a fine woman, although weak and terrified of her husband. She knew César-Auguste must leave her home, connived at it, was willing to bear her own sorrow at being parted from him because she wanted above all his happiness. She believed perhaps in his love for Félicité, or Félicité's love for him, a love she was herself too frightened to give. One Sunday afternoon it was all arranged: on a Sunday afternoon because that was when Monsieur and Madame Franck took their weekly stroll. César-Auguste stole away then, leaving behind his manuscripts, his fine grand piano which he had won for the Grand Prix d'Honneur at the Conservatoire. And worst of all, such was his conscience, he gave a written undertaking to pay off all his father's debts which the bloodsucker said he had spent educating the ingrate. Eleven thousand francs! And César-Auguste paid back every sou. From then on he signed himself C. Franck.

Georges woke with a start. 'Isn't he here yet?' he asked, and checked his own watch with the ormolu clock on the chimney piece. 'Oh, maman, this is too bad –'

She rang the bell to interrupt him and when Arlette appeared, said, 'We will eat in five minutes whether Monsieur Franck is here or not.'

Georges said, 'I'll just go and wash,' and quickly followed the maid out of the door. Félicité heard the girl suppress a giggle, smiled fondly at the thought of Georges' virility, decided then and there to sack the maid. The smile vanished; her face became troubled: she was trying to remember why Claire came to live with them all those years ago. Something to do with Claire's father wanting to sing and needing an accompanist. César was to improve Cousin Claire's piano-playing – but Félicité was confused: could she be right? When Claire's father, Féréol, retired to Orléans was he not made Captain of the Fire Brigade? Such an odd fate for a lyric tenor. But whatever the reasons, Claire came and there was, for a time, happiness in the house of the Family Desmousseaux with their two lodgers, César and Claire. And he was again teased and called the young women's oracle.

The front door banged. Félicité looked up, startled. The chestnut-seller had gone. The winter sun was trying to break through. She heard Georges greet his father, heard Arlette singing in the kitchen and, under some compulsion from the past, was obliged to continue her memory, obliged to remember the songs he now wrote for Claire - 'To Mlle Claire Féréol', 'To My Cousin Claire' and then 'To My Dear Cousin Claire' – *Robin Grey* and the melody with the 'cello obligato *Le Sylphe*, signing himself CSRGSTFRNCK. And what of *The Angel and the Child*? Ripped to pieces by his father, savaged by a mad dog. Yet, did he not write it out again? But to whom did he dedicate the second copy? Not to Félicité. He had only the one way of expressing himself. Who, then? Who?

'You should see him,' Georges said, entering like a ringmaster announcing the next act. 'He's soaked to the bone.'

On cue, César stepped into the salon and stood like a naughty child, a droplet of rain running down his nose and falling to the carpet. His trousers were sodden to the knees and round his feet a puddle formed. He smiled benignly.

Félicité said, 'Franck, what do you think you are doing? Look at the mess you're making. You'll ruin the carpet.'

'I thought I'd change before lunch.'

'Absolutely not,' Félicité decreed. 'We can't wait any longer. Georges is famished. You'll just have to sit in your wet clothes. That'll teach you for being late. Anyway, what kept you?'

The moment he had been dreading since leaving the Conservatoire had arrived: what would he say? He couldn't possibly tell them that an unseen, unknown young man, reputed to be a composer of great promise, had hidden in a cupboard in his classroom, kept out the other students, listened alone to the improvisation, left a card with his initial in César's hatband and thrown him into such turmoil that he had walked in circles trying to fathom why someone should behave towards him in this fashion? Could he tell them that his equilibrium had been disturbed at the sight of Victor-the-pumper guarding the cupboard door, that long-forgotten names and faces had invaded the present? Even as he rehearsed for the thousandth time the sequence of events, he knew his tale was absurd. The morning had been tinged with the quality of a dream. César understood there was meaning, but what meaning? All he wanted to do now was to go to the piano and play through the setting of the psalm he'd been sent, to see if he could uncover clues about the composer, perceive what kind of man it was who would act in such an illogical manner. He said, with a vague gesture towards the windows, 'The rain, the rain, my dear.'

'Did you not use your umbrella?' Félicité demanded while Georges smirked and César smiled like an idiot-child. 'Well, no matter, let us eat luncheon.'

'I'll just go and change,' César said and was on his way before Félicité could stop him.

'We're not going to wait another minute,' she called and then quite as loudly said to Georges, 'You see? He doesn't listen to a word I say.'

César changed speedily, trying to give himself time to go to his studio and to play through Zenta's music quickly, but twice Félicité called to him to hurry and he dared not disobey. By the time he joined them in the dining room, Georges was on his second helping of vegetable soup.

'I hope you like your soup cold,' Félicité said, dipping the china ladle into the tureen.

'I don't want any soup, thank you,' César said.

'Nonsense,' she said and placed a steaming bowl before him.

42

He did not touch the soup and gazing absently into the thick, opaque surface recalled his father's warning when he confessed his wish to marry Félicité. Don't forget what happened to Monsieur de Praslin, the vulture had shouted. Monsieur de Praslin had been poisoned by his wife.

Georges said, 'Papa, I've brought you a book.'

Félicité asked eagerly, 'For an opera?'

'No. To read.'

'Your father never reads anything.'

'Papa, you must read this,' Georges said, taking from his pocket a small, bulky volume.

'Books bore him,' Félicité said.

'He won't be bored by this. I wasn't.'

'Yes, but you have an intellect, Georges.'

'Nevertheless,' Georges said by way of agreement, 'it is important that he try to read it. Everyone should read it. You may find it difficult, papa, but you must persevere.'

'Now, why should you give me a book? It's not my birthday. Is it?'

'No, papa, it is a book you ought to read.'

Félicité snorted.

'A novel? A play? Something for an opera, perhaps?' César said, taking the volume and then searching for his pince-nez.

'No –'

'What, then?'

'Kant's *Critique of Pure Reason*.'

César did not bother with his pince-nez. He said, 'Now what sort of book is that?'

'Philosophy.'

'Philosophy?'

'Of the highest order.'

'He won't get past page one,' Félicité said.

'It's an improving book,' Georges said.

'To my knowledge people have been trying to improve your father for thirty years. Without success. Let us hope Monsieur Kant is more successful.'

'*Herr* Kant.'

43

Over coffee and eructation, César judged the time right to excuse himself, but Félicité spoke sharply, 'Sit down, Franck,' she said. 'You're forgetting.'

'Forgetting?'

'Get the dictionary, Georges.'

César tried to hide all the expressions of weariness which swept over his face. The torture was only just begun. He had indeed forgotten about the dictionary which Georges fetched from the glass-fronted bookcase in Félicité's boudoir and rejoined his parents now in the salon where César was already seated; Félicité placed a notebook and pencil on a table beside Georges' armchair and resumed her place at full stretch on the chaise-longue. This was all routine, the beginning of a ritual which had developed between them and which Félicité insisted on preserving because, she believed, it was one of the practical measures open to her for bringing about the realisation of her deepest longings.

Georges opened the heavy tome, *The Dictionary of Greek Mythology: a complete study of the legends and personages, together with a commentary on their significance* by Professor Josef-Marie Marcel, Paris, 1842, and found the place they had reached the previous week. A shiver ran down César's spine and he shuddered. Félicité tilted her chin and gazed at the ceiling, slowly running her fingers down her meagre neck: she was preparing to be receptive.

Georges began. 'Hades.'

'No. Too depressing,' Félicité said.

'Haemon.'

'Don't know him.'

'Betrothed of Antigone. Creon's son. After Antigone hanged herself, he took his own life in despair.'

'Worse than Hades.'

'Halirrhothius.'

'Mmmm?'

'Son of Poseidon.'

'Ah, the sea. Good.'

'Murdered by Ares.'

'One wonders how the human race survived.'

Hamadryades, Harmonia, Hebe, Hecabe, Hecale –

Félicité suddenly held up her hand, eyes wide, struck by an idea. Georges, taking note of her dramatic gesture, read from the dictionary. 'Hecale was a poor old woman who gave Theseus hospitality when he was out hunting the Bull of Marathon.'

'No, no, not Hecale. Penelope!'

'Penelope?'

'I thought today of Penelope—' she announced.

'Penelope who?'

'Penelope and her shroud.'

'Penelope,' he repeated, consulting the book. 'Pelopia, Peloponnesus, Pelops, Pelorus, ah, Penelope, wife of Odysseus. What was that you said, maman, about her shroud?'

'Didn't she weave a shroud for eternity?'

'I can find no mention of it here. She made a robe for her father-in-law, Laertes, but unpicked the work each night.'

'Why should she do that?'

'To keep at bay a crowd of suitors led by Antinous,' he said, paraphrasing the entry before him. 'She promised to wed one when she finished the robe. She saw to it that she never finished. She did not want to be unfaithful to Odysseus.'

Félicité sat upright. 'A frisson has run down my back,' she said. 'An infallible sign we are on to something, Georges.'

He showed no excitement, but read on. 'Oh dear,' he murmured.

'What now?'

'Penelope as faithful wife is but one tradition. There is another, less savoury.'

'Tell me.'

'Some say she became the mother of Pan, either by Hermes or by all the suitors.'

Félicité's hands flickered with irritation, brushing aside Pan, Hermes and any number of others. 'We will ignore the lascivious side of her temperament. We will concentrate on fidelity. That appeals to you more, does it not, Franck?'

César smiled; could he slip away now, he wondered?

Georges said solemnly, 'But the important question is: is Penelope a suitable subject for an opera?'

'There are possibilities,' Félicité said. 'It seems more commercially attractive than Alomaeon returning to slay his mother,

Eriphyle, in revenge for her vanity and deceit towards his father and himself.'

'That, I thought was a proper subject for a grand opera,' Georges said huffily. 'Penelope is for the Opéra-Comique.'

'I do not want to sound crass, Georges, but there is more money to be made at the Opéra-Comique.'

'Penelope,' Georges said again. 'I suppose it is a good title.'

'It is a fine title. And there are wonderful opportunities for songs. The Robe Song. The Suitors' Chorus. An aria for Penelope, "I will never betray thee, Odysseus", or some such.'

'Does it appeal to you, papa?'

'Penelope? Excellent, very fine,' César said, rising.

'Sit down, Franck,' Félicité ordered. 'We must discuss this fully.'

César remained standing, shifting his balance from one foot to the other.

'Since we are not being crass, maman,' Georges said, 'would it not be better to consider Penelope the mother of Pan, ravaged by Hermes and a chorus of muscular Greeks?'

'Certainly not. Your father can only write about what he understands. And therefore we are limited in our choice of subject. Fidelity, he can manage. Lasciviousness we must leave to Jacques Offenbach and all those other Jews.'

'Shall I write out the myth in simple form?'

'Do. You will read it tonight, Franck.'

'Of course, of course, my dear, and I really must hurry. So nice to see you, Georges. Splendid, splendid, Penelope, splendid,' he said, reaching the door and, to encourage them, hummed a few atonal notes and was gone.

Georges began to write. Félicité said, 'Life is very extraordinary and always unexpected. There I was, rather desolate, gazing out of the window when a chestnut-seller took shelter across the yard. To anyone else, I suppose, she would have been simply a chestnut-seller. But not to me. I thank God my parents educated me properly. And, you know, the theatrical tradition is to think in symbolic imagery. When I looked at the chestnut-seller I saw at once, just from the way she passed her hands over the glowing coals, that she was Penelope weaving her shroud.'

'But Penelope didn't weave a shroud, maman.'

'Even so,' Félicité's eyes became glazed. She could already see the bills outside the Opéra-Comique: *Pénélope* by C. Franck. Her imagination skipped nimbly to the première. She was in a box, inclining her head and hand royally. The reception for the work was thunderous, triumphant. She would employ Jules Gouffé to prepare a lavish dinner for a thousand guests at the Jockey Club; they would dance until dawn to the Act II waltz, *I will wed you when the robe is done* – stitched? finished? Georges must decide; she humiliated Camille Saint-Saëns with her devastating wit – 'You are a homosexual and a Jew' – and had her breasts stroked by the Abbé Gounod. But her dreams were interrupted by the sound of César's piano. 'What *is* he playing?' she asked. She listened a moment longer, then rose and marched down the corridor to César's room: there he sat, his back to her, his grey hair curling over his worn coat collar, his shoulders salted with dandruff, his hands at full stretch to accommodate the sombre chords. 'Franck, what are you playing?' she asked.

'Zenta,' he said.

'Zenta?'

'Hermann Zenta.'

'German?'

'Yes. A disciple of Wagner's, I think.'

She shuddered. Wagner reminded her of flesh and pubic hair. 'It's an awful noise,' she said and shut the door on him.

'Not awful,' he said aloud after she had gone. 'Promising, but odd, very odd, not to say rum.'

He studied the words of the psalm, 'When Israel went out of Egypt, the house of Jacob from a people of strange language', he read, and the language was strange indeed. 'The mountains skipped like rams, and the little hills like lambs'. Trust Herr Zenta, César thought, to choose the obscure. And what sort of tune, César wondered, had the composer given to those ambiguous words? He sang the melodic line in that particularly unmusical voice only gifted musicians can produce. He was puzzled. The accompaniment was Germanic enough, quasi-Wagnerian, but the melody suggested something else, a different sort of mystery altogether, not Teutonic, but even more mysterious if possible, hidden, misty, a suggestion of cruel sentimentality, of wind and

47

the keening of woman. Puzzling, César thought.

In the salon, Félicité stood in the doorway and listened to her husband's voice intoning the strange tune. 'Do you hear that, Georges?' she asked.

Georges looked up and he, too, listened. 'Not much of a tune,' he said, 'Does he mean that for Penelope?'

'No, no, no,' Félicité said and motioned for him to be quiet. 'Does that sound like Wagner to you?' Georges shrugged. Félicité said, 'No, that's not Wagner. It's more like – like Mendelssohn, yes, Mendelssohn, surely: that overture he wrote, you remember, Georges, the sea, islands, caves, seagulls, waves smashing against rocks, you remember –'

'No –'

'Yes, you do.' She listened again and although she could not recall the title of Mendelssohn's piece, she remembered reading something about it, something to do with the feeling and atmosphere. 'Yes,' she said, 'Celtic, that's it, Celtic.'

And César played and sang the psalm once again. Herr Zenta intrigued him more and more. Not quite right, he thought. No, not quite right.

5

Not because he needed the money, but because he craved the activity, the afternoons César spent hurrying from one end of Paris to the other teaching amateurs to play the piano, the organ, to appreciate music. From Auteuil to the Île Saint-Louis, to Vaugirard, to the Faubourg Poissonnière, in private houses, institutions and colleges, on foot, by omnibus, on foot again, he hurried, bustling, chuntering, conducting an eternal inner debate, question, answer, question, and on this day his mind haunted by the unknown, invisible, mysterious Hermann Zenta. He was greeted by acquaintances, laughed at by strangers, was aware of the aching silence in his head; smiling benignly, brows furrowed, mumbling and muttering, César pursued his daily round. And towards evening, weary of all the wrong notes played that afternoon, he shuffled along the rue de l'Université. Paris was shrouded in dusk:

the domes, the steeples, the pillars and porticos, the squat, tumble-down houses and the great hôtels lost their shapes as the en-croaching darkness inked them out like a dissatisfied painter: only the plane trees remained, sharp with winter stars for leaves. César loved this hour as he had loved the stillness and cleanliness of his mother's kitchen before the evening meal was begun: what dishes will be concocted this night? what tastes? what smells? who will eat well and who will eat ill and who will not eat at all? The best hour this, the apéritif, the prelude; to him, all existence was a prelude – but to what?

He walked through the small square garden that fronted the massive, twin-steepled church of Sainte-Clothilde where he was organist. He dragged himself up the worn stone steps and, at the entrance, dipped his hand in the font and crossed himself. He reached into his pocket, took out some coins and dropped them into the box for the poor of the 7th arrondissement. The light in the large church was dim and grey. Here and there candles flickered. The wide, Gothic arches down each side aisle cast unsteady shadows across the nave and choir, but left the altar, which was modest and serene, in light. César sat on one of the chairs at the back. He turned his eyes towards the high, vaulted roof and breathed rhythmically.

Each evening he came here and sat alone and quiet, leaving outside the church the bustle and business of the day. Sometimes he would stay no more than ten minutes; tonight, being Monday, he would remain for an hour at least, before setting off for Camille's weekly soirée.

César loved Sainte-Clothilde. He knew people said that it was too large and lacked any feeling of holiness, that even when thronged with worshippers it seemed empty. But the place suited him as though its duality matched his: an impressive edifice apparently devoid of life, yet, he knew there was life; a Christ resided within. He shut his eyes. All thoughts flew from his mind. Claire appeared to him. I love you, she said and cried; in silence, of course.

'César?'

Gardey, the curé, peered at him through the candle-lit hush, a guardian angel in search of a ward. 'You're late today. Unusual for you.'

'I got off to a bad start.'

'Too many lessons?'

'Yes, far too many.'

'You do too much.'

'Yes, I do too much, and not enough.'

'May I sit with you?'

'Please do.' The priest took the chair in front of him, half turned so that César addressed his profile. 'And you, father, are you well?'

'Yes, well, always well.' Gardey brought his hand up to cover his mouth, appeared to squeeze his long nose between thumb and forefinger, saying softly, 'César, there's been a man looking for you.'

'For me?'

'Keep your voice down. He may still be about.'

'What sort of man?'

'Youngish, foreign accent –'

'Wearing a cloak?' César asked, knowing what the answer would be.

'A cloak? Yes, yes, yes indeed and a large hat pulled low over his eyes. Do you know him?'

'Not exactly know him, no –'

'He had a letter for you.'

'A letter?'

'Wouldn't let me give it to you. Wanted to deliver it himself. Didn't seem a trusting sort. Rather sinister, I thought. I had the strong impression he was dangerous.'

'What did he look like?'

'I didn't get a good view of him,' Gardey said, 'but he was young, certainly, clean shaven, heavy-jawed. Wanted to know if you still lived at No. 95. Asked all sorts of questions: did you play here only on Sundays? did you visit the church during the week? was it true you came here each evening to pray? I was evasive, of course, I –' The priest broke off mid-syllable. He began to drum nervously on his cheek with his fingers. 'Don't look now,' he said, 'but he's standing beneath the organ loft.'

Slowly, as though the muscles in his back and neck had stiffened with some affliction, César turned: in the doorway, beneath the organ, the great pipes soaring to heaven like arrows, against the blackness of night, the silhouette of a man, cloaked, floppy velvet hat at one with the hidden face. César wondered whether this was dream or nightmare. 'What do you want?' he barked. The echo in Sainte-Clothilde played its tricks: 'want-ant-ant-ant.' The figure raised a white-gloved hand, touched the brim of his hat, seemed to bow and César was certain that the man smiled; then, he was gone, heavy footsteps on stone, speeding into the dark. César and Gardey rose and hurried after him, paused in the portico, looked out into the square, saw nothing. Slowly they went back into the church when Gardey cried, 'Look!'

'What?'

'The letter.'

An envelope, the pale green of spring grass, lay on a flagstone as though carefully placed. The priest stooped to retrieve it. The envelope was addressed: To C. Franck. By Hand. 'Open it,' Gardey said.

In the light of votary candles burning, aptly, beneath the stained-glass window to Sainte-Cécile who, red cloaked and clutching a miniature organ, gazed balefully heavenwards, at the First Station of the Cross where Pilate washed his hands, César tore open the envelope and read:

We will come face to face at the next meeting of the Société Nationale de Musique. You *will* teach me, you know.

Z

'Who is he?' Gardey asked.

'I don't know.'

'Obviously a maniac.'

'Obviously.'

'An odd way to behave.'

'Yes, odd.' But César could no longer pretend to be alarmed or displeased or anxious: for some as yet unfathomable reason he felt a sense of occasion, auspicious, awesome. One must expect mysteries and portents in the hour of dusk. Not quite right, no, not quite right. The man used the language of dreams in a world of reality. César looked to where the stranger had stood: through the arched door nothing but a gentle, wintry mist filled the porch;

51

beyond were the shapes of trees or demons, the statues of petrified angels.

6

'How extraordinary! You've just missed him.'

'He was here?'

'A most peculiar young man. Kept his hat on. The Prussians never have had any manners, not what I call manners, don't you agree, Monsieur Franck?'

César smiled. He sat on a delicately scrolled sofa beside Madame Saint-Saëns, the ugliest woman he believed he had ever seen. Her son was her image; each possessed of the identical nose: gross, bulbous, hooked. She smelled of lavender and garlic. Every Monday evening César was placed beside her. She was a dozen or more years older than he, but the two were regarded by all as contemporaries and there they sat like chaperones for the young, near the fire, beneath the large Revolutionary clock with calendars decimal and Gregorian.

César's enigmatic smile behind which he so often hid, concealed now inward amazement which he did not feel the need to confide to the old woman. It was odd, he reflected, that one could go through life without ever hearing a word or a name or a particular harmony, and then suddenly, in a single day, one heard nothing but. Like Zenta, for example. César had been sitting, idly gazing on the company, watching the old manservant, Théophile, pass amongst the guests with drinks and cakes, when someone near had spoken the name. César was shaken from his reverie. Madame Saint-Saëns had asked if he was quite well. César had replied by enquiring if she had ever heard of the young German composer, to be told that he had just left the party. Truly, it was astonishing the way incident and coincidence weaved in and out of life. He was resigned to the belief that the only certainty was the unexpected.

'Well, don't you, Monsieur Franck?' She tapped her silver-handled ebony walking stick impatiently.

'Don't I what, madame?'

'Agree with me.'

'On what subject?'

52

'Manners and Prussians.'

'Manners and Prussians, now that's a very interesting topic,' César said. 'I'm not sure Prussians have any manners.'

'My point precisely,' the old woman said: she was even more hideous when she smiled. Fortunately, her attention was taken at that moment by the pianist, Mademoiselle Poitevin and the two women talked of the new fashion of shrouding ladies' hats in silk net – 6 francs at the Bon Marché, the older woman advised.

César half-closed his eyes and viewed the room as though through a distorting lens. Both this and the adjoining salon were crowded, the babble of conversation constant. Someone, Camille probably, was playing a musical joke on the piano, a theme of Gluck in the style of Offenbach; there was much sycophantic laughter. What am I doing here, César wondered? Why, he asked, did he regularly inflict such boredom on himself week after week? He knew everyone; no one knew him – the cross of the unsuccessful. Some few acknowledged him but they were as insignificant as he. Bussine there, for example, who had spotted César and was coming towards him, Romain Bussine, Professor of Singing at the Conservatoire, young, tall, spiky, languid. Camille's friend, co-founder of the Société Nationale de Musique, and joint President, but still a nonentity. 'Ah, maître,' he said, 'I always think that the sight of you and maman side by side is one of the sweetest in Paris.'

Peculiar, César thought, for a man to call a woman not his mother maman; but then, he was after all a very close friend of Camille. César said, 'Is Duparc here?'

'In the music room.'

'Romain, dearest!' Madame Saint-Saëns had noticed him with obvious pleasure and held out both skinny hands for him to take. 'You must join us. We're discussing millinery. Romain is so interested in everything, Mademoiselle Poitevin, especially ladies' fashions, aren't you, Romain? Now. Where shall you sit?' she asked looking pointedly at César.

'It's all right,' César said, rising. 'I'm just off on a jaunt.'

He crossed the room, which always seemed tidy no matter how many guests there were. It had the atmosphere of a museum to Madame Saint-Saëns' youth: Louis XVI full-bottom chairs, tapered legs, intricate scroll-work, acajou panels, sparkling marquetry, Rouen china on shelves marred by a monstrous, tasteless black statuette of Diana, the huntress, and by the old woman's fading paintings of faded flowers. There was no hint of Camille's energy, no evidence of the modernity to be found in his music: Maman dominated all.

In the adjoining salon where the piano was hidden by a closely packed semi-circle of guests, César found Henri Duparc, a little apart from the others but beaming happily as the pianist passed from parody to a Liszt Rhapsody and was then joined by another pair of hands, and another until all six were, to cheers, foot-stamping and clapping, banging out the piece at an impossibly frenetic tempo. Seeing César, Duparc yelled joyfully. 'What artists do to art is unforgivable.'

'Let's go somewhere quiet and talk,' César said, and the two wandered off to find an unoccupied corner in the main salon. 'You seem to be enjoying yourself.'

Duparc's eyes had a way of shining with wonder. 'I do so envy Camille,' he said but with admiration not bitterness. 'Everything comes so easily to him.' He was a handsome man in his late twenties and looked more like a cavalry officer than a musician: bristling moustache, assertive chin, clear eyes, he was always scrubbed and neat as though he had just emerged from a bath. But his manner was gentle, his presence warm and reassuring. César had been the first to spot his musical gifts. Duparc had, as a boy, been his pupil at the Jesuit College of Vaugirard, and had graduated to César's private composition class. He had published some tender, haunting songs, *Cinq Mélodies* five years before; since then, nothing. Composition was an agony for him but he never discussed his difficulties, never confessed to pain, not even to César. The two had much in common. The malicious said they shared the same creative block.

César said, 'I want to ask you something. What do you know about a fellow called Zenta?'

Duparc's reaction confounded César: had he asked after Bismarck he could not have received a more agonised response. 'Zenta? Zenta? Oh God,' Duparc said shutting his eyes, screwing up his face and shaking his head as though the name filled him with doom.

'You know him obviously,' César said.

'No, not know him, no, but –' Duparc's voice trailed off. He was obviously uncomfortable.

'What about his music?' César asked.

After a long pause, filled by the fury of the rhapsody from the next room, Duparc shrugged helplessly.

César was a little shocked. The younger man was usually forthright about people, never devious, always generous towards those with gifts, brutally frank about those who were lacking; he had a good instinct for talent. César could not ever recall seeing him at a loss when it came to passing an opinion of another's music. 'I take it you've heard his work?'

'Never!' Duparc cried as though he were on oath in a court of law.

'But you know Zenta's name?'

'Yes.' A strangled sound this, truncated, wrenched from a hostile witness.

'Henri, what *is* the matter with you?'

Duparc was saved from answering by a sudden explosion of cheers and applause from the music room; both he and César turned to see Camille, who had cut through the group round the piano like the prow of a ship through water. He paused in the doorway, cool, superior, and glanced mischievously at his guests; in his deep, booming voice – he spoke with a marked lisp – he said, 'Wasn't that fun? Liszt for six hands,' and with a peculiarly energetic gait, bouncing on the balls of his feet, crossed the room at speed to join his mother and Romain Bussine. When César turned to resume his conversation with Duparc, the younger man was gone, slipped away evidently behind César's back. Zenta, César concluded, had a surprising effect on people.

Almost without realising it, he wandered, crab-like, towards Camille. César was forced to admit that he was ineluctably drawn to him, was fascinated by the man's talent and intelligence, by the curious magnetism his personality exerted. The mother's nose, so gross on her face, was somehow more acceptable on her son's. The beard helped, and the mysterious eyes: he looked positively rabbinical, though he was not a Jew, whatever the envious might say. Just forty years old, he was industrious to the point of lunacy,

César thought; music flowed from him, as though beneath his feet the earth was a treadmill of unceasing melodic harmonies. Yet the man himself was controlled, icy, remote, and, in noting that, César wondered if Camille possessed some secret which made creation possible. There was a chance, César speculated, that Camille's detachment and his own separation were not so very different; he had often been of the opinion that much of Camille's music lacked, as his did, a truly profound engagement of the man to the artist, as though Camille, like César, was too much the mechanic. Yet, obviously he was not troubled as César was; music, in all its forms, poured out of him. Why? How? In those questions lay the heart of Camille's attraction for César, as though he might one day hear Camille let slip some magic formula that would unlock the floodgate. César frequently felt the desire to question Camille directly on the subject, but never did. Camille seldom talked seriously about himself, he preferred to tell stories of others or quote from books he had read: he had a prodigious memory for both. And of course, César was forced to admit, music, even at its most obtuse and technical, held no secrets for Camille. Possessed of perfect pitch, the rhythmic accuracy of a metronome, the complexities of counterpoint, harmony, tone, structure had never needed explanation. They were his to command and use. In every way, César thought, Camille was to be envied. What sort of Christ, César wondered, resided in the man?

César found himself behind the sofa on which Camille was nose to nose with his mother; Romain sat on the floor, hands clasped round his knees, looking up at them – and inadvertently at César – with concern. César could tell at once there was tension between the three. Romain was anxious; Camille lisped more than usual and his mother talked loudly.

'But I've told you, dearest,' she said, 'that I will not have that girl in my house.'

'Well, it's too late now, maman.'

'You've behaved disgracefully, Camille,' she said fidgeting for a handkerchief in her sleeve. 'You should not have allowed her in the house.'

'She's been here before –'

'She is not to come again –'

'What do you want me to do? Put a sentry on the door?'

'Please don't speak to me like that, Camille.' The handkerchief was lost in her nostrils.

Romain said, 'Don't cry, maman, please –'

'She's an awful, vulgar, common little girl. Who brought her?'

'Hermann Zenta,' Romain said.

At this, Camille looked all round quickly and nervously, saw César and smiled. 'Yes, she came and left with Zenta.'

'Zenta? That awful little Prussian? Why did he keep his hat on? Is he a Jew?'

'No, maman –'

'How anyone with any breeding can be seen with that girl is a mystery to me –'

A young man – rather highly-strung, César thought – rushed in and from the doorway called 'Camille, Madame Fuchs is going to sing one of Duparc's little ditties and wants to know if you'll accompany her?'

'Yes, all right,' Camille answered; to his mother, he said, 'Maman, will you come and listen? You know how you love Duparc's songs.'

'No,' she said, 'I'm too upset.'

Without another word Camille rose and bounced out of the room, Romain followed but not before giving the old lady a sympathetic pat on her hand. César, too, was about to follow when Madame Saint-Saëns asked him to join her again. When he was seated beside her, she said, 'I feel in need of a companion who understands. We, of the older generation have much higher standards than the young people of today, don't you agree?' César tried to smile but failed. She said, 'Do you know this Holmes girl?' She had difficulty pronouncing the name and offered something that sounded like 'Ol-maize'.

'Augusta Holmes?'

'Awful girl.'

'No, I don't know her. I believe I've met her once or twice. As a matter of fact she wrote to me earlier this year, wanting to join my composition class.'

'You turned her down, I trust?'

'Oh yes.'

'I should hope so.' She replaced the handkerchief in her sleeve. 'Had she any talent?' she asked as an afterthought.

'A little, yes, quite promising, but, you know, if you'll forgive me, it's quite inconceivable to me that a woman could compose worthwhile music.'

'I absolutely agree,' the old woman said. 'Women are not cut out to be composers. Who has ever heard of a great woman composer? Look at that awful Vicomtesse de Grandval. Camille liked her, too. I don't know why he's so drawn to female musicians. Women can never be great in any of the creative arts except one where men are absolutely useless.'

'And what's that, madame?'

'Having babies.'

'Ah yes, yes, of course.' He nodded sagely but was inwardly afflicted by the memory of his two dead children and a pain, black as the grave, clawed at his heart.

Madame Saint-Saëns said, 'Camille can be a very disobedient boy sometimes. Oh, now I suppose you'll think me too protective, after all, I know he's forty but I believe that men of genius need special care. After that disgraceful concert, I forbade him to bring the Holmes girl into my house. He took no notice. Were you at the concert?'

César struggled to rid himself of the ache. 'What – what concert was that?'

'At which the Holmes girl sang Camille's *Danse Macabre*?'

'No, but I heard about it, of course –'

'They booed *her* not the song. I fainted.'

'Yes, so I believe. I was very sorry –'

'She appeared looking like a harlot.'

'Oh dear –'

'I've never seen such a dress. So vulgar and indelicate.' She shuddered at the memory.

The touching strain of Duparc's song filled the room; a welcome peace descended over César; thoughts of death faded from his mind. He imagined soothing hands on his brow, remembered Claire saying, I love you, and was, for a moment, warm. And when the song ended there was not the boisterous applause that had greeted Camille's earlier bravado, but a sort of sigh went up from the listeners, a sound of gratitude and approval. Presently, the Revolutionary clock struck eleven and the guests began to disperse. César was among the first to take his leave. At the front door, Camille said, 'I hear you're going to teach Zenta. Lucky fellow. You, I mean.'

'Nothing's settled yet,' César said.

Almost an hour later, Camille closed the door on Romain, the last to go; he fastened the chain and turned the key in the lock.

'Camille?' his mother called from her bedroom.

He did not answer. He was angry with her and would punish her by not going in to say goodnight.

'Camille, dearest, come and see me.'

He was determined not to answer her but, turning from the door, he saw the glow of candle-light down the passage and thought at once of childhood and how, from his cot, he could see the night-light in her room, a protective glow against infant terrors. He hesitated, and heard her creaking bed, imagined her sitting with the aid of her ebony walking stick, silver-handled, engraved: 'To Maman, from her loving son, Camille', and, with a staccato grunt of effort, swinging her legs, her yellowed feet unslippered, to lie prostrate; a moment to catch her breath, 'Camille!' she called.

Slowly, resigned, he walked down the passage to her room. No matter how much she angered him, he was unable deliberately to hurt her. At her door he paused before entering, before embarking on the nursery ritual of a man in his fortieth year.

She looked at him and did not look at him. 'You're angry with me,' she said.

'Yes.'

'Because of what I said about that girl?'

'Yes.'

'Don't be, my darling, I can't bear it when you're angry with me. I apologise, I apologise, I do, I do.' She raised her face to be kissed and always, no matter how often, at this moment of putting his lips to her cheek he never failed to be startled by her ugliness which was also his ugliness; their noses touched; *Psittacus erythacus, semiticus*. What hope was there for him looking as he did? How could he ever expect his love to be returned? How could anyone in the act of coition, look up into such hideousness? Cruel, to be

59

created with a dazzling gift that had never before shown itself even remotely in his forbears, yet to inherit this grotesque lump on his face from his mother, like a curse. Always at this moment of kissing her.

'Am I forgiven?'

He smiled, sat on the edge of the bed, crossed his legs, folded his arms on his chest, smiled again. 'Yes, you're forgiven.'

She patted his knee. Head and happy eyes tilted, she said, 'Shall we have our chocolate?'

'I'd like that, maman.' He stroked his beard, crooked his forefinger to smooth his moustache, the silken sensation of a baby's comforter.

She pulled the bell cord, then reached for a book on her bedside table, Camille's diary of appointments. 'Oh,' she said with a frown of surprise, 'you appear to be free tomorrow. Except, of course, you have the string quartet to finish. The first movement should be back from the copiers on Friday.'

He did not show his irritation. He hated days when there was nothing. He loved to be busy, to drown himself in activity: societies, publishers, colleagues, pupils, committees, to be busy; and to enjoy the results: recognition, fame, lively tumult. These last few weeks, all had gone quiet, hushed, worrying. Or were these his night-time terrors, he wondered, to be soothed by a candle burning late, by a mother's kiss?

She said, 'Camille, why were you so very angry with me?'

He stiffened. He did not want these matters discussed. 'You've already apologised, maman. And I accepted your apology. We need not talk about it any more.'

'Oh but we must, Camille. I can't go to sleep with this unpleasantness between us. I must know why I angered you so deeply.'

'You know why.'

'I don't, I don't, I promise you I don't. All I did was criticise some common little singer who was booed and hissed –'

'My music was booed –'

'Nonsense. It was she. I've never seen such a vulgar dress. I know shoulders are meant to be fashionable but not the entire upper torso. I was outraged. So were the audience –'

He refused to listen, but allowed her to prattle on, his mind returning to the Salle Pleyel, to Augusta singing his *Danse Macabre*, to the whistles and catcalls and his strange enjoyment of the fiasco. He remembered seeing Augusta at rehearsal, their first meeting for God knows how many years: how excited he had been, lisping incessantly. Since adolescence, three women only had possessed the power to stimulate him, and he had forgotten that one of them was Augusta. And suddenly she had impinged on him again, glowing, magnificent, a giver of life. And how divinely she sang; and her dress, always more daring than any woman's in Paris, flaunting, teasing, inviting. Had they exchanged a dozen words the day of the concert? Not as many, perhaps, faster–slower, louder–softer. And afterwards, when the audience howled their disapproval, and she fled from the platform, he ran after her and, so sweetly, passionately, she told him she wanted to change her life, to become a *serious* composer. He promised to help and help he did, but to no avail. He tried to see her again but her apartment was empty, she had gone away. No one knew where. And then, tonight, she reappeared uninvited, audacious –

'Camille, why are you so upset?'

He snapped back into his mother's room, recognised the anxiety on her face. 'I'm not upset,' he said sharply.

'Oh yes you are, I always know when you're upset. You never stop tugging at your beard as though you're trying to pull it off.'

'The more you ask why I'm upset, the more upset I become.'

'You see? You are upset, you're lisping dreadfully.'

'Oh, maman!'

'All right, Camille,' – more gently, softer – 'we won't discuss it. I know how painful the memory of the concert is. I don't know how we ever got on to it.'

'It's not painful.' Why did they both persist so? 'Anyway, I'm going to transcribe the work for orchestra. I've decided it should not be sung.' He paused trying to get the esses under control, to speak more slowly. 'The Cazalis poem is, to put it at its highest, second-rate. I shall allow the idea of Death fiddling in a churchyard, at midnight, in winter, with skeletons dancing and, no doubt, rattling their bones to *work* on the audience's imagination. They do not need to be *told* the story. Not in song.'

61

'And not, if I may say so, Camille, by an Irish singer who insists on wearing a dress designed to show off the muscles of her diaphragm. I don't care what you say, that was the real reason why the piece was booed. I know it was the real reason why I fainted. It was all too explicit.'

'She isn't Irish,' God, why could neither of them leave it alone? And he knew so well his mother's technique, knew she would prod the open sore until the pus oozed out. And why couldn't he learn to keep silent? Why did he feel obliged to answer and argue?

He was rescued by Théophile, old, gentle, bent, who entered with hot chocolate in a silver jug on a silver tray with two Sèvres cups like lilies standing on square saucers. 'Ah, good *morning*, Monsieur Camille,' the old man said pointedly. 'Will there be anything else, madame?'

'No thank you, Théophile. You may go to bed now.'

'Oh, thank you *very* much, madame. How very kind.' He shuffled out, master of irony.

'You must talk to him, Camille. He's becoming impertinent.'

'Too late now, maman. You should've listened to me ages ago, to poor Aunt Charlotte, to everyone.' He prattled like a hostess at a failing party.

'What, and get a maid? What, with you alone in the house? An only boy? My dear Camille, you are very naïve. Maids are extremely dangerous with young boys in the house. One hears so many cases of disease.'

Mother and son sipped their drinks. The moment, he thought, of danger had passed: there would be no further mention of Augusta. He was wrong.

'What d'you mean she isn't Irish?'

'Who?'

'That singer who likes to show her midriff.'

'No. Not Irish.'

'Not? But the name certainly –'

'French –'

'French? You surprise me.'

'Her father, I believe, was Alfred de Vigny.'

'Vigny?'

'That is what the lady claims.' He kept his eyes firmly fixed on the window, watched the wisps of Opéra-Comique clouds chasing the moon, but knew all along that the old woman was leading to the questions he wanted to avoid.

'Have you been seeing her, Camille?'

'No.'

'But you've been trying to, haven't you?'

Curious, how he could feel her disappointment without even looking; the wounded stare, the dark eyes filling with tears. 'You might have told me, Camille.'

Told her what? That he wanted Augusta, so passionately wanted her that he could neither sleep nor eat, that he walked the streets of the city at night in the hope of catching a glimpse of her? Tell his mother that he wished to see Augusta lying on his bed, legs apart, naked – 'It's nothing serious,' he said. 'Nothing serious,' with more care.

'Are you in love?' she asked.

'Maman, you ask such old-fashioned questions. No one talks about being in love any more.'

'More's the pity. What do people say now?'

Want, need, must have. 'Relationships are more' – draw breath – 'sophisticated now.' God, maman, if you only knew how sophisticated relationships were now, how many lovers she's had, has: but not me, maman, and no surprise when you look at me. Or you.

'Do you have such a relationship with her?'

'Of course not, maman. We are fellow musicians. Professionals. Nothing more.'

'I detect more.'

'Then you are wrong.'

'Where you are concerned, I am seldom wrong.'

'It's late. I'm tired.'

'I don't want to see you hurt.'

'I don't either.'

'She is not a suitable woman, Camille. You will promise to take my advice before doing anything rash?'

'Maman, you know I'd never do anything without consulting you.'

'Promise.'

'Promise.'

'You will find someone soon, I feel it, who is loving and gentle and not – not strident. A man should never marry a woman who has ambitions for herself, only for him.'

'Maman, whose marriage? You jump to conclusions –' he said with disapproval as though he had eaten something sour.

'I am concerned for you, Camille.'

'I know that, maman.'

'I want you to be happy.'

'I want that, too, maman.'

'Your nature is your nature.'

What was she saying? What was the old witch saying? Was she really concerned for him or for herself? 'I do not want to continue this conversation,' he said unable to keep the bass voice even any more.

'Be true to yourself,' she said, arthritic fingers fidgeting with folds of her dressing gown; it was her turn to look away.

'Enough, maman, enough, enough, enough!' He rose, clasped and unclasped his hands.

'Don't get upset,' she said. 'There's no need. I only want you to know that –' tears now, running, as they always did, towards her cavernous nostrils – 'what you do is your own affair, it isn't for a mother to interfere. I know that, but it isn't for a mother to condemn either. Men of genius don't have to conform to society's rules for ordinary people. You are what you are. You don't *have* to marry.'

He began to shiver. He had not escaped. She had invaded forbidden territory; the candle-light pained his eyes. 'It's late,' he said softly, more to himself than to her. 'It's terribly late.'

She held out her arms to him; he knelt, buried his face in her lap, felt her embrace, sinewy, agitated, constricting, like being bound by steel. Silence in the room but for the wind rattling the window panes; from the street, the sudden sound of running footsteps, diminishing at speed, someone escaping, Camille thought. He stood, passed a hand through his ruffled black hair. 'I must work,' he said.

'Don't be angry with me, Camille. I have to say what's in my heart. You are impulsive and that frightens me. I'm not the only one concerned for you. Romain, too –'

'Yes, Romain,' he said curtly.

'Treasure your friends,' she said.

'Goodnight, maman.' Again he kissed his own ugliness.

'Goodnight, my darling. You do forgive me, don't you?'

He went straight to his studio at the far end of the passage and was startled and pleased to find a note from Augusta. She must have slipped into his room before leaving the party, scribbled on manuscript paper in thick pencil and placed the page on the piano:

Camille, glorious Camille, was it very naughty to come without being asked? I couldn't help myself. I was in a dangerous mood tonight – I know what you'll think – that I've been avoiding you since the concert but it isn't true, Camille, I swear it isn't true – I've been away – I can't tell you why – not in the letter – perhaps not ever – don't be angry – help me – help Zenta – on Friday next – Duparc is in on it – so too a dear called Emmanuel Chabrier – speak well of Zenta, please, please, glorious Camille – help – if you do – I know you will – you may ask of me *anything* and it will be granted – I swear – *anything* – Ars Gallica – help me – Friday – A

He read the note twice: each time her voice, her vitality, her madness flooded his consciousness. His impulse was to reply at once, to steal from the apartment, deliver his response in person at dead of night. So typical of her to create mystery, drama, excitement out of what was mundane and commonplace. 'You may ask of me *anything* and it will be granted.' What anticipation of pleasure those words conjured. Everything she had ever wanted was bought at terrible cost to herself. Camille knew she paid for life in the basest coinage, but even so he was under her spell and helpless. You are impulsive and that frightens me, his mother had said. Yes, yes, he wanted to act now, this instant, disregard consequences, the future, anything that did not feed his immediate needs. He took writing paper and, standing at the piano, wrote:

Astarte!

I will help Zenta. I want you to be my wife.

Camille Saint-Saëns

65

He addressed the envelope and left it on the marble-topped hall table for Théophile to deliver by hand first thing in the morning. In the salon, the Revolutionary clock chimed one, and he could hear his mother's snores.

As though life were a series of unconnected, self-contained incidents, Camille, having proposed marriage, thought no more for the moment about Augusta Holmes. Out on the narrow balcony that ran the length of his studio, he sat peering through a telescope, scanning the stars which he loved and knew by name, Argo Navis, Cassiopaeia, Eridanus, Cygnus, Delphinus. He swivelled the instrument slowly until he found the gibbous moon, adjusted the focus on the mountains, the plains and craters a million miles away and thus, by looking at the sky, he put aside the need to look at his own nature. Know not yourself, he seemed to say.

He gazed on the heavens and then he worked, the one activity divorced from the other. He sat at his desk, the piano in reach, and began to write down the notes that perhaps his demons sang to him. For, Camille composed music not in the sense that the sounds and harmonies, the melodies and themes needed invention: they were there, constantly; all he must do is record them, put them down on paper with pen and ink, scribble the hieroglyphics for others to reassemble into intelligible sound. He lived in a sea of music in which he submerged himself. His talent was his protection from life. At work, his pen scratching at such speed he could barely control it, he was, he believed, fully himself, protected from pain, immune to disaster. Gone from his mind was the ugly and vulnerable captive who had proposed marriage on an insane impulse; gone were the stars. Camille worked, plunging into the warm water of his imagination. By morning he would complete the slow movement of the quartet for strings and pianoforte. The demons sang.

And across the city, heedless of stars, mute demons his companions, César struggled for sleep. Some child-like excitement, and anticipation of the future, kept his senses awake. He could not rid his thoughts of the cloaked figure in the church, could not wait to meet the man on Friday face to face. The dull and grinding routine of life had been rudely shaken. Suppressed memories had risen from the past, Josquin at the window, smiling. César tossed and turned and buried his face in the pillow. But even as sleep at last overtook him, he was aware that new themes were hard to come by, that life was cyclic, that tomorrow he would wake in silence and hear on rising the music he could not write. He would give himself up to an alien Christ. The hours had one more surprise in store. He dreamed. Not for many years had such vivid images invaded his subconscious mind. He saw himself on a precarious mountain road, a sheer and terrible drop to one side. Some distance ahead was his guide, Claire wearing a cloak. She led him, always from afar off, to a cave which was dark and frightening. Summoning his courage, he entered and saw lying on a rough-hewn catafalque, a shroud stained with blood. He was compelled to uncover what lay within and slowly he began to unwind the sheet, expecting all the while to find a rotting corpse. But there was nothing, except a dazzling white moth which, in escaping, startled him. He tried to catch hold of it but the moth flew to the light, and César stood at the entrance of the cave watching it ascend higher and higher until the shining white creature was at one with the stars.

7

Ars Gallica.

In the small upstairs room above the offices of Georges Hartmann the young music publisher, at 17 boulevard de la Madeleine, Chabrier tacked up the motto of the Société Nationale de Musique to one side of the improvised platform on which stood two Zimmerman grand pianos. 'Arth Gallica,' he said lowering his voice an octave.

'Camille won't come. I just know it. It's already dark,' Vincent d'Indy said grimly, arranging chairs in semi-circular rows for the Friday evening concert. Slender, haughty, eloquent, an aristocrat with a Van Dyck beard and burning eyes, he was unusually nervous, for this evening was to be the first performance of his sonata for two pianos which he and, he had hoped, Camille were to perform. But Camille had not attended the customary afternoon rehearsal and now there was barely an hour and a half before the concert was to begin.

Chabrier said, 'Unfortunately, maman had to be kithed and put to bed. I had to compothe a thymphony, thix thextets, a thong, a thonata, a thcherzo and a thoprano tholo before theven.' His impersonation was cruel, accurate and caused even Vincent to smile.

Duparc, who was helping to set out the chairs, said, 'Camille will turn up, have no fear. Anyway, he's the best sight-reader in the world. He'll be all right without rehearsal.' Duparc's instincts were always to look on the best side of things.

Vincent's nervousness was not to be easily assuaged. He was only twenty-four, the youngest of the three, and the most ambitious. Prone to passionate outbursts, his voice easily lost its cultivated tone. 'Sight-reading is a superficial gift,' he said, 'but in any case I believe he should do me the courtesy, since he is meant to be playing my piece this evening, of rehearsing beforehand and, therefore, make the effort to understand a work which after all may be, I say *may* be, the most complex he has ever encountered. But then I do not expect Jews to display courtesy or, indeed, to understand the meaning of that peculiarly French word.'

Duparc knew he ought to keep silent yet persisted, nevertheless, out of a punctilious regard for accuracy. 'Camille is not a Jew,' he mumbled but just loud enough for Vincent to hear.

'He has a Jewish nose and his mother is a Jewish mother.'

'Boyth! Boyth! Thith ith no way for memberth of the Thothiété Nathionale de Muthique to behave,' Chabrier called, hammering extra loudly.

'*Ars Gallica*,' Vincent said, 'not *Ars Judaica*!'

Chabrier said, 'Oh Vincent, don't be a bore, there's a good man. Just be yourself: arrogant, and aristocratic. Camille founded the Society. We wouldn't be here if not for him.'

'Founded it,' Vincent said, 'to hide his Jewish nose behind. He doesn't care about *French* music. He cares about Camille Saint-Saëns. All over the world Jews do this, behave like chameleons. They have no true colours, except Jewish ones. It's a brotherhood, a fraternity, like Freemasons. Just come with me one day and listen to Charles Maurras. His lectures will change your lives as they did mine. You will understand only too well why French music is so decadent. Because impresarios, Jews of course, have misused opera by corrupting Art into Commerce, and have been aided by so-called creative men, Jews, of course, like Scribe, Auber, Hérold, Offenbach, Halévy and not forgetting Meyerbeer whose real name is Jakob Liebman Beer.'

'You don't mention Saint-Saëns on that list,' Duparc said stiffly. 'I wonder why.'

'Because I am not fool enough to deny the man is talented. But I deny that his talent is pure,' Vincent replied with a satisfied superior nod which seemed to ensure he had spoken the last word on the subject.

'It's not the first time he's missed a rehearsal,' Chabrier said, stepping back to admire his handiwork. 'And it won't be the last.'

'Exactly my point,' Vincent said, beginning another row of chairs, 'unreliable, highly-strung and very probably a pervert.'

Chabrier and Duparc responded simultaneously and angrily. A man's private habits were a man's private habits – from Chabrier. Who was to say what was perverted and what wasn't? – from Duparc. Vincent hissed again about *purity*, said that homosexuality was expressly forbidden by the Church, and it was a disgrace that Saint-Saëns was allowed to play his organ in the Madeleine. At this last remark Chabrier burst out laughing and began to sing, 'I was playing with my organ in the Madeleine, what a jolly time I had, what a jolly time I had. There'th no one there who theeth, but oh how it doth pleathe, it giveth me wobbly kneeth, to play my organ in the Mad-e-leine ...' Duparc chuckled, but Vincent, who believed dignity to be a virtue, carried himself erect and continued unsmilingly to set out the chairs. Chabrier never knowing when to stop, placed one hand on his fat hip, the other, with bent wrist, flapped in the air like a mannequin, and proceeded to take mincing steps up and down the platform, weaving in and out of the pianos, while continuing his improvisation. His impersonation of a ballet dancer and a male homosexual was indistinguishable. 'You have to get your hands around your organ, what a jolly time you have, what a jolly time you have, up and down your thing you go, it'll make you sing, you know, when you manage to get your hands around your organ!' He did not understand the frantic entreaties of Duparc who was snapping his fingers: Chabrier thought the man was keeping time. 'It's really best in church, in your organ loft or perch, it's like playing with a doll, it was built by Cavaillé-Coll–' He stopped because he had turned and understood why Duparc had become so animated: in the doorway stood Romain Bussine. How much he had heard of Chabrier's song was anyone's guess, but enough to cause obvious and thin-lipped disapproval. At Chabrier's embarrassment Vincent smirked; Romain ignored the fat man and greeted the other two.

'Isn't Camille with you?' Vincent asked.

'Evidently not,' Romain said quietly.

Chabrier said, 'He's missed rehearsal. Again.'

'Are you expecting many this evening?' Romain asked.

'The usual. Between twenty and thirty,' Duparc answered.

Removing his gloves and coat Romain said, 'Oh, by the way, Holy Father Franck is walking up and down outside. He must have been there for hours. His nose is a bright ultramarine.'

Immediately Vincent hurried across the room and opened one of the windows, which overlooked the broad boulevard de la Madeleine. On the far side, under the plane trees, César paced, hands behind back, occasionally stamping his feet like a soldier on ceremonial guard. Vincent called 'Pater seraphicus!' César did not respond. Closing the window and turning back to the others, Vincent said, 'I'd better go and get him.' He sped from the room. The moment he was gone, Chabrier said, 'Now, remember, Romain, Vincent knows nothing about Zenta.'

'Oh?'

'No. He's humourless. He wouldn't see the joke. And he's very protective towards the old boy.'

Duparc said, 'To be honest, I'm not very happy about it either,' and wandered over to the window to look down on the boulevard busy with pedestrians and César pacing.

'Why not?'

'It's because it's all at the old boy's expense that I'm worried,' Duparc said. Down in the street, Vincent appeared. He called and waved to César but to no avail.

Chabrier said brightly, 'You all treat him like a saint. And he's not, I promise you.'

Romain, who was paging through Vincent's score which lay on

one of the pianos, said, 'I wish I worshipped him as you all do. To be perfectly honest, I find him a terrible old bore.'

Duparc held his tongue. Romain was not talented enough to be argued with; but Chabrier said, serious for once, 'He is a great teacher and I owe everything to him.'

'Everything,' Romain said with a degree of smugness that suggested Chabrier's everything wasn't very much.

'I'm not the only one,' Chabrier said.

'It's all so holy,' Romain continued, and pointed to Vincent's score. 'Look at this.' He affected a shudder. 'In imitation of the master. It's so monastic. It makes me think of choirboys.'

Chabrier murmured to Duparc, 'Everything makes him think of choirboys.'

'At least,' Duparc said trying to ignore the interruption, 'Vincent's music is French.'

'But the French have a soul, don't they? We have feelings, and emotions and passions. With Vincent if it's not politics, it's piety. There's no wine in his music, no garlic, no sunshine.'

'Don't blame César Franck for Vincent d'Indy,' Chabrier said.

'But you claim he is a great teacher,' Romain retorted.

'So he is,' Chabrier answered quietly and with conviction. 'So he is.'

Almost to himself Duparc said softly, 'Yes, oh yes, the music tells him everything about one,' and watched Vincent begin to dodge the cabs and carriages in a bid to reach César on the far pavement.

'Pater seraphicus,' Vincent called again, half-way across the busy thoroughfare.

César had heard him yell the first time from Hartmann's upstairs room, had seen him waving from the shop doorway with a spluttering gas lamp overhead casting across the young man's face dancing, diabolic shadows and he had heard him call again now, 'Pater seraphicus' from the middle of the street. César pretended to be preoccupied. He did not want to be noticed, did not want at this moment the company of others. Inwardly, he could barely contain his agitation: tonight was the night Zenta promised to materialise, and the prospect had excited him to fever pitch. What days he had lived through since Zenta had, like some wild buccaneer, taken his imagination captive. César needed time to bring his thoughts, his emotions, his nervousness, his fear, under control: he wanted no one to see the state he was in. For two hours he had been pacing up and down in the bitter cold: no matter which way he walked, the sharp, cutting wind seemed to be against him, but he had not really noticed. His mind was on the promised confrontation though why Zenta should provoke in him such turmoil, he could not discover. César wanted more time to compose himself –

'Pater seraphicus!' Vincent cried scurrying on to the pavement, 'you'll catch pneumonia in this ice wind.'

'I'm a little early, you know,' César said.

'But you should've come in, Father, and sat with us in the warm.'

He wished Vincent would not call him Father or Pater seraphicus; it made him sound so old; but then, he reflected, he was old and the old must be protected from too much excitement. 'Who's up there with you?' César asked suspiciously. Vincent told him. César's eyebrows beat a polka. 'No one else? You're sure there's no one else?'

'No,' Vincent said a little bitterly, thinking of Camille, but he did not believe it fitting to criticise an eminent and senior colleague in front of César. 'Let me take your arm, Father, and we'll cross the road –'

'Are you not rehearsing?' César asked. 'You wouldn't want me to hear the rehearsal, would you?'

'There hasn't been a rehearsal,' Vincent said, cupping his hands and blowing into them.

'No rehearsal? You must be very confident.'

'No. Camille failed to appear,' he explained reluctantly.

Typical of the man, César thought, but kept silent. He did not believe in encouraging the young to criticise their elders. 'He'll turn up. He usually does.'

Vincent was beginning to stamp his feet, 'We can't stand out here all night, Father,' he said trying to stop his teeth from chattering.

But César made no move. There seemed to him something so final about entering Hartmann's for the concert. His instincts and his intuition told him that an auspicious event was about to take

place, but auguring good or bad, he could not say. Entering Hartmann's, he felt, would be either like walking into a trap or emerging
from a tunnel. He almost gave in to an impulse to turn and run
away, perhaps would have done so had not Vincent taken hold
of his arm and said, 'Come in, Father, please. I'm frozen.' César
allowed himself to be guided across the boulevard. The going was
dangerous; each time César spoke, he stopped.

'You're sure there were only the four of you up there?'

'Quite sure –'

And: 'No strangers about?'

'No, Father –'

And: 'Vincent, tell me something. Ever heard of a man called
Zenta?'

'Zenta?'

'A composer.'

'We'll talk when we get inside, Father –'

'Have you heard of him?' César demanded.

'Zenta? No, can't say I have. Watch the curb Father.'

César stood dead still as the cab passed within inches. 'Never
heard of Zenta?'

'No. Watch out, please, Father –'

'Well, you're the first man I've met all week who hasn't.'

'I've been busy –' Vincent said absently, managing with a tug
of the sleeve, to pull César to safety. He hurried to Hartmann's
door opened it and, with a gesture that managed to combine court-
liness and impatience, urged César to hurry.

They entered the shop, passed the displays of sheet music –
mostly Camille's – spread on boards like fans. The secretary, an
adenoidal, conscientious youth with red hair, poked his head out
of a cubby-hole and said, 'Shall I tell Monsieur Hartmann you're
here, Professor Frick?'

'Franck!' Vincent said sharply, but the boy merely smiled and
nodded.

The mistake brought César down to earth with the authentic
thud of reality. He was suddenly reminded of his anonymity: in
his own publisher's office they did not know his name. His excitement plummeted. And then, Hartmann himself appeared out of his
office at the back, the doorway partially concealed by the

raised lid of a Pleyel grand. César observed he had that look of anticipation, peculiar to publishers, which seemed to expect the delivery of a new work, and not just any new work, but a masterpiece that would be acclaimed throughout the civilised world.

César said, 'No, not a thing, I'm afraid, not even a song.'

Hartmann's eyes betrayed uncertainty, his smile unease as one who's had his mind read. He quickly recovered and became his usual zestful, bright self. 'Well, Vincent, you have to forgive me. I won't be able to hear your sonata this evening. Wife's parents. But leave a copy on my desk won't you? My God, Vincent, you're shivering. You're not that nervous, are you?'

'No. Just cold,' Vincent said politely.

After the briefest hesitation – Hartmann was made uncomfortable by silence – he said too cheerfully, 'Talking of songs,' as though he could not bear life to be illogical, 'here's a curious fact. A sudden and unexplained demand for Camille's *A Voice By The Cedar Tree*. Can't print enough copies. They sell and sell and sell. Amazing, isn't it? A fortune for Camille, of course –'

César smiled. This was the real world all right, the reminders of anonymity and failure and everlasting silence. And will *The Beatitudes* ever be finished?

Vincent quickly changed the subject, as though to spare César more pain, 'Have you seen Camille today, Hartmann?'

'Seen him? I hope not. Must keep him working, you know. I have to pay the rent somehow.'

His laughter carried them up the narrow wooden stairs to the room where the concert was to take place. César paused as he entered, looking all around to make sure no one was lurking in dark corners. Chabrier waddled over to greet him. 'Maître,' he said, a long drawn out sound in his mouth, doubling the warmth of the welcome. 'Is it true that you've been standing out there in the street speaking to strange women?'

Vincent, humourless as prussic acid, raised protective hands as if ready at a moment's notice to cover César's ears. César said huffily, 'I do talk to myself. Sometimes people think I am addressing them. I didn't see any women.'

'Ah, but you were looking for women, were you?' Chabrier said.

'No, no, no, no, no, no, no –'

'Sit here, Father,' Vincent said, 'near the front.'

'I really do prefer the back, by the window,' César said. 'I like to be a long way from the sound.'

'Me too,' Chabrier said with feeling.

Duparc joined them and shook hands, 'Ah, maître,' he said with his sweet smile, César held on to his hand. 'Sit with me for a moment, Henri. I want to talk to you.'

César led the way to a seat at the back by the window. Duparc sat beside him. César said, 'You're hiding something from me, aren't you, Henri?'

'I, maître?'

'About our friend Zenta.'

Duparc shrugged expressively and uncomfortably.

'I've been studying the music he sent me.'

Duparc said, 'Any good?'

César blinked busily, knit his eyebrows for several moments twisted his hand to and fro in the air as though he was screwing something into a wall. 'Not good exactly, not bad either, but puzzling.'

'Puzzling?'

'I thought you might be able to help me solve the little riddle I find in his work.'

'And what riddle is that, maître?'

'Well, the young man's obviously taken a stroll through the streets of Bayreuth with Tristan as his guide. Or Isolde. But I have the feeling he's travelled further afield.'

'Oh?'

'Can't place it, can't place it, thought you might be able to help. You see, there's a sweetness to the music, soft light in which gremlins lurk.'

'Is there?' Duparc said non-committally. He caught Chabrier's eye and winked.

'You can't explain that?'

'Not really,' Duparc said.

'Also, I have the impression, though this is nothing to do with the music, mark you, of a slight mental imbalance in the composer.'

'I – I couldn't say.'

75

'Likes a mystery and a drama does Herr Zenta.'

'Does he,' Duparc said in a flat voice.

'Now, Henri, no running away this time. I want you to tell me everything you know about the man.'

Duparc shot a desperate look in Chabrier's direction but the fat man had turned his back. It was Romain who came unwittingly to the rescue. He said, 'And how is Madame Franck?' resting his lanky frame on the back of a chair. He lit a cigarette and elegantly removed bits of tobacco from the tip of his tongue.

'Well, thank you,' César said.

'You must bring her to Camille's one Monday evening. I feel sure she and Maman will get on frightfully well together.'

César agreed with a vague nod, put out his hand in an attempt to stop Duparc from again slipping away, but Duparc was too quick. He hurried over to Chabrier and whispered, 'The old boy's nobody's fool.'

'Why do you say that? What were you talking about?'

'Zenta of course.'

'Is he on to us?' Chabrier asked.

'No, but – but he understands more than anyone I know about the life of things. I do find him very touching,' Duparc said and coughed to conceal his emotion; he was genuinely moved.

César was irritated with Romain for interrupting his conversation with Duparc. Duparc was, César knew, a scrupulously honest man and would not have lied; if he knew something he would have confessed. And thinking those thoughts, César wondered why he regarded Zenta in terms of criminality, why he should even question the truthfulness of an old friend, or use words like confess as though a murder had been committed.

Romain was saying, 'Camille is a special case, of course, with all that talent, but it's you I envy. You lead such a disciplined life. Do you advocate a strict routine, is that the answer, do you think?'

'Routine,' César repeated thoughtfully.

'For example I noticed on Monday evening you left Camille's on the stroke of eleven, as you always do. Presumably you rose at the same hour the next morning, sat down and worked. Your life is always just the same, is it not?'

'Oh yes, just the same,' he said and, while Romain continued to talk, César thought, of course, that is how it must look to the outside world: just the same. What other answer could he give? How could he explain that since Monday so much had happened that he could barely control his thoughts. What would it matter to Romain, for example, if he were to confess that he had dreamed on Monday night for the first time in many years? had woken in a state of exultation and, although now, he could not recall clearly all the details, he remembered the mountain pass, Claire in a cloak, the dark and terrifying cave, and looking upwards at the heavens, at the stars, but the reason why was lost. How would Romain react to the incident concerning Victor-the-pumper, the guarded cupboard, the note pinned to a door, the half-concealed reflection in a looking-glass of a man listening to the organ? These were major and mighty events in his life. Yet, to others his life appeared just the same. Suppose he were to tell of Zenta in the church: would Romain not consider the tale ridiculous? How would the admission be received that he felt unaccountably haunted by a shadow? Surely as the babbling of a madman. The days that had just passed were as full as any he had known, charged with unceasing inner activity. And even if he did unburden, who could explain his excitation? Why, for example, had he remembered Josquin's face? Or, now, this moment, the peasant woman at her spinning wheel?

He remembered: in adolescence, on one of his eternal concert tours, walking alone through a village – perhaps it was a second dream, he now thought, for he could not recall the exact circumstances and it was unlikely that his father allowed him to walk unaccompanied – but he clearly remembered the village, and himself sweating under a summer sky heavy with close cloud. He came upon a woman, quite young with a square, peasant face, spinning at a wheel, singing a wonderful descending melody, a falling lilt of great beauty. César stopped and asked what the song was. She had made it up, the woman informed him but with an open, friendly smile, said that she now presented it to César as a gift. You may have it, she said, if you like it so much. And she sang the haunting phrase again. At that moment, a man appeared, a wiry, wild-eyed man, and he struck the woman hard across the face: seeing César's fear and bewilderment, he explained that the woman was his wife, and that she had been unfaithful to him; he knew because she only sang that melody after she had been loved, and he that day, the man confessed, had not loved her. Obsessions.

'Oh yes,' César said, 'that's the secret. My life is always just the same,' but Romain was no longer standing there. He had gone off to help Chabrier and Duparc usher the first arrivals to their seats.

Singly, and in twos and threes, the members of the Société Nationale de Musique had begun to wander into the pokey, make-shift concert hall. Hartmann's upper room was not an ideal place for a recital – the straight-backed wooden chairs were uncomfortable and creaked, the air grew quickly stale, a true *pianissimo* was difficult to hear at all, and to sit near the window, as César did, was to be pricked by icy needles of wind. But César, in spite of the mild physical ardours, loved the Société's meetings, loved to watch the members and their guests arriving, the waving, the nodding, the laughter. *Ars Gallica*, was their motto, French musicians dedicated to French music, pure music, not opera or operetta which now held public taste captive. And would anything come of it, César wondered, of this little society that Camille and Romain had founded? Would French music revive? would they create an audience for what was serious and not spurious, what was lasting and not transient? would they, he wondered wryly, create an audience for themselves? Such an odd collection of men: why did musicians always look so dull and unprepossessing? But how should they look? It was enough that they were recognisably human and that their names were musical: Guiraud, Fissot, d'Indy, Bourgault-Ducoudray, Duparc, Fauré, Chabrier, Lalo, but not as yet Saint-Saëns. The recital should already have begun but Camille had still not arrived. Vincent had ostentatiously taken his seat at one of the two pianos, rested his hands on his lap and literally twiddled his thumbs to demonstrate publicly his displeasure. Briefly he discussed with Romain the possibility of a substitute but they decided to wait a little longer. The audience, César included, did not mind the late start: the conversation hummed along punctuated here and there by warm springs of laughter as though music was not the main purpose of the gathering, but rather the communal spirit, the comradeship, the coming together of men who, in the course of an ordinary day, toiled long hours in solitude. César, although in daily touch with his students, appreciated the contentment that the presence of his colleagues bestowed. Of the leading lights, he was by far the most senior, and so was treated with a certain courtesy, respect, even affection. And often, César noted, he was treated with a certain solicitude, too, sympathy for the plight of a talented failure, as though the younger men were aware that he had never fulfilled his great promise; they must have felt he was in need of comfort and, to be sure, he was comforted.

Twenty minutes late Camille arrived, made no apologies, greeted no one, but swept through the room trailing an opera cloak lined in green silk, and mounted the dais to take his seat at the piano opposite Vincent who at once rose and approached him with sharp, marching steps as though his feet best expressed his anger. Camille pretended not to notice. 'Good evening, Vincent,' he said as a master might to a recalcitrant pupil, and pointing to the score on the piano, asked, 'Is this it?'

Vincent, clenching and unclenching his fists, managed, after considerable effort, to control his resentment, telling himself that the performance of his music must not be endangered by petty emotion, but he was not helped in the exercise of self control by the sight of Camille leafing through the music as though the pages were blank. 'That seems perfectly straightforward,' Camille said.

'There are one or two things we ought to discuss before we play,' Vincent said, and began to instruct Camille, warning him of the more complex passages and indicating expression-marks of vital importance. At this, the audience, which numbered about twenty-five, fell silent and, as one, strained forward to hear the exchange.

'In the adagio,' Vincent was saying, 'there is this passage marked *mezzo forte, molto espressivo*. The theme here is meant to recall a visit I paid in youth to Blois, and it expresses the earth that is France, the sky that is France, the rivers and the fields that are France, the Christian spirit that is France. You have to look upwards to heaven, and downwards, reach down into the French earth, dig, dig, dig.'

79

'But I'm a composer, not a coal miner,' Camille said.

The audience roared their approval. Someone cried, 'Vive la France!' And another 'Vive Saint-Saëns!' and yet another, 'To the barricades!' Camille was delighted, but Vincent remained rigid as a religious statue. Camille said, 'Beat the tempo you want in the adagio.' Instead of beating time, Vincent made a wide, sweeping arc with his arm. 'Adagio ... molto ... mol ... to ... ad ... a ... gi ... o,' he intoned in a funereal voice. Camille nodded sagely, reached into his inside pocket for a slim, gold pencil and while writing on the score said, for the spectators' benefit, 'Very slowly,' and received another burst of laughter and applause. Camille then rubbed his hands to warm them, stretched his fingers and said, 'I'm ready,' now glancing round and greeting those he knew who were many. Meanwhile, Vincent, trying to give the impression of unmolested dignity, resumed his seat at the second piano. Romain rose to read from the Société's statutes: 'The aim of the society,' Romain intoned, 'is to aid the production and popularisation of all serious musical works, whether published or unpublished, of French composers: to encourage and bring to light all musical endeavour, whatever form it may take, on condition there is evidence of high artistic aspiration on the part of the composer. In brotherly love, with complete forgetfulness of self and with the firm intention of aiding one another as much as they can, the members of the society will co-operate, each in his own sphere of activity, in the study and performance of works they shall be called upon to select and to interpret.'

He sat down to murmurs of approval. The ritual concluded, Vincent raised his hands above the keys and then, as though he had waited for that precise moment, a tall, raven-haired man, aged thirty perhaps, handsome with fiery black eyes stood in the centre of the room and cried out, 'Scoundrel!' pointing dramatically at the pianists. Vincent looked at Camille. Camille looked at Vincent. Which of the two did he mean? 'You have ruined my life,' the man cried, without throwing further light on the mystery.

The mood of the audience, which was already boisterous and good-humoured, soared to new heights: shouts, applause, cheers, foot-stamping, the scraping of chairs, the snare-drum of boisterous conversation erupted in a tumult carelessly orchestrated. To this

80

accompaniment, Duparc and Chabrier pushed their way through to the man, took him by each elbow and attempted to propel him towards the door.

César took no part in the furore, but sat nodding and smiling as though this was just the sort of behaviour to be expected of a music society. His neighbour, however, Alkan, whose real name was Valentin Morhange, had risen to see what was going on. He was a fierce, impressive man, a pianist and composer whose energy and output made even Camille appear sluggish. He prided himself on knowing everything and everybody. 'A-ha!' he cried, 'a poet!'

'Who is?' asked César.

'The young fellow. Name of Mendès. Catulle Mendès. Married to Judith Gautier.'

'But which of our pianists is the scoundrel?' César asked.

The member behind them, a viola player in Pasdeloup's orchestra called Madinier, a grubby, furtive man, said, 'Which one's the scoundrel? The one who's screwing his wife, I suppose.'

César turned to him. 'Is one of them in love with his wife?'

'I don't know,' Madinier said, 'but I bet you one of them's screwing her.'

The ushers, by then, had managed to manoeuvre Mendès half-way down the aisle, but the poet who was taller and stronger than both Duparc and Chabrier, broke free and darted towards the pianos. 'I'll kill you,' he shouted. 'I'll kill you and I'll kill Zenta!'

'Zenta? Did he say Zenta?' César asked of Alkan who was standing on tip-toe to see the fun.

Camille, for the first time, became alarmed. He took cover behind the raised lid of the grand piano and, using it as a shield, peeked round from time to time as though he expected it to protect him from flights of arrows.

Once more, Duparc and Chabrier captured the man. Hooking their arms under his shoulders the musicians faced the door while the poet continued to face the platform. Backwards he was again propelled down the aisle. As the party reached the door, Mendès screamed passionately, 'I'll see you both in hell!' was bundled out, while an instant hush possessed the audience who then greeted with renewed cheers the noise of splintering wood and thudding which was the unmistakable sound of someone falling heavily down a flight of stairs. A moment later, Duparc and Chabrier re-appeared, the fat man dusting his hands with exaggerated disdain in the manner of a Harlequin.

Resuming his seat, Alkan said, 'Who's this Zenta?'

César began the answer with vague and ambiguous shrugs and grunts. At last he said, 'Not a bad young composer.' He hoped all would understand he did not know the man.

'There can't be anything between *Vincent* and Judith,' Alkan said after some consideration. 'It must be Camille. Well, I don't know what women see in him. And I suppose this fellow Zenta's been there too.'

Madinier leaned in between them. 'Probably a threesome. That's what goes on these days. Dirty bastards. Mind you, I wouldn't mind having a go at Judith Gautier myself. I may be sixty, but I can still get it up.'

If there was one quality César disliked about his fellow musicians it was their coarseness. 'What was the poet's name?' he asked with industrious eyebrows.

'Mendès,' Alkan said. 'Catulle Mendès. A symbolist, I believe. Writes novels. I've never read them.'

'I have,' Madinier said. 'Germanic themes. Lesbianism, black magic and incest. Good stuff if you like that sort of thing. I do.'

'Funny how out of touch you can get,' Alkan said sadly. 'I thought Mendès was living with Augusta Holmes.'

'Now *she's* got big tits,' Madinier said as if the matter was in dispute.

César said, 'Well, for a poet, Monsieur Mendès does not behave in a very poetic way.'

The audience had come, more or less, to order. The pianists sat once again at their instruments. Camille preserved a façade of indifference; Vincent covered his eyes with a hand and appeared to be deep in prayer. Duparc and Chabrier stood guard at the door. Calm eventually returned and presently the music began. César was instantly overcome with weariness, an inability to listen, similar to a sort of blindness he suffered when confronted with certain books. Not that Vincent's sonata was downright bad or, worse, downright indifferent; no, it was forced: you had the feeling that here was someone who had *made* himself into a composer, that music perhaps was not quite natural to him. César believed that what he had said to Vincent the first time they had met still held true: My dear fellow, César had said, you know nothing about music whatsoever.

Lightness was what was needed, champagne instead of sacramental wine, and even while Vincent's mournful first movement droned on and on, César recalled Zenta's setting of the lines, 'The mountains skipped like rams, and the little hills like lambs', and there was gaiety, yes, lightness, the air through which one couldn't quite see, not of a piece with the rest of the composition, but there nevertheless to be encouraged. Perhaps Zenta would be a good balance to Vincent. César's students, like a circle of children twirling with hands held tight, were reluctant to admit newcomers to the dance. But Chabrier and Duparc seemed to be in favour; and Camille had spoken well of him. A powerful character, Zenta, contriving mystical appearances in church, his name on the lips of impassioned young men. César listened for a moment: the end of the first movement was nowhere in sight.

He focussed his attention on Camille who played effortlessly as though he had studied the piece for weeks. How free of conflicts Camille seemed, so devoid of effort, strain, will. César was suddenly consumed with envy. Lisping gargoyle, he thought, how dare you be so famous, so rich, so prolific? And yet, for all Camille's accomplishments, César believed, as artists will, that his own way was the true way, that the struggle, the battle was a means to a glorious end. But what if to struggle with one's longings and aspirations, difficulties and spiritual mortification, one's compulsions and obsessions, yes, and one's doubts, all to be expressed, remember, in sound, what if it mattered nothing? God forbid.

Uneasy, César wiped for himself a spyhole in the condensation on the window-pane, looked down at the dimly-lit street and was at once intrigued by what he witnessed. No sounds penetrated the window, and Vincent's sonata reverberated in the room, so that the charade César observed was like a ballet danced to ill-matched music. First, he saw the poet, Catulle Mendès, leaning against or clinging to a street lamp; the man lit a cigarette and blew a long thin stream of smoke up into the glow-worm light, and the smoke was there suspended in a twisting spiral, a spectral sword above his head. Twice he looked towards Hartmann's, as though he sensed César's eyes on him but, all at once he stiffened, alerted by something in the street. Tossing away his cigarette, a dragonfly in flight, he retreated into shadow. In the room, the pianists had begun the adagio, the attenuated phrases colouring César's anticipation of what was to happen next; he wiped the pane to widen the angle of his vision and gasped audibly: he saw Hermann Zenta coming up the street. Although the face was hidden, there was no doubting who it was: the floppy hat, the cloak, the white gloves César vividly remembered in the porch of Sainte-Clothilde. Down the street towards Hartmann's the unsuspecting figure walked jauntily, César thought. Then, like some Count Albrecht confronting the woodcutter, Hilarion, Mendès reappeared in the spot light, held up his hand, may even have said something, and Zenta stopped, frozen in his tracks. Mendès advanced. Zenta stood his ground. César had now to twist his neck, to crouch almost in order to see the action; his back was to the pianists, and his neighbour, Alkan, observed him with mild but sympathetic astonishment.

Between two circles of street light Zenta and Mendès met. Zenta tried to pass, but Mendès took a sideways step to block his path and Zenta held back. An occasional, and sometimes wild gesture, indicated that the two were exchanging words. Suddenly, they assumed unnaturally casual attitudes, Mendès looked heavenwards, and appeared to whistle, Zenta stared into one of the darkened shop-windows. The reason was soon evident: a barrow was being slowly pushed towards them by an aged chestnut-seller. She halted near Mendès, held up a newspaper cone that contained her wares: he refused to buy with a curt shake of his head. The old woman trundled over to Zenta and offered him the chestnuts. Zenta declined, an elegant wave of the hand, but he reached into his pockets for coins and gave them to the chestnut-seller who blew him a kiss and returned to her barrow to trudge wearily out of César's line of vision. A moment later the two men took up their former position, Mendès now assuming the classic stance of a pugilist, Zenta approached his opponent cautiously and, when he was close, a clarinet length away, lifted the brim of his floppy hat

84

to show Mendès his face. César strained forward, narrowed his eyes and just managed to glimpse a straight nose and a determined chin: the revelation was too quick, the night too dark to form any clearer impression. But the effect on Mendès was startling: he stepped back a pace as though he'd been struck, dropped his guard and seemed about to collapse. Without another word, Zenta hurried out of sight directly beneath where César sat, presumably entering Hartmann's shop. Alone, Mendès stood, helpless and bewildered, crumpled. He set off down the street, a disconsolate, defeated figure. For no reason at all, César chuckled.

The finale, prestissimo, was nearing its end. César beamed, his eyes bright with pleasure. What a fascinating man Herr Zenta is, he thought. A glimpse of his face was apparently enough to rob poets of their passion. And counterpoint to Vincent's erratic themes, César hummed Zenta's mountains skipping like rams and his little hills like lambs.

Alkan whispered. 'What's that you're humming?'

'*In Exitu Israel.*'

'Israel? Good God, not while Vincent's playing.'

'Ssh,' from somewhere.

Alkan again, a little later, 'I'm thinking of setting the Talmud to music.'

'All of it?'

'Well, as much as possible.'

'Ssh.'

When, César wondered, would Zenta confront him? He felt as though he could no longer contain this dread anticipation. Seeing the man enter Hartmann's, knowing he was in the very building filled César with frantic excitement. He squeezed his knees together and shut his eyes tight.

'Clap,' said Madinier from behind.

'Hmm?'

'Clap. It'll look bad if you don't applaud your own pupil.'

'Ah.'

César hadn't noticed that the performance was over. Arms outstretched Camille and Vincent were bowing to the audience and to each other. Camille with that special display of humility the famous have when being generous towards the unknown and untalented. The applause was polite but unenthusiastic; both performers made the most of it but Romain, sensing the dying fall, rose to thank the pianists, gave notice of forthcoming events and brought the proceedings to a close. But the members lingered to discuss the performance, Vincent's sonata, the prelude provided by Catulle Mendès, and mostly what they themselves were doing and writing and planning. Hartmann's red-headed secretary began to extinguish one at a time the lights, in the hope that the ensuing gloom would drive the members out into the crisp night, or into the warmth of the Café Tortoni, but they continued to talk and to expound.

César's eyes were never still, expecting Zenta to materialise at any moment. A delightful excitement pervaded his being, but, to his annoyance, Duparc and Chabrier fell in either side of him and seemed to have no other purpose but to detain him. Their conversation was, César thought, unusually inane, but like gaolers they stuck to him, accompanied him when he tried to catch Camille, but Camille was locked in conversation with Romain. While César and his cohorts hovered, he heard Romain hiss, 'Zenta, Zenta, I know all about Zenta. You're not fooling anyone, Camille. You'll make an ass of yourself again. It's best to be with people who understand you.' Camille couldn't have heard it all, for he strode angrily from the room before Romain had finished, pausing as he reached the door to swirl his green-lined opera cloak in the air before wrapping it tightly round him. Turning, César came face to face with Vincent.

'Well, Father?' Vincent asked hopefully.

'Well, well, indeed.'

'You liked it.'

'Liked what?'

'My sonata.'

'Ah, yes, your sonata, well, well, indeed.'

'You did not like it.'

'It'll be a splendid thing when it's finished.'

'Finished?'

'Pleased you agree with me. Mustn't leave a note unturned, must we?'

Vincent, too, left abruptly.

86

César said, 'I must hurry,' taking out his pocket watch.

'Do you know what Massenet said to Vincent?' Chabrier said hurriedly.

'What?'

'I must get the story right,' Chabrier said, 'Vincent congratulated the Professor on his oratorio. Heavenly, he called it.'

'Vincent called Massenet's oratorio heavenly? Well, I suppose he would,' César said.

'To which Massenet replied, "Oh I don't believe in all that creeping Jesus stuff."'

Chabrier alone laughed. Duparc contrived to appear embarrassed. César said, 'Yes, yes, I must hurry. We're the last here. There's no one else.'

The red-headed secretary stood patiently under the one light that was still flickering. 'Yes, there is,' he said, 'I'm here, Professor Frick,' and laughed a nervous laugh.

With Duparc leading and Chabrier behind, César was escorted down the narrow stairs to the shop which was in darkness. 'Careful of the bottom step, maître,' Duparc warned.

There was a pale glow from somewhere in the back, from Hartmann's office, which suddenly brightened like a northern sun; Camille's silhouette was framed in a doorway behind the Pleyel grand.

'This way, if you please,' he said.

'Who does he mean?' César asked.

'You, maître,' Camille said, avoiding as ever César's name which he found impossible to pronounce.

'Me?'

'If you please.'

'Go on, maître,' Chabrier said, 'you're in for a pleasant surprise.'

Carefully, César felt his way towards Camille, sidling past the displays of music, and sliding around the Pleyel grand until he reached Hartmann's office door.

'Enter,' Camille said.

As though expecting to be given a fright by unruly children, César stepped into the office in which one candle burned and standing behind the light, head bowed, was a familiar figure.

'Allow me to present my protégé,' Camille said, 'Hermann

87

Zenta,' and like a wicked fairy slammed the door to so that César and the young composer were, for the first time, alone.

8

The candle stood on Hartmann's desk with Zenta behind it, suffused in the unsteady, flickering haze, an apparition, silent, head bowed, cloaked, face hidden by the floppy hat. Like a moth, ever the moth, César was drawn towards the flame. The alarm which Camille's dramatic gesture had first aroused quickly gave way to disappointment. César had hoped Zenta might have arranged a more stylish meeting-place than Hartmann's cramped office, littered with sheets of music piled from floor to ceiling, on shelves, even on the window-sills and, with some uneasiness, César noticed on the floor to Zenta's right, a stack, waist high, unsold copies, hundreds, of *Redemption*, César's symphonic piece which had been such a melancholy failure that he had all but obliterated the memory of it from his mind. The omens for the meeting were not propitious. The word *Redemption* on the top copy loomed out of the darkness like a warning in a fog. Yet, César's first instinct to be angry soon gave way to a more accommodating reaction, a sort of prim smile that suggested he was about to indulge Zenta's eccentric behaviour.

– Well, well, Herr Zenta, allow me to introduce myself, although I'm sure it's unnecessary and you know only too well who I am. Nevertheless, I believe in preserving certain formalities. My name is César Franck.

César extended his hand which remained outstretched, and untouched. Zenta did not look up.

– Permit me to say that you do not now appear quite as confident as when making mysterious appearances in church, or writing letters, eh, hmm, what?

Stillness.

– Come along, Herr Zenta, you have contrived this interview. The least you can do is to say something.

Nothing.

– What is it? Nervous? That's understandable and, if I may say so, well deserved. You are hoist with your own petard, a victim, please forgive my bluntness, of all this Teutonic melo-drama.

88

César crouched a little, trying to see under the brim of the hat; he caught a glimpse of the very point of Zenta's chin, but it disappeared with a sudden jerk and the floppy hat quivered like a demented bat on the wing. César closed his eyes.

– I have said this to others and I'll say it to you, sir, to your face: Your music is not as Teutonic as you might like us to think. I have the impression we have travelled a little further afield, into a landscape just a touch more whimsical. Am I right?

A soft sound, a rustling made César open his eyes: Zenta was slowly, very slowly, removing one white glove, finger by finger.

– What is it, Herr Zenta? Are we waiting for an old man's verdict on *In Exitu Israel*? Are we anxious to know what the teacher thinks of the pupil's work, is that it? I do wish you'd say something, sir. It is very tiring for me to make the going.

On to the desk Zenta dropped one white glove, and then began on the second.

– Shall I start by saying that the work is promising? Yes, that's where I shall begin. And you are anxious, I suppose, to know whether or not I will take you on as my pupil. Before I give you an answer, Herr Zenta, you must admit me to your confidence. Was the work unaided? I ask, because it seems to me, a poor old teacher of music, that you suffer from what one might call a mixture of styles but then, perhaps, *you* are a mixture of styles, hmm, eh, what? Mysterious in your appearances, impudent in your approach, brave when threatened, generous to chestnut-sellers, but miserably timid when face to face with reality. Oh yes, I know a great deal more about you than you think.

The second glove joined the first in a careless heap on the desk. Zenta's hands were pale, translucent, elegant.

– Yes, yes, a mixture of a great many styles, and that comes from not knowing who you are or what you are. If I were to take you on I should insist that you be yourself, whatever or who ever that may be.

Stillness.

– Come now, Herr Zenta, do say something. I cannot stand here all night. And I ought to add that if, *if* I take you as my pupil, allow you to join my circle, my composition class, then I shall demand very high standards of your private behaviour. I cannot have dashing young poets breaking in and interrupting our lesson with vulgar passion, outbursts and accusations of an unsavoury character. Is that understood? I am not suggesting for a moment that you are not to be allowed a private life, that would be presumptuous of me, but I do demand that you keep your private life private. And, permit me to say, moral. I do not know what you get up to, I do not want to know what you get up to, but, alas, I can guess what you get up to, and I would rather you did not get up to it while you were my student, do I make myself clear?

Zenta's fine white hands came together as though to pray, or to entreat.

– I have to say, however, that it will be difficult for me to teach you anything, that is if I am to teach you at all, should you insist on remaining completely silent. Teacher and student must converse otherwise, perhaps, no doubt I state the obvious, communication is impossible. You must learn to overcome your natural timidity. I see now that all your elaborate theatrical inventiveness is a shield to hide behind. You are unable to face people, is that correct, have I hit it? Well, well, dear Herr Zenta, I am a shy man, too. I understand shyness in others. I understand what it is to be tongue-tied, awkward, at a loss for words, incapable of putting together a single coherent sentence, especially at a first meeting. I communicate, as I suspect you do, in other ways. Well, well, well. But I urge you, no command you, to speak to me, otherwise I will have no way at all of knowing whether or not we are in the least compatible, and compatibility is the key to any relationship, be it husband and wife, father and son, master and student. So, come along, Herr Zenta, let us make an effort. What do you have to say for yourself?

Outside the office, listening at the door, crouching in the shadow of the Pleyel grand, Chabrier said, 'I wonder which of them is going to speak first?'

Duparc said, 'We shouldn't have left them alone.'

'Perhaps I ought to go back in,' suggested Camille.

'No, wait,' Chabrier said urgently. 'The old boy's cleared his throat.'

César suddenly said, 'Mountains skipping. Odd.'

Camille came to Chabrier's side and also tried to hear. 'What did he say?'

Chabrier shrugged. 'Something about mountains.'

'Mountains?'

'Ssh.'

From the motionless attitude of prayer, Zenta's fingers began to move, became interlocked; the hands tightly clasped together, rocked to and fro, trembling, imploring.

César said haltingly, 'What? What – what is it, Herr – Herr Zenta?'

Again the gesture of fervent supplication.

'You – you want – you want something from me?'

An eager nod: the hat brim shook.

'What is it?'

'Your ... opinion ...' The voice was hollow, sepulchral, barely audible.

'My – my opinion? Of what?'

'Your opinion ... of ... my ... music.' Slow the speech; careful, foreign precision.

'Of your music?'

Another nod.

'Well. Now. Let me say, what? Promising. Yes. Promising. Decidedly.'

The hands relaxed; limp, they disappeared inside the cloak.

'Is that what you wanted, Herr Zenta?'

Zenta bowed his head.

Outside the door, Chabrier said, 'They've broken the ice. He says the music's promising.'

Camille clapped his hands excitedly. 'Good, good!'

César asked, 'Did you hear something just then, Herr Zenta?'

From Chabrier: 'Ssh!'

César answered his own question, 'The wind, I think, only the wind. You were about to say, Herr Zenta?'

Camille hissed impatiently, 'All that needs to be said is, "I'll take you on as my student", that's all that needs be said.'

'Ssh, for God's sake, Camille.'

César said, 'I think there are mice in this office, Herr Zenta, eating *Redemption*.'

'The old boy's laughing,' Chabrier said.

A chuckle, a kind of hissing sound issued out of César at the idea of *Redemption* as food for rodents. But he stopped abruptly because he thought Zenta had spoken. Zenta had.

'Maître.'

A whisper; barely that; a voice without timbre, so quiet that César had to peer through the dim light in the hope of seeing the other's mouth move, but mouth and face remained hidden.

'They've gone quiet again,' Chabrier said.

'Maître, I must ask you one more question –'

'Yes, another question, yes?' Inadvertently César whispered, too.

'Am I to be your student?'

'I thought I had said as much.'

'No.'

'Yes.'

'Yes?' A tremble of hope from Zenta.

'I beg your pardon, my dear boy?'

'Am I to join your circle?'

'Classes are in the evenings. At my home. Come next week.'

'You think my music worthy?'

'Could you speak up, my dear young sir?'

'Worthy? My music. Is it worthy?'

'A lot to learn, a lot to learn, and a great deal more to unlearn.'

'But am I now a pupil of César Franck?'

'You are. I've said so. Yes, yes, yes.

Chabrier said, 'I couldn't hear a word of that.'

'I heard "Yes", three times,' Camille said.

César was unexpectedly overtaken by dreadful disappointment. He saw himself as though from a great height, standing opposite a frightened, insecure young man from whom he had expected – what? He felt suddenly ridiculous, chiding himself for having allowed this boy to affect him so deeply; he regretted his own eternal hopefulness: he cursed the inaction of his daily life. If only more happened to him in the exterior world, he would, he believed, grow more used to the unexpected: one needed, he realised, to judge critically events quite as much as one needed to discern between good and indifferent music, and a critical faculty of any worth is founded on experience and knowledge. Blaming himself for his unfulfilled expectations, César turned towards the door and reached for the handle.

'Wait, please, maître,' Zenta said, the whisper a little stronger, higher pitched.

When César turned once more to look towards the candlelight, Zenta's white hands were unfastening the hook that held the cloak in place.

'My dear young man –' César said with some anxiety.

The cloak dropped to the floor and in that same movement, or so it seemed, Zenta whipped off the floppy velvet hat. César sucked in his breath, biting his bottom lip. Hair, golden hair, too much for a young man, fell to Zenta's shoulders, and César, eyes wide, saw for the first time the young composer's face.

Mademoiselle Holmes, he said or thought.

She wore a man's suit, but underneath the jacket César saw a blouse, cut very low, frilled at the edges, tightly fitted which made it look as though her breasts, to César, wondrous and large breasts, were bursting to be free.

Mademoiselle Holmes, he thought or said.

She smiled, and it was a smile of relief, and of affection. Was there, in that instant, more light in the room? Her beauty glowed like some astonishing star: her eyes sparkled; generous, intense, amused eyes that seemed to grow as one looked at them and César was transfixed, as though they held some hypnotic hold over him, he could not look away. He did not want to: he beheld a face that, by a trick of creation, was perfectly composed of imperfect features – the nose a touch too long, the mouth too wide, the chin too assertive, the cheeks too round, but all of a compelling harmony. And the impression he received was so quick and startling, the transformation so unexpected that he began to laugh, noiselessly, to himself at first out of some uncontrolled, superficial embarrassment as though intent on covering a social gaffe.

Augusta said, 'I wanted you to judge my music without being prejudiced by my sex. I wanted to be judged on an equal footing with your other pupils. I wanted to be accepted for my music and for no other reason.' She was, he remembered, a dramatic soprano.

93

The charade she had devised and the role of dupe he had been obliged to play ignited an infantile spark in him; his innocence, naïveté, even the disappointment of a moment before, were all combustibles: like a child at a circus he saw the acrobat-clown fall only to catch himself and dangle comically in the air. The glorious enjoyment of finding himself in a pleasure garden erupted in laughter, no longer inward, but rich, swelling laughter. And she laughed, too; and he knew she laughed not at the spectacle of him helplessly convulsed but because she must have understood intuitively that she had touched a secret source in him.

Camille said, 'I don't like the sound of that,' and brushed Chabrier aside to open the door and enter Hartmann's office. There, he discovered César seated on the pile of scores for *Redemption*, some of which lay scattered across the cheap, worn carpet alternately wiping tears from his eyes and holding his forehead. Augusta, hermaphroditic in her revealing blouse and tailored suit, stood over him, her face expressing childlike amazement, joy and concern. Both continued to laugh and the appearance of Camille, closely followed by Chabrier and Duparc added to the fun.

Augusta said between spasms. 'He's agreed – to – teach – me –'

'I have, I have,' César said helplessly.

'He likes – my – likes my – music –'

'I do, I do.'

Camille did not derive pleasure from the spectacle of others' happiness, unless he had been the cause of it. He observed César and Augusta coldly, thinking to himself that this was no way for his future wife to behave. And the sight of César, white-haired and, to Camille, slightly senile, giggling like an infant, was almost obscene. 'Wasn't it clever of me to bring you two together?' he said. Neither took any notice.

At his shoulder, Chabrier said, 'It was all Augusta's idea,' and giving Camille as wide a berth as possible edged his way to Augusta, and kissed her hand. 'You're frozen,' he said, 'but congratulations. Welcome aboard.' When he laughed, his whole frame shook.

Duparc, more reserved, level-headed and sensitive, was relieved that the comedy against which he had warned had not misfired: he had imagined all sorts of disaster, the worst of them being a refusal by César to teach him for allowing such a practical joke to be played. But the old boy obviously had not minded; on the contrary, he appeared positively to have welcomed the prank as though, perhaps, he felt that to be treated by the young as their fellow was an enriching and rare experience. Duparc congratulated her, but not as warmly as Chabrier; Duparc still nursed faint misgivings which he could neither define nor voice.

'Well, won't you say thank you?' Camille asked.

Chabrier said, 'Augusta needs to thank no one but herself.'

The laughter never really died: even after the two had more or less regained their composure, it continued to lurk mischievously beneath the surface, always in danger of breaking out once more and rendering either or both helpless.

'And the little hills like lambs,' César said, his eyes closed but the lids somehow stretched as though they were the only means he had of controlling his inner state, and, on opening them, encouraged by the warmth of Augusta's smile, he added, 'I knew there was something not quite right.' He hummed the tune she had written, like a jig, and she seemed to him amused and flattered.

Camille said brusquely. 'I'm glad it's all settled,' and then, going closer to Augusta, added more quietly and urgently, 'I must see you alone. I must know your answer.'

'Answer?' she said, puzzlement clouding her wide generous smile.

Camille shivered as though an icicle had slid down his back. For, the expression of bewilderment on her face, the silliness of her smile, her total lack of comprehension, instantly told him that his proposal meant nothing to her. Had she thought he joked? Had he not made it plain that he wanted her as he had never wanted anyone else? Had she not promised anything – *anything*, the word had been underlined – if he would help her to become a pupil of this foolish, failed old man? In the lightning process of realisation, Camille believed he hated her, but even as he turned, as always on the impulse, and walked furiously out of the office into the street banging Hartmann's door behind him, he was aware, too, that she would always have some place in his heart and, in a way, he hated her the more for that.

'What's the matter with Camille?' Duparc asked, but no one answered.

Chabrier said, 'Let's all go to Tortoni's. Everyone'll be there. We can celebrate. Tell you what, maître, you can buy us champagne.'

'Not me, I fear,' César said, the laughter still trapped in his voice, 'oh dear me no, I must be getting home. Too much excitement for one evening.'

'I'll walk with you,' Augusta said, eyes bright, as though the decision thrilled her.

Chabrier, looking all around, asked where Camille was: the question, like a wrong note, brought a sudden stop to the momentum of the proceedings. Duparc answered that Camille had gone; a brief uncomfortable pause ensued.

César said, 'I must go, too,' standing. For the first time he saw her as a danger to his peace of mind. Obsessions.

Augusta said, 'This has been the most wonderful evening of my life and no one is going to spoil it.' And, to César's surprise and embarrassment, she linked her arm in his and escorted him out of the shop into the street: once outside, César carefully disengaged himself; her eyes like bright beacons never left his face: he looked up at the clear night sky.

Chabrier had the key from Hartmann, and Duparc reminded him to lock the outer door. While César and Augusta stood in the empty street, the fat man bent over and poked about for the key-hole; Duparc whispered to him, 'Emmanuel, do you think we should warn the old boy?'

'Warn him? About what?'

'About Augusta.'

'What about her?' Chabrier asked, straightening up.

'Shouldn't we tell him that she's a little mad?'

'Don't be a fool. She's not mad, she's a woman. And besides I forgive her anything. And do you know why?'

'Why?'

'Because where Augusta is, there's life.'

The icy wind unabated whipped down the boulevard de la Madeleine. César stood gazing at the sky, breathing the night air as though it were spring. 'Oh,' he said, 'what an amusing evening.' He turned to Augusta who was still watching him, saw her raise a hand as though she meant tenderly to caress him; he drew back.

She said, 'Do you mind if I walk with you?'

He smiled; and she smiled, too. By then, Chabrier and Duparc had joined them. Chabrier said, 'You're sure you won't come with us to Tortoni's?'

Augusta looked to César. He shook his head, then smiled again. Chabrier and Duparc each kissed Augusta's hand and saluted César like a comrade-in-arms, and then they watched the music master and his new pupil begin their journey, he hurrying as usual and she running to keep up.

9

Half-way down the narrow rue Duphot, Augusta said, 'Please, could you not go so fast?'

He apologised, tried to take a slower pace, but soon was back to normal speed. His enjoyment of the evening had given way to uneasiness the moment they had parted from Duparc and Chabrier. He was pricked by the beginnings of panic: what if anyone he knew should see him walking at this hour with such an extraordinary companion? True, there were not many people about except for the comings and goings outside the cafés, but you never knew who you would meet, a friend of Georges, for example, or worse of Félicité. You could not easily explain away someone as startling and as eye-catching as Augusta Holmes who insisted on allowing her cloak to fly from her shoulders revealing her jacket, her frilly, low-cut blouse and tightly fitting male trousers. The few passers-by, no matter what sex, glanced her way, while she hardly looked where she was going but walked, trotted, turned to César, her lustrous hair loose under her hat and streaming like her cloak, her eyes, bright as any stars, rarely leaving his face.

When they reached Notre Dame de l'Assomption which stood in a small, oddly shaped close, she said, 'Please, could we rest a moment?' and without waiting for a reply sat down on the church steps, legs spread wide like a man and took a cheroot from her jacket. 'Do you smoke?' she asked.

'No.'

While she lit up, César impatiently paced the length of the steps eyes down, intent, looking up only at the approach of footsteps.

'I have so many questions to ask you,' she said after a moment.

'Have you?'

'Well of course I have,' she said. 'And you must have questions for me.'

'Perhaps. One or two.'

'Ask.'

She had an imperious way of speaking, more commanding than any man. She alarmed César. He said, 'Your name.'

'How funny.'

'Funny?'

'Never mind, go on, I'll explain later.'

César paced; nearing her he said, 'Is Holmes a Hebridean name?' Holmes: he pronounced it like Camille's mother 'Ol-maize.'

'Hebridean? No. Irish.'

'Ah!' he exclaimed, raising a forefinger. 'Irish!'

'I'm thinking,' she said, 'of adding an *accent grave* to the e.'

'Holmès,' he said. Ol-mess.

'Yes! That's right! Holmès. Do you think I should?'

'Should what?'

'Add the *accent grave?*'

'It is easier.'

'Then I will.'

'Are both your parents Irish?'

'My mother's dead.'

'I'm sorry.'

'My father lives in Versailles. He's retired now.'

'From what?'

'The army. He's a general in the Irish Guards. General Dalkeith Holmès.'

'A general? That's a grand thing to be.'

'He's a grand fellow,' she said. 'A saintly man.'

'And you were born where?'

'In Versailles.'

'In Versailles, were you?'

'Why do you sound so surprised?'

'Well, because I guessed you had gazed on some other landscape. I detected that in your music.'

'No. Wrong. Only France.'

98

'Impossible,' he said.

'And I say it's true.'

'But you're Irish, mademoiselle.'

'But I've never been to Ireland,' she protested.

'It's there even so. Is it a misty place?'

'Yes, they tell me it's misty. It's a prison, too.'

'I am sorry.'

'There's a conqueror in Ireland. And my people want to rule themselves. And must. And will.' She leaned forward now, elbows resting on her thighs, puffing deeply on the cheroot.

'You see,' César said, 'there you are, you say "my people". I heard that in your work.'

'Good!' she cried and with her thumb tipped her hat to the back of her head.

'I'm a foreigner, too. A Belgian by birth, though when I was born Liège was in France.'

'Now, shall I tell you why I thought it strange when you asked about my name?'

'I think I ought to be getting on my way,' he said, walking on so fast that she only caught up with him when he turned right into the rue de Castiglione. 'You see,' she said a little breathlessly, 'I was about to ask you what I should call you?'

'What you please.'

'What do the others call you?'

'Mostly maître. Vincent d'Indy calls me *Pater seraphicus* and sometimes Father.'

'Now, that's a funny thing,' she said.

'What is?'

'For someone who isn't your son to call you Father.'

Her words struck an unsettling chord of memory, but he could not bring to mind exactly what. He said, 'I'd rather you didn't call me Father.'

'I won't. That's the last thing I want to call you. I have a father –'

'Ah, the General, yes –'

'I'll call you something of my own. I'll think about it.'

'Maître will be perfectly acceptable.'

'Maître, maître,' she repeated as though she had never heard the word before. 'No, I don't like it. No, we'll find something else.' But she never did; from that moment on, she never called him anything. 'Have you any daughters?' she asked suddenly.

'No—'

'Sons?'

'Yes. Two,' and two dead, he wanted to say, 'Why?'

'My father always says that if a man has sons it's because he's the dominant partner in the marriage.'

In spite of himself and of knowing it was untrue, he was flattered. 'But your own father had a daughter.'

'Ah, but soldiers are as soft as silk, didn't you know that? Especially generals.'

They walked in the dark shadows of graceful arcades and on the diamond patterns of tiled pavements: insects, moths probably, attacked a dim street lamp; somewhere, behind them and to their left in the direction of the Place Vendôme, a drunk sang passionately of Barcelona. She talked of her father, General Dalkeith Holmès, the Irish Guards, of the uniforms he wore and the medals he had won. César did not listen. He was only now conscious of being victim to a sliding sensation, a descent. Why, he wondered, had he expected so much? Why had Zenta, or whom he still thought of as Zenta, stirred such apprehension and eagerness in him? Why, hidden in a cupboard, had Z loosened thoughts of Josquin? The intimations of a wonderful event had, he concluded, been infantile. Here he was walking beside a girl who was given to masquerading as a man, a girl, moreover with a reputation for being modern with lovers and affairs and so on and so forth, and he had, almost unwittingly, admitted her to his circle. How would he explain it? What would he tell the Actress? He consoled himself with the knowledge that she was a general's daughter: that, at least, was respectable. He rehearsed: I've decided to teach a general's daughter, Félicité, my dear; it sounded well enough, one could almost say impressive. Why then, he asked himself, had he succumbed to this depression; the inescapable anti-climax?

Abruptly, he stopped. She was saying something about military parades, how she loved to see the soldiers in scarlet; he interrupted: 'Why?' he asked sharply.

'Have you ever seen the regiment on parade?' she asked incredulously.

'No, no, no, no,' he said, dismissing with an impatient gesture the entire army. 'Why did you do what you did?'

'I don't know what you mean,' she replied indignantly.

'Stalking me, at the Conservatoire, cancelling my lessons, sticking messages in my hat, appearing in the church – that was you, wasn't it?'

'Oh yes,' she said, laughing warmly, 'that was me all right.'

'Well, why?'

'Because of your letter.'

'*My* letter. What letter?'

She reached into her back trouser-pocket and took out a folded sheet of César's writing-paper. 'This letter,' she said, 'written to me in March, turning me down for your composition class.'

'Oh yes,' he said, remembering.

'Oh yes all right. Operatic, theatrical, you said.' She unfolded the letter and leaned into the light of a café window. Inside they were shutting up for the night, piling table upon table, chair upon chair.

'Your own music was quite different from – from Herr Zenta's,' he said stiffly.

'Not at all,' she said. 'All that was different was my *sex*!' She read from the letter, putting on a pompous voice, ' "Your compositions are, in my opinion, superior to those of the Vicomtesse de Grandval, the only other lady composer whose work I have had the opportunity of hearing." ' She thrust the page at him as though to condemn him of a capital offence. 'If that doesn't prove your prejudice, I don't know what does!'

Was she truly angry, César wondered, or was she play-acting? He said, 'Prejudice? How?'

'How, he asks! Prejudiced against woman, of course –'

'Not at all,' César said, hurrying on.

She ran beside him. 'Of course you are. You turned down Augusta Holmès, but you didn't turn down Hermann Zenta. That proves my point. I bet you didn't even bother to play through Augusta's pieces. You thought, oh a woman, bound to be no good. And to compare me with the Grandval woman! Compare me to

Mozart or Schubert or Wagner, I'll stand that comparison. But to Grandval! She couldn't compose herself for sleep let alone a decent piece of music. I thought to myself, I'll show him, I'll tie him up in knots, I'll mystify and bedevil him, I'll make it impossible for him to say no!' And then, after the vehemence, she tugged at César's sleeve and eyes wide, mouth trembling, a little girl, said, 'You're not angry with me, are you? Oh don't be angry. It was only fun. You enjoyed it, didn't you? Oh, say you enjoyed it. You did laugh, after all.'

'Yes, I did laugh,' he said.

'And I did so want to be your pupil.'

'Did you?'

'Ask anybody. Ask Camille. I told him I wanted the world to take me seriously as a composer. Who could I study with, I asked him, that would prove that I wasn't playing at it? Who do people take seriously as a teacher? He said at once, César Franck.'

And did he say, but he's a failed, old composer who was once thought promising, but who hasn't written anything for years because he hears nothing but silence? He said, 'That's very flattering.'

'I know I can be a great composer,' she said. 'Truly great. Not because I'm a woman, but because I have the sounds of the angels in me!'

He winced: such belief in self embarrassed him. 'We shall see,' he mumbled.

They crossed the rue de Rivoli and entered the Tuileries Gardens. The rows and rows of plane trees with luminous dappled bark, some still with dead leaves and balls of seed, twisted, gnarled branches, clear against the night sky, a military parade of trees. The drunk whom they had heard in the Place Vendôme seemed to have followed them, for now they heard his cracked, unmusical voice again, singing no more with longing for a city, but with despair for some lost love.

Augusta said, 'And you really, really, honestly, honestly think my machine good?'

César winced again. She had used the modern painter's slang for work: machines, they called their creations. He abhorred the word; it struck too near home. He said, 'Good? Well now, that's a very difficult question. I think it's quite good enough for you to learn more.'

'Oh yes, I know that of course, it's only –'

'What now?'

'It's only, I don't want you to be prejudiced. I don't want you to make it harder or softer for me because I'm a female. I want you to treat me exactly the same as you treat the others.'

'Prejudiced, indeed,' César said tetchily. 'I believe I'm able to judge music as music.'

'No, no,' she said, 'you think you can but you can't. No man can. It's not your fault. It's the way things are. You're bound to be prejudiced.'

'I am not prejudiced!' César said, halting and raising his voice. 'Anyway, I've always believed my prejudices are my greatest virtues. I don't, for example, hold any prejudice against good composers, men or women. But I'm deeply prejudiced against bad composers.'

'Who's to say they're bad?' she asked defiantly.

'*I* am!' To his astonishment, he found himself shouting. 'I,' he continued, a little less loudly, 'I, after fifty years of study and practice of informing my faculties with the highest standards of listening to J. S. Bach, to Mozart, to Beethoven, I say to you what in music is good and bad. Not because I like such-and-such, or dislike so-and-so, but because I tell you by the standard of the past and the present what is good is good, and what is bad is bad. How old are you, mademoiselle?'

'Twenty-three.'

'Twenty-three, yes, well, when I was twenty-three I believed that what I liked was good and what I despised was foul. And I tell you, thirty years later, it is not so. I was wrong then, I am right now.'

'Yes,' she said, 'but how many women composers do you know?'

He stopped short; her change of direction momentarily baffled him. He said, subdued, 'Not many.'

'It's difficult, you see, to be a woman composer.'

He wished she hadn't said that: too glib. 'It's difficult to be a composer,' and he wished he hadn't said that: too glib.

'Ah, but I've had no formal training, no Conservatoire, no prizes –'

'Someone must've taught you –'

'Mostly myself, but there were two glorious men in my life, my musical life, that is. Captain Klosé, a friend of the general and bandmaster of the Artillerie de la Garde Impériale –'

'Klosé,' César said, 'did he not teach clarinet at the Conservatoire?'

'He did indeed, and a finer teacher there never was. A dear old boy he was and is. Retired now. And the other dear soul was the organist at the church in Versailles, Lambert –'

'Ah yes, Lambert –'

'Those are the two: Klosé and Lambert. Army and church. Scarlet and black, that's what's made me.'

'And, perhaps, a Bavarian gentleman, too?'

'Who? I don't know any Bavarians –'

'No? I thought I smelled a little German sausage in the chords.'

'German sausage? Oh!' she said, 'you mean Wagner? Oh, Richard's all right. But I'm through with all that.'

Richard, indeed, and through with all that: how fortunate, César thought. He said, 'Good, good,' and then she held his arm again, stopping him from going on. He was not used to being touched. He said, 'What is it?' Her face was lit by the faint rays of the moon; he thought he detected some anguish in her eyes, a stricken look, an ache. He said, 'What's the matter, mademoiselle?'

She said, 'You'll hear terrible things about me. Don't believe them, will you? Please don't. People gossip, and lie, don't believe them, please. Just believe I want nothing more in this life than to be a composer and one that'll do you proud. I'll be a serious student, oh, I will, I will. I'll work harder than anyone. I'll be dedicated and disciplined. I'm going to change my entire way of life just so that I can learn and learn and learn from you.' Her ardour gave way abruptly to a practical tone. 'By the way, how long is the course?'

'The course?'

'How long will it take?'

'For what?'

'For me to learn what there is to learn.'

'This life,' César said, 'and the next.'

She laughed. 'The impossible fascinates me,' she said. 'I'd rather die than fail. But I won't fail. I will write music that will free me, my sex, France, the country of my birth, and Ireland, the country of my ancestors. My whole existence has but one purpose: to write music that will liberate.'

Is that all, César thought? It would be enough, he reflected sadly, simply to write music. 'We shall see,' he said, 'we shall see.'

'I'm going to leave you here, is that all right?' she asked like a young beau to his girl.

'I'm perfectly capable of crossing the bridge on my own,' César said, amused.

'When must I come?'

'Next Wednesday.'

'What time?'

'Eight o'clock.'

'Where?'

'My apartment.'

'Will there be others?'

'Oh yes, we all meet on Wednesdays.'

'I want private lessons, too, you know. I haven't the patience to learn in a group –'

'I shall be the judge of that, mademoiselle.'

'Augusta,' she said. 'Call me Augusta,' she vanished.

When César reached home he was exhausted. He could not think. He sat heavily on his bed, staring at Kant's *Critique of Pure Reason* which lay on the table by his side. Wearily, for want of an action, any action, he reached out and opened it at the first page: 1. *Of the difference between Pure and Empirical Knowledge.* That all our knowledge begins with experience there can be no doubt, he read. He repeated the words aloud. He read them again silently. Experience experience – the word had resonance. What did his experience tell him, he asked? Slowly, like a dripping tap, thoughts entered his consciousness. Experience told him that he made a terrible, horrendous mistake. The moment the girl revealed herself he should have refused to teach her, then and there, in Hartmann's office. But the laughter was misleading; he cursed himself for laughing. And then, with a picture of her in his mind, he realised what an intense creature she was; he had forgotten that the real world, if it was real, could be so oppressive. He had built around himself thick protective layers of routine, innocence, eccentricity, yes, saintliness even, in order to keep the world from entering his well-guarded compound, and now he felt the world, a raffish, dangerous world was about to impinge. Charged emotions were not for him: he wanted no part of them, but a conviction took hold that, willy-nilly, he would be dragged down into some unimaginable, deadly quagmire. He wanted an undisturbed life although he knew there were others who needed to feel that life was a great drama – the Actress was like that, wasn't she? – people who needed affairs, deceit, anguish, yes, violence, and he was certain, but without proof except for instinct, that Augusta Holmès was one, and no teacher of any value can detach himself from the life of the pupil – no master can ignore his student's unhappiness or joy and still hope to be master. And César understood how insidious were the whirlpools of young lives: how attractive it must seem to parents to live the life of their children, and how dangerous, as dangerous, he reflected sadly, as the young living the life of the old.

The wind found the open window, billowed the curtains and rattled the panes, a sound like warning thunder. At random he turned the pages of the book. Section III. *Of Opinion, Knowledge, and Belief*. The holding of a thing to be true is a phenomenon in our understanding which may rest on objective grounds, but requires, also, subjective causes in the mind of the person judging. The salon clock chimed the half. The Actress turned in her sleep. César tried to remove his jacket, managed one sleeve and then sat like a half-dressed doll.

He heard Augusta's voice now, the flow of words lost, but the energy and passion at high tide. True, her voice was melodious and pleasant; she had a strange, charming lilt but the talk poured out of her in torrents, spurts, jets, waterfalls. Talk about hopefulness: I can compose great music, she had said – had not César believed that of himself once? – and she had summoned angels and all the Saints to be her amanuenses.

Exerting himself, he was able to remove his jacket: he fell back on the bed and stared vacantly at the ceiling. He thrashed out wildly now to try to find some good in what had taken place: did Zenta's transformation mean something? a symbol? a chrysalis, perhaps? He replaced Kant on the bedside table, believing there is no pure reason in the inner world: no matter how well ordered the brain, thoughts themselves were subject to a higher law.

Sleep did not come easily; he had passed the point of deep slumber. Instead, confused by a mosaic of imagery, he saw Claire, Zenta, Augusta, the curé in Saint-Eustache and, repeatedly, like a centre-piece, Victor-the-pumper guarding the cupboard door. He was disturbed and frightened, struggling to prevent her sexuality from entering his consciousness. Towards dawn, he dozed off for a few minutes but woke with the name of Josquin on his lips. Later, when the first light of day was creeping beneath the velvet curtains, he went to sleep to the sound of the peasant woman singing and he dreamed of Augusta naked. He woke and saw Augusta naked. Augusta, naked, followed him into his study, down the boulevard, to the Conservatoire. Augusta, naked, pressed her awesome breasts against his lips even as he prayed for peace and quiet in Sainte-Clothilde. Augusta, naked, haunted him by day and by night. The obsession was a tyranny. He tried to tell himself that the indecent images would quickly pass as all the others had done, but he was mistaken. On two separate journeys he embraced Augusta naked on an omnibus, was stricken by an erection, was obliged to hold his umbrella half-open before him like a monstrous cod-piece to hide his passion. The same torture occurred at luncheon with Félicité and Georges.

'How do you find Herr Kant?' Georges had asked.

'Kant?'

'The *Critique of Pure Reason*.'

'Ah yes, pure reason, yes, well, I find it very amusing,' he said as Augusta, naked, sat astride him, smiling, begging him to kiss her nipples. César rose from the table.

'Franck,' Félicité said. 'Pray, take your napkin from your waist and replace it in its ring.'

He pretended not to hear. He smiled, walked round the table until he was calmer.

'What are you doing, Franck?' Félicité demanded.

107

Hiding an erection, my dear, nothing to worry about.

So the days passed. How long could this go on, he asked himself. Augusta would come soon for her first lesson. Would she arrive naked? He prayed for relief, but his prayers went unanswered.

PART TWO

'Augusta Holmès is a very décolletée person.'

Rimsky-Korsakov

Augusta, naked, said, 'He told me he *loved* my music. He said I was by far the most promising young composer he'd heard for ages and ages. He said I had the sound of the angels in me. He *begged* me to be his student.'

Mendès, dressing, muttered, 'I don't believe you.'

'What, what did you say?'

'I don't believe you.'

'It's the truth. He told me. It's the truth. I swear it. He *loved* my music. Why should I lie?'

'Because you always lie.'

'Oh get out, you make me sick.'

'How old did you tell him you were? Twenty-five?'

'*Get out!*'

'Twenty?'

'Get out!'

The crash of glass and the reverberations of piano strings punctuated their exchange. Augusta threw back the bed-clothes, grabbed her green silk robe, and while wrapping it round herself, hurried from the bedroom. Calmly, Mendès tied his cravat. He heard her cry, 'Holy Mother, what d'you think you're doing?'

Adjoining the bedroom was the one other room to the fifth-floor apartment, what Augusta called the studio. Before her tenancy a painter had installed a pitched skylight in the roof. There were no chairs, but the floor was an archipelago of cushions; saucers with candles, carelessly placed, looked like abandoned sailing ships. There was clutter everywhere. On the walls hung more than a score of portraits, all of Augusta, nude. In pride of place were studies, one in charcoal, the other in oil, of two men, Alfred de Vigny and George Moore. A smaller frame contained a silhouette of Mendès, cut from black paper by an old man in the Place Pigalle. Yet another frame held the first page of *Danse Macabre* inscribed to her from Camille. When she burst in, two of Hartmann's workmen were at the open window that overlooked the rue

Mansart. Glass lay shattered on the floor. Outside, suspended from a block and tackle on the roof and tied with thick ropes, a Pleyel boudoir grand swung dangerously to and fro. Augusta pretended not to notice another couple of men at the skylight peering down at her. She tied her silk robe loosely.

'We lost our grip,' one of the workmen said.

'The window pane is to be repaired before evening.'

'Well, I don't know about that,' the man said, 'we'll have to get hold of a glazier —'

'The window will be repaired before evening. And Monsieur Hartmann is to pay.'

The man nodded vigorously. 'Of course, Monsieur Hartmann will pay, but it's a question of getting hold of the glazier.'

'If the window pane is not replaced by five o'clock this evening, you may tell Monsieur Hartmann that the piano goes back tomorrow. I will take my custom elsewhere.'

Augusta turned to go, but stopped to look up at the two men ogling her from the roof. She smiled bewitchingly. One of the men blew a clumsy kiss, the other clutched his heart. She marched back into the bedroom — a cell, spare, clinical, austere — where Mendès, now dressed but for his jacket, lay on the bed admiring the high polish of his shoes and smoking a cigarette. 'How are you going to pay for the piano?' he asked.

'I'm not,' she said, sitting at her dressing-table to brush her hair. 'Hartmann's given it to me.'

'Has he,' Mendès said flatly.

'He wants to publish my music.'

'Does he.'

She turned to him, head tilted, screwed up her eyes while she brushed out a knot. She said, 'You think my music's a joke, don't you?'

'No. I just think that a grand piano requires a grand favour.'

She gave him her back, eyed herself in the looking-glass. 'Julie should've returned by now. Where is the girl? My arm gets so tired brushing.'

Mendès allowed smoke to trickle up his nostrils. 'Will you come with me on Sunday to Nanterre?'

'No.'

'When did you last go?'

'I hate institutions,' she said.

'She is your child.'

Augusta changed the brush from one hand to the other. She had not seen their daughter for more than six months. She said, 'The nuns advised it was better not to visit often.'

'And you always take the nuns' advice.'

'I don't like small children. Babies revolt me. When she's older –' She stopped, remembering the agony of giving birth; she hadn't been able to sing for a month her voice was so strained from screaming. And she remembered the stretch-marks on her breasts.

Mendès said, 'And in April, will you come to Bayreuth?'

'Just you and me?'

'No. Judith will travel with us. But we won't see much of her in Bayreuth.'

'I don't think I can go.'

'Why not?'

'I promised I'd discipline myself and work.'

'Writing music?'

'Yes.'

'And you always keep your promises.'

'I intend to this time.'

He stubbed out the cigarette and immediately lit another. 'I am going to ask you something, Augusta, and I don't want you to lie this time.'

She flicked a glance at him in the looking-glass; he was staring at the ceiling, his expression, solemn; rhythmically he stroked his moustache with the back of his thumb. She said, 'Ask anything you like, but for God's sake don't be pompous.'

He said, 'Where have you been this past month?'

'Away.'

'Where?'

'Away.'

He inhaled deeply. 'I wish to know, Augusta, where you've been.'

In the studio Hartmann's men were calling, 'Easy now, let her swing, slowly, up a little –' Augusta rose. 'I must see what the piano looks like,' she said.

113

Mendès said sharply, 'Augusta –' but she was gone and he heard her admiring her new acquisition.

'Beautiful!' she cried. 'It must have a shawl, a flowered shawl with a black fringe. Turn it round, I must have a view of the street.'

One of the men leaned across the piano, which rested on the sill half in, half out of the window, and called to his colleagues on the roof. 'Right, one of you come down here,' then, to Augusta, 'We'll bring her in now, then we're home and dry. All we have to do is get the lid and legs on.'

The keyboard faced into the room. Augusta fingered a broken chord, C minor, sad, a key in which to tell a lover the affair was at an end.

A workman said, 'That's pretty,' with a hint of insinuation.

Augusta looked at him, her eyes darkening. 'Tidy up the mess,' she ordered. 'And remember what I said about the window pane. It's to be fixed by five.' As she turned she loosened her robe a little more so that the man left on the roof was rewarded for continuing to watch her. In the bedroom, Mendès had swung his legs off the bed and was seated with his elbows resting on his knees, hands clasped, cigarette dangling from his lips. Augusta said, 'You look like a retired Apache dancer,' laughed and then held out a hand to him. 'Come and see the piano. It's perfect in the studio.'

Mendès said softly, 'I want to know where you were. A whole month, Augusta, no word, no letter, nothing. Why didn't you tell me you were going away?'

'I just wanted to be by myself,' she said irritably, resuming her seat at the dressing-table.

'For Christ's sake tell the truth for once in your life.'

Brushing fiercely she said, 'It *is* the truth.'

'You're a congenital liar. You wouldn't know the truth if you ate it for breakfast –'

'Very funny –'

'Where were you?'

'I'm not going to tell you.'

'With Camille?'

'Oh God, no.'

'Hartmann?'

'Please, what do you take me for?'

'That's best left unanswered.'

She dropped the brush, held up both hands in mock admiration. 'Your wit is like a rapier this morning.'

He stood, hands thrust in pockets, jangling his change. Slowly, he crossed to a chair in the corner near the dressing-table on which Zenta's suit was laid. From the floor he picked up the floppy hat, examined it, tossed it on the bed. 'You're not going to tell me, are you?'

'No.'

'But what if I were to tell you that I *know* where you were.'

'This is a ridiculous conversation,' she said brightly. 'If you know why do you ask? God, I wish Julie would come. I want my bath run.'

'You should've told me you were pregnant again,' he said.

The brightness did not leave her voice. 'That's clever of you. I thought I'd been rather discreet. How ever did you find out?'

'Dr Ollendorf is also Judith's doctor.'

'Oh, was your wife having an abortion, too? What an odd coincidence. And what a loss to music. The father may have written another Idyll, like the one to Siegfried.'

He looked out of the window at the courtyard surrounded by other apartments. A child was skipping. A woman swept a door-way with a twig broom. There were still puddles from yesterday's rain reflecting the grey sky. He said coldly, 'I want you out of this apartment, Augusta. The rent is paid until the end of the month. That gives you three weeks.'

'*You're* lying now.'

'I'm not. I want you out of here, I don't want to see you again.'

'I'm sure that's true, but I meant about the rent. You paid a year in advance. Madame Laurant told me. You were always too hopeful.'

He said, 'It's my apartment. You're to be out at the end of the month.'

She glanced secretly at him: he was trying to light a cigarette but his hands were trembling and he could not easily take the match from the box. She said, 'You'll have to throw me out. I've no money. I've nowhere else to go.'

'It's my apartment,' he said again, his voice hollow.

'You took it in my name.' She sat still and calm, gazing at her own smile, her chin defiant.

Mendès said, 'No money? How are you going to pay for your lessons?' He struck the match but the end snapped.

She saw the stricken look in her own eyes. The dreadful thought of her father cast a shadow across her face. She said, 'I'll find a way.'

'How? Money doesn't grow on trees. Dr Ollendorf isn't cheap. You have your father to keep, Julie's wages to take care of. How are you going to manage, Augusta? Or perhaps someone will pay for you? Camille, perhaps, he's doing well. No, I know, your teacher, what's-his-name, he'll teach you for nothing because you're so promising, isn't that it? I hear he's rather old so you won't be able to oblige with your usual services, but that rather suits you, doesn't it? Old men are rather in your line. Vigny, Klosé, all they want is a little feel now and again, and that won't bother you, will it? It never has.' He lit the cigarette, tossed the match on to the floor. In the courtyard the woman with the broom scolded the child who began to cry.

Augusta said, 'Why do you always talk about money? Is it because your father's a banker?'

Julie, Augusta'a maid, knocked and entered carrying a stack of newspapers and journals. She was black, from Cayenne, with innocent eyes and a serene temperament.

'Get out,' Mendès said.

'No, wait, I want to see the papers, Julie,' Augusta demanded. 'Have you looked at them yet?'

'Yes,' Julie said, eyes on Mendès, watchful.

'And?'

'Only the *Guide Musical*.'

'Oh.' Augusta was disappointed. 'Show me.'

'On page three,' Julie said, handing over the papers to Augusta who opened to the place and saw the headline, ZENTA'S IDENTITY REVEALED. She read, 'Last night, Mademoiselle Augusta Holmès –'

Mendès, enraged and growling, swept the dressing-table clean

116

of objects, knick-knacks, powder-puffs and scent. 'Get out! Get out!' he screamed, then turned and in one savage movement wrenched the curtains from the window, half covering his face so that he had to wrestle to free himself. 'Get out!' he bellowed once more but Julie was already gone. Augusta sat calmly pretending to read the item about her escapade. Mendès grabbed the newspaper from her hands, scrumpled it up into a tight ball and threw it across the room. 'Murderess!' he yelled. 'Whore! Rotten, stinking bitch!' He stood over her now, seized her by the shoulders and shook her hard. 'Are you capable of anything? Absolutely anything? Are you going to destroy yourself and everybody else? Don't you live by any law, moral or human, other than expediency, ambition, appetites and impulse? Bitch!' She broke free of him, stumbled towards the door but he caught her by the waist. 'You're a liar, you're ruthless, cruel, treacherous –'

'Let go of me'

'You can't do anything straightforward, can you? No, you have to create drama, get your name in newspapers, do everything for effect. Christ Almighty,' he said with a great sweeping movement that propelled her towards the bed, 'I thought I knew you. I thought you were generous and kind and loving and even, Jesus Christ, honest in your own way, but you're not! You're a vile bitch. No one can know you or understand you because you're a chameleon, you change from minute to minute. How could I believe it was possible to know you when there's no one there to know?' Augusta tried to rise but he pushed her down again. 'Sit down, I'm talking to you –'

'Leave me alone –'

'Bitch! That was my child inside you! Murderess!'

She made a dash for the door but stumbled and, in falling, reached out to Mendès for support. He held her, put her at arm's length, then struck her hard, twice, across the face. She screamed and the noise suddenly arrested his rage. He stood for a moment still, panting, looking at her as though she were a stranger. Then, cupping both hands he clasped her breasts, tears running freely down his cheeks. 'Oh God, I love you,' he whispered.

'Julie!' Augusta screamed, 'Julie!'

Mendès slapped her a third time and, as the maid opened the

door, he pushed past into the studio. Oblivious of the workmen who watched wide-eyed, he tore one of the nude paintings from the wall, picked up a screwdriver from the piano and ripped the canvas to shreds, flinging the remains to the floor. Then, he marched back into the bedroom where Julie was comforting Augusta and, ignoring them, collected his jacket, hat and cloak and ran from the apartment.

A silence settled. After a few moments, one of the workmen cleared his throat and said, 'Well, shall we call it a day?' and awkwardly he began to pack up tools and belongings. As he and the others were leaving he heard Julie saying, 'Hush, don't, stop it now' and he guessed Augusta was crying. He called out, 'Don't you worry, we'll have the window fixed by five,' and hoped he had comforted her.

But Augusta was not crying. While Julie, on hands and knees, began to clear up the scattered debris, Augusta, who had been leaning against the wall, slid slowly to the floor until she was seated, legs outstretched, head back, arms limp, laughing.

'Hush now,' Julie said, casting anxious glances at Augusta, 'don't laugh, it'll turn to tears –'

'No, no, no,' Augusta said, her laughter rich and enjoyable. 'I'm so relieved, we got off so lightly. He's gone and I'm free. I'm free. I'm free.'

'Didn't he hurt you?' Julie asked.

The question applied a brake to Augusta's relief. She fell silent, stared vacantly, and, at last, said, 'What did he mean it was impossible to know me because there's no one there to know?'

'People think you're for the good time, that's what.'

'Can't they see that I've got more in me than that?'

'They see what they want to see.'

More to herself than to Julie, she said, 'I'll show them. I'll make them grovel.'

Julie said, 'I'll run your bath, then I'll try to fix the curtains.'

'I must succeed,' Augusta said, but with a note of fear as though the prospect of failure was more real. The mood snapped. She said, 'Is the *Guide Musical* the only mention of last night?' and crawled to retrieve the scrumpled newspaper which she smoothed out to read in brief of her transformation from Zenta into the newest member of César Franck's private composition class. The item ended: 'The habitués of the Café Tortoni may not be pleased to learn that Herr Zenta also managed to enter the hallowed precincts of the Conservatoire where "he" obtained a private lesson from the Professor of Organ. We are reliably informed that this fulfils all the conditions of a wager made by some who frequent Signor Tortoni's establishment and that, therefore, Mlle Holmès is now their creditor to the tune of 50 francs.'

'You must go to Tortoni's and collect the money for me,' Augusta said, watching Julie pour steaming water from a kettle into the bath.

Julie said, 'Will you go on singing?'

'I'll have to from time to time.'

'I have money saved. You don't have to pay me, you know that.'

'You're kind,' Augusta said and caressed Julie's cheek.

'A couple of painters want me to pose,' Julie said. 'I don't mind earning a bit extra.'

Augusta hesitated before saying, 'I have to be so careful. I have to be serious and I have to be *seen* to be serious. It's a tightrope.'

'We have a year rent free,' Julie said.

'And the baby's cared for. Catulle will go on paying for her, he's so full of guilt.'

'If only –' Julie began but stopped herself.

'If only what?'

'If only you didn't have to send your father so much every month –'

'I don't want to think about it,' Augusta said in a rush.

'Did you write to him to say you couldn't go on with the payments?'

'I don't want to think about him,' Augusta said, but the shadow, for the second time that morning, had darkened her face.

'I'll get the stuff for the lotion,' Julie said.

'Mix it in here,' Augusta said. 'Don't leave me alone.' Her eyes grew huge and childlike and repeatedly she bit her bottom lip.

'Get in the bath. I won't be a second.'

Alone, Augusta remained motionless; to herself she murmured, 'I have so much to give up.'

2

Melted white wax, spermaceti, oil of almonds, rosewater. Julie sat, patiently mixing the ingredients while Augusta, suffused in steam, lay in the bath, arms languidly at rest over the enamel sides. Julie best loved Augusta in moments like these, relaxed, easy, the mood confessional, disconnected: passion, will, stridency all absent. Augusta talked, Julie listened, sometimes interjecting but mostly silent as if it was tacitly understood between them that this hour was Augusta's therapy.

Augusta, eyes closed, said, 'After I left him last night in the Tuileries Gardens, after he'd agreed to teach me, you know what I did? I walked into the Place de la Concorde, stood looking up the Champs-Elysées, up the hill towards the Arc de Triomphe which always seems to me quite out of proportion, too big, too monstrous. Anyway, I raised my fist, I did, and I said aloud, louder than the wind, I said, "Right, Paris, you bitch, I'm on my way now. You'll prostrate yourself before me sooner than you think. You have been warned!"'

'Did you? Really?'

'I did! Paris is a bitch, a real bitch, God forgive her. And you know, the funny thing was, it was freezing last night and I wasn't cold at all. I had a fire in me. As though I was already there –'

'Where?'

'There! There! Anyway, if I wasn't actually there I was on the road, wasn't I? I'd taken the first steps to fame and glory. Dangerous moments when dreams are about to come true. Ah, but I knew it was only the beginning. I've a long way to go.'

'And you liked the professor!'

'The professor?'

'The teacher –'

'Oh, he's a dear old boy, mad as a March hare, but they say he can teach and, by God, I'm going to learn. I'll take everything he's got to give. And more. It's going to be hard, Julie. We have to economise. I have to give up the old ways, all the friends and the fun. Life mustn't be allowed to intrude. Not like this morning. Ah well, we've seen the last of him.'

'Why did you let him in last night?'

'Why? Why? Because he took me, that's why.' She paused, reflecting on her weakness, her inability to resist being pirated; the savagery, the force was itself the excitement. Love-making in any other form was too tame for her.

'And Camille?' Julie asked gently.

'He was angry with me because I laughed at his proposal of marriage. He's a fool, and an iceberg to boot. He doesn't really care about anything except himself. He wants me as a disguise, a camouflage, so he can hold hands with Romain Bussine and have a good conscience. Ah, to hell with them all. They'll all come running when I'm a success.'

Success: the word was a magic incantation, conjuring up all the pleasures of the known world. She could repeat it to herself endlessly to feel at peace and hopeful, to pass into another delicious awareness of self: success, success, success.

Julie finished stirring the mixture and said, 'I'll let it cool now –'

'Bring me a glass of champagne,' Augusta said dreamily.

'But –'

'All right. White wine. And give me a cushion for my head.'

Comfortable, sipping the cool white Burgundy, her body floating in the hot water, Augusta's mind also floated. I will be a success, I shall be famous, I can compose.

What, she wondered, did success mean to her, really mean? Who of her friends were successful? Were fame and success one and the same thing? Could one be successful and unknown? Could one be famous and unsuccessful? Ah, God, she thought, success is a trick requiring technical skill: all you have to do is understand the mechanics, study its workings as a watchmaker faced with the most intricate, delicate clock. The whole bloody society was subject to the mechanical laws of success: some formed opinion, others bowed to opinion; but most bowed to success itself; there were the springs, the cogs and wheels of the machinery which had to be oiled, repaired, cleaned, adjusted. People said she was successful, but then, fools, they didn't know the extent of her ambition. All right, she was not unknown; she was sought after; she regularly found her name in scurrilous pieces written in the newspapers. Any man seen with her was instantly thrust into her light. Entering a café she was easily recognised; waiters fawned on her; whispers and gossip attended her. And what she knew about success she readily acknowledged she learned from Vigny.

Vigny had known it all: success, he told her, was other people's illusions but, God, he knew how to help it along, shutting himself up in Charente at Maine-Giraud, creating mystery and intrigue, the very stuff of illusions, placing on his head the aesthete's crown, clothing himself in sackcloth and ashes, and even getting poems written about him – 'And Vigny more withdrawn, Returned ere noon, within his ivory tower'. And what went on in the tower? how austere in reality was the anchorite's life? The women came and went, his last mistress – also called Augusta – bearing him a posthumous son. It's all a bloody sham, she concluded. And wasn't it Vigny who had encouraged her own style, the outings to Fontainebleau, the hints of depravity? 'Take lovers,' he had said, 'but only the famous. Never love a nonentity.' The bastard, Augusta thought, I was fifteen when he bought me, the bastard.

But he had launched her, there was no denying it, and the life in her responded all too readily to the life outside. Soon, she realised she could not exist without the constant activity, the parties, the chatter, the concerts, the cafés; yet she knew those were the very things she now must sacrifice – but could she? did she have the strength? She must find the strength. Perhaps, she bargained with herself, all need not be surrendered. Poems and songs would, she was certain, still be dedicated to her; she would again sit naked for an artist and thus heighten her belief in her own beauty and, like a reflection of the reflection of Narcissus, her erotic senses would be unhealthily pleasured. Men would continue to grovel – how she loved the word, grovel. Before she was twenty she learned that men, no matter how famous or clever or talented were all, without exception, susceptible to the thought of her naked beside them in bed. And what wild promises they made and sometimes kept in order to make that thought reality. And how she used and misused her sensuality and how that, in itself, the very act of tempting others, excited the temptress.

The game she loved more than the winning or the losing. For long periods she was indifferent to the sexual act – she was passing through such a period now, she reflected – and when the need arose it was quickly satisfied. But the chase was eternally fascinating. The sudden daring of a man unable to control his passion any longer, putting a frightened hand to her breasts, a darting tongue to her ear, pleading, trance-like, to bed her; and others, affecting a sort of superior sexual dexterity, who would run an elegant forefinger down her neck, gently pull her dress lower, astonished to find her unresponsive; and some – these she most enjoyed – who, like Mendès, at the sight of her naked, lost all control and were punished with terrible self-reproach: all were fuel to her sensuality, not theirs. Each time, she held back enough of herself to retain command; there was no man whom she did not feel she could eat and spit out as pulp. The web she had spun, the life and celebrity she had created was self-generating. With success nothing succeeds like promiscuity.

The water in the bath had begun to cool, the wine to warm; the steam was no more. Augusta's pleasure also diminished. Unwillingly she measured the cost to herself, the time wasted, the work delayed, the music unwritten. To maintain success required all her energy and imagination, and left her creativity bereft and exhausted. Worst of all, she became less practised at entering into friendships or relationships with any depth to them; acquaintances and liaisons flourished; the many were preferred to the few and so the judgment of people's worth, true worth, was blunted: she courted the useful and influential, believed liars, trusted deceivers, admired the untalented, was amused by bores, loved by cynics. Love itself, whatever definition was put on it, was a word, a concept to deride: if ever she was made to feel more deeply than she believed was safe, she accounted herself victimised, not privileged; the bearing of a child was a penalty, not a prize.

Fame, of which she had no knowledge, she guessed was different in kind from success. To no one, not even Julie, had she ever confessed the violence of her drive for fame because, she admitted, she was secretly ashamed of such ambition, at times thought it ridiculous, yet could not free herself of it. Fame, she supposed, was not bought or engineered like success. Fame had perhaps to be earned. How dare Mendès say it was impossible to know her because there was no one there to know? Her respect for fame

123

was her saving grace – why could he not perceive that? The going had been hard and rough, she had been buffeted and bruised, but her respect for fame she had kept, as though here lay her integrity, small yet perfectly preserved, flying the banner, Fame Must Be Earned. She bore no envy for the famous; the successful she despised.

And if fame was to be earned she had no other means than her music. But here, too, she discovered conflict. What music? From day to day her need to compose altered. On Monday she would write what she thought would sell; on Tuesday, what she thought would be considered serious; on Wednesday, she wrote music to prove that women can write music; Thursday, she wrote to liberate Ireland; Friday, to rescue single-handed the music of France; Saturday, she sought commercial success again; on Sunday, of course, she dedicated her music to God. In all this profusion of sound she knew that she herself remained hidden and obscure. From her earliest years, when the tunes first ran free in her head, she had, perversely, compulsively, set them down not as she heard them but as she thought others would want to hear them. Klosé, at Versailles, her first teacher, bewitched by her prettiness, liked the military marches she could endlessly invent; Vigny demanded love songs and eternal themes. She could hear him now encouraging her as he undressed her. George Moore who wrote poems for her to set, odes to his native Ireland, who painted her nude and whose thin, tortured face disgusted her even to this day with its expressions of guilt and repression, he had been one of the furtive ones: in the Café Nouvelle-Athènes, once, he had pretended to spill wine down her, wiped her clean, trembled, giggled and fled. And Catulle Mendès who believed that poetry and therefore art must be controlled and elegant, absent of emotion – and look how *he* had behaved today – for him, she had written music without feeling, imperfectly formed. And Camille? Camille was always puzzled by her total lack of technique, astonished when she confessed ignorance of such essentials as counterpoint and harmony. All he wanted was to accompany her to the sunlit woods of Fontainebleau, watch her remove her woman's clothes and dress as a man. Always he gave the same advice: write what's in your head, Augusta. Yes, all very well, but her courtship of worldly success had distanced the tunes which were once so powerful and harmonious. The music she composed seemed to her no longer truthful. The life she led had dulled her standards of what was good and bad in herself. So, she performed more, sang, accompanied, gave recitals, which was the easy way out, for it demanded little except her physical presence. To produce music she had to surrender too much else and that, until recently, she had not been prepared to do. She cursed herself: she acted perversely out of compulsion not because she didn't know better.

How had the determination come to break the pattern of her existence? She remembered now, as she sipped the last of the tepid wine, the moment of resolve to change her way of life. She had learned she was again pregnant. She told no one except Julie; she agonised for almost three months about what she should do. On the evening she sang *Danse Macabre*, the decision to rid herself of the baby became unshakeable as though abortion symbolised the severance from the past. The audience's reaction that night had caused her to flee the platform, not because her pride of performance had been wounded but because the unexpected boisterous and crude tumult had washed over her producing waves of nausea. Camille had laughed at her and at the reception of the song; the only time he became serious was when he was told his mother had fainted. I want to change my entire life, Augusta remembered saying, I want to be a serious composer. He had promised to help and she had departed the hall with the booing still in her ears. She had not gone home, but into a cheap hotel in the rue de Londres; she had lain all night vomiting, crying, fretting, utterly alone. She did not know why the promise of motherhood should bring her to hysteria: the prospect of pain was terrifying, and she hated her slender waist misshapen, her breasts, her wonderful breasts, suddenly overblown and pendulous. She experienced that night for the first time the fear that youth was transitory, that those resources upon which she had in the past so heavily relied were ephemeral. Some time in the early hours of the morning, when her anguish was most acute, she resolved that the need she had spoken to Camille would be satisfied; she would disjoint the past from the future; she must rid herself of the insane terror that time was running out by filling time with what was important to her. She determined to impose herself on the world, to fulfil what she believed to be her destiny, success, fame, music.

The glass was empty. Augusta's thoughts were suspended in lazy speculation of what might be – vague, pleasurable longings. César's face came into her mind – he was laughing. Do you want something from me? she remembered him asking, and: I say to you what in music is good, what is good is good, and what is bad is bad. She recalled those particular words because they were unexpectedly fierce, uttered with such stern conviction. And he had agreed to teach her. Because her music was good? She smiled but the smile was brief. Had she not tricked him into accepting her as a pupil? Had she not contrived it? Was she not partaking in an elaborate pavane of her own choreography? Was she not paying lip-service to her aspirations? The questions, rippling flutes, trickled through her consciousness but strangely did not disturb her. She was on the road to glory, and no misgivings would undermine the blast of trumpets.

Presently, Julie returned carrying a towel and rosewater in a tall, thin-necked bottle. She said, 'Come now, let me help you,' and as Augusta rose from the bath Julie covered her in the towel warmed before the studio fire. A little light-headed, Augusta gently patted her body dry while Julie added the rosewater to the substance she had previously mixed and which was now congealed into a thick, soft cream. Augusta let the towel drop to the floor and stood admiring herself in the looking-glass. She began to pull at the flesh around her stomach, cupped her hands to lift her breasts, turned sideways to view her waist and hips. 'No,' she said, 'there are no stretch-marks any more. The cream is good.'

'All the women of Cayenne use it,' Julie said, and dipped her fingers into the preparation beginning gently to massage her mistress from neck to ankle, long, sweeping movements, caressing the area around her naval, and oiling her nipples. Augusta watched Julie's dark hands on her pale flesh, like streaks of honey in cream, and a memory returned from adolescence: when first her breasts began to form she would for the hour before bed lower the light, stand or sit in front of the looking-glass, run her hands over her body as though performing a dance learned in an oriental bazaar, her arms Cleopatra's asps, her hands Salome's veils. Once, she remembered, when she had discovered the new, soft hair at her thighs, her father entered the room. Frightened, she had pulled the quilt from her bed and covered herself. He stood in the open doorway, his face contorted, as if in pain. 'Jesus, Jesus,' he said, 'God help me,' and fled. For a long time afterwards he seemed cowed in her presence as though weighed down by a dreadful secret. She shuddered, feeling the cold of the shadow.

Her skin glistening with the thin film of lotion, Augusta began to exercise, movements she had learned from a ballerina, bending and twisting in all directions, swivelling her hips, stretching her legs, standing on tip-toe to extend her arms, hands, fingers to their limits as though an invisible prize hovered just out of reach. And after Julie placed over her a robe, she settled for sleep, not in the bedroom but on cushions set before the fire in the studio. The maid drew the curtains to cover the window with the broken pane, and tugged thin strings which lowered blinds to cover the skylight and shut out the grey noon sky.

In the semi-darkness, watching the scarlet coals, Augusta's eyes grew heavy. Wrapped in her robe she imagined the sensation of birth, her own birth, the coming into light. She was warm with well-being. The violence of the morning was forgotten. The break with Mendès symbolised the end of the old way. The thought of César, the symbol of the new, brought comfort. Her determination to change felt immovable. Life would not be allowed to intrude, but in that movement before sleep, when terrors encroach, she had the impression of falling and the notion, brief yet sharp, that the past could never be cleanly severed from the future; and, as if to confirm her fears, she woke to Julie stirring the fire, saw the flames escape and die, felt the transient shadows across her face and learned that a messenger had brought news from Versailles that her father, Dalkeith Holmes, had been arrested for causing bodily harm to Captain Klosé, retired bandmaster of the Artillerie de la Garde Impériale.

3

Dalkeith Holmes had, the previous evening, lost his precarious foothold. He reached out for the iron railing, missed it and plunged headlong down the flight of stairs, crashed into the first-floor landing, spun like a top before again cascading down another flight and coming to rest on the flagstones in the courtyard. The bottle in his trouser pocket had been crushed to pieces in the fall; he felt liquid running down his thigh to his knee; he did not know whether it was absinthe or blood; he did not know whether it was night or day, dawn or dusk. He did not care.

'*Augusta! Augusta!*'

A door opened an inch, a little wider, wider still: the wedge of light crawled across the yard until it found the back of the fallen man and rested there. A voice said, 'It's the Irishman again,' and the light vanished. Holmes breathed heavily, spittle trickling on to the flagstones.

'*Augusta! Augusta!*'

Like repeater-rifles, all around him, doors opened and shut, voices bellowed disapproval and requests for silence.

'*Augusta! Augusta!*' And then: 'Oh, Christ Jesus, Augusta, come back to me!' loud enough for the concierge in her hole to hear.

Madame Auguez tall, emaciated, severe, hovered over him, the Angel of Death.

'Stand up, monsieur,' she ordered.

'I cannot.'

'You are disturbing all the tenants.'

'Augusta! Augusta!'

'Stop it, monsieur.'

'Major, not monsieur, Major, Major,' he barked, screwing up his face as though the effort pained. 'Major Dalkeith Holmes, madame.' He began to cry, like a child afraid of thunder.

'Major Holmes,' the concierge said, obliging him, 'you are not to be so naughty. I am responsible for the respectability of the pension.'

'Then why the hell am I lying here? That's not very respectable,' he said through his tears, wounded by indignity.

'You have fallen down.'

'Who has?'

'You have, Major, and you are lying in the courtyard. Get up.'

'Who's that? Oh Christ, whose voice is that?'

'It is me, Madame Auguez.'

'I'm bleeding, madame. I've a wound in my upper leg,' he said and lost consciousness. Blackness, stars, a racing moon. He came to and saw a second pair of legs, wrapped in winter clothes.

'Augusta? Augusta?'

'No,' said Madame Auguez.

'Who is it, then?'

'My sister-in-law.'

'I want Augusta.'

'You are to stand up, Major Holmes.'

'I cannot stand, madame. I want my daughter, for Christ's sake.'

'She is not here.'

'Augusta! Augusta!'

'There is no use calling for her. She is not in the house.'

'I'm done for, Holy Mother of God. I'm done for!'

The sister-in-law, another Madame Auguez, but softer, said: 'Don't cry, Major Holmes, I beg you not to cry. You are a soldier.' He could see neither of them, only feet, courtyard, spittle.

The concierge: 'Do what you like but stop your noise.'

'I want my daughter!' He started to wail, a terrible lament, long, extended notes of lonely anguish. Doors opened again, angry voices resounded, doors closed, a pack of cards collapsing. 'I want Augusta. I want to see her before I die.'

'Your daughter is not in this pension, Major Holmes. She has never been in this pension. Get up and go to your room.'

Hands gripped his shoulders. The world spun. He was on his back. He saw the two faces, one a skull close to him, the other a shining disc a million miles away. The skull suddenly recoiled. 'Ugh,' it said. 'He smells of absinthe.'

'Gangrene,' Holmes said.

'You are drunk, Major.'

'Who is?'

'You are.'

'The hell I am. I'm hurt, madame. I'm dying.' He drew back his coat to reveal his thigh. 'I'm bleeding, can't you see?'

'Hold our hands, Major, and we will pull you to your feet.'

He emerged from the grave: he screamed. The women no longer spoke to him in a language he understood. 'Pa, pa, pa!' said the first: 'Tsch, tsch, tsch!' said the second.

129

Limping, holding on to Madame Auguez' bony, brittle hand on his left side, and to Madame Auguez' sponge of a forearm on the right, he allowed himself to be led over the uneven, cracked stones, under the archway into a smoke-filled cell. A pot rested on a stove: a ladle in the pot. Where was the third witch?

'Get some newspaper. Cover the chair. He's bleeding badly.'

'Put him on the floor, then.'

'We can't do that, oh no, we can't do that.'

The two women helped him to sit.

'What time is it?' he asked, eyes closed.

'Nine o'clock.'

'Day or night?'

'Night.'

'Where's Augusta?'

The women exchanged a helpless look. The soft one approached the chair. 'Do you want a priest, Major?'

'What about a doctor?' said the skull.

The answer evaded him; he felt wonderfully drowsy. He slept, woke, saw a hand, hairy, on his bare thigh. 'Where are my trousers?' he asked.

'Madame Auguez is getting you another pair from your room.'

He found difficulty in raising his head. 'Vigny,' he said. 'Augusta knows. Klosé told her.'

'You are delirious.'

'He doesn't stop about his daughter.' The soft Madame Auguez.

A second hairy hand, matching the first, began to help bandage the thigh.

Holmes asked, 'Why are you bandaging me, Vigny?'

'I am not Vigny. I am Dr Coquard.'

Holmes looked up too sharply, glimpsed the doctor only briefly before the world again spun at alarming speed, sending him off into yet another oblivion.

'Where is this daughter of his?' he heard Dr Coquard ask.

'I don't know. I've never seen her. She's never visited this house to my knowledge. No one gets past me without my knowing.'

'Ah. He's coming to.'

The Angel of Death said, 'I once heard, only gossip mind, that the –'

'Tsch, tsch, tsch.'

'What?' from the doctor.

'Some scandal. An older man. I don't gossip. I hear a lot, of course, but I keep it to myself. They lived the other side of the town then.'

'*Lies!*' screamed Holmes.

'Stop that, Major,' ordered the doctor.

'Augusta, Augusta, Augusta.' Over and over and over again.

'Major Holmes.' The doctor again. 'This is Dr Coquard. Can you hear me?'

'Of course, I can hear, Christ love us.'

'You are ill. You've had an accident. Your leg is cut, but that's not serious. You have a high fever and I am going to get you to hospital first thing in the morning. I don't want you to move, do you understand? Madame Auguez is going to allow you to stay here. You're to lie as still as possible.'

'Pa, pa, pa pa.'

A moth against the window-pane. He opened his eyes. The sister-in-law was beside him in a halo of light, staring anxiously, a look he had seen before, on the face of a trooper on the field at Pegu. He had survived then; he didn't think he would survive now.

'There, there, soldier-boy.'

'Madame?'

'Monsieur?'

'Do you know Captain Klosé?'

'I can't say that I do, sir.'

'Rue d'Anjou.'

'Here in Versailles, Major?'

'Yes, he's a soldier. Was.'

'What regiment?' This from the Angel of Death.

'Artillerie de la Garde Impériale.'

'A Captain, you say.'

'Yes, Captain Klosé.'

'What about him, sir?'

What about him? What about him? 'I want a drink.'

'No, Major. The doctor said no.'

'Klosé will bring me a drink.'

131

'You must lie still and rest until they come to take you to the hospital.'

'They call him Franz-Josef.'

'Franz-Josef?'

'He looks like the Emperor.'

'A fine old man, then.'

'Tell him Dalkeith is dying. Tell him there's no need to bring his clarinet.'

'He doesn't know what he's saying. He's mad.'

'Tsch, tsch, tsch. Let him talk if he wants.'

'Jesus Christ have mercy on me.'

'He will. He will.'

'Remember: no clarinet.'

'I'll remember.'

He opened his eyes. There was no one there. He was in solitary. I must get to Klosé, he thought. Thank God, I'm wearing trousers.

Like a blast on a church organ the light pierced his eyes, a winter sun, colder than ice. He stumbled, fell, picked himself up, ran, walked, staggered. He tried to hold himself erect, to look fearless, as only an old, failed soldier can. People pointed; people stared; he pretended not to notice; he walked on head held high: if only his knees wouldn't buckle. He kept his objective firmly in mind: to get to Klosé. He had no money for drink; they'd left what little he had in his other trousers.

The street was narrow, the houses closely packed, the plane trees either side a guard of honour. He heard the clarinet at once and was reassured. Plaintive, seductive, beckoning, reedy. He paused, held on to one of the trees, looked up and down the length of the street, trying to detect from which house the sound emanated, and was drawn like a snake by a charmer to one that bore the sign Pension de la Reine. A window on the third floor was ajar allowing a dancing net curtain and the strain of music to escape. Holmes came to attention: forward march, left, right, left right, past the concierge – why did they all have cauldrons? – left turn, up a covered, stone stairway, towards the source of the sound, the lilt of a lament for a love long lost; or a daughter.

The ruler of the Austro–Hungarian empire, clarinet in hand,

opened the door, barking, 'I cannot play softer. Fart more loudly you won't hear me.'

'Klosé.'

'Dalkeith!'

'Let me in.'

'Forgive me. Thought you'd come to complain.'

'Never. Not me.'

'Come in.'

Holmes fell forward into the tiny third-floor room: music piled from floor to ceiling, bed, chair, table, all covered in music. Where did the man stand, sit, eat? And the smell of damp, mould on sour milk.

'Here,' Klosé said, 'let me make space for you. Didn't recognise you. Thought you were the fellow below, foreigner, American, writer, does nothing but complain about my noise. Sit here, Dalkeith. Pleasant surprise. Haven't seen you for almost a year. My God, what's the matter with you? You look awful.'

'Give me a drink, Klosé, for the love of God.' Klosé's face fell: only a refusal out of kindness can bring such regret. Holmes knew the look on a thousand faces: pitying, abject, irreversible. And normally such a generous man.

'Don't ask, Dalkeith. Know you mustn't. Know what they said. Said it'd kill you. I'm not an assassin.'

'I'm so dry it hurts.'

'Don't ask me to kill you, Dalkeith.' Smiling.

'Just a sip.'

Klosé stroked his white mutton-chops feverishly, a sure sign of inner agitation – of relenting? 'No, Dalkeith, not even a sip. Give you something to eat. Do you more good.'

'I'm not hungry,' Holmes replied savagely, knocking over a pile of music with an angry fist.

Klosé didn't seem to hear or notice, or didn't want to. 'Bread, bought an hour ago, cheese – Caprice des Dieux – grapes, hot black coffee you could march the regiment across.'

'No wine? No absinthe?' Holmes crooned.

'Lots of butter. Lines the stomach.'

Holmes watched the man disappear behind a rancid curtain, saw his round shape make grotesque bulges in the thin material.

133

Easier to ask him now, while invisible. 'Klosé, what have you been telling Augusta?'

The bulging curtain froze. Pa, pa, pa, pa. Rain on the windows.

'Augusta?'

'That's what I said.'

The bulge moved again. 'No. Haven't seen her.'

'You wouldn't lie to a dying man, would you, by God?'

'Haven't seen her. Swear it.'

'Do you know where she is?'

'Augusta?'

'Who in the name of Christ do you think I'm talking about?'

'Augusta, yes.'

'Where is she?'

Klosé reappeared, plate in hand. 'Coffee won't be long,' he said.

Holmes looked at the food: bread, butter, cheese, grapes. Were all French kitchens so dirty and the food so clean? 'I'm not hungry,' he said.

'Eat all the same.'

'I don't want to eat.'

'Must. You look half-starved.'

'Half-dead, you mean.' Weird, thought Holmes, to be fed like a baby by a man who had stood before the Band of the Imperial Guard beating four-four. 'Have you ever fed a dying man before, Klosé?'

'You're not dying. Irish all exaggerate.'

'My daughter, too?'

'Your daughter, too.'

'You're sure about that, are you now, Klosé?' Holmes watched closely the other man's mutton-chops which seemed to move on their own, bristling, like choristers standing to sing. 'She wouldn't just be repeating lies she heard elsewhere now, would she?'

'Coffee'll be ready,' Klosé said.

'How else could she know about Vigny?'

'Milk?' Klosé called.

'Absinthe, for God's sake.'

Klosé brought to him a steaming mug held like a torch. 'Drink it black,' but before he could hand over the coffee, Holmes covered his face, and hissed through tears, 'You shouldn't have told her, Klosé. I have to see her, have to see her before I die.'

'You're not going to die, Dalkeith.'

Holmes looked up at him; with the heel of his hand he wiped his eyes, his nose. He said, 'She sent me a letter, Klosé.'

'Letter?'

Holmes began to search in his pockets. 'Yes, a letter,' he said, 'an obscene, blasphemous, debauched letter.'

'From Augusta?'

'I've said so.'

'Saying what?'

He found a crumpled piece of paper in his breast pocket. 'Read it,' he said, thrusting the letter at Klosé who took it gingerly, putting down the mug as he read:

You swine, you are no more father to me – I know what you did – I've heard from witnesses – The only thing I don't know is how much Vigny paid you for me – 10 francs? 15 perhaps, one for each of my years – sold me for a harlot aged 15 you swine, and made me pay you interest on it – Well, not another penny do you get from me – understand? – sink in your own bog – I will never see you again.

By the time Klosé had finished reading, Holmes was crying again. 'She doesn't even write "Daddo darling", doesn't sign her name, nothing, just vileness. Oh Christ, what have I done to deserve this?'

'Pretty plain, I'd have thought,' Klosé muttered.

'You're the villain here, Klosé, you're the Iago here all right,' Holmes said desperately.

'Me?'

'Witnesses, she says, witnesses. Well, Klosé, you and I know there was only one witness in that room, and that was you, Iago.'

'Not guilty, Dalkeith,' Klosé said, turning away. He picked up his clarinet and fingered the silver keys nervously – pa, pa, pa, pa.

'Well, how in Christ's name did she find out?' Holmes demanded, and then, crumbling again, 'I have to see her, Klosé. I have to make my peace with her. I have to explain –'

135

Klosé glanced over his shoulder angrily. 'Explain? What? That you took money from Vigny and drank it in a week. You behaved like a cheap pimp, Holmes. Look at you! You were an officer in the Irish Guards! Look at you!'

'It *was* you who told her, I know it—'

'Stop snivelling. Can't bear to see an officer so degraded,' and he looked away.

'Oh Christ, when the world's hard, the world's hard. I have to see her, Klosé—'

'She won't see you.'

'That's why I'm here, Klosé darling fellow,' Holmes said with an imploring smile. 'She won't come for me, but she'll come for you. Go fetch her, Klosé, there's a good man. Atone for driving a wedge between father and daughter.'

'She was fatherless!' Klosé shouted. 'Don't care if you did sire her—'

Holmes was stunned by the old man's venom. For a while he stared at the bandmaster's rotund back but could not focus for long, and began to wail again, covering his ears as though he could not bear to hear the sound of his own misery. He did not hear the thumping through the floor from the room below, was unaware of Klosé marching out on to the landing and shouting down the stairwell, 'Yankee-doodle-dandy', did not take in his surroundings until he became conscious of Klosé seated beside him speaking with gentle passion now, but not gently enough to stop his tears.

Klosé said, 'A man squanders gold, must expect to be punished. Augusta was, is, most extraordinary female I ever set eyes on. You'd expect to find such beauty in salons and palaces. But not in the military barracks here in Versailles. No. Me, I taught clarinet at the Conservatoire, so came into contact with lots of young people, lots of musicians. Never one to compare to Augusta. When she came into my room, sun shone. When she sang, gods listened. And when her hands touched the piano keyboard, Franz Lizst trembled with envy. Wild she was, certainly, unmanageable, wilful, obstinate, devious, unpredictable, everything a woman of talent ought to be. Or man. Men, great artists, don't care who you mention, would give their right arms for her temperament. You don't understand artists, Dalkeith. God's jewels. Most extra-ordinary and worthwhile people on earth. Not fathered by ordinary mortals, and certainly not by officers in the Irish Guards. They come into the world like a thunder-crack. The world is me, that's what they say. They create themselves.

'Why, then, you ask, and it's a fair question, why isn't she brightest comet in sky? Why isn't Paris at her feet? Why isn't her music played by every orchestra in the world? Tell you why. She's a woman. It's a curse. A woman. Simple, no? God help her. Take away talent and she'd be a queen, an empress. Beauty alone entitles her to glory. But house in that beauty the passion, energy, gift, she possesses, and you have a crippled human being. You have a woman of talent. In this world, *unforgivable*.'

'Have you finished?' Holmes asked through his tears.

Klosé sat, hands on knees, panting. On the clarinet he could still sustain anything they cared to throw at him, but speaking as passionately as he had done robbed him of breath. 'Yes, finished,' he whispered.

Holmes said, 'A father is a father, for all that, Klosé.'

'You haven't listened to me.'

'I have, I have, I understand all about artists, I wasn't bad on the flute myself, you know, but I'm speaking of my daughter, my little baby, my child –'

'Go back to bogs of Ireland, Dalkeith. Can't stand your sentimentality.'

'Go and bring her to me.'

'Don't know where she is.'

'You do, you do, I know you do.' The old man shook his head, smoothed his moustaches as though that eased his breathing. Holmes said, 'Klosé, I'm going to tell you something. I'm as sober as a judge, a hydropathist, that's me. God knows when I last touched the stuff. I'm telling you the truth. Ask Dr Coquard. I'm a dead man, Klosé. God knows how much more of the yellow stuff I'm allowed before I drop like a stone. My liver's eaten away. I'm going blind. I see everything through tears and mist. I have pain all up and down my back. Each time I take a sip, the stuff goes straight to the liver and it just crumbles away, offal for dogs. I want to see Augusta before I die.' He did not dare look away

137

from the old man, wanted to see whether he had moved him, noticed the lips pursed and unpursed, saw no change in the bandmaster's eye. 'Fetch her for me, Klosé, for the love of Christ!'

'No. Not even for love of Christ.'

'Oh Jesus, I hope you confess that, Klosé, and I hope they – I hope they–' Holmes could no longer express his hopes: except to be with Augusta again; and oil for his throat.

Klosé said, 'Leave Augusta alone. You're an alien in her world.'

'How can you say that to a father?'

'Too old to lie, Dalkeith. She may, as they say, have come forth your fatal loins–' the bandmaster smiled to himself at this – 'but she's a free spirit, unattached, independent of fathers.'

'Oh, but don't you understand, Klosé, she's cut me off. She doesn't want to see me again. She's left me to die. It's barbaric, Klosé.'

'No, she's left you because she's left you. You could have been most dearly beloved father in whole of Europe, still she would have left you. You don't understand talent, aspiration. They're her parents. Honour thy talent and thy aspiration, and thy days will be long upon the earth which the Lord thy God hath given thee.'

'Blasphemy!' Dalkeith snapped. 'Blasphemy! She used to talk like that and it's all lies. It's an excuse for not living in the world, as if anybody wants to. Who wants to live in the world? Who? Who? *Blasphemy!* Klosé! Great turds of blasphemy, that's what all of you talk! Art, talent, fame. Blasphemies! Drives children away from parents. It's all self, self, self. Klosé, self. Self, self, self, self, self,' the word became meaningless, self, self, self, self, self, self.

Klosé put a hand to his bald, domed head, held it there firmly, as though his cranium were in danger of disintegrating. 'I know what I'm talking about, Dalkeith. Had such a small gift myself, blowing air through a black wooden tube. Tiny pearl, almost valueless on open market. I risked nothing. Took no chances. Avoided danger. Taught others to blow through wooden tubes. Kept time for marching men. Not much of a life. One accident saved me, chance of fate, gods playing dice. In barracks at Versailles, a girl, teach her, spy gold. Give her sense of her own value. What more could indifferent clarinettist, a dull, boring bandmaster ask for? I have entered Paradise clinging to your daughter's skirts.'

'Blasphemy, pure and unadulterated. You live life. You go from one day to the next. That's all, that's all.'

'No,' Klosé said obstinately, 'I taught Augusta Holmes.'

'Yes, taught her to hate her father –' A hammer tapping, tapping away at a bruise: pa-papapa-pa-pa. Was it night again? Holmes wondered, or had he simply closed his eyes? He blinked. No change in the quality of light or darkness. 'I must have a drink,' he said. He stood, or had he fallen?

'Go home, go to bed, sleep. You're not well.'

'Get Augusta for me.'

'She won't come, Dalkeith.'

'Yes, she will for you. She'll do anything for you. She likes old men, she'll do anything for any old man except her father. I only want to explain that what I did I did for her good. I needed the money, Klosé. Vigny was good to her, educated her, taught her to like fine things, what harm was there?'

'She was fifteen years old, Dalkeith.'

'Oh, Iago, Iago.'

'She wants nothing to do with you,' Klosé said. 'And you only want her to pay for your drink. You don't care a jot for her. You're losing your keep, Dalkeith. That's all you care about. You don't love her, you never loved her, you sold her and can't buy her back!'

Holmes was conscious of Klosé's fat old neck between his hands and knew he was choking the life out of the man: regicide, he thought, and then he was out in the narrow street, the rue d'Anjou, in the rain, mouth open trying to catch the drops, licking his dry lips. He heard shouts from the house, and saw windows raised and shooting stars, and stumbled forward, propelled by the need to escape but he could not remember from what. He was aware of footsteps in pursuit, of a pissoir, and temporary oblivion.

The next he knew, a whore took pity on him. He sat on the pavement, leaning against a pissoir decorated in grey posters, grey buildings, grey pavement, grey sky. 'I can't see a thing,' he said to a shape that passed, but no sooner were the words out of his mouth than he saw the letters S–E–M–L at eye-level on the

139

pissoir wall. He worked along, using a finger to point the line: S–E–M–L–O–H–A–T–S–U–G, then he slipped and caught his head on the kerbstone. They first drive mad, he thought: why should she have her name spelled backwards on a pissoir? 'Help me!' 'Who can read?' 'Help me!' The whore:

'You must have been a handsome fellow.'

'I'm looking for my daughter.'

'You're the second today.'

'The second?'

'Looking for a daughter.'

'I am, I am.'

'Anything you say, sweetheart. Does she work these parts, then?'

'Where are we?'

'Versailles.'

'Oh Christ. I thought I'd got to Paris.'

'I know what you want.'

'What?'

'I can tell by your eyes. Here have a nip. Better?'

'Ah, God, that's art.'

'Art?'

'Can you read?'

'No, I can't.'

But, suddenly, he could read: in a light too bright, yellow, golden, the words: Danse Composer Soprano Macabre Holmes Camille at piano Saint Augusta. He screamed, screamed to be rid of chaos, screamed for his daughter, beat the tin pissoir with his fists, was suddenly gripped by strong male arms, and afterwards, found that he was hugging himself in a tight, constricted embrace, his own arms immovable. Was he in a coffin? Terrifying laughter answered him, the screeching of wild birds. In greyness again, worse than grey, he saw her: Augusta, my lovely one, my daughter, my own darling. He knew it was her, seated on a bed – his bed? – because he experienced such tender warmth as only her presence and absinthe produced, and he knew he had had no absinthe since the whore allowed him a shallow sip. Augusta, it is your father. I am your father.

4

Augusta could see he was trying to speak, but the sounds were unintelligible. His eyes were open though they appeared to her sightless. He seemed so thin and shrunken it looked as if he could easily slip out of the strait-jacket. She sat at the end of the narrow, rickety bench on which he had been laid in a small cell at the rear of the gendarmerie. In another cell, which she could not see, one man laughed and another cried. She listened to her father, gurgling, and looked into his blank, pale eyes. She regarded him coldly; she had no pity for him.

Dr Coquard, small, bald, sallow, entered the cell. He said, 'Are you his daughter?'

'Yes.'

'He's pretty far gone.'

'Yes.'

'You had better get him into an asylum. He's a danger to himself and everyone else.'

'You've found that out, have you?'

The doctor did not know if he was meant to smile. He said, 'You want me to arrange somewhere?'

'He hasn't any money,' Augusta said, 'and I certainly can't afford to keep him.'

Coquard said, 'I know a place, not far, run by nuns, Saint Marcel-le-pauvre. The Medical Superintendent is Dr Cantagrel. We studied together. He's a good man. Used to be an assistant to Dr Blanche in the rue Berton in Passy.'

'How much will it cost?'

Coquard shrugged. 'Whatever you can afford.'

'I can afford nothing.'

'Then they will keep him for nothing,' he said.

'What would we do without nuns?' she asked, squeezing a smile.

'Madame –'

'Mademoiselle.'

'Mademoiselle,' Coquard said with a polite inclination of the head. 'I was called out last evening to your father, and, of course, I had to attend him here. My bill will have to be settled.'

'Present it, and it will be paid,' Augusta said grandly as she rose from the bench. She gave the doctor her address and, without looking back at her father, left the cell. In her head she heard a door slamming shut.

Outside in the street, Klosé, his neck bandaged, waited for her. She ran to him and they embraced warmly; she kissed his bald pate a dozen times. Anxiously she asked, 'Are you all right, my little one?'

'Can't speak very loudly,' he said in a strained whisper. 'And can't turn the neck too well.'

'Oh my dear,' she said and tenderly touched his cheek.

His eyes glowed with pleasure. 'Wonderful to see you. Wish it were under happier circumstances.'

'God, I could do with a drink,' she said.

'I know a place, not far,' he croaked. 'Want to talk to you anyway.'

Jouvier, who owned the stables in the Place de Clichy and who had brought Augusta to Versailles, was waiting by the trap and horse, walking up and down the pavement blowing into his hands and sniffing. On Klosé's instructions he took them to a café near the Gare de Chantiers and not far from the rue d'Anjou where Klosé lived. 'Not the Grand Hôtel,' Klosé said, holding the café door for Augusta to enter, 'but at least it's warm.'

The café was crowded with evening customers: Augusta and Klosé were squashed into a mirrored corner, side by side on a banquette. 'Versailles isn't what it used to be,' Klosé complained. 'Should never have moved the Assembly here. Town's full of politicians.'

Augusta removed her gloves and the muslin from her hat which, unadorned, had a jaunty, male look to it, like a bowler. In the angle of the mirrors she could see her image full face and in profile, and she narrowed her eyes to appraise herself.

Klosé said, 'You look wonderful, Augusta.'

She put a hand on his. 'And you, my dear, you've had an awful time.'

'All your fault,' Klosé said with a twinkle.

'Mine?'

'All that stuff about Vigny. Dalkeith accused me of telling you.'

142

'So you did.'

'Yes, years ago, but you already knew about it. I remember you saying so. Vigny himself –' He was interrupted by a frail, elderly waiter; Klosé ordered a beer for himself and a plum brandy for Augusta. He said, 'Didn't Vigny himself tell you?'

'Yes.'

'I remember our conversation clearly. Something about Vigny wanting to be your father. He had some rum ideas about incest, didn't he? Never understood it really.'

'Nor did I,' Augusta said with a sort of finality, as though the subject were exhausted.

But Klosé, easing his neck carefully from side to side, said, 'Why did you write to Dalkeith as you did?'

'I don't know.'

'You must know.'

'Very well. I need to save all the money I can. I thought it was time to stop keeping him in absinthe.'

'Money, ah, yes, but you shouldn't have thrown Vigny in his face.'

'Don't scold me,' Augusta said with more ill-temper in her voice than she would have liked; quickly but no less edgily she went on, 'You know what it's been like between him and me. He saw me as a bread-winner and that's all. He'd have put me on the streets if that was the only way for him to have a comfortable life. It's odd. When I'm nowhere near him, I've only to think of him to feel miserable. But sitting there just now, looking at him, that emaciated, shrivelled muscle, I thought, my God, I'm glad I did what I did. I felt no guilt, no responsibility at all. I thought that's that. End of the movement, *march funèbre*. I'm getting rid of the past.'

'Hope not.' Klosé did not like Augusta when she was hard and insensitive.

'Not you, my dear, oh no, not you. If it hadn't been for your encouraging my music –'

The waiter put their drinks before them. Klosé had difficulty swallowing his beer. He said, 'What's to happen to Dalkeith now?' She reported her conversation with Coquard. 'An asylum?' Klosé repeated. 'Did you agree?' His alarm was evident.

'Yes,' she said. 'It's for his good.'

To Klosé, Dalkeith's committal seemed too hasty, too convenient, but he said no more on the subject. Augusta had the effect on him of stifling criticism; he did not like to offend her; he preferred their relationship to be without tension. His regret that Dalkeith should be confined he hid by saying, slyly, 'I've been reading all about you.'

'Oh? Where?'

'In the *Soir*. About your disguise, *genus masculinus*.'

'Was there something in the *Soir*?' she asked excitedly. 'I must've missed it —'

'Oh yes, there was. So, at last, you're going to take yourself seriously.'

'What a funny way of putting it.' She smiled crookedly.

'What d'you mean? Putting it that way since you were thirteen. Like a sou for every time I wrote, pleaded, begged in past fifteen years: take yourself seriously! I'd be a rich man.' They sipped their drinks. Klosé winced each time he swallowed.

Augusta said, 'It's always other people, never oneself.'

'Nonsense. This chap Franck. Serious fellow?'

'Very.'

'Second-class composer.'

'First-class teacher,' she said. 'Anyway, he's only the means, the beginning —'

'Of what?'

'Of realising all those dreams we used to have.'

'Not dreams. Plans.'

She studied her profile in the mirrors, saw herself imposed on the other customers as though she existed in another perspective, caught the eye of a man with a monocle who could not hold her gaze. She said, 'I have to learn how to discipline myself.'

'Always known that,' Klosé said. 'What's this chap Franck like?'

Augusta thought for a moment about César and remembered him laughing. But she was not good at giving brief appraisals of people. She was gifted with instinctive reactions to others, rather than the ability to observe with clarity. She said, frowning, 'Timid, uncertain. Also quite fierce. Do you know what I mean?'

'No.'

'I think he's a good man. They say he's a godly man.'

'More music less God. Chap'd be better off.'

'We all have to find a use for our gifts,' she said, downing her drink.

Klosé did not answer because he did not understand, and Augusta disturbed the isolated nature of the silence. 'I must be getting back,' she said.

'Have another.'

'No.'

His throat hurt. Carefully he twisted his neck this way and that. 'Bruised the windpipe,' he said. 'Won't be able to blow, don't suppose.'

Augusta said, 'I feel as though a weight has lifted.'

Klosé nodded but that, too, hurt. He said, 'Something to say to you, Augusta–' but she obviously did not hear, for she was busy catching the waiter's attention and she mimed that she wanted the bill. Turning to the mirrors she re-tied the muslin around her hat. She said, 'I'll see you home, my dear.' He paid.

They returned to the rue d'Anjou in silence, strolling arm in arm, each feeling they were protecting the other. Jouvier followed with his trap and horse at a respectful distance. At the Pension de la Reine, Augusta and Klosé took the stairs slowly up to Klosé's room. On the landing outside his door he invited her in; she declined. She clasped his hand and gazed warmly into his eyes. 'I really must go,' she said.

But he held on to her. 'Something to say.' His voice was fainter than in the café. 'Question to ask. How – how –' he broke off, flapped his free hand in the air as though trying to erase a mistaken start. 'Money. Nuisance. Lessons to pay for. How will you manage?'

'None of your business,' she said lightly, her head and smile to one side.

'Is my business. Selfish. Want to be footnote in your biography. I have a little money. Pension. Not much. Never married. No children. Only self. Want money, ask me.'

She kissed him on the forehead. 'I'll give concerts, I'll do some copying. Don't worry about me.'

'Do worry. Composers need health. Don't want you up day and night earning sous. Want you energetic.'

'I am energetic. You know I have more energy than anybody in the world.'

'Take my advice: don't squander energy. Valuable commodity. Don't think too much. Do, don't think. Write music. That's all.'

Taking his face in her hands so that she flattened his exuberant sideburns, she said, 'No one has ever been kinder to me than you, and that's true.' Again she kissed his forehead and he suddenly clasped her round the waist and held her close, turning his face to rest his cheek against the frills of her blouse, smelling her scent, welcoming her softness. She did nothing to deter him, but stood gazing over the dome of his bald head at the peeling paint on his door, her hands by her side, passive, as though to be embraced by the old man was an obligatory human function which she acknowledged with indifference. A minute may have passed. When Klosé released her, she noticed that his eyes were moist; she smiled tenderly at him, and quickly departed. By the time she reached the street she could hear, from the third floor window, Klosé trying to play his clarinet, not a tune, just a single note, broken by squeaks and silence. She began to hurry away but on reaching the corner where Jouvier waited, she paused to hear the clarinet come again, in lilting phrases haltingly played that somehow she knew was meant to be a stately sarabande for unrequited love.

Jouvier took her back to Paris and the rue Mansart. Seated in the rear of the trap, Augusta allowed herself a genuine sigh of relief. I feel as though a weight has lifted, she confessed to Klosé, and she recalled, coming out of the gendarmerie, the sound she imagined or heard of a door slamming. She was cutting off the past as though she travelled down a long dark corridor into the light, closing behind her one door after the other. Mendès had been the first, and now Dalkeith: both she had shut out, and she marvelled at the turn of events, knowing that she herself, by some mysterious instinct which guided her actions, had contrived their departure from her life. But this belief in her own powers, the certainty that she was in control of her own destiny was momentarily undermined by a letter from Camille which was awaiting her return:

Sappho!
I am deeply disappointed in you. You have no decency in you
at all, no, none. You will destroy yourself. You cannot go
through life using people and then discarding them. *You* will
end up used and discarded. I shall never cease to love you as
long as I live, but I shall marry someone else.

C

She tore up the letter and said nothing to Julie about the
contents. When the maid asked what had happened in Versailles,
Augusta said, 'Tomorrow, tomorrow,' and then began to undress
for bed occupying herself with practical matters – had Julie
collected her winnings from the Café Tortoni? had the glazier fixed
the window pane? did they have a suitable shawl with which to
cover the piano? Julie handed over the 50 francs, drew the curtain
aside to reveal the mended pane, said she'd look in the morning
for a shawl in the market, and brought a cup of hot soup to Augusta
seated, naked, before the dying fire.
Augusta, only vaguely aware of Julie's presence said, 'I will
not destroy myself,' and tossed the pieces of Camille's letter on
to the coals.
'Who says you will?'
'I can't expect help from anyone, and don't want any. They all
have to be locked out. The door must be closed and bolted.'
'The door is locked,' Julie said.
Augusta continued to be self-contained. She thought now of
the future, and experienced a pleasurable stab of excitement, of
expectation. A picture of herself at the piano busily, intensely
writing music came into her mind, and the strings, lush and overwhelming. And César nodded his approval. Success, fame, recognition of the sounds she heard seemed to be an arm's length away,
hers to reach out and snatch. The past was done with. The future,
unsullied and golden, was hers for the asking.

147

5

The future, Augusta decided, would begin with her first lesson, and so the whole afternoon she agonised over what she should wear for such an auspicious event. She settled finally for a dull brown dress she had had especially designed to impress the Mother Superior of the convent in Nanterre when handing over the baby. She had worn her hair in a bun on that occasion, and would have done so again had not Julie said she looked ridiculous. By the time Augusta was satisfied with her appearance she was already late; she took a cab to 95 boulevard Saint-Michel and arrived almost an hour after the class had begun.

When she entered the music room, all the men, except César, rose. He said, 'Ah, Mademoiselle Holmès, ah yes, you must forgive me if I do not – er – rise, but I have – I have the cramp.' He smiled a sickly smile which gave no indication, she thought, of pain.

Augusta, in turn, apologised for being late, was graciously forgiven, and then introduced to those members of the class she did not know: Albert Cahen and Paul de Wailly, both young, both awkward. Cahen, shaking her hand limply, said, 'I am working on a musical poem to be called *Endymion*,' and then blushed; Wailly said nothing.

César suddenly rose. 'Ah, that's better,' he said and invited Augusta to sit.

'I like the floor,' she said and, accepting a cushion from Chabrier, squatted as near to César as she could manage. She noticed then, being able to see beneath his work table that, when he resumed his seat, he placed a heavy pile of books on his lap, the one on top, she read, was Kant's *Critique of Pure Reason*; she was impressed.

César cleared his throat, sat back in his chair, closed his eyes, pressed his finger-tips together and said, 'I hope the others will not mind, mademoiselle, if I were to break off the interesting discussion on harmony which we were pursuing before your arrival, to tell you something about our methods in general.' Murmurs of agreement from the men. 'Let me say at once our method is that we have no method. The individual is free to develop at his

– or her – own pace in whatever the chosen style. But – and this is the paradox – no individual is allowed to set his – or her – own goals above the good of all.' Collectively, he explained, they might influence the course of French music whereas individually each was doomed to loneliness and failure. As with the Société, the aims of the class were the complete forgetfulness of self so that much could be learned from the mistakes and success of others.

To all this Augusta nodded fervently. The complete forgetfulness of self, yes, yes, she thought, she longed for that: music was all. She said, 'That is what I most want.'

'Good,' César said, 'and have you brought some recent work for me to see?'

'Yes,' she said modestly, reaching into her music case.

'I will look at them after class. You would not mind staying behind a minute or two?'

'No, of course not.'

'Excellent. I have no doubt we will all get on well together. And so, Vincent, let us return to the interesting point you were making. About the key of B major, to which I am very partial.'

Augusta listened enraptured, absorbed in the arguments and the incidental instruction which arose from them. Once or twice César asked her opinion which she offered reluctantly but was relieved not to have said anything silly; for most of the time, however, she remained silent.

After the class, the men took their leave, all of them wishing Augusta well; alone with César, she handed over two or three manuscripts which he studied with a deep frown of concentration. 'Yes, yes,' he said, 'you have to unlearn everything and learn everything. Not easy, I'm afraid. It is a slow process, Mademoiselle Holmès –'

'Augusta –'

'– I'm afraid that you must forget Ireland for the moment, you must forget womanhood, and think only of *pure* music. You must write fugues, fugues and more fugues. You cannot speak until you have a language. The fugue will give you a word here, a phrase there, perhaps even a sentence or two. Slowly, I say slowly, you will with diligence acquire the language.'

'How slowly?'

'I beg your pardon?'

'What do you mean by a slow process? How slow?'

'That is entirely dependent on you. A year of fugues. Another year of fugues. A third year – who knows? – we may begin to discuss other things.' He smiled reassuringly.

'Three years!'

'You will still only be twenty-six, mademoiselle.'

Thirty-one, she thought. 'Yes,' she said.

'I, Mademoiselle Holmès, have been at it for almost fifty years and I know nothing, absolutely nothing.'

A year, two years, three. To Augusta patience was a debilitating disease: she wanted all now, yesterday, last week. She said, 'I will do whatever you say. I place myself in your hands. You must make me into a great composer.'

'I will attempt to help you to make yourself into a composer. The word great is not one I often use.'

'But you like my machines?' Reassurance she needed like a drug.

'You are my pupil. And I will show you no special favour. I will work you until you drop,' but his expression belied his words: he gazed on her, she thought, with great tenderness. 'Well,' he said, 'there endeth the first lesson.'

She gave in suddenly to an irresistible impulse to kiss him. She darted forward, kissed his forehead and dashed into the hall. She was about to let herself out of the front door when a voice behind her said, 'And, pray, who are you?'

Augusta, startled, turned to confront a tall woman, thin and sinewy with severe, suspicious eyes. Augusta was reminded of the Mother Superior and felt her heart pounding: she could cope with the fiercest man; women terrified her. 'My – my name is Augusta Holmès.'

'Has there been a party?'

'No. I – I –'

'No party? You are the wife of one of my husband's pupils then?'

'No. I *am* one of your husband's pupils.'

'Indeed.'

'Yes.'

'I was not informed he had a new pupil.'

'Yes.'

'Of composition?'

'I beg your pardon?'

'Are you a pupil of composition?'

'Oh yes, yes, of composition, yes.'

'Franck?' Félicité called, but never looking away from Augusta; the narrowed eyes raked her like rifle fire.

The response was miraculously speedy. 'My dear?' César answered, halting mid-stride in the doorway between hall and music room still carrying the books which he now held at waist level. He cleared his throat, exercised his eyebrows, said, 'Ah have you introduced yourself to General Holmès' daughter?'

'I did not know you had a new pupil.'

'This,' César said, 'is Madame Franck.'

Instinctively, Augusta bobbed as she had done to the Mother Superior after giving over her daughter into the nuns' care.

Félicité said, 'Franck, put down those books, you look ridiculous.' To Augusta: 'What is your particular forte, Mademoiselle Holmès? Songs, tone poems, symphonies' – all spoken through clenched teeth as if she were controlling an impediment. 'Are you, perhaps, a believer in the cyclic form?'

Before Augusta could answer, César said, 'Mademoiselle Holmès has a flair for operatic music, my dear.'

Félicité's eyes examined Augusta from crown to toe. 'One might have guessed,' she said, but there was the faintest suggestion of a softening about her manner. 'I am not without ideas for suitable operatic subjects myself.'

'My wife is an accomplished musician,' César said.

'The Greeks and the Israelites are the best inspiration for opera,' Félicité said. 'I am not an admirer of the Bavarian. Are you?'

'Oh,' César said airily, 'Richard's all right.'

Félicité raised an eyebrow. To Augusta she said, 'I seem to recall the word "poison" written across Franck's copy of *Tristan*.'

'We mustn't keep Mademoiselle Holmès,' César said. 'She's had a long, hard lesson.'

Augusta took his words as her cue to curtsey and go. Later, in the rue Mansart, to Julie she said, 'He is wonderful,' and still later: 'He is the gentlest man I know. And the most strict. He is a great teacher.' But what she said to Julie, and to others were affirmations of loyalty, not articles of faith. Augusta admitted only to herself that she did not know whether he was wonderful or gentle, strict or great. Those were the attributes she wanted him to possess; her decision to enrol as his student must be proved to have been correct; her pupilage had to be a success; with Augusta every undertaking had to be a success: she endowed César with perfection.

Sometimes, when at work on the fugues, the endless fugues, the truth impinged. Battling with the mathematical intricacies of music, she would realise that the struggle to please him was immense and that to please him was her only means of measuring her progress. If he said, 'I like that, oh yes, I like that,' her days were filled with the strength to write more. 'I don't like that at all, *not – at – all*,' brought bleak despair. Despair, not hopefulness, proved to be Augusta's more enduring companion. For long periods she seemed unable to do anything right, and César's criticism could be brutal. About her fugues: 'Too much combination, not enough expression.'

'I don't know what you mean!'

'I felt sure I was making myself clear. We are musicians not mathematicians.'

'But one day you say that I'm to forget myself and what I feel and concentrate on *pure* music, the next that you want expression. I'm hopelessly confused. I don't know what you want!' She banged the keys of his piano with her fist.

'It is best, and I say this as a general warning, not to put words into my mouth. I do not believe I have ever said that you're to forget what you feel. That would be impertinent of me. But you are right to remember my words about pure music. Let the music speak. Do not do to your music what you have done to me and put words into its mouth. Let it speak for itself. As to this latest fugue, you have gone too far in the opposite direction. You have denied that it is a piece of music. Your fugue says to me that two plus two makes four. Now, while that is true and, no doubt, very interesting, it is not music. Try again.'

'Yes, yes, I'm sorry, I'll try again.'

And again and again and again.

'They would not let you do this at the Conservatoire,' he said, 'but I like it very much.'

To Julie: 'He liked it! He liked it!'

The notes multiplied: four fugues in a month.

'Ah, yes, yes, we have been working, I see. A little advice, Mademoiselle Holmès, which I give to all my students. Do not write much but let what you write be very good.'

Despair, and for long periods, too: not only in response to criticism, but also to neglect.

'He doesn't know I exist, Julie. I have handed in two machines in the past three months and not a word, not a single word. Today I went up to him and asked what he thought. He said nothing but smiled that stupid smile of his! I swear he's lost the work!'

In her blackest moods, when anonymity and a sense of her own inadequacy entombed her, the dangers within were greatest. Julie knew the warning signs: Augusta talked and laughed too much, too loudly; her toilette would last hours, long, indolent baths; she would cover her face and eyes in too much paint, and for class she would wear her old dresses, the necklines plunging, and she would douse herself in scent, adopt a bright, glittering manner more reminiscent of the Moulin Rouge than the Salle Pleyel. In those moods she ignored the economies necessary to her and Julie's existence. She haunted the Café Tortoni at night, sitting at the table of the male homosexuals, known to the clientèle as *Tortoni's castrati*. The men at this table adored her. They found her witty and amusing and thought her beautiful beyond words; paradoxically, some detected a motherly quality in her and loved to confide in her and to seek her advice; in turn, she confided in them. They believed that she had suffered deeply as many of them had suffered the anguish of broken love affairs, the torture of impermanent relationships; she encouraged the myth of herself as one victimised and preyed upon by men.

One evening, during a period when César had been oblivious to her for more than a month, Augusta confessed her desperation. An Italian boy, Alfredo, said, 'Do something outrageous!'

'Like what?'

'Oh, I don't know, go to your next lesson naked in a carriage

153

pulled by leopards with peacock feathers in your hair and a diamond in your navel, your pubic hair dyed the colour of the Florentine sky.' He pursed his lips provocatively.

'Alfredo's right,' another said. 'You have to shake the old man out of his dull, boring bourgeois world. If you want my opinion, Augusta, he's not your style. He's so terribly shabby.'

And although Augusta insisted that César was even so a fine teacher, the seed of an idea began to implant itself in her mind. At the next lesson, after César had called the class to order and was about to give his attention to Albert Cahen, Augusta said, 'I have something I want to sing,' and turning to Paul de Wailly, asked sweetly, 'Will you accompany me?'

She sensed the consternation from Vincent but turned her back on him. César repeatedly looked over his shoulder as though someone was about to come on him unexpectedly; Duparc studied the rug; Chabrier smiled; Cahen said, 'I thought we were going to discuss *Endymion*.' Before any answer could be given, Augusta said, 'Play, Paul' and Wailly struck a rumble in the bass that was meant to be a timpani roll before the rise of the curtain.

Augusta had put together sketches she had once written for an opera about Zeus giving to Hermes supreme power over the animal kingdom. Now, to Wailly's frantic accompaniment, she sang all the parts, tenor, bass, soprano and coloratura, arias, duets, even in one frenzied passage a quartet. Standing, kneeling, imploring, defenceless, with gestures grand and tender she enacted the work, imitating from time to time the trumpeting of elephants, the roar of lions, the screech of birds. For Zeus she placed a brass fruit bowl on her head; for Hermes she used one of the curtains as a toga; as Ganymede she trapped a pencil between upper lip and nose. The performance was frenetic, vital and irresistibly funny, and presently her small audience were convulsed with laughter, César becoming quite as helpless as he had been in Hartmann's office at their first meeting. Only Vincent remained solemn, disapproving.

And when it was all over, and Augusta had been much congratulated, she marched triumphantly into the hall to reclaim her cloak and hat to be met by Félicité Franck who introduced to Augusta her son, Georges. His reaction pleased Augusta: he was obviously dazzled by her. 'Bravo,' he said, kissing her hands with moist lips.

'A little life,' Félicité said, nodding her approval, 'very welcome. We listened at the door.'

Augusta hardly slept that night. To Julie, she said, 'I believe I made them aware of me as a person, as someone who has life in them. He won't ignore me so easily again.' Her excitement was irrational, she knew; she had done nothing but show herself off in a vulgar, glittering way. She did not care. Her energy could not be for long suppressed. She would not have her individuality smothered. She was heady with triumph. But two days later Chabrier paid her a visit in the rue Mansart, and Augusta detected at once that his jollity was assumed, and the purpose of the interview clumsily disguised.

'I see Camille's married,' he began, chuckling inanely.

'So I believe,' Augusta said, on her guard, wondering where she was being led.

'You heard the manner of his proposal?'

'No.'

'He wrote a letter to the girl's brother! "Would you like me as a brother-in-law?" he asked. The fellow said, "Yes"!'

'What's she like?'

'I'm glad you asked that,' he said, his podgy forefinger dotting an imaginary i. 'She is rather plain, rather dim, very young. They live with Maman who gives the girl a terrible time. She is very modest, never opens her mouth. Puts up with all Camille's nonsense. A very flat girl in every way.'

An awkward silence. Augusta said, 'He's written an opera.'

Chabrier agreed ruefully. 'Yes, trust Camille to do an opera about a harlot cutting off a man's hair to emasculate him. You know what the symbolists say about it? They say it is a symbol of Camille's own castration,' and he lapsed into his impersonation, forgoing the booming bass for outraged falsetto, 'Oooh, maman, it'th thore!'

Augusta said, 'Is Romain still a friend?'

'Oh yes. More than ever. I was talking about Camille to the Maître the other day. The old boy said a very fine thing: Camille is all outward show, he said. Some people think they are before

155

an audience all the time, when it's the work that matters, isn't that so, Augusta? It's something I have to learn, too.' He was unusually thoughtful, subdued. 'It's something we all have to learn. We don't have to *be* anything so long as the work's good, eh, Augusta?'

Augusta smiled. 'You're trying to tell me something. What?'

The fat man lowered his eyes and studied his knees. What he had to say next, he found difficult: 'You – you put yourself in a dangerous position, Augusta.'

'I did? How?'

'Don't misunderstand me. I loved the little opera. I loved the performance. And so, I think, did the others, the old boy included. But Vincent didn't. He's a pompous prig, but powerful. He said – you won't like this, Augusta – he said that you ought to be dropped, that you lowered the tone, weren't serious, *etcetera*, *etcetera*. Duparc was non-committal. I spoke up for you. But the old boy was half-inclined to agree with Vincent. So we left it with the Maître saying he'd think about it over night, but it was plain to me that you were unlikely to go on being his student.

'Then, this morning, I met him on the Pont Saint-Michel, as I sometimes do on my way to work. Usually I have a bit of fun with him, but I was upset, I confess it, Augusta, I didn't want you to be hurt or to suffer such a set-back to your career. So I asked him outright what he intended to do about you. And he said he would give you another chance, and he told me that his wife had intervened on your behalf, and, as you know, the old boy's terrified of her and does what she tells him. She hates Vincent, too, so it was a way of getting at him. But still, it was a dangerous moment, Augusta. You have to be more careful. You mustn't disturb the peace. You've made an enemy of Vincent and he'll pay you back one day, I promise you. So, please, be careful, my dear. Just see to it that the work's good, then nobody can touch you. I'm in the same boat. Unfortunately, it's the work by which we stand or fall, not ourselves.'

She wept after he had departed. Julie tried to comfort her but for the rest of the day Augusta was inconsolable. For more than a week she could not face the unpleasant truth that there raged inside her a battle from which she could expect no peace, as if she were both victor and vanquished, Augusta defeating Augusta. But which was which? She had known she had much to surrender; she had known that self-discipline was not easily acquired; above all she had known that to channel her vitality and energy into her work rather than into her life was a see-saw struggle for her very survival. And even in these moments of painful inner conflict she believed that the composer was more worthwhile than the woman, and the idea of sacrifice became suddenly attractive. As though reinforcing her battered forces, she summoned all her reserves. She drew up endless time-tables and schedules of work. She tried to find the stillness in which to compose, tried to find escape in her music.

Believing in some instinctive way that her very identity was under siege, she sought to make her identity the subject of a composition. She began work on an *Ode*, a hymn to herself in which she attempted to bring together all the strands of her tangled existence, as though the piece was an autobiography in sound. She experienced great elation from the work and waited in torment for César's opinion.

In front of her fellow-students, he said, 'Oh dear, oh dear, the military are marching again, I see, and here a church organ plays, oh dear, and here we have *Rheingold*, I believe – is the quotation intentional? – and ah, as I suspected, the leprechauns have made a return visit to Paris.'

Vincent sniggered.

It was too much for Augusta. She lost all restraint. 'How dare you!' she cried, 'I have worked for weeks, slaved to get it down and you dismiss it just like that? Mother of God, that's *me* in there, that's *me* you're trampling underfoot. All the things that make me, yes. I'm glad you detected that. And I'm not going to be denied the privilege of my talent to express myself. You and your *pure* music, *pure* music, there's no such thing! We sit here in comfortable seclusion playing with sounds as if they were for our ears alone. God, there's a world out there, a whole world, and we sit here and ignore it.' She fought to control her tears, but her cheeks were flushed and repeatedly she bit her bottom lip. She stared hard at César who was nodding and smiling his inane smile. The others in the class were cocooned in embarrassment. Vincent shut his eyes and pinched the bridge of his nose as though to meditate.

César said, 'That's it, of course. Music should be musical and, above all things, expressive. That's very true.'

'Expressive of *what*?' she demanded.

He did not answer her directly but talked of his own present occupation. He had put aside *The Beatitudes* and had embarked on a symphonic poem called *Les Eolides*, inspired by a poem by his neighbour, Leconte de Lisle, who lived on the opposite side of the boulevard. 'The verses which inspired me,' César said looking directly at Augusta, 'were those addressed to the daughters of Æolus. "Floating breezes of the skies caress both hills and plain with a capricious kiss". It is good, you see, to be buffeted.'

In a letter to Klosé, Augusta wrote, 'I don't know how long I can go on with him. I don't understand him. I feel as though he wants to smash me into little pieces. God knows why he ever took me on. I believe he hates my music. I believe he hates me.'

6

Augusta. Awake, eyes shut; five o'clock and time for the waking game, senses confused, but what could he hear? Silence, to his sorrow. Thank you O Lord for giving me life this day. He must hurry. Blessed are the meek for they shall inherit the earth. The Actress turned in her sleep, a horse urinated, a floorboard creaked, silence rushed, cracked, rolled on a faraway sea. Blessed are the poor in spirit. He was condemned to listen to emptiness. *Gott ich danke Dir*. Rejoice and be exceeding glad. I am in my fifty-sixth year and it is late. He must hurry.

Augusta.

A great swelling sound, pure, perfect, still-born. Always at the moment of rising: a sound that refused to be captured or recorded, an accompaniment to the stirring of the senses, so brief, so transient, so triumphant and sensuous, so unlike any sound he had ever heard or imagined that he questioned each dawn reality itself. Bare floor beneath bare feet, hands beneath buttocks, the diminuendo, a moth's wings, silence.

Augusta.

Summer sunshine. The boulevard Saint-Michel worked in gold, and trumpets at the bathroom window panes. How long was it since he'd last cut himself? The Actress tinkled E natural. The maid, new, Clementine, a scarecrow, breastless, said, 'What time do you want breakfast, maître.'

'Half-past seven. Always at half-past seven.'

'Half-past seven.'

Alone, windblown notes before him, he sipped the hot black ink. Always at this moment before lifting his pen, an intrusion: I love you. Claire's voice. Augusta's face. 'But you're married.' *Il maestro e lo scolare*. No one else, not his mother or his father, not his wife or his children, no one but Claire had ever said to him those words, I love you. Certainly not Augusta. Augusta, Augusta, breasts to suckle, life to be caressed. Why was he so hateful to her? Why not pretend her music was perfection, as she was perfection, why not win her by kindness and love instead of distancing her with unnecessary severity, uncharacteristic cruelty? How could he make his feelings known? How could he see more of her? How could he be alone with her? He lifted his pen, dipped it in the ink and asked Claire forgiveness for his betrayal.

Later, to Félicité, he said, 'It's a slow process.'

'It's warm out. There's no need to take your coat today.'

'No, no, no, no.'

'And don't hurry. You always arrive everywhere too early.'

They sat, to begin with, in silence.

Félicité asked, 'Will there be a class tonight?'

'A class? Tonight?'

'Do concentrate, Franck. Are you giving a class tonight?'

'A class, yes, I believe there is a class tonight. Here, yes, I believe so, here, yes, tonight.'

'You must tell me. I can't be expected to guess.'

His heart sang: a class tonight, and Augusta.

'Will Mademoiselle Holmès be coming?'

'I believe so.'

'I hope so. She is a good balance to d'Indy.'

A balance? What does she know of balance? Could she see that he walked upside down, on air, weightless at the merest thought

159

of Mademoiselle Holmès with or without the *accent grave*. Imbalance, more likely. Could Félicité detect the remorse in him for hurting Augusta, for being so destructive of her music? He wished he understood why he was able to be gentle with the others, but was always vile towards her. Did he expect more of her? Was he punishing her for obsessing him? He wanted to show he was kind and tender, but could not or dared not. And for long periods he forced himself to ignore her; for his own peace of mind he had to pretend she did not exist; and when she again intruded he punished her cruelly. And how he had adored her for arguing with him so passionately. There's a world out there, she had said, a whole world, and we sit here and ignore it. Oh, such passion, such beauty, such youth.

Passion? What did he know of passion? Oh, but with Augusta you had only to sniff her to know she was passionate. And what had he done about it? Nothing, of course. There was nothing to be done except to look at her, or not look at her, smell her or hold one's breath. And touch her? No. Not touch her, no. Never? Never. She was a child, searching and vulnerable, and he was old, and a fool.

An uncontrollable, unasked-for rush of thoughts, images, impressions, dreams remembered: the way she sometimes dressed – we are composers, not members of the corps de ballet at the Opéra Comique, d'Indy had said – and then, for no rhyme or reason, she altered her appearance, took on a more severe, serious, studious look – why? And sometimes she wore scent, and sometimes she did not, but always she pulled the cushion off the big chair by the fire, placed it near to his feet and sat looking up at him – I hate chairs, she said – and when he had some point to make about her music – sometimes he invented points to make – she came round to behind his desk, leaning over his shoulder, her breath warm on his cheek, her scent sweet, her presence invigorating. Yes, and when she sat, she showed her ankles, and he had dreamed once of her ankles, of her bare feet walking through deep sand near the sea, and he had heard the peasant woman's song, the descending phrase, and Augusta had said, in the dream, I'm yours if you want it so much, and he had slapped her, and he awoke, crying out. For weeks afterwards he was too ashamed to say a word to her, or even to look at her. And the way the boys, even d'Indy, fussed round her; and Duparc with his new cravat each week, and Chabrier jolly and vulgar, and Cahen, eyes agog: bees round honey never buzzed so attentively. And she? how did she respond? as though they didn't exist, and always the troubled little frown at the bridge of her nose, two straight lines and one diagonal, a pucker of concentration and doubt.

Félicité said, 'D'Indy maintains Art is Life.'

'Ah yes, so he does.'

'Then why does he manage to write music that is dead as a doornail?'

'I don't know. I don't know anything about those things.' All he knew was that Augusta excreted juice where he was dry, was luxuriant where he was arid. The only thing they had in common was music. He had nothing else to give. He had nothing else.

What was there for him as a man in the world apart from music? He did not drink excessively, he did not like the theatre, he could not read books, could not make things with his hands, could not talk to people and only recently he had counted up the times in his life he had made love. Seven. Seven times. Always to Félicité. And how many times had he said 'I love you' to another human being? Not once. Not once in words. Not even to his own children, and not even to himself. And how many times had the words 'I love you' been said to him? Once. Once only, by Claire, furtive, blushing Claire, little fingers touching, Claire whose face he could no longer bring to mind. What life was there for him if he did not exist in music? He was too old to soldier, politics bored him, what else was there? What else? Answer me, for Christ's sake, don't just sit there sipping coffee as if that was the only thing that really mattered. Only one thing matters in the entire universe –

'*Music!*'

Félicité quivered with fright and spilled her coffee. 'Franck,' she said, 'please warn me when you are going to shout.'

'Shout? Did I shout?' Was that the sound he heard echo and re-echo in the empty caverns where there was no music? All within him was hushed. How could he explain that without music he was lonely and desolate?

Félicité said, 'Franck, you must visit the eye doctor.'

'The eye doctor? Why?'

'Your eyes are watering.'

– I am crying.

'It is an unseemly sight at breakfast.'

He was crying for himself, for his loneliness. Yes, that must be an unseemly sight: to watch tears drop into an ice-bucket and freeze. Who could melt them? Augusta? But how could he contrive to see more of her? Give her extra lessons? Alone? Oh God, the dangers. Say, just say, he could not restrain himself in her presence and that he reached out, grabbed her, kissed her, felt her breasts, her thighs. Josquin, crouched at the entrance to the cave, hissed. He must stop this. This must be stopped. He could not betray himself, his wife, his family, bring disgrace down on their heads. He would have nothing, not even the pretence of life. He may as well be dead. Perhaps he was dead. No, no, no, no –

'*I am not dead!*'

Félicité said, 'If you do that again I shall leave the room.'

– Don't leave the room, don't leave me alone. He was too cowardly. He had always been too cowardly. Life was frightening. But he believed, had to believe that what he was lay hidden inside him, as it was in every living thing. He must struggle to find it, perform an act of faith, a sacrifice of life to life –

'Sacrifice and struggle.'

'Franck, you are quite incoherent this morning.'

– Let he who is without sin cast the first crotchet. He had never even so much glimpsed what was hidden, though he knew he must thrust downwards, deep, downwards, deep. Had he had a vision once of what it could be like, when Claire whispered –

'I love you.'

Félicité's jaw dropped and her eyes grew wider. 'What did you say?' she whispered.

A variety of smiles flitted across his lips. He tapped his temple with a forefinger. 'A puzzle, a musical puzzle,' he said.

'Oh,' Félicité said, her face sagging. 'I thought –' but she did not say what she thought.

Was it Claire or Augusta who had blushed golden? Had something in him broken out, to be sure, something suppressed and tortured, some part of him that needed blessing, the frozen waste in need of warmth, Claire had brought the spring thaw. How brief, long ago, nearly forgotten. Now it was autumn though the summer sun beat down, and only winter to come.

'Franck, will you please wipe your eyes?'

We are what we do. And he did nothing. He was a useless, tired, dead old man. And yet, it would be glorious to pretend that spring was coming. All was repetition. He had not the courage then to answer Claire word for word. He remained silent. He was engaged to Félicité. An excuse. If he had known the meaning of courage he would have told Claire what she had told him. He wrote her a song. That was his way. But she was too shy to understand. And now it was summer out, autumn in, and he had never said I love you to anyone. From Augusta he must expect nothing, only silence. He must not hope, he must not dream, there was cause for neither. The moth danced round the flame, and he watched from the darkness, but who was it beside him? Josquin?

'Who's there, for God's sake?'

'Franck, what *is* the matter with you?'

'Nothing, nothing, I assure you.'

'Is it nothing to shout "music" without warning? Is it nothing to whisper – what ever it was you whispered? Is it nothing to clutch your heart and hiss, "Who's there, for God's sake?"' She tinkled the bell vigorously.

'I'm perfectly all right,' he said. 'It's the blowing of the winds, you see, my dear.'

'You should've finished *The Beatitudes* first,' Félicité said as Clementine entered, a scarecrow more frightened than frightening. 'Fetch the thermometer I keep in the bathroom cabinet,' Félicité ordered.

'I have no temperature, I promise you, my dear.'

'Fetch it, Clementine.'

The maid curtsied and left. César rose from the table, quickly swallowing the last of his coffee. 'I must be off,' he said.

'Franck, allow me to take your temperature.'

'Don't forget,' he said, 'there'll be a class tonight.'

'You're not going out with your coat on, are you? It's warm out.'

'Is it? Warm out? Is it?'

'For heaven's sake, Franck, at least take the napkin from your collar and use it to wipe your eyes!'

The postman with the forked beard said, 'Good morning, professor.'

'Good morning,' César said. 'And how is your wife progressing?' Is it an affectation, he wondered, to be concerned for strangers?

'The fever's down, but it'll be a little time yet.'

'But on the mend, eh, on the mend?'

'Oh, yes, definitely.'

'Anything for me?'

While the postman searched in his bag for César's letters, he said, 'Takes a catastrophe to find out about things.'

'Does it, does it, indeed?' A variation, César thought: what now?

In his hand the postman held a large bundle of letters which he sorted through, but continued to explain to César, 'All the while the old lady's been ill, I've had to do the shopping and the cooking. Didn't much care for it at first, but I got used to it, soon enough.' One letter. 'Ah, here we are, from Orléans.'

From Orléans? From Claire? César took the letter too quickly, snatched it almost, and began to tear open the envelope.

'Well, where was I?' the postman said. 'Oh yes, so, the funny thing is, it turns out I'm rather a good cook. They say the best chefs are men, don't they? But, according to my old lady, and to my brother-in-law who visited me from Arles, I'm a little above average, well, even if I say it myself, I seem to have a talent for cooking—'

The Angel and the Child: César recognised his own musical handwriting on the faded, folded paper; he could feel his heart pounding too fast, his temples throbbing. Was Claire saying, I love you again? A letter; not her hand—

'My brother-in-law runs a small inn near Arles, so we're giving up Paris, giving up the Post, and moving down to Arles, I'll do the cooking, my wife can serve.'

Dear Professor Franck,

It is with a heavy heart that I have to inform you that Madame Claire Brissaud, nee Féréol, passed away after a long and painful illness, bravely born. She left very little, but there was a Will, which has now been proven. Among her bequests was the following: To my cousin, Monsieur César-Auguste Franck, 95 boulevard Saint-Michel, Paris, I bequeath my copy of *The Angel and the Child* which he so kindly presented to me many years ago.

I would be grateful, esteemed sir, if you would be kind enough to acknowledge receipt of the manuscript.

The postman said, 'So, you'll have to train another fellow in your ways, professor. At the end of the month you won't see me again. I shall miss you. But, as I say, it takes a catastrophe to find out about things.'

César said, 'I am very sorry.'

'Well, no one's indispensable.'

'No.' He could not stop the letter from trembling. Could he stop himself from fainting? He smiled. Oh God, the only one ever to say I love you and he could not bring her face to mind.

The postman said, 'Don't you want your coat on this morning?'

'Yes. I feel the cold.'

Cold, he passed the day in a dream, a state without feeling, absent of grief. He wandered lost. Not Chabrier, fatter, jollier, more refreshingly irreverent, not the sunshine, not the bright blue sparkle of the river, not Paris bustling could touch him. He had not seen Claire for more years than he could count, but had believed she resided in him, believed she warmed him. But he did not grieve. Against his will, he experienced a light-headedness as though an invisible thread had snapped. And in Sainte-Clothilde at twilight, the familiar anticipation possessed him more intensely than ever.

'Why do I feel like this?' he asked in the still, empty church. 'Why don't I weep? Why don't I mourn?'

Gardey, the curé, who was in the vestry, heard a noise, thought it was a cry of pain and scurried into the church to see César seated as usual near the door. César heard the priest's business-like footsteps in the empty place, looked up and said, 'I thought – I thought I was alone.'

'I did not mean to disturb you,' Gardey said.

'Sit by me.'

'What is it?' Gardey asked, taking a chair in front of César.

165

'I lost someone today.'

'Oh my dear friend, I'm sorry –'

'No. Don't be. I hadn't seen this person for more than thirty years, although I believed she was important to me. But I feel nothing.'

'Tell me her name. I will pray for her.'

'Claire Brissaud, nee Féréol.'

'I'll remember.'

'I feel, to my shame, free.'

'Free?'

'I cannot explain.'

'You are not obliged to mourn the dead. You may give thanks that they're with God.'

'Yes.'

'I will pray for her.'

'Thank you.'

Gardey, after a moment, rose. 'Perhaps now is not the time, but there is to be a marriage on Sunday week. The couple hoped you would be free to play for them.'

'A marriage? Yes, of course.'

'Thank you. I'll tell them. They'll be pleased.'

'Father –'

'What?'

'Pray for me also.'

The mood of insensibility continued into evening. Guilt that he should be so unfeeling only accentuated the void. But when the class assembled he was victim to an unpleasant sensation which to begin with he could not identify, a sort of fretting as though nothing were in the right place, or as if he had forgotten something important – whatever it was – a minor matter but irritating to a ridiculous degree. He fidgeted with his hands, stroked his sideburns, pinched his eyebrows. He sat first in one chair, then another. The students could not fail to be aware of his uneasiness. Vincent was the spokesman. 'Pater seraphicus, you are obviously bothered by something. Would you prefer to postpone the lesson?'

'No, no,' he said absently, wishing he knew what troubled him. 'Let us begin. And, Mademoiselle Holmès, no operas this evening.'

'Augusta's not here, maître,' Chabrier said.

Like air rushing into a vacuum, César suddenly understood. Augusta was absent. What had passed for irritation was transformed into concern, and the need to see her grew quickly and uncontrollably. He was puzzled and shocked by his own emotion. And when the class began, his senses were attuned not to the music but elsewhere: outside, every footstep was her footstep; a carriage stopping, a knock on a door, a rustle in the passage were heralds of her arrival, but she did not arrive. What is happening? he asked himself, what is happening? He could not rid himself of the desire to see her, to partake of her presence, smell her smell, irrationally convinced she was the only one alive who could and would comfort him. Was he so fickle, he wondered? The moment he learned of Claire's death he admitted feeling free to a priest, suffered no grief and longed instead to be with Augusta whom, until this moment, he had thought of as unobtainable, forbidden fruit. But it was not now his senses he believed Augusta could satisfy, but rather that she would replace Claire and inhabit the emptiness within him.

When the students were taking their leave, he asked, 'Does anyone know where Mademoiselle Holmès is?'

'In Tortoni's, probably,' Vincent said. 'She's there most nights, I am told, drinking too much and talking too loudly.'

Chabrier said, 'That's unfair, Vincent. She's lonely. I don't believe she's close to anyone except for Julie.'

'Julie?' César asked.

'Her maid. Augusta's not used to working alone, to devoting all her time to composition. It's easier for a man. Hell for a woman.'

'One is either disciplined, or one is not,' Vincent said.

Duparc said, 'You know, maître, I think she needs more encouragement.'

'One only encourages work that is good,' César said, regretting the words instantly; so arrogant and without credentials.

'No, I don't mean her work. Of course she has a lot to learn. Who hasn't? No, she needs to feel more a part of the circle.'

Vincent snorted.

After they had gone and a hush had settled over the apartment, César stood in his music room without moving, lost in thought. The maid, Clementine, locked her cell door; the Actress twisted and turned, creaking the bed springs until she slept. César remained motionless, his mind on Augusta, compelled to rehearse every word he had spoken to her at her last lesson: he squirmed at the memory of how harsh he had been, how cruel and destructive with his sarcasm about military bands and leprechauns. Perhaps he had discouraged her forever. Perhaps she would never again attend a lesson – and who could blame her? Oh God, he knew he must see her as soon as possible and apologise. Yes, yes, she needed encouragement and all he had provided was scorn. She must be coaxed back. The idea that he had driven her away plagued him like an incurable rash. He wanted to be with her. He wanted to be with her *now*.

He tried to be calm, tried to reason himself out of this absurd impulse to rush out into the night to see her. Tomorrow would be time enough, he argued. Tomorrow he would call on her and offer his apologies for all the thoughtless things he had said. But having found what he knew to be a sensible solution, he succumbed to disappointment and provided himself with reasons why the morrow would not do. What if he were seen entering or leaving her apartment in broad daylight? How would he explain himself? After all, he did not call on Vincent or Duparc or any of his other students unless for a professional purpose and he could not think of a professional purpose for calling on Augusta. And did not want to. Now, now, he must see her now. He must. Had not Vincent inadvertently told him where to find her? Did he not say she was nightly to be seen at Tortoni's? The very thought of the café, however, alarmed him: could he risk so public a place, so many prying eyes? But they would be meeting in a crowd, he reassured himself, which is not quite the same as visiting a woman alone in her apartment. Yes, but even so, what if the Actress were to find out? He did not dare contemplate such dreadful misfortune. He glanced at his pocket-watch: not yet midnight; time enough.

He tip-toed into the darkened hall, reached for his hat, stopped, frozen: what if Augusta suspected that his motives for encouraging her were less than pure? What if she perceived in him his passion for her, his obsession? He understood he was passing through a sort of delirium, close to madness. She was young and beautiful. He was old and mad. Go to bed, he told himself. Yet, reason as

168

he might, the ache to comfort her intensified, more agonising with the passage of every second. There was nothing he could do but surrender to his longings.

Silently, he slipped out of the front door, marvelling at the ease with which he did so. Deeply he inhaled the fresh night air, and even as he set off down the boulevard another warning sounded but was ignored: he remembered all those years ago escaping from his father's house, a similar sense of glorious freedom, but ending ensnared by Josquin. Too late, too late now. He sped towards Tortoni's.

7

Tortoni's was reality, Augusta liked to believe. Tortoni's was the world. The café surged with vitality, exuded warmth, friendliness, all the countless easy pleasures of life. She had only to make her way through the rows of snare-drum tables, three deep on the boulevard, to be transported into a familiar, welcoming, densely-populated terrain. Resentment of César, which she had nursed since her last lesson, vanished. The intensity of his narrow little conclave lifted. The pinprick of guilt she had felt for missing the class that evening subsided. This was the great world and she was at home in it.

Beneath the lanterns, waiters in ankle-length white spotless aprons spun like teetotums with miraculously balanced trays held high overhead, prizes bearing gâteaux and pâtisseries, wafting the smell of freshly-ground coffee, of steaming chocolate, and alcohol potions subtly flavoured. And entering the salon behind, she was bewitched by the intimacy, the hubbub, the constant cachinnation of plates and saucers, cutlery and glass, the irresistible babble of assignations made, of trysts broken, of reputations extolled and destroyed; the heady worship of success, the disparagement of failure, the secrets of life, God, morals, all expounded with artificial passion or artificial disdain, all in the closely packed confines, beneath the murals of Tarantella dancers of the Café Tortoni.

'Augusta! There's Augusta! Augusta!'

Tortoni's castrati rose to her, but as she weaved her way towards

169

them a hand tugged at her sleeve. She stopped and turned.

'Augusta.'

Camille gazed up at her, wistful, amused. Beside him sat Romain Bussine, neither wistful nor amused: he inclined his head politely but as though his neck were stiff. Camille said, 'It's been too long.'

'I've missed you,' she said, realising it only at that moment.

'Have you?' he said, obviously pleased. 'Have you?'

The *castrati*, excited as banshees, screeched, 'Augusta, Augusta, there's a seat for you here – doesn't she look divine? – Augusta – I prefer her hair loose – Augusta!'

Camille stirred his *café liégoise* with a long, silver spoon, licked it clean and using it like a conductor's baton, pointed to an empty chair at the table. 'Join us,' he said.

She hesitated, cast a sideways glance at the banshees and called to them, 'I have to talk to Camille. I'll come over in a moment.' Like a carefully orchestrated passage, their excitement plummeted; they sat, curls touching, hissing at each other, 'Camille! She's back with Camille! Augusta's talking to Camille! Oh la!'

Languid and reluctant, Romain helped Augusta off with her cloak and held her chair. 'What will you have?' he asked.

'Cognac,' she said, sitting.

Camille said, 'You look beautiful. Lovelier than I remember which proves what a poor thing memory is.'

'How sweet you are,' she said, squeezing his hand, and asked what he was up to. He told her of the thousand-and-one engagements, commissions, performances, past, present and future he had arranged. His chatter delighted her; the café warmed her; she had not known such gaiety for weeks.

Romain asked, 'And how are your lessons?'

She launched at once into a racy, exaggerated account of César's methods, giving a grotesque impersonation of him, overdoing his grimaces until Camille and Romain were helpless with laughter. But while performing, suddenly, a refrain ran through her mind, an insistent accusation of self by self: you are a betrayer, the inner voice said, a betrayer. And although she continued to lampoon him, the accusation did not cease and her energy gradually subsided. The entertainment had turned sour in her mouth. She broke off abruptly.

'What's the matter?' Romain asked.

'I don't know.' She shuddered. 'Someone walked over my grave.'

Like a portrait painter Camille squinted at her. 'How very odd you are. I'd also forgotten you were very temperamental.'

She continued to hold his hand but did not look at him. 'I have an awful feeling,' she said, 'that I'm changing. And I don't want to.'

'Well, don't,' Camille said lightly.

'Have I, do you think?'

'Have you what?'

'Have I changed?'

Romain said, 'I've noticed one thing.'

'What?' she said.

'You look so much younger.'

Camille sniggered. 'I wonder,' he said. 'Do people change?'

A waiter, as though executing a balletic flourish, placed Augusta's glass before her and was gone. The two men watched her drink. Romain said, 'There's another thing, of course: one never reads about you any more. And that's not so much a change as a relief.'

Augusta affected to laugh. Romain had touched an exposed nerve. 'Yes, but people *know* what I'm doing. Everyone knows,' she said, but added on a note of too much hopefulness, 'Don't they?'

Romain asked lazily, 'Shall I be beastly?'

'Oh, *do*,' Camille said.

'People are no longer interested in you, Augusta. The world detests earnestness and you've become earnest. We've all noted the change in style, that your neckline is several inches higher, that men don't threaten to commit murder on your behalf and that you don't change lovers twice a week. All that has been noted. And people think you've become dull. You're a bore, Augusta – I'm only saying what people think. They resent not being able to witness each and every episode of your life because in days gone by you used to take such pains to see that they did. You are no longer attended by spectacle. You used to provide us with drama for our dull little lives. If you want to know what people think about you, the truth is they don't think about you at all.'

'Oh dear,' Camille said, 'you *have* been beastly.'

'Have I?' Romain asked innocently, mocking her again. 'I thought that was what Augusta wanted to hear.'

The café violinist, old Pastinado, began to play *La Solitaire*, the song Camille had dedicated to Augusta. With a royal salute Camille acknowledged the compliment and Augusta turned to smile at the old man who played reverently and with much vibrato, shuffling from table to table, swaying passionately, his chins shimmering. The knowledgeable among the *castrati* sighed audibly, approving Pastinado's sense of occasion and his instinct for romance. Augusta turned her smile on Camille. He said, 'Romain didn't offend you, did he?'

'Of course not,' she said. 'May I have another cognac?' Eyes closed, she listened to Pastinado playing the tune more sadly than was intended. 'Oh, those were lovely days,' she said.

'I'm glad we met tonight,' Camille said.

'So am I.'

Camille toyed with the spoon in his empty glass. 'Oh God, how quickly the years go,' he said. 'Can we do nothing to slow them down?'

'Nothing,' Romain said.

Pastinado timed the final phrase at the composer's table. Camille stuffed a note into the old man's hands. He said, 'Play something vulgar. Play Offenbach.' Pastinado obliged with a weary, knowing smile and moved on with his famous little skipping step in time to the *Trio Patriotique*. Camille said, 'I bet old Franck won't allow you to write any vulgar little tunes, will he, Augusta?'

Impulsively she said, 'Will you look at some of my pieces, Camille? Mostly fugues, I'm afraid.'

He seemed surprised by his own response. 'I'd rather not,' he said, 'do you mind?'

Augusta shrugged. 'Well,' she said, 'the old boy likes them. He thinks I'm awfully promising.'

'That's all right then, isn't it?' Romain said delicately.

Camille asked about the atmosphere in class. 'Is it really like a religious service? Do you all compose at a prie-dieu? Technically it's all lovely, but there never seems to be any laughter or, God forbid, passion.'

'That's not true, Camille,' Augusta said. The tug of loyalty was strong. 'Duparc writes beautiful songs.'

'Yes, one every decade.'

'He has problems. He has to – to find himself.'

'Oh God, how pretentious,' Romain said.

'And you, Augusta, do you have to find yourself?'

'Yes,' she said curtly, and swallowed her drink. She wished she could say she hoped she never would find herself, that she was afraid of being unequal to the struggle, that she wanted nothing more than to sit here night after night talking rather than doing, being loved rather than giving of herself. But the words, perhaps the thoughts themselves, were censored by the inability to face failure.

'I think she's become a reluctant disciple,' Romain said, stifling a yawn.

'And what about the old boy? Is he really as dotty as you make him out to be?'

Romain said, 'I hear that none of you ever talk of the pleasure in writing music, only the difficulties.'

'He is a wonderful teacher,' Augusta said quietly.

'Oh very definitely a reluctant disciple,' Romain said. 'I can tell.'

'I was told that women found him attractive,' Camille said. 'Is that true?'

'Who said so?'

'Maman.'

Romain guffawed. 'Maman!' he cried.

'I do not find it all that funny, Romain.'

Augusta asked, 'Does your mother know him?'

'Rather. They sit together on my Monday evenings. Maman does not approve of the way he looks at women. She thought that inside he's probably rather ardent.'

'Ardent,' Romain repeated, mocking.

'I haven't noticed,' Augusta said. When she came into a room César appeared to shrink from her.

'Obviously he needs bringing out,' Romain said.

'He's a bit old, isn't he?'

'Not for Augusta,' Romain said.

Pastinado played Meyerbeer. Camille said, 'Romain, be a dear and find someone to talk to.'

Romain obeyed instantly without looking at either of them. He sauntered across to the other end of the café, paused at a table, stopped to talk.

As though removing a mask, Camille's manner altered. He became unusually serious; even his lisp was less noticeable. 'Romain can be very cruel. It's part of his charm.' And more quietly, tenderly for one who resisted his own tenderness. 'I'm glad we're friends again, Augusta. It's been too long to be angry with anyone, especially you. And I know Romain mocks all the talk about finding oneself, and he'll go on about it tonight to me, and say it's all romantic rubbish, but, I'll let you in on a secret, Augusta, and you must promise never to tell anyone ever. I believe in it. I believe everybody has to find themselves. I know, because I've taken great pains to make certain I never shall.'

'Oh, Camille,' she said affectionately, head to one side. She had never known him gentler.

'I think about you, Augusta, often. Too often.'

'But, Camille, you're a married man now.'

'I love you, Augusta, I will never stop loving you,' he said as if it were a reprimand. 'And if you ask me why, I answer with Montaigne: because I am I and you are you.'

'Nonsense, my dear.'

'No, no, perfectly true. I often think of the days before the war, when we all used to go to Fontainebleau. You were really very wicked. And I loved you. And there's one memory of you I shall carry with me all my life. I have only to think of it and then I want you with awful pain and longing –'

'What, what memory?' she asked, intrigued, engaged.

'When you give another party at Fontainebleau I'll tell you.' He took her hand, played with her fingers.

'No, tell me now.'

He gazed into her eyes. 'You wrote in the earth that you loved me. Do you remember?'

'Yes,' she said, 'Augusta loves C.'

'And then that awful idiot Catulle Mendès came into the clearing and nearly choked the life out of me.'

174

'And me,' Augusta said, smiling fondly.

'What a tragedy for music if he'd done it.'

She caressed his cheek. 'There is nothing quite like being told one is loved, is there, Camille?'

'Or wanted,' he said. 'I want you, Augusta. Give another party at Fontainebleau.'

She withdrew a little. 'And is it true that you proposed to your wife after you had sent me that beastly letter?'

He smiled, pleased she remembered the note he had written. He said, 'Yes, I believe it was two days later.'

'And is it also true you proposed by letter?'

'Quite true. And to her brother, you know, not to her,' he explained as if it was a cause of pride to him. 'She was my pupil. Very young and very pretty. I wrote to her brother asking if he wanted a brother-in-law.'

Augusta laughed fondly. 'You didn't, Camille, did you?'

'Yes, I did.'

'Are all composers dotty?' she asked.

'Not you, Augusta, not you.'

'Ah, Camille, that's the nicest thing anyone has ever said to me.'

He was about to kiss her cheek when Romain returned. Augusta said easily, 'And you have two sons, I believe.'

'Yes. Two fine boys.'

Romain said, 'When they grow up they're going to be very pretty.' He sat and stretched out his legs.

'Like their mother, thank God,' Camille said smiling.

'Said all you want to say to her?' Romain asked as though Augusta were not present.

Without warning and apparently for no reason, Camille erupted, suddenly castigating Romain not for his rudeness to Augusta but for some slight to Maman. Camille developed the theme with what seemed to Augusta unnecessary savagery, lisping dreadfully, raking up past incidents, reminding Romain that he had omitted once to write a thank-you letter to Maman for a week spent under her roof. Augusta took no part; embarrassed, she gazed into her empty cognac glass, privately enjoying Romain's discomfort. Romain, too, did not speak. He stared at Camille with an interested, polite look as though fascinated by what Camille would say next.

175

A gypsy halted Camille. A young woman with a baby asleep in her arms thrust a posy of violets under his nose; he waved her aside angrily and lost his train of thought. The three of them were caught in a pocket of silence; all around them, the laughter and chatter continued unabated. Romain said as if all were sanguine, 'I'm going to make a prediction.'

'Oh?' Camille said, tapping his foot noisily.

'I predict that by the end of the year Augusta will have given up all this nonsense.'

'What d'you mean?' she asked.

'Oh, all this finding yourself nonsense. I predict that within six months you'll have had enough of César Franck. You'll give up wanting to write music.'

'Never.'

'Oh yes, you will.'

'I won't.'

'You will.'

'Why are you so sure, Romain?' she asked testily.

'Because you're not cruel enough to be a composer.' He smiled crookedly at Camille.

Augusta said, 'It's late. I must go.'

The men stood. Camille whispered, 'Remember what I said about Fontainebleau.'

'Remember my prediction,' Romain crooned.

'Let's meet soon,' Augusta said, quickly kissing Camille on the forehead. She turned, stopped, gasped. Camille and Romain looked up to see what had so startled her. She was gazing at the café entrance but neither of them noticed anything unusual.

'What now?' Romain asked.

'I thought I saw –' she began but did not finish; for a brief moment she believed she had seen César in the street, peering into the café, looking at her. An illusion, she decided, as before in youth, with Vigny, her father's image haunted her.

'You really have become very eccentric, Augusta,' Romain said. 'I do believe Father Franck is an infection.'

She tried to smile – his words were so disquietingly apt – but covered her unease by blowing a kiss and making for the door.

The *castrati* cried, 'Augusta! Augusta! Aren't you going to join us?'

'I really must get back. I have work to do!'

'Oh Augusta! You promised!'

She waved and was gone.

'She looks flushed, she looks upset, Camille's fuming, Romain's delighted, what happened? are they friends again? we'll find out from Romain –'

The whispers of speculation carried her out into the street; just in case she really had seen César, she looked this way and that but he was nowhere about. She could not afford a cab, so she walked and grew more and more depressed. A weight lay heavy on her which she could do nothing, it seemed, to alleviate. Past the sleeping concierge, up the stairs to her rooms: only then, seeing the piano, did she feel her depression transform itself into an irresistible need to compose. Hurrying now, she ordered Julie to keep the fire going and sat at the piano fingering a theme, discovering harmonies, jotting down the notes and chords that pleased her. She called the piece *Serenade* and believed while in the process of creation that the sounds were pure and musical, that they exposed some essential part of her she was able in no other way to express. Towards dawn, when half the work was done, she inscribed the title page, 'To C. Franck', and then slept before the hushed fire, her head on Julie's lap. She woke with a start. Through the skylight the dawn clouds were streaked with the early, faint pink rays of the sun. Quietly, she played through what she had composed and detested every note. She consigned the manuscript to the dying embers in the grate; the flames briefly warmed her. She stared, vacant, lost, at the ashes which twisted and coiled as though they had a life of their own. Julie stirred, but did not open her eyes. Barely audible, Augusta murmured, 'What shall I do? Oh, Mother of God, help me. I believe I hate him. I never want to see him again. I don't care if Romain and the others do gloat. What stops me from making the break? I don't want to go back to the old way, and I don't want to embark on the new. And somehow, Julie, I know he's the reason. He doesn't help me to express all that's in me.' She was crying. She said, 'I don't want – I want – oh, I don't know what I want and don't want. Oh Jesus, help me, I really think I do hate him.'

Her eyes closed, Julie asked, 'Who?' as though still asleep.

And in the morning, as though to endorse and recall her previous resentment and anguish, the concierge handed her a note scribbled in pencil on a torn piece of newspaper.

> Please do not miss your lesson next week.
>> C. Franck

To Julie, she said, 'It's like being in prison.'

8

César had lost his courage, He had expected her, for some reason, to be alone in Tortoni's; but there she was with Camille and Romain of all people. Things always turned out differently from the way he imagined. He cursed his foolishness for embarking on a wild night-errand, walked on past the café and glimpsed her laughing. He scampered by a second time to see her now alone with Camille, foreheads touching. César feared for his own sanity: this girl would drive him mad. A third time: she was leaning over Camille – kissing him, perhaps? – and, on looking up, seemed to gaze straight into César's eyes. He skidded away and when he passed the café a fourth time she was no longer there.

What now? Must he trudge wearily home? Must he wait another week in torment? Would she or would she not appear at the next lesson? He must see her again, there was no denying the need. He must somehow encourage her back into the fold. He found himself walking in the direction of the rue Mansart. I am mad, he thought.

He heard the tinkling of the piano from the street, wished the chords less emphatic, contemplated entering the building and knocking on her door. No. He was too timid. What would he say? I have walked half across Paris in the dead of night to tell you to come to class next week? No. He stood in the shadows and listened. A clumsy key change, he thought.

A note was the only answer, but he was without paper. A café would, no doubt, sell him a sheet. But nearing the Place Pigalle he bought chestnuts from a chestnut-seller, shared the contents of the cone among astonished urchins who stood near by, and scribbled his note on the newspaper wrapping. The old fat concierge was asleep. He put the note on her lap and as he turned to go, fancied he smelled Augusta's scent.

Augusta. Asleep or awake, in darkness or in light, he thought of little else. He saw her perpetually, imagined her voice, the look in her eyes, the sweetness of her smile. The silence was blacker, deeper than ever. No longer did he hear, on rising, the crescendo; the hush was absolute, a coffin entombed. Even the pious, sickly Christ was absent. Augusta alone occupied his thoughts.

And when, as though nothing had happened, she appeared at the next lesson without so much as a fleeting reference to his note, his excitement was so great that he was obliged to keep silent lest his voice tremble and betray him. If he could find it in himself to encourage her, he did so unhesitatingly, earned her smile, nursed it in his heart. When he was harsh, he shared her despondency. And he discovered that rarely now did he allow himself to think of the physical act of love: the daydream had been poisoned by the realisation that there was always an afterwards to love-making; the lying motionless beside the object of love; the revulsion, the turning away, the hiding in the cave with Josquin on guard. He dared not think of it. He was content to be in her presence once a week, but soon that did not suffice. He wanted to entice her deeper into his world and to hold her there. But how? how?

TEN LETTERS

'He excelled in his power to penetrate his pupils' thoughts and to take possession of them ...'

Vincent d'Indy

FROM CESAR FRANCK TO VINCENT D'INDY:

c/o M. Sanche
Arille, Aude
2nd July 1876

Dear Vincent,

I thought you would like to know that I have finished the full score of my symphonic poem *Les Eolides*. I would be grateful if you would alert the Société and arrange a performance. The poem (by my neighbour Leconte de Lisle) is a little more gentle than my piece. I have perhaps erred on the side of violence, but, I assure you, the wind, in my experience, is extremely rough. (I mean, of course, in the spiritual, mystical sense.) My Eolides sometimes get out of temper.

I will now go back to *The Beatitudes*.

Your teacher,
C. Franck

Your letter arrived just as I finished this. I beg you not to be too hard on Mlle Holmès. She may not have written anything for six months but yet I believe her to be talented. Remember, dear friend, what you were like at the beginning. We must be loving and patient.

CF

I mean, of course, we must be loving and patient to *all* who learn, not just to Mlle Holmès.

CF

FROM ROMAIN BUSSINE TO
CAMILLE SAINT-SAENS:

Paris
July '76

Camille,

And how is Bayreuth? I read your reviews of *The Ring of the Niebelungen* which were carried prominently here. I am so pleased you find The Great Man dreary. Is his house, Wahnfried, (does it really mean Peace from Illusion? God help us!) as hideous as you say? I trust you did not, as that buffoon Chabrier did, buy a Wagner cravat which, I am told, by pulling a string causes The Great Man's face to appear from under one's lapel; did you wear a *Parsifal* hat? do you write your critique with a *Siegfried* pen?

Paris is empty, hot and tedious. I cannot afford to go away this year. The only other person in the city is Augusta. I have seen her twice at Tortoni's. Her high complexion was due, I fear, not only to the hot sun. We met also in the Luxembourg Gardens. She was with her 'maid'. Augusta said she was hiding from Mendès who is pursuing her again. I thought how constant are the men in her life! But she explained she is terribly poor and Mendès is pursuing her in order to repossess her apartment which apparently is his! She says work with Father Franck is very dispiriting. She says he will not let her be herself! (Whoever that may be.) The man has obviously some sense after all.

No doubt you had reports of his symphonic poem, *Les Eolides*. Wagner is jocund in comparison. I have heard only the piano version which the old boy has done. Instead of spring breezes we get an Atlantic gale. I fear the composer is as untalented as I've always said. All musical knowledge and no music. I begged the Société not to perform the piece, but Franckists are powerful. (Duparc and d'Indy are now joint secretaries, did you know?) I fear we will be buffeted by a full orchestral version before long.

Maman, Marie and the boys are in good health.
I cannot wait for your return,

Romain

3

FROM AUGUSTA HOLMES TO CAPTAIN KLOSE:

11 rue Mansart
8th September 1877

My dear,

Thank you so much for sending me the money so promptly – You will never know how much I appreciate it – you saved my life – I have been able to hang on to the apartment – Mendès has behaved like a boor.

Do not scold me for not visiting Dalkeith – I hear regularly from Dr Cantagrel who says his sight has gone and his bouts of violence are more frequent – I cannot bear to think of him – If only he had been more of a *father* to me, I would have begun to study composition at a proper age – 14 or 15 – instead of being sold off like a whore – and I would not now be having to endure the struggle, the misery of my present state – I'm not sorry for myself, believe me, but I am paying the penalty now for his indifference.

You ask how I am getting on – I suppose you mean with Franck – I pray God I did the right thing in going to him – he is a hard task master – the trouble was that for a year I did not understand a word he said – the trouble now is that I do! – I wrote nothing for almost 10 months – but now I am working on a programme symphony called *Lutece* – (I mean to enter it for one of the municipal prizes and I mean to win) – I must establish a position – I must show the males what I'm made of – (Lutece was the original name for Paris so I hope to appeal to the judge's civic pride!)

Thank you again – I will repay you as soon as possible – I am giving some concerts soon (as a singer) and so will be in funds again.

With love
Augusta

4

FROM CESAR FRANCK TO AUGUSTA HOLMES:

By hand: Thursday

I am sorry you were out when I called. I wanted to congratulate you in person on winning second prize for *Lutece*. You would, I'm sure, have taken first, but I have many enemies. The winners were Dubois and Godard.

C. Franck

FROM ROMAIN BUSSINE TO AUGUSTA HOLMES:

Paris
9th July '78

Dear Augusta,

It is my sad duty to write to you of tragic news concerning Camille. Although we have tried to keep the matter private you may have already heard some of it, or none of it. I will assume the latter.

In the spring, Camille remembered he was rather late with a Requiem Mass that he'd been commissioned to write. He dropped everything and ran off to Berne where he locked himself up in a hotel and managed to compose and orchestrate the entire Mass in eight days. Shortly after his return, on 28th May, at about 3 p.m., Marie, his wife, was in her room dressing. Maman was asleep in the dining room. A servant, who was doing the washing in the kitchen, opened a window to let out the steam. Little André, Camille's elder son, heard some friends in the apartment below and leaned out of the window. He overbalanced and fell the four storeys into the street below. He was killed instantly. An hour later, Camille came back from rehearsals and I am told hugged the body of his dead son for several hours without speaking.

But there is worse. Marie became very ill as a result of the tragedy and was unable to feed their younger boy, Jean, who had to be taken to her mother's house to be looked after. The child, who was in any case, frail, contracted some illness and died two days ago, within six weeks of his brother.

Camille is in need of friends. The recriminations in the household are terrible. Marie is much blamed. Camille feels – I don't know what Camille feels, but I believed that you as one of his oldest friends may want to write or see him.

Yours,
Romain B

His address is 14 rue Monsieur le Prince.

6

FROM AUGUSTA HOLMES TO
CAMILLE SAINT-SAENS:

11 rue Mansart
10th July 1878

Camille my dearest,

    I have heard from Romain of the terrible news. If you feel I
can be of any comfort to you, you have only to say so and I will
be with you. I pray for you and for your peace of mind. My heart
aches for you. Do, do let me help. My sympathy for you is deep
and abiding.

With love,
A

7

FROM CAMILLE SAINT-SAENS
TO AUGUSTA HOLMES:

14 rue M. le Prince
27th July 1878

Dear Augusta,

Thank you for your kind letter. I see in the press that you are to sing *Danse Macabre* again. Do watch the phrasing, and do not attack the opening passage too violently. Perhaps, before you sing, you ought to explain the poem to the audience. I think last time mystification played an important part in the reception. Who is to accompany you? Whoever it is tell him to watch the staccatos: *all* are intentional!

You send me the expression of your deepest sympathy. I thank you. I have just lost two children in the space of a month and can assure you that my gaiety is notably restrained.

Yours as ever,
C

8

FROM AUGUSTA HOLMES TO CAPTAIN KLOSE:

11 rue Mansart
6th February 1879

My dear,

   Can I go on owing you for a little longer? I am so dreadfully
short at the moment – I may have to move to something smaller
– Chabrier is helping me to look for somewhere – all is gloom
here – I wish the winter was over – I am considering giving up
my lessons with Franck – he has taken to staring at me for minutes
on end without saying a word – he makes me feel as much of
a failure as he is – he has also taken to delivering notes by hand
– I hide from him – I am riddled with disappointment – my cantata
Les Argonauts received only an honourable mention from this year's
judges – Duvernoy won – my dreams, our dreams, seem no nearer
of fulfilment – let us meet soon –

A

9

FROM CESAR FRANCK TO AUGUSTA HOLMES:

By hand: 95 boulevard Saint-Michel
                                        2nd April 1879
   I enclose a copy of a song I wrote in my youth, *The Angel and the Child*. I heard from Emmanuel Chabrier that you were giving a song recital shortly and looking for works to sing. I thought you may want to include mine in your programme. Do say if it is not the sort of thing you are after.
   I hear, too, from Emmanuel, that you are thinking of moving to a smaller apartment. If it would be of any assistance to you, I am quite prepared to waive my fees until you are more settled. I would hate to think of losing you as a pupil especially as I believe you are on the brink of great things.

                                        Yours sincerely,
                                        C. Franck
Scribbled in haste – I am so sorry to have missed you.
                                                        CF

FROM DR CANTAGREL TO AUGUSTA HOLMES:

> Saint-Marcel-le-Pauvre,
> near Pontoise
> Val-d'Oise
> 11th April 1879

Dear Mlle Holmès,

I pray God this reaches you in time. Your father is desperately ill and cannot have long in this world. I beg you to visit him. He collapsed yesterday after a particularly violent outburst which much weakened him. He asks for you when he is conscious. I have moved him to a private room where he may suffer his last with some dignity. Please come as soon as is humanly possible.

> Yours respectfully,
> Paul Cantagrel
> Medical Superintendent

PART THREE

'A mystic? Go and ask Augusta Holmès.'

Maurice Emmanuel

I

Julie asked to accompany Augusta on the journey to Dalkeith's death bed, begged, pleaded, wept; Augusta refused. She wanted no sympathy, no comfort. 'Don't go, don't,' Julie cried, as though terrified by some ancient memory of death and all things related to death.

'I must.'

'Why? Why? You didn't go to him once, not once while he's been there. Why go now when he's dying?'

Augusta did not answer, because she could not. She was unable to discover in herself the reason for her journey, except to say, 'He is my father,' and not to say that she positively needed to witness his death. The compulsion was undeniable; she was driven by confused forces which were both frightening and yet exciting. A part of her shunned the idea of death; a part of her wanted confirmation of its finality; a part of her hated the dying man; a part of her loved him. She held him responsible for all her misfortunes; she craved independence from him; and, to her, strangest of all she had a strong desire to comfort him and to make her peace with him.

The carriage sped at night through the Porte de Clichy. The city, unnoticed, gave way to villages, the villages to hushed, straight tree-lined roads, until at last they came to great, rusted wrought-iron gates. The driver descended, his boots on gravel-chips a regiment marching, and taking hold of the gate he shook it like an inmate wanting to be freed. A human shape, small, bent, carrying a naked torch, emerged from the gate-keeper's lodge. 'Who is it?' the shape asked in a kindly voice which quickened Augusta's fear: she did not want to be made welcome here.

'Mademoiselle Holmès to see her father,' the driver said.

'Holmès, oh yes, we're expecting her.'

The driver ran back to the carriage – soldiers retreating – and mounted to his seat; the shape turned a heavy key, pulled what seemed like an unending length of chain through the railings, and the gates creaked open, scraping the gravel to set Augusta's teeth on edge. The horse, flanks silver in the moon, lurched forward, snorting. Passing the shape who held the torch so that Augusta saw a face remarkably young, no more than a boy, with a lick of fair hair across his forehead, smiling with great sweetness. 'The priest's already there,' he called, eyes urgent; she heard him close the gates, the chain length running, the heavy key turned.

Slower now, up the curving drive; the horse, too, was reluctant. Augusta looked out to her right, but saw nothing except tight clusters of trees; swaying with the movement of the carriage, she glimpsed, through the left-hand window, on raised ground, barren against the sky, the dark, imposing outline, like a fortress, of the old monastery of Saint-Marcel-le-Pauvre, out of which the shattered bell-tower grew, the stone pillars which had once supported the small cupola like a ring of flagpoles. She could see the heavy stone walls that guarded the forecourt, and above and beyond them, like distant, unsteady stars, blotches of yellow light and isolated candle clusters in the upper floor of the house itself. From the moving carriage, there was no sound but the wind in the trees, the horse snorting, and the rasping of the brakes as the driver reined to a halt. This time he did not descend, but said to her, 'We're here,' leaning back to open with some trick of his whip-handle, the near-side door for Augusta.

'You'll wait for me,' she said and stepped down. Recessed in the thick outer walls was a huge solid wooden gate, inset with a smaller door. An iron ring at the end of a pole she presumed was the bell pull, but when she tugged at it, there was no answering sound except for the chafing of the pole against the wood; but it was evidently enough to cause a second porter to open the smaller door: a fat, unhealthily bloated face peered out through a narrow opening. Augusta gave her name, stated the purpose of her visit. 'Pass,' the second porter said and drew wide the door to admit her.

Ducking – the lintel was low even for her – Augusta stepped into a covered walk that led straight to the front door of the house thirty yards away. To right and left were square neglected gardens open to the night; one, Augusta guessed, had once produced herbs, the other, perhaps, had been more formal; in both, weeds and wild flowers now proliferated. These twin wildernesses were bordered by cloisters where pillars supported the sloping slate-tiled roof, and the old cell doors were visible. Ahead stood the house, two-storeyed, three large, wide windows at ground level, six smaller ones above, some filled with the light Augusta had seen from the drive, all barred. Steeling herself, Augusta began to walk towards the front door. Sheltered here from the wind, the silent vows of the past, she thought, continued to haunt the place, but as she drew nearer the building she was increasingly assailed by the noise of human voices, loud and distressing, terrible howls and wails, and one voice, above the others, ranting incessantly. By the time Augusta was half-way to the house, the front door was already open and three or four close-packed faces atop one amorphous body, watched her approach. A woman's voice from within called loudly but sweetly, 'Now come along, my little ones, keep away from the door,' and the single body with many heads vanished, and was replaced by the silhouette of a nun, unusually tall.

'Mademoiselle Holmès?' the nun asked uncertainly.

'Yes,' Augusta said, reaching her: an unwrinkled face, large innocent eyes, a perpetual smile of regret.

'I am Sister Martha. Please come in.'

The hall was deserted but the noise from all over the house was deafening and unceasing, giving the impression of a vast, rioting mob. The nun did not seem to notice, but Augusta felt herself to be immobilised by the unrelenting onslaught: she could barely find the impulse to walk forward; she managed to raise her hands to unfasten her cloak. Sister Martha said, 'I should keep that on. It's cold in here. Perhaps you'd like to wait in the library.' She led Augusta to a door, saying, 'I'll find Dr Cantagrel.'

'How is my father?' Augusta asked as though she had only now remembered Dalkeith lay dying in the house; perhaps already dead.

'The priest's with him,' Sister Martha said and hurried off down the hall to the far end where twin wooden staircases curved gracefully to the upper floor. Augusta was about to enter the library when she saw, in a doorway on the opposite side of the hall, the faces again peering at her, four of them, wide-eyed with interest: one, a man, was elegantly dressed in an apple green suit and a tall dove-grey top hat: he quizzed Augusta through an eye glass;

the others could have been men or women: all had hair to their shoulders, matted and unruly, and each wore a long, shapeless smock. Briefly, and a little fearfully, Augusta took note of them before hurrying into the library and closing the door.

There were no books, only row upon row of empty shelving. The windows were without curtains. The painted ceiling, dark with age and neglect depicted an Italianate Christ turning water into wine at the marriage in Cana of Galilee. An oval walnut table stood in the centre of the room; there were no chairs. The noise of the house was intrusive here, too; somewhere upstairs, perhaps directly overhead, a man railed in anguish against President Patrice MacMahon. Augusta tried vainly to stop her teeth from chattering, tried vainly to think, but the place and the awful sounds conspired to produce in her uncontrollable panic; she did not know which fear was greater: the conviction that once in this place she would be forgotten and left to rot, or the certainty that on the other side of the door, the four wretches lurked and she was helpless. In an attempt to occupy her mind, she studied, with exaggerated interest, the walnut table-top and deciphered some of the designs and messages carved or scratched on the surface: hearts pierced by arrows, several crosses, 'Help Me', 'Antoine loves S', '1 Sam 21, 13'. And, as she turned her head this way and that to read, so the door began to open. She looked up sharply: slowly, slowly, the door moved until, at last, it was wide enough for her to see the four faces, the eyes staring, long shadows stretching across the floor towards her. Terrified, Augusta tried to smile but managed no more than a twitching movement of her mouth. The elegantly dressed man tipped his topper and said, confidentially, 'The food isn't good. They let us do what we like, but that isn't what we want. We need a firmer hand. We need a leader. I had a fight yesterday –'

'And the day before,' whispered one of the others.

'Yes and the day before, but I wasn't hurt. The great thing when fighting is not to get hurt. There's a fellow here, a disruptive influence, who cuts himself all over at the earliest opportunity.' He put a finger to his lips to imply enough had been said.

'Which one's that?' asked another.

'The man who calls himself I can't remember his name, but

if it wasn't for the four of us the place wouldn't exist. We have to do everything. Lead, follow, work, play, walk, run, stand, sit, eat, shit. It's a lot to remember. But we do what's required. There used to be five of us.'

'How long will you be here?' asked the third of Augusta but she was saved from answering by the terrible raving from above which smothered her ability to think. Her mind became numb, and yet, prompted from some deep-seated source, she remembered inexplicably the giving of birth, as though the shouts from above were her own, recalled the unbearable pain and the long-forgotten thought, when this is over I shall be freed. Damn Dalkeith, she thought. Damn all fathers.

Suddenly the four at the door scattered like birds at the sound of gunshot. A short, square energetic man entered the room in a rush, something frantic and driven about him. 'I am Dr Cantagrel,' he said, coming to an abrupt stop and bowing. He talked in a loud, hoarse whisper that was somehow deafening. 'I'm sorry to have kept you waiting, mademoiselle, but – but –' he brushed aside the unspoken explanation, pointing to the ceiling, 'I apologise for our friend upstairs. He's been at it a week.' The doctor beckoned Augusta to follow him. 'We've moved your father into a smaller room we keep for –' again the sentence was unfinished. 'Upstairs,' he said, opening the door to the hall to allow her to pass. 'We never lock doors,' he explained.

They hurried the length of the hall towards the twin staircases: the walls were adorned with painted panels showing scenes from the lives of saints; the ceiling was Saint Theresa's, her apron heavy with bread, her feet deep in rose petals. Dr Cantagrel talked all the while, shooting occasional glances at Augusta as if to make sure she was keeping up. He had fine, intelligent eyes but with heavy black rings of sleeplessness beneath. He said, 'I'm glad we've been able to help your father. A decent sort. But God knows where he used to get the stuff from, smuggled a bottle in his boots once – takes some doing. First year he was a model patient, one or two lapses the second. This last year he's been ill. A few days ago – Wednesday, was it? – he just keeled over. Talked about you a lot. All the time, in fact. Very proud of you. Said you were a composer. Is that true?'

'Yes.'

'Odd for a woman. I used to work for Dr Blanche in Passy. Blanche liked artists who had come apart. Here we have all sorts. Politicians, soldiers, a judge from Rouen, a couple of medical men, all hoping to be made whole again. Not much chance, I'm afraid. Lost souls, you see, lost souls. Once lost not easy to find. But you have to keep on trying, don't you?'

Between the staircases Augusta saw through open doors to the old chapel. The nave was bare and there was no cross on the altar. An old woman patient was sweeping the floor with busy, fussy strokes. Dr Cantagrel, noticing Augusta's interest, said, 'No one prays any more. Not here, anyway,' and was about to mount the stairs when he paused without warning, and looked back down the hall. Augusta only realised he had stopped when she was on the second or third step and saw his attention had been caught by the top-hatted man and his three companions who had been following fast behind. Dr Cantagrel said, 'You should be upstairs, shouldn't you?'

The top-hatted man said, 'We were told to welcome the new arrival.'

'No, this is Mademoiselle Holmès, Dalkeith's daughter. She's a composer.' The information caused the four to look more furtive than ever; they huddled together and whispered excitedly. Dr Cantagrel said, 'Make yourselves scarce,' and continued up the stairs towards the source of the continuous clamour.

Reaching the upper hall, Augusta was shocked by what she saw. The area was crowded with men and women wandering about aimlessly, shouting at the tops of their voices; two men were fighting and a third was begging them to stop. Amidst the tumult, the nuns were easily visible, some with medicine bottles and spoons, others feeding patients from bowls; Sister Martha, who had admitted Augusta, was seated on a low wooden form beside a young girl to whom she read from a missal.

Dr Cantagrel, his hoarseness rising above the din, said, 'Don't be alarmed. None of the patients are sufficiently dangerous to be locked up. You see those over there –' he indicated with his chin the two men in combat screaming abuse at each other and the third trying to separate them – 'they'll all be friends in a moment. I don't believe in unnecessary discipline. I believe in allowing them to get their problems out in whatever way suits. You'll see, they'll be like new people in a minute or two. I deliberately employ very few keepers, too few, in fact, to keep order. It's part of the plan, you see, mademoiselle. Let them work it out of themselves. And it seems to be succeeding. I believe I will soon have some amazing results. My methods may even be taken up by people on the outside, in the everyday world, so to speak. Of course, the good sisters don't always approve. They keep telling the patients to bear with each other, to love each other even, but that's hardly the point. Still, where would we be without them, eh? They take care of the food and the hospital and what they like to call our spiritual needs.'

He guided Augusta down a passage which led off the main concourse. Here, the voice of the man who raved against President MacMahon was loud but his words unintelligible. Dr Cantagrel said, 'Poor fellow. His wife gave birth to a monstrous deformity and it turned his mind. For some reason he thinks the President was responsible. But he'll work it out, he'll work it out.' Either side the passage were doors. 'Private patients,' Dr Cantagrel explained; pointing to each door as they passed, he said, 'A vicomte, a judge, a girl who saw the Virgin in Le Havre, a leading member of the Commune of Paris, a Professor of Obstetrics –' He paused, turned to Augusta, smiled as though to apologise for what he was about to say: 'Madness is no respecter of persons. We're all in danger of monstrous births.' They came to the last door in the corridor; Dr Cantagrel knocked and entered, then beckoned Augusta to follow.

In the glow of a melting candle, Augusta saw Dalkeith lying on a low cot covered by a dark grey blanket; his face was pinched and yellowish with the bloom of death. The cell was small and bare. The priest, who was young with a mass of curly hair, had his back to the door and was gazing out of the barred window at the night. By the bedside a nun, Sister Marie-Louise, knelt to wipe Dalkeith's brow. Although the walls of the cell were of thick stone, the row of the inmates continued to intrude. The moment Dr Cantagrel and Augusta entered, the priest turned to them: he reminded Augusta of Chabrier. 'Are you his daughter?'

he asked. She nodded. 'He's been calling for you.' Augusta did not move, but stood at the foot of the cot, gazing at her father's wizened face: had she not been told this was Dalkeith, she would not have recognised him.

The priest continued, 'He has made a sign that he is sorry for his sins. I gave him absolution. I've anointed him with holy oil, and I've blessed him. Look how beautiful he is. That's the Grace of God.'

Augusta perceived no beauty: she saw only the sunken cheeks, the hollow eyes, the wisps of dull white hair already lifeless. She said, 'He wasn't a believer. He blasphemed and brought nothing but unhappiness to those who tried to love him.'

Her harsh words, harshly spoken, caused the nun to dab more energetically. The priest flushed a little, and said, 'He made a sign that he was sorry, and Christ came to call sinners to repentance, not the righteous. Look how beautiful he is.'

Augusta was in no state to deny her perversity free rein. The sight of Dalkeith, helpless and tranquil, fed her resentment of him. She said, 'Well, I'm here. I've come. What's expected of me now?'

Dr. Cantagrel said, 'Just sit with him until he –' The unspoken word rasped in Augusta's mind; but her resistance was steadfast. The priest sat on the edge of the cot which the nun understood as her cue to rise and step back as if she expected Augusta to take her place. The priest said to Dalkeith, 'Major Holmès, your daughter's here now. Augusta's here.' No movement but for his irregular, shuddering breath. Again the priest tried, again there was no response. 'You talk to him,' he said to Augusta.

Augusta looked straight ahead, at the barred window, but she felt the scrutiny of the priest's eyes, the nun's silent disapproval and was aware of Dr Cantagrel squinting at her, appraising her conduct as though she were a case which interested him. After a moment, Dr Cantagrel, close to her ear, said, 'He must have done something pretty bad to be denied comfort on his death bed.'

'I am not denying him –' Augusta said hoping to sound vehement but she caught a sudden and unwanted emotion in her voice and broke off: in loosening feelings whose roots were deep and arcane, she was shaken, momentarily, by a falling sensation, and saved herself in time before crashing. Dr Cantagrel, like an alert rooster, poked his head towards her. 'Oh, for God's sake, let yourself be moved,' he implored.

She fought against crying, but even so looked now at Dalkeith through irrepressible tears; struggled with herself, determined to preserve her hatred and resentment as though they were the most precious things she owned; but she was losing the battle, in danger of being moved in spite of herself, not because his death was a reality but because she was reliving a separation from him years ago, when she had put out her hand for him to hold but he had declined, turned away, told her that what he did was for the best; the longing for his embrace was so powerful then and now, that she required all her strength to resist; in summoning will that was already wavering, she endangered her ability to control herself. And she became conscious again of the awful noise in the house, the violent babble of human voices each demanding its own existence.

Another sound, closer, gentler, but no less insistent, intruded: voices, from behind. The priest was looking past her to the door; so, too, the nun and Cantagrel. Augusta turned to see, in the doorway to Dalkeith's cell, the top-hatted man in the apple-green suit with his three companions: they stood in a tight knot and they were singing meaningless words, to atonal, elongated notes, a weird ethereal lilt, a dissonant threnody of their own devising. Seeing that Augusta had noticed them, the top-hatted man said, 'For the composer,' and then resumed the song. Another said, 'We have to do everything.'

The choir penetrated Dalkeith's receding senses. Soldiers, he thought, and then wanted to call for Augusta but couldn't move his lips: a hiss of spittle escaped instead. Death was yellow.

Standing, the priest said, 'Please take his hands, child, he hasn't long now.'

Why, Augusta wondered, should he be embraced when it was she who was in need of his protection? The self-pity dissolved what little resistance remained. Calmly, she came to Dalkeith's side, and sat on the cot. The priest reached under the blanket and took Dalkeith's hand for her to hold. She recoiled at the touch, as though she gripped bones without flesh, her flesh.

Dalkeith said, clearly, 'Augusta.'

205

'Yes,' she whispered, 'I'm here.'

'You're my child,' he said.

'Yes, I am.'

'Will you sing for your Daddo?'

'No.'

'Is it not you singing?'

'No.'

A hiss of air.

'Is he gone?' she asked.

Dalkeith said, 'Gone where?'

'Nowhere,' she said.

'Will you sing for your Daddo?'

'No.'

'It's for the best,' he said.

'Yes.'

'I'm your father, y'know.'

'I know.'

'Are you singing, Augusta?'

'No.'

'Are you dressed in gold?'

'No.'

'I'm dying for a drink,' he said.

The priest smiled.

Augusta said, 'There's been wrong on both sides,' and wanted to say, I forgive you, but as the words formed in her mind, so came the thought, that she must ask, not bestow, forgiveness. In that second of indecision the priest said, 'He's gone,' and parted their clasped hands. The nun murmured prayers; the choristers sang in cracked, tuneless voices; the uproar in the house did not cease; Dalkeith's passing went unmarked in the world; his daughter sat and stared at the corpse.

Cantagrel turned on the singers. 'That's enough of that. Go on now, find things to do.' They stopped at once and were gone. He glanced at Augusta who had not moved. 'Mademoiselle Holmès,' he said, 'you'd better come, too.'

Augusta tried to rise but could not; her eyes were fixed on Dalkeith's face as though mesmerised by the sight of death. Reason told her that it was over; one insignificant life had ended; a man

206

she had hated, whom she had wished dead, was no longer able to inflict pain. But reason took no account of a primitive outrage that welled up in her, an ancient, savage cry of protest against death, against its speed, stealth, cruelty, and indifference; and reason neglected to assuage the guilt that afflicts survivors when they allow death to perpetuate conflicts life can reconcile; and reason is helpless in the face of remorse and shies away in terror from a child's grief at the loss of a parent. Augusta wept unwillingly, sobs of protest, guilt, remorse and mourning.

The priest said, 'He's with God. Give thanks, child.'

And Cantagrel, at the door, said, 'Well, well, who'd have thought.' From his back pocket he took a silver flask, removed the stopper and approached Augusta. 'Have a little brandy,' he said. He put one arm around her shoulders and tried to help her to stand, but she was too distracted by her own wretchedness to know what was happening. 'Don't touch me!' she yelled, and flailed her arms wildly almost knocking the flask out of Cantagrel's hand. Both the priest and the nun came to the doctor's assistance, one either side of her and they managed to pull her to her feet.

'Come on, my dear,' Cantagrel said, 'sip some of this –' and he forced the flask to her mouth; the liquid burnt her lips and tongue, but still she fought. 'Let's get her to my room,' the doctor said. They pulled her out into the passage where a bald, corpulent man with a shaven head stood before one of the private doors and said as they passed, 'May the Lord have mercy on your soul,' and coming once more into the concourse where the frenzied gabble of the inmates, the fits of violence, the spiritual misery and incoherence enveloped her like a locust swarm, Augusta lost all sense of time and place; she fainted and had to be carried – she did not know by whom; she awoke to hear the man ranting overhead; she sipped brandy, too much brandy, so that the world span dizzily; she had a blinding headache, vomited out of the carriage window, fainted or slept, woke to see Julie and although Augusta knew she must now be home in the rue Mansart, she remained somehow in Saint-Marcel-le-Pauvre, a throbbing in her head heightened by the memory of the awful noise of human suffering. Awake or asleep, uppermost, was a yearning to be embraced by her dead father, a physical need to feel his arms round her, and the more she struggled to rid herself of that need, the more it intensified. Her confused perceptions prevented her from understanding whether unhappiness came in dreams or in some disordered reality; she slept fitfully. She remembered opening her eyes in a pale, shadowy light that could have been dawn or dusk, and seeing hovering above her suspended in the air César's face surrounded by stars, remembered feeling intense and violent hatred, remembered clawing out to smash the icon, and Julie intervening and César crying, 'Josquin! Josquin!'

2

Chabrier gave César the news on the Pont Saint-Michel. 'Have you heard about Augusta?' the fat man said with such a depressed look and tone of voice that César was seized by an awful panic, fearing the worst and, in rapid succession, imagined her mangled by an omnibus, saw her pale in her coffin, walked from the grave trying to conceal his grief. He said, 'You mean Mademoiselle Holmès?'

'How many Augustas do you know, maître?'

'Well, come along, come along, I haven't got all day. What about Mademoiselle Holmès?'

'Her father's dead.'

César turned his face to the sun, closed his eyes, revelled in the warmth, all's well with the world. 'The general, oh dear. Killed in action, was he?'

'I don't know. Is there a war on anywhere?'

'The Irish are always fighting wars, I believe.'

'Confidentially, maître, between you and me and five hundred other musicians, I heard he was confined to an institution,' Chabrier said embracing himself with both arms in imitation of a straitjacket.

César stared hard at him with disapproval. 'Who told you that?'

'I'm not thaying,' Chabrier replied, grinning.

'Calumny,' César said. 'I have it from the lady herself that her father was a distinguished soldier, a general and a hero.'

'Ah well, Camille, who shall remain nameless, must've got it wrong.'

'Yes, I daresay, he gets a great deal wrong,' César said and wanted to be gone but Chabrier detained him, tugging at his sleeve.

'Maître, I'm sorry to ask this, but things are a bit tight at the moment. I really don't like asking you, but any chance of a loan?'

'A loan?'

'Fifty francs.'

'Fifty francs? Where should I get fifty francs from?'

'From the bank.'

'That's a very large sum, Emmanuel.'

'I'm trying to get to Spain.'

'To Spain?'

'A girl I met, Rosario's her name, a tightrope walker in the circus. You know I can't resist muscular legs.'

'Please!'

'But it's not only her legs, maître, I love her. She doesn't speak a word of French, but her father was a clown so she's good at mime.'

'And how do you speak to her?'

'I play love songs on the piano.'

'And not too much thumping, I hope. Your pianissimo is another man's forte. And watch the sustaining pedal.'

'Rest assured, maître, I never thump more than three times a night, and I use the sustaining pedal only when exhausted.'

César thought for a moment. 'It's an interesting theory but I am not absolutely certain it works. Something you picked up in Bayreuth, I daresay.'

'No, maître, I met her here in Paris. But now she's gone back to Spain. And of course we can't write to each other, so I *have* to go and see her. Only fifty francs, maître. In the course of true love?'

'Well, well, well,' César mumbled happily, 'true love, eh?' and reached for his wallet. He counted out the money.

Chabrier said, 'Maître, this is very decent of you. I'll pay you back next month.'

'Next month? Yes, that'd be convenient.'

Chabrier, taking the money, narrowed his eyes in an exaggerated way, and peered at César. 'You seem in high spirits today, maître?'

'The sun is shining. I play banker to Cupid, yes, yes, my spirits are high.'

Chabrier smiled. 'Nice to see you happy, maître,' he said warmly.

Happy? Yes, César had to admit as he set off across the bridge that he was blissfully happy. He walked on air; he skipped, trotted, twirled his umbrella. Fifty francs? He would have lent Chabrier a hundred had he asked. All because of a man's death; terrible, César acknowledged, to rejoice at another's passing, but there was no escaping the conclusion: the demise of General Holmès with an accent decidedly grave, had provided César with a heaven-sent or hell-bent opportunity to call upon the sorrowing daughter. The circumstances had presented themselves without effort: he had found yet another excuse for trying to see Augusta alone.

The day passed full of expectation, though there were moments of misgivings: should he at luncheon tell Félicité that Augusta's father was dead and that he intended to visit her? No. No, no, no, no, no. Should he summon a Conservatoire messenger and send him to the rue Mansart with a letter informing Augusta of his intention to call on her? He had known no luck when delivering his own letters; she had always been out; he had not even seen the inside of her apartment; perhaps it would be better to warn her of his visit. But what if she replied she did not wish to receive callers? Best not to risk rejection. But if she should think him socially graceless for paying a visit without warning? No, no, he was a musician not a man of fashion: musicians weren't expected to be versed in etiquette. If she should think his call odd or rude or indelicate, he could always hide behind his professional manner and pretend it was she who was eccentric. Having reassured himself, the clouds dispersed, the sun shone again in anticipation of dusk.

At twilight, the witching hour, faster than ever he walked, stumbled, trotted, running the gauntlet of tramps and crones, pimps and whores, a city's derelicts crawling from beneath their stones, braving the dark. On he went startled by scuffling in alley-ways, by hurrying footsteps of unseen fugitives, alarmed by screams of predators and the cries of a child savagely beaten. His anticipation protected him. Slower now, the way growing steeper, the boulevards rising, the streets darker as he climbed towards Montmartre and came at last to the rue Mansart on the very edge of the Place Pigalle.

The concierge at No. 11, a bulky old woman in her cramped lodge had nodded off; a gas lamp, turned low, popped and spluttered; a dead moth was seared to the shade. His excitement at the prospect of seeing Augusta he could barely contain; he climbed the stairs which creaked and groaned with every step, thinking that in a moment, in a moment, he would be in her presence. On the top landing he paused to catch his breath. It was pitch dark but for a slither of pale light, piano-string slim, at the end furthest from where he stood. He could just make out Augusta's door and felt his way towards it, raised his hand to knock, but froze. From within there came the sound of a woman singing – odd, he thought, for a house of mourning – a strange, barbaric chant, high-pitched, piercing. He listened more intently, and heard another sound, whimpering like that of an animal in pain. The singer was not Augusta, of that he was certain, and he could not tell if the other sounds were even human. He remained, hand poised to knock, immobile.

Footsteps ascending the creaking stairs shook him from inaction. He felt his way to the bannister, peered down through the gloom and saw a bald pate, a shadowy form reaching the floor below, heard heavy, laboured breathing, and a knock on a door. The door opened.

'Doesn't Mademoiselle Holmès live here?'

César did not know the voice.

'Upstairs! She lives upstairs!'

'Oh! I thought I'd reached the top. Is there another flight?'

'Must be, mustn't there, if she lives upstairs.'

'Can't see a thing –' the man complained as the door slammed to, and stepped uncertainly towards the staircase. César let out a grunt of annoyance. He wanted to see Augusta *alone*, and the thought crossed his mind that he could hide somewhere, wait for the man to pay his respects and leave. The man had reached the half-landing, rested a second and began up again. César glanced around hurriedly, and started towards the crack of light at the far end of the landing. He put out his hand to investigate and found himself pushing open a narrow wooden door; he stepped through, and gasped. He was outside the building, roof high, on a ledge looking over the rue Mansart. Light from the street and the evening stars encircled him. He dared not move. He heard the man knock on Augusta's door.

'Ah, Captain Klosé!' he heard Julie say.

'I've come to see Augusta '

'Ah, but she sleeps. She's not well. Best not to see her.'

'Oh. Not well?'

'No. She cries, she wakes, she screams. I sit with her all the time. I'm frightened in case she does something stupid.'

'Bad as that?'

'Terrible. She shouldn't have gone to that place. She's not herself.'

'But I would so like to see her.'

'No, Captain. She sleeps and she needs sleep. Best not.'

'I'm staying in Paris tonight. May I come tomorrow?'

'Yes, yes, tomorrow.'

'Tell her I was here.'

'Yes, of course. You are kind.'

The door closed. Klosé shuffled off, beginning the descent. Balanced on the ledge, César strained to listen. Below the street lamps were brightening sluggishly as darkness came on. Then, César heard again the mysterious singing, curiously nearer than before. Turning, he saw to his right, a pitched sky-light aglow it seemed with small islands of light which could have been the reflection in the window-panes of the stars. He had only to take a step to see through the glass which was patterned with dust and grime, and pounded by moths drawn, as he was, to the light. Through the window he saw a room warm with the dying, unsteady flames of candle-ends in saucers and the crust of a neglected fire. Before the fire Augusta lay on cushions covered in a pale blue sheet and kneeling beside her was the black girl, Julie, dabbing her forehead with a cloth, singing or chanting her outlandish, nasal melody as if summoning spirits who would comfort her mistress. Augusta was not still for long; suddenly, she flailed her arms about her, shouted out, struggling with unseen demons. And César remembered that when his second child had died, Félicité had rampaged through the house smashing cups and saucers and plates and ornaments, and had to be restrained. Where, he wondered, was the reason in grief? Augusta fought her invisible tormentors and while she did so opened her eyes, looked directly at César, a face at a window in the night. Then she lay, squirming, while Julie comforted her, singing more quietly now a weird Circean incantation. And César, above, was consumed with jealousy: he wanted to be the one to comfort Augusta, and he resented the maid's ministrations, her gentleness, her kissing of Augusta's forehead, her savage lullabye. Involuntarily, as though the maid's magic worked on him also, he was drawn along the ledge, back the way he had come, through the small opening on to the landing. He knocked on Augusta's door.

'I have come to see Mademoiselle Holmès,' he said.

'She sleeps,' Julie said.

'I would like to see her even so.'

'No, monsieur, it is not the right time. She —'

'I wish to see her,' César said and pushed past Julie into the room, astonished by his own impudence but knowing he was unable to resist the compulsion.

He had not been prepared for the nude pictures of Augusta on the wall: like an artillery bombardment they besieged him. He kept his eyes downcast, and said, 'I will sit with her for a while.'

Julie hesitated, shrugged. She said, 'Don't wake her, please, she needs sleep,' and collected from the floor her bowls and cloths, leaving César with Augusta.

He knelt beside her, and gazed lovingly on her face. He had never seen anyone so beautiful: he studied the arch of her eyebrow, the imperfection of her nose, her lips slightly open and he gazed on her slender neck and her naked shoulders. Barely audible, haltingly, punctuated by long silences he said, 'I am here. I have come to comfort you, if I can. I know how terrible grief is. Grief may last a lifetime, there is no use hiding the fact. But I'll tell you what once came to me when I was listening to Saint Matthew's Passion and which comforted me. Grief is the end of something and also a beginning, not only for the dead, but also for us, the living, the mourners.' A long, long silence. He yearned to touch her, to kiss her in repose. He said, 'Birth follows death surely as

213

night day. For us, I mean for *us*. We have to go on and on being
born. We have to go on and on grieving. You will hear that in
the music, I promise you. It is the triumph.' He leaned over her
and kissed her forehead and she woke suddenly, eyes wide, startled,
agitated. César was for a moment paralysed. And then, Augusta
with terrible savagery lashed out at him and screamed, 'Leave
me alone, can't you, leave me alone!' Hard she slapped his face,
raising herself up so that the sheet fell from her to reveal her
nakedness. And he fell sideways, his arm raised to his head to
protect himself. He tried to crawl away out of her reach but crazily
she pursued him, clawing at his face, crying, 'What do you want
from me? For Christ's sake leave me in peace! Mother of God,
give me some peace!'

She was on top of him; naked, she was on top of him, pressed
against him pulling at his hair, screaming unintelligibly until Julie
ran in to help, tried to pull Augusta off but was herself brought
down. In that instant, the two women across his body, he remembered the cave, the two girls, the one with sores around her mouth,
and Josquin laughing. 'Josquin! Josquin!' César cried.

Julie managed to quieten Augusta, pulled her back on to the
cushions, forced laudanum between her lips. Meanwhile, César
had risen, struggled to his feet to discover a cut above his eye
where Augusta's fingernails must have scratched him; a trickle of
blood obscured his vision.

'She's not herself,' Julie said, 'she's not herself.'

'I'm so sorry, I – I –'

'Go now, please. Go.'

He stumbled out of the door, down the dark stairs, heard the
maid singing again, exorcising Augusta's demons. Out in the street
he vomited. How he reached home he never knew. He locked
himself in his bedroom, sat on the edge of the bed, holding a
handkerchief over his eye. And although his head ached, and the
delayed shock caused him now to tremble uncontrollably, he was
excited by the memory of Augusta's body on his, of her breast
against his face, the feel of her flesh. And he was nauseous again
and roused as he could never before remember, except the once
so long ago, when Josquin in the cave held his legs.

Josquin: a boy twice César's size, muscular, cunning, dangerous.

Always when César practised, at the sound of the piano, giving time for César's father to leave the room, Josquin at the window, teasing and tempting the protégé-slave. He was handsome – or so César's mother thought, he remembered her saying as much – and once he had overheard the maids confiding to each other that Josquin was beloved by all the women in the town, young and old alike. A knowing, insolent manner, eyes sharp with mischief, an indolent way of moving but if danger reared he could be quick as a cat. Whenever César saw him in the town he forever seemed to be leaning, lounging, cap low over his eyes, whittling wood, surrounded always by younger boys like anxious terriers.

Why did Josquin torture him? Unfathomable the reasons why he should resent César's gifts, why he was intrigued by a boy his own age who would be locked up for six, seven, eight hours a day simply to move fingers more nimbly across a piano keyboard. Not many words passed between them, not even in spring or summer when the window was open. Always he appeared suddenly, out of the shrubbery, silent as a thief, grinning as if to say, 'Here I am again,' lean against the sill, knife in hand watching César practise.

Josquin: We've got some horses, Franck. We can ride out to the caves. The girls will bring food. Just you, me and the girls, hey, Franck? Ever seen a girl's tits? Ever seen a virgin's beard?

Oh, Augusta.

Josquin: What's the matter with you? You mad or something, sitting indoors in this heat? Come on, come with us, out to the caves. We'll swim naked.

Leave me alone, leave me alone, stop it, please, my father will kill me.

Josquin brought two girls to the window, silly, giggling girls who made faces at César; one, an ugly little creature with sores round her mouth and blackened teeth listened in wonder to the music César made and it was she who Josquin slapped hard on the crown of the head, knocking her cap askew. At night, before sleep, César thought of Josquin, imagined the naked swimming and darkened caves; at night, asleep, he dreamed of Josquin and of nude girls with beards, and twice he dreamed that it was he Josquin slapped so hard his eyes had fallen from their sockets.

215

In spite of the terror Josquin invoked, the sinful, forbidden pleasures he conjured up in César's mind, César wanted to be his friend, longed to escape from bondage, and sometimes, in his day-dreams, wanted to be Josquin.

He had felt Augusta's breasts.

A summer of pain, the agony of temptation resisted. The old widowed pastor, in his sixties, took a young wife, a pale, blonde girl, just twenty, with round blue eyes in fear and awe of the world. She taught the stories of the Bible at the school and her favourite, César learned, was the story of Ruth. In his adolescent fancies, César watched her swimming naked, lay close to her in darkened caves, imagined her whisper as clearly as if she were standing beside him at the piano that she loved him, would run away with him to live in the forests where they would never be found. And at church, on Sundays, he would gaze on her in prayer and in song, and, emerging into sunlight, would watch for some sign, a smile, a nod, a greeting, anything that he might interpret as awareness of his existence. But she gave no sign: her eyes were fixed on some distant point from which she seemed to fear either danger or delight. And then, when autumn came, he saw her no more in the church; and Josquin came no more to his window. The grown-ups whispered and fell silent when children entered rooms, the church was closed on Sundays, the pastor sent away; the maids talked of a cellar beneath the school-house where the pair were caught in the act, but César did not know what the act was, and could not imagine, except to see them dancing like ill-worked puppets at a country fair. And often César thought of the pastor's young wife, and of Josquin, and he remembered writing a song of longing which he called *The Alien Corn* and which his father burned in fury.

He had seen the inside of Augusta's thighs.

He ran away in winter. No farewell note, trusting no one, wrapped warmly, César set off, walking without set purpose but found himself heading towards the woods outside the town. He crossed a frozen stream, cut his knee on a jagged stone, and limping saw, a little way off, Josquin at the entrance to a cave, crouched on his haunches, low to the ground, guardian of a forbidden universe, Victor-the-pumper at the cupboard door, Josquin calling

to him, inviting, and César was unable to resist. Josquin's grip
was tight and strong. Inside the cave, a fire smouldered; a smoke
haze filled the enclosed space and the smell was foul. The two
girls who had been at his window sat cross-legged passing a bottle
between them. César drank, too, and was quickly dizzy, nauseous,
shivering with cold. Josquin ordered one of the girls to warm him
and kicked her hard when she disobeyed. César wanted to escape
but could not. The second girl caught hold of his leg and pulled
him down, holding him on the cold ground while the other, the
one with sores round her mouth, warmed him. He struggled and
kicked but he was savaged. And Josquin held his legs while the
girls raped him, and Josquin's laughter resounded in the cave.

Augusta. He had kissed Augusta sleeping.

Better than practising, Josquin said. César hobbled home. His
father locked him in a cupboard, in the dark, for two days and
two nights, despite his mother's pleas. For months afterwards,
César had nightmares, feared disease, for a period was dumb and,
when he found his voice again, stammered and lived in silence.

Oh, Augusta.

To his regret he realised the memory brought no relief. The
images of the girls in the cave confused with Augusta and Julie
whirled continuously through his mind. He was in turn repelled
and stimulated. The days that followed he endured as though he
were being tortured for information he was forbidden to divulge.
He was compelled to relive not only the agony of his adolescent
outrage but also the spectre of Augusta rising up at him, clawing
his face – in his mind grief excused her violence – and always
her nudity infinitely echoed by the paintings on the wall, her weight
and Julie's bearing down on him. The tumult licensed his imagination to riot and he came to believe himself capable of all manner
of things. He could, he was confident, summon enough strength
to smash the wall, the invisible barrier behind which he felt himself
incarcerated, and escape into the world. To be born. To partake.
He cursed his own cowardice, accounted his behaviour lunatic for
trying to comfort a sleeping, insensible woman, but he glimpsed
briefly a truth: quiescent, Augusta offered no threat to his conduct
real or imagined; only when she reared up, human, driven, mad
from grief, did she shatter his private universe. He resolved the

217

next time he saw Augusta alone he would declare himself to her. And afterwards? Afterwards, he would look her in the eye; and she him. Afterwards, they would look at each other.

He developed a heightened sense of the future, anticipating an inevitable climax, but as though the variations were being played before the theme. As he neared the Conservatoire one morning, a carriage stopped beside him and Camille leaned out of the window.

'The very man I want to see!' Camille said with a hideous grin. 'I say, you wouldn't like to write a requiem, would you?'

'A requiem? For Mademoiselle Holmès' father, do you mean?'

'Good God, no,' Camille said, amused by the thought. 'But, odd you should mention him because I'm just on my way to see the daughter. No, I agreed to a commission which I don't want to do now. I haven't the time. I should never have agreed to it, but there you are, that's me. The last time I wrote a requiem I had an awful run of bad luck. I thought perhaps you might like to do it instead.'

'A requiem mass?'

'It could be valuable. You know how people love anything to do with death.'

'No, no, no, no,' César said. 'I've made it a rule to avoid requiems for as long as possible.'

'Ah well, very sensible.'

And a day or two later, after class, Duparc asked, 'Any news of Augusta? I heard she wasn't well.'

César shrugged.

'Not well?' Vincent said. 'She behaves curiously for one who isn't well.'

'Oh?' César said. 'I heard she was confined to bed?'

'Not so. I heard yesterday in Tortoni's that she's giving one of her famous parties. In Fontainebleau.'

'Fontainebleau?' César repeated, raising his eyebrows.

'She'll bring disgrace on all of us. She'll degrade us,' Vincent said.

'Why?' Chabrier asked sharply. 'Just because she gives a party in Fontainebleau?'

'You know what goes on at her parties. They were infamous

before the war. I'm told it's all Camille's idea. He has invited the whole corps-de-ballet from the Opéra-Comique. Enough said.'

'Enough said,' César agreed.

Chabrier said, 'Fontainebleau, eh? I might postpone my trip to Spain.'

3

Camille when offering sympathy be it for a bad notice or the death of a loved one, believed that the gratification of the senses overcame the deprivation of the spirit. Loaded with packages garishly wrapped, he knocked on Augusta's door, pushed Julie aside and burst into the studio scattering his gifts like rose petals. 'Open them, open them,' he ordered, standing over Augusta who, warmly wrapped in a red flannel dressing gown, sat by the window. She looked scrubbed and vulnerable. She was drowsy and gave a false impression of being almost unnaturally relaxed, for she still heard, albeit distantly, the tumult of Saint-Marcel-le-Pauvre and saw an image of Dalkeith's shrivelled face but somehow overlaid, like a shoddy print, on César's likeness with a halo of stars.

Camille who had been smiling expectantly observed her dull state, sniffed the air suspiciously and said, 'Oh, Augusta, you've been doping,' with regret.

Julie said, 'She needed calm, Monsieur Camille. Only a little laudanum.'

'A little? She's taken enough for a whole opium den, if you ask me. I forbid her to have another drop, is that understood? Open a window—'

'It's cold, Monsieur Camille—'

'Open the window.' He took from his overcoat pocket a bottle of Krug. 'Now, be a good girl and cool the champagne.'

Alone with Augusta he gazed sternly at her. 'You're not to dope anymore. That's an order.' He began to tear the fancy paper from the packages he had brought. 'If you won't open them, I will,' he said, uncovering chocolates, scent, a new novel by Zola, tickets for an opera – his – a packet of Lapsang Souchong tea, sugar-coated almonds and a signed copy of his *Romance in D major* for 'cello and pianoforte. He deposited all the gifts beside Augusta, then

219

sat gracefully on a cushion, and leaned over to kiss her lightly on the forehead. He said, 'Now tell me all the gory details.' She wanted to smile, but tears came instead. Camille frowned. 'You *have* taken it badly,' he said without attempting to conceal his surprise.

'I know,' she said, shuddering to control her crying, 'much worse than I ever thought possible.'

'Why?'

She shrugged. She found it hard not to think of Dalkeith without seeing César. No two men could be less alike, yet she saw them as one.

'I remember,' Camille said, 'oh, a long time ago, before the war, I remember you telling me how much you hated him.'

'Yes, yes,' she said, but shaking her head, wishing it wasn't true. 'I said it a thousand times, and believed it what's more. But, oh, Camille, it was so awful to be there when it happened, to be in the room – when he – when he–' Her tears got the better over her.

'Do you mind if I smoke?' he asked and pulled out his silver case in which he kept English cigarettes, a habit he had acquired in London after fleeing to England at the outbreak of the war. He tapped his cigarette thoughtfully as Julie entered with the champagne stuck in a zinc bucket, placed it beside him and then left them together. 'People like you and me,' Camille said, putting the cigarette in his mouth to muffle his next words – artists, musicians–' – people like us oughtn't to have parents. We should be free to do what we like, when we like.

Augusta, using the corner of her sleeve to wipe her eyes, said, 'I had such a strange sensation. I wanted him to reassure me. On his deathbed, I wanted his reassurance.'

'How d'you mean? reassure you about what?'

'Just reassurance,' she said, her voice tremulous.

'Don't cry. It won't do any good, unless you're prepared to scream and shout and tear your hair in grief like they do in Arabia.'

'I'm afraid I've already done that,' she said with her little-girl smile.

'Oh?'

'I don't remember much. Julie says I attacked Father Franck. Evidently he was just sitting with me and suddenly I woke and went for him.'

Camille guffawed. 'I saw him not an hour ago. He did look a bit battered. Tell me, tell me, tell me all. Attacked Father Franck! How rich!'

She began to weep again. 'I hope he understands. I meant nothing against him.'

'Didn't you?' Camille asked not without malice. 'We do odd things, you know. Nothing is an accident. I wonder if it wasn't your way of deliberately getting at him.'

'But why should I? He's harmless.'

'That's not what you told Romain and me in the Café Tortoni.'

She made no answer, but felt again the burden of César's presence, as though her conscience pricked her for a sin she had not committed. César bore down on her; she could not breathe.

Camille said, 'You admitted something intriguing a moment ago –'

'What?'

'Explain to me, why did you want your father to reassure you?'

She buried her face in the pillow as if she wanted to hide, mumbling something which he asked her to repeat. 'I can't explain,' she said dully, 'I don't know what I wanted, but watching him die so unspectacularly, he just took one last breath and that was all – just in that moment I felt something so powerful, Camille, I just wanted him. I just wanted my father with all that implies. My *father*. I just wanted him to hold me and say it's all right, it's all right.'

Camille blew a thin stream of smoke at the ceiling and said in a calm, detached voice, 'It's *never* all right, haven't you learned that yet?' but quickly realised he was in danger of taking himself too seriously, so changed course. 'And no amount of opium will make it all right.' To show off, to amuse her, he quoted de Quincey: ' "Thou hast the keys of Paradise, oh just, subtle, and mighty opium!" Utter rubbish!' he said. 'Don't believe it, Augusta.' He had the best prescription for overcoming unhappiness or the threat of unhappiness, and brusquely offered it to her: 'You mustn't lie here and mope. You have a life to lead. You have work to do. You have a *career*.'

His advice filled her unaccountably with even greater despair and produced a sort of mental and physical weariness, as though she had been labouring days and nights on end without sleep and, stopping suddenly, surrendered to insensibility. In an exhausted voice she said, 'It's all so wretched. Everything seems to have gone wrong. The very moment Daddo died, it was as though all my misery weighed on me—'

'Misery? You make too much of it—'

'No, listen. I've made every mistake it's possible to make. A leopard can't change its spots, Camille. I should never have tried.'

'You've lost me—'

'I don't think I can go on being his pupil. I feel as though I'm without any identity at all. And the moment I walked into the asylum where Daddo was, I was so frightened, because it seemed so right for me to be there, as if I hadn't got a mind of my own any more, as though my talent had left me. You can't be what you're not. And I want my music to be triumphant and joyous, not *pure*, I don't care about purity. I've never felt so defeated in all my life.' She was crying again and Camille poured champagne into her glass. 'Perhaps you're right,' she said. 'Perhaps I did mean to lash out at him.'

He said, 'If you feel like that, you had better tell the old boy immediately you no longer want him to teach you and stop wasting his time and your money.'

'That's another thing. I don't know if I have the strength to make the break.'

'Write a letter.'

'Yes, I suppose I could do that. I've no energy, I've nothing.' There was a void of which she was aware, but of which she could not speak, a terrible emptiness, without expectation and without possibility. She thought of the feeling as grief for a dead father. Yet, vaguely she reflected she had known this vacancy before, could not remember when, for some reason, in retrospect, understood that good would come of it. Or was that a forlorn childish hope?

Camille said, 'If you mean what you say, that you want to make a new beginning, then you ought to make a public show of it.

222

Let everyone know you're entering the world again. Being a nun doesn't suit you, Augusta.' He sipped his champagne, eyeing her over the rim of the glass; he was up to mischief and it amused him. 'I'll give a party for you. We'll invite everyone who is anyone.' His ugliness was more acute when he was plotting, like a misshapen imp. 'You leave it to me. I know how the world works. Yes, I'll give a party for you on Friday week in the forest of Fontainebleau.'

Augusta lay back and stared at the skylight. Camille smiled.

4

Why doesn't he move, Félicité wondered, why doesn't he speak? Even to cry out, I am not dead! would be a welcome sign of life. But nothing. He barely ate. All her hopes plummeted to earth, dead on impact, a bird shot in error.

'You must eat something, Franck.'

He sat and stared. She turned away, picked up a fan, cooled herself vigorously as though twinges of self-reproach – should she have him see a doctor? a priest? – needed blowing away. 'When will you be finished with *The Beatitudes*?'

—

'I listened this morning to you. The same theme endlessly repeated. I do not approve of this cyclical, circular nonsense,' in music or in life, an endless repetition without variation. Are you going mad, Franck? Is it your madness to be imprisoned eternally in the same sound?

—

'For thirty-one years we've been married, Franck. I expect to ask questions that are never answered, to raise interesting topics which are ignored,' but this rigid immobility is utterly terrifying. I do not believe you are working any longer. Your gifts have atrophied. I see the future bleak.

—

'I miss Georges. I wish he still came. He writes so rarely. Poor Georges,' married to a pale English girl with a pale English mind who spoke no French and who cooked beef grey. Poor Georges. 'I am going to get the dictionary.'

She rose, went into her boudoir to fetch from the glass-fronted bookcase *The Dictionary of Greek Mythology*, but when she returned to the dining room, César had gone. 'Franck? Franck?' she called, opening the door to the hall. 'Franck?' He had gone leaving behind his silence.

Aimlessly, she wandered back to her boudoir carrying the dictionary like a tray. She lay on the chaise-longue by the window, gazed out at the leafy poplars, bathed in warm sun. The courtyard beyond was empty. She was empty. She had lost everything, she thought, even her dreams. Now, when in her mind's eye she entered her box at the Opéra she waved regally and looked towards the stage, but the stage, too, was empty.

She opened the book: Thyia, the first woman to sacrifice to Dionysus – no; Thiades, Thyone, Thyrsus, Tisphone, Titanesses, Titanomachia, Titans – no; Tithonus. Tithonus?

Tithonus: son of Laomedan and Strymo, was half-brother to Priam. By the prayers of his lover Eos was granted by Zeus immortality, but as Eos had omitted to ask for perpetual youth, he shrank away until he became a cicada. (The English poet, Alfred Tennyson has written a poem *Tithonus*. Ed.)

Félicité looked up cicada, learned it was an insect that made a shrill, sharp sound. A shrill, sharp sound. A chorus of cicadas. A plea for immortality. An aria of reproach: stupid, stupid, Eos, why did you not ask for eternal youth?

The fan dropped from her hand; her head lolled; she snored. She dreamed. A creature, half beast, half woman, costumed by Fragonard, danced in a sylvan glade, ageing visibly, until she could dance no more and Félicité, naked, equally old, laughed and swam out to sea. And then she was in a theatre, but not the Opéra, and César was Tithonus, a tiny, cardboard cut-out jiggling on invisible strings. The applause was deafening, the cheers tumultuous. 'Bow!' she cried from the darkened box, 'Take your bow!' And a voice, César's when young, answered, 'I have shrivelled and shrunk,' repeated it several times, faster and faster, until there was nothing to be heard but a sound shrill and sharp.

She woke. The dream images remained with her. Had Georges been there she would have told him a frisson had run down her back. It was a good omen, she was sure, to dream of Tithonus, just what was needed to shake César from his apathy. Hurriedly she rose, scribbled out the bare bones of the legend, not forgetting the chorus of cicadas and the plea for immortality, folded the scrap of paper and was taking it into César's studio when in the hall she paused, seeing on the corner table an envelope addressed to her in her husband's hand. Inside was a note which startled her:

I will not be home for luncheon and may be late for dinner. I have had to go to Fontainebleau on urgent business.

CF

5

The afternoon sun pierced the shade of the wild pines and the beech trees, cast tessellated leaf-patterns of fine lace on the broom and heather, and caught the pink and golden tips of the long fingers of grass. A girl's laughter, loving and content; the vibrato of insects; a flute from deep in the copse lightly tempted any who would venture into the woods. So strange a day César had never known. He lay in the shade of a stripling oak, his tall top hat perched on his chest, his arms and legs spread wide, smiling lazily. He had drunk too much; everyone had drunk too much. When he opened his eyes a little, just enough to get a blurred picture of the world, he was soothed by the cavorting of a small bird in the tree-top, sharp, darting movements that enhanced his own sense of stillness. He lowered his eyes so that he could see across the sheltered clearing, and Augusta came into view, elegant and cool in a long summery white gown edged in black – out of respect for her father, he supposed; a parasol, black edged in white, lay beside her. She leaned against a tree-trunk looking up into the canopy of leaves; she seemed sad; she put out her glass to be filled. At her feet, leaning on one hand, pouring the wine with the other, sat Catulle Mendès, the poet César remembered from long ago passionately threatening Vincent and Camille, the man he had seen accost Zenta outside Hartmann's. His beard was fuller now and he wore a tassled hat that gave him a respectable, middle-aged look. He talked continuously to Augusta: César could hear the rise and fall of his voice, never the words and occasionally he laughed at one of his own jokes. But Augusta did not laugh, nor did she reply or interject, just gazed towards the unblemished summer sky, only where she looked there was no sun.

So strange a day: the distant flute caressed César's thought. In the forest the girl no longer laughed. Nearby, to his left, someone indolently strummed a guitar. Like a dream. The day had all been like a dream: so many people, few of whom he knew, the little chorines from the Opéra-Comique, a dozen other girls with foul mouths and accents from the rue de Poissonnière, men in straw boaters, all assembling before the portico of the Opéra and setting off in the carriages and cabs, like a snaking Arabian caravan to Samarkand.

Uninvited, César had simply joined them. He had learned of the arrangements from Chabrier. No one questioned his presence. He smiled now at the thought of his impudence. Where did such courage come from? Love is the mother of necessity. A butterfly settled on the crown of his hat. What would Félicité say if she could see him now? What would she say if she could see the women? Especially the one with purple hair who had said to César she liked old men, and another, young and unwashed, in reply to something a cabby had whispered in her ear, had screeched, 'What? And smell of horse shit all day?' Félicité would not have approved. The thoughts glided sleepily through his mind. He was at peace. He no longer worried about the silence in his head; he no longer felt the compulsion to write music for the sake of writing music. Augusta was all he cared about, and he was in her presence, all was well with the world. They had not exchanged a single word, but she was there, he knew what she was doing, saw her when he wished – what more could he ask? And he was certain that this day would be a fateful day: the opportunity would come, he knew it, and he would declare his love for her, and they would lie together in a sylvan glade. Through the summer haze he gazed at her: had she ever looked more beautiful? She was loveliest in white, loveliest when forlorn.

A round heavy shape cast a shadow: Chabrier, flushed, untidy, grinning, leaned over to refill César's glass. 'No, no,' César murmured half-heartedly.

'It'll do you good,' the fat man said, adding inanely, 'What and smell of horse shit all day?' All the way in the carriage, from Paris to Fontainebleau Chabrier had laughed at the remark, speculating on what the cabby could possibly have said to prompt it. 'What and smell of horse shit all day?' over and over again, laughing each time he uttered the words. Chabrier tottered on. César sipped his wine. Augusta was there staring at her sunless sky.

Should he take his jacket off as the others had done? No, the sweat felt good. Besides, he didn't have the energy. So strange a day. And such a collection of people, smart people whose names César did not know – could they be famous if he hadn't heard of them? – dressmakers and decorators mostly, furniture dealers and jewellers and those awful, stupid actors from the Comédie. Félicité would enjoy them. I, always I, I, I. Ghastly as the mother, brilliant as the father, did you see me as Phèdre, and the laughs I got, and such exquisite timing. Why did they always talk about timing? I, I, I, I. And that grubby little painter, whose fingers and hair were stained like a palette, talking of light and depth, and of giving a *feeling* of people and objects. So boring. The flute was nearer now: too many breaths, César thought, but perfectly acceptable. The girl laughed again. Augusta sipped her wine, Mendès droned. Chabrier, somewhere, said, 'What and smell of horse shit all day?' and giggled like a woman. For a moment, César watched the top hat on his chest rising and falling. The butterfly danced by. Then Camille's voice, booming, 'Come on, Augusta! This is my party.' Augusta did not move, but Mendès fell silent. So strange a day.

And strangest of all had been the behaviour of Camille. César, being the first to arrive at the Opéra, had seen everyone else arriving – the foul-mouthed girls, the men and women flaunting their own celebrity. The morning was heavy with heat and low cloud but, as if by magic, the sun broke through the moment Augusta appeared. César had tried to keep out of sight, but she had seen him and she had blushed – why, why, he wondered had she blushed? Could it be that she didn't want to see him? that she despised him? He buried the unanswerable questions. But why blush? She had turned away, sharply, turned to the black maid, Julie – overdressed, César considered, for a maid, dazzling in yellow

– and said something that caused the maid to look at César too, and to bite her lip, plainly troubled. Oh, why, why did Augusta blush? Could he dare hope – no, best not to hope. Catulle Mendès had turned up next, a dashing entrance, raising both arms like some operatic hero and crying 'Augusta!' at full voice. At the sight of him, Augusta's eyes grew round with surprise and fury; it delighted César to see her turn away from this man and enter one of the waiting cabs. When Camille's carriage drew up in the forecourt, the celebrities were transformed into sycophants and like courtiers at a palace gate buzzed and bustled with self-importance hoping to catch the rays of reflected glory. Camille, wearing a straw boater, an English blazer and beaming hideously, was half out of his carriage, a large, beribboned box in his hands, when he saw Catulle. He froze. His smile vanished. His displeasure was apparent to the waiting court who, in sympathy, fell silent then seethed with questions. Camille's eyes narrowed to oriental slits. 'Romain,' he called imperiously. As though stepping to a languid oboe obligato, Romain sauntered over to Camille. Words were exchanged. Romain laughed, or sneered – César couldn't quite be certain which. Camille angrily retreated into his carriage thrusting the beribboned clothes box into Romain's hands. Romain, sauntering still, never quickening his pace, pushed through the guests like a *chef de protocol* and passed the box through the cab window to Augusta. It was then César noticed the name ZENTA printed in large type on the box. Animated discussion erupted: was the outing still to take place? Did Camille not want to go? What did he intend? Camille's booming voice gave answer: 'Fontainebleau,' he said to his driver. At that everyone made a rush for their vehicles and César more or less fell in with Chabrier. So strange a day.

He looked again at Augusta – and she was looking at him. He smiled a foolish smile. She glanced away. 'Come on, Augusta, it's *my* party!' Camille boomed. César could no longer resist the heat, the wine, the drowsiness. His eyes grew heavy. The girl in the forest laughed. The flute played B instead of B flat. The bird fluttered above. Chabrier whinnied. Was it Romain who said, 'Come on Augusta, Father Franck won't mind,' before César surrendered to dreamless sleep?

A chord on the guitar, excited shouts, clapping woke him. His head ached, a severe pain that distorted light and made him retch. Gingerly, César took stock of his surroundings, made certain of the ground beneath his body, opened his eyes but because of the sun prismatic in the leaves shut them again immediately. He thought of Augusta, and, by cocking his head, put the world in danger of spinning senselessly. Augusta was no longer there. César became alarmed, struggling to sit. All that remained of her was the black parasol edged in white; Mendès was gone, too, the tassled hat left in evidence. César, using the trunk of the oak to stand, looked out across the shaded clearing to see where the others had been: there was no one, he was alone, the place was deserted: nothing but hats and bonnets, canes and parasols, picnic baskets and rugs, jackets and shawls, Zenta's beribboned box open and empty, scattered débris, a sort of devastation, as though an army had marched through while he slept destroying all life before it. Alarmed, César leaned against the tree and held his head for fear it would roll from his shoulders. Had they gone and left him? What time was it? He fumbled for his watch: a little after four. Another chord on the guitar, another shout, cheers. César stumbled towards the copse from which the sounds seemed to come, passing from afternoon sun into cool shadow. Now he heard the guitarist playing a passionate Spanish rhythm, a fandango perhaps, and, a yard or so in front of him, he saw the backs of some of the men who were clapping in rhythm. To his right he spotted a gently rising knoll and, using the branches of trees, pulled himself up the incline until he could see over the heads of the men.

He saw first a flash of yellow and, narrowing his eyes to peer through the uncertain light, he saw Julie swirling her skirt and stamping arrogantly, arms extended above her head, wrists proudly angled. He watched with interest for more than a minute before he realised she wore no bodice, was bare from the waist up. These black women, he thought, have no shame. But after his eyes grew more accustomed to the scene, he noticed that all the girls, freely interspersed among the male audience who stood in a generous circle round the dancers, were also naked. César held his breath. He had never seen so many bare bosoms all at one time in his life. He searched the spectators for Augusta, but he could not see her anywhere; Mendès was visible and that reassured him. But where was Camille?

A shout of approval signalled the end of Julie's dance, but only momentarily. Flapping her hands she beckoned to the others to join her and a weaving chain of girls developed, the guitarist accompanying with a stately gavotte. To much laughter Chabrier joined in. He had taken off his jacket and shirt, and wore only a grubby woollen vest with sleeves to the elbow. He looked ridiculous, with his braces slipping off his shoulders. What fools men make of themselves, César thought.

Suddenly, from out of a clump of bushes behind the circle of onlookers, Camille appeared and waved a warning to the guitarist who broke off what he was playing and struck three dramatic chords. At once the girls rejoined the men, though some, to César's surprise, stood with their arms round each other. One girl playfully kissed her companion's breasts. Meanwhile, Camille cleared a path, officiously pushing people aside, and then, out of nowhere it seemed, Augusta appeared. She was fully clothed. There was a groan of disappointment. She stood in the centre of the circle, hands on hips, slowly regarding her audience – defiantly, César thought, perhaps even with a certain coldness of which he had never before known her capable. Without any warning she lifted her long skirt only to reveal tight-fitting male trousers, Zenta's trousers. There was much laughter at this.

Augusta said, 'I want a drink!' and Chabrier, clumsily pouring champagne, staggered towards her, presented the glass, made a courtly bow and resumed his place in the circle. Augusta drank, but kept her eyes on the audience. She swayed a little: unintentionally, César decided. She tossed the glass backwards over her shoulder scattering some of the girls.

'Silly bitch,' one of the chorines cried. 'You could've cut us to pieces.'

Julie slapped the girl. There were tears. Distracted by the incident César had looked away from Augusta, but when he returned his gaze to her, she was undoing the buttons of her bodice. With each button a shout went up, and when finally she allowed the dress to slip from her shoulders to the ground, the cheers shook the leaves. Hands on hips, in Zenta's trousers, she slowly stepped out of the dress and turned to show her breasts, so that all in the circle could admire the wondrous sight. Now Camille approached carrying a jacket that looked like a Spanish bolero, and Zenta's familiar floppy hat. The guitar player discovered a new, more frantic rhythm. To whistles and cries of approval, Camille helped Augusta on with the jacket, buttoning it up for her. It was a tight fit and Camille made much of his moment. César was intensely jealous.

At last, Camille presented Augusta with the hat. She placed it on her head at a rakish angle, bowed to the sustained applause and then in a rather thick voice said, 'One minute. One full minute. Beginning ... *now!*'

No sooner had she uttered the word than she ran off into the forest. What followed astonished César. All the other girls ran after her, laughing and giggling at the tops of their voices while the men, in unison, began to count, but long before the minute was up Camille had set off in pursuit, closely shadowed by Mendès and in no time at all César was alone in the glade.

Out of the forest, among other voices, he heard Augusta's, ringing clear, 'Come and find me,' she called, and more distant, with laughter, 'Over here, over here.' Birds fluttered overhead; butterflies danced. And César, setting off in search of her, determined to be the one who found her: the opportunity for which he had been waiting, he knew was at hand.

'Come and find me,' she called.

The forest was filled with laughter.

'Auguthta!'

'Augusta!'

Augusta!

Deeper into the woods he tramped, the path scattered with abandoned clothing, the trees ringing with shouts of triumph, screams of enjoyment, and the perpetual laughter of the hunters and the hunted. Twice he came upon loving couples: the woman with purple hair in the arms of a young boy who wept – 'Never mind, never mind, dearie,' César heard her say – and Julie the maid, entwined to look like some barbaric monster with the girl she had slapped.

'Auguthta!'

'Augusta!'
Augusta!
Urgency entered César's pursuit. Pushing through overhanging branches, tripping in the undergrowth, falling, half-falling, he stumbled blind in the forest. But then, from what direction he could not tell, he heard Augusta singing, the words as clear as though she stood beside him, a mysterious, ethereal melody:

> 'Oh, come, the dusk no more shall stir,
> Come now or I will miss you in the fading light,
> Be brave, trust my embrace,
> Enter, be welcome, behold the sight
> Of you and me, of you and her.'

She was near all right, but not near enough, for she was moving, apparently encircling him, an ever decreasing noose.
'Auguthta!'
'Augusta!'
Augusta!

> 'I am the flower of the field,
> The bearer of love, of knowledge and of trust,
> The cold shall be warm, the dry wet,
> The soft shall harden, and from the dust
> We shall be made and never yield again.'

So long as he heard the voices of Camille and Mendès calling her, César still had hope. So long as he heard her voice he knew she was free and his for the finding.
'Auguthta!'
'Augusta!'
Augusta, Augusta, Augusta –

> 'Oh, come, I am the prophet and the priest,
> Come now, or I will miss you in the fading light,
> I will kill and I will make to live,
> Enter, be welcome, behold the sight
> Of you and me at peace, of you and her.'

He did not hear her again. He did not hear Camille or Mendès. Beset by panic, by desperation, he began to run. A branch whipped his cheek; a pair of birds exploded from a nearby bush and soared above the trees. A terrible, ominous silence descended over the forest. He was sweating but shivering, too, struggling up rising ground when he saw Zenta's hat caught on a branch. He stopped panting hard, strained to listen. She was near, he knew she was near.

The fierce roar of a man's voice immediately below him caused César to reach out for support. Augusta screamed. César stumbled forward, hearing a violent snapping of twigs and branches, heard Camille cry out for help, then cry out in pain. Mendès shouted, 'Rotten bitch!' and again Augusta screamed. One step more and César found himself looking down on a deep hollow surrounded by the gnarled roots of ancient trees laid bare, where the heather was dense and where a secret stream meandered. There was little sunlight, but enough for César to see Camille on the ground crying in anguish, blood pouring from his nose with Mendés standing astride him, growling furiously, fists clenched. Augusta howled, short and savage, terrified bleats but stopped abruptly, now too frightened to scream, as Mendès turned his fury on her. 'You bitch,' he said, 'you rotten cock-teasing bitch, I'll kill you! *Who is it you mean?*'

Augusta desperately looked all round for a way to run from him and in doing so, saw César standing above. He was aware of her terror; instinctively, he could not do otherwise, he put out his arms to her, a gesture of succour. Up the rough incline she scrambled with Mendès in pursuit, but she reached César in time, embraced him with all her strength, and he her. Seeing César, Mendès stopped. Camille sobbed. César held Augusta, her warm cheek in his neck, her body against his. It passed through his mind fleetingly that this was the closest he had ever been to another human being, and would ever be. Frozen, a tableau of suspended passion, the quartet remained.

'Thank you, thank you,' Augusta murmured.

Camille whimpered. Mendès fumed.

And then César saw over Augusta's shoulder near the meandering stream printed letters a foot high scrawled in the soft sand. He could see the word, LOVES, could not take his eyes away, was oblivious to movement and cries of concern about the place, was unaware of Romain helping Camille to his feet, of Julie gently disentangling Augusta from his embrace, of Chabrier trying to calm Mendès who stalked off into the forest.

Alone, César continued to stare at the word LOVES. So strange a day, like a dream. Slowly, never looking away from the word, he slithered down into the hollow, found himself on all fours and crawled towards the stream, to see in the sand the message AUGUSTA LOVES C. He put his face close to the ground, one hand outstretched tracing each letter like a blind man reading Braille. He cried out or stifled a cry. 'Augusta loves C,' he murmured aloud, and, closing his eyes, he could feel again the warmth of her body against his.

6

In the carriage returning to Paris, Augusta hid her face in her hands. She did not want to see anyone; she did not want to be seen. Night had fallen; even in looking out of the carriage window there was the danger of seeing her own reflection, of confronting herself. She doubted if she would ever know inner peace again. She was filled with self-hatred. She was bitterly ashamed.

Beside her sat Julie. Opposite Romain, hands clasped behind his head resting against the padded upholstery. Not for the first time he said with a supercilious laugh, 'Well, well, well, I just can't get over it. Pater seraphicus to the rescue! Well, well, well.'

Augusta moved her hands to cover her ears, but could not shut out self-reproach. Why, she wondered, had she allowed herself to be persuaded by Camille to go to Fontainebleau? What self-destructive wilfulness caused her to bring down this sense of shame? She was not, she insisted to herself, a whore like the vulgar girls Camille had paid to do what they were told. Why had she given in to what was tawdry in her, to that strident, grasping creature who did not know bad from good, right from wrong, who persisted and pushed and drove as though hell-bent on an early death? Why could not the superior being in her take command? Grief, she decided, played vile and unpredictable tricks.

Julie said, 'Oh, it was lovely, Monsieur Romain, just like the old days.'

'Camille's right. No one ever changes.'

'*He* don't, that's sure.'

'And Catulle Mendès? He is just the same. Violent, jealous, mad. Is it true, Augusta, that before the war, they also fought over you?'

Julie said, 'Oh yes, that's true.'

Augusta asked, 'Who invited Catulle?'

'I did, of course,' Romain answered gaily. 'But, tell me, who invited Pater seraphicus?'

Neither woman knew the answer. When Augusta first realised César had joined the party, she was suddenly made to feel guilty as though he were a reminder of her excellence, a conscience figure whose image hovered before her, the icon she had wanted to destroy. She would write an apology to him in the morning. She would beg his forgiveness. For the hundredth thousandth time she resolved to change her ways, but raising her head, she looked out at the darkness, saw instead her own reflection, irresolute and untrustworthy.

Morning shattered her good intentions. Shortly before noon, she and Julie were awakened by a knocking on the door. Head aching, nauseous, Augusta rose to admit Vincent d'Indy, righteous with anger. Neglecting to greet her, he said, 'I do not intend to stay long. I have only come to tell you that because of your outrageous and obscene behaviour, Father Franck came close to death last night.'

'What happened?' she asked dully.

'On his way home from Fontainebleau the cab in which he was travelling, together with Emmanuel Chabrier and an unnamed woman, met with an accident. The driver was doubtless drunk. Pater seraphicus, it appears, was not badly hurt, but when going to find help was set upon by thieves and savagely beaten up. He is running a high fever. The doctor says he has concussion. He could have been killed.'

Augusta sank down on to a low cushion, hugged her ankles, rested her forehead on her knees, wept silently.

Vincent said, 'I have discussed the matter with my fellow students and I cannot conceal from you our outrage. You are not worthy to be his student. Since Pater seraphicus is in no condition to make a decision, we have agreed to make the decision for him.

You are dismissed from our fellowship. You cannot continue to be his pupil. You have brought disgrace on us all. And because of you Pater seraphicus has come close to losing his life.'

7

César lay in delirious excitement. Was it a dream or reality? He did not know, did not care. Whether the experience was of the inner or outer world was not important: all that mattered was his ecstasy, his joy unconfined. While Félicité, the maids, the doctor, son Georges, fussed over him, César, doing nothing to alleviate their concern, wore his seraphic smile, was mostly silent, dozed on and off, moaned a little from time to time, and relived over and over again the events which began in the forest of Fontainebleau where Augusta Holmès had written in the sand that she loved him. The fever had begun then.

Not since Claire. Augusta loves C. She holding him, her face in his neck. And that was only the beginning, not all, by no means all. There was a terrible, oppressive need to compose, a compulsion he had never before experienced: the silence in his head remained but insanely he longed to record it. To record the silence. And that had happened to him after the accident, after he had been robbed and beaten by thieves, or because of it, he could not be certain which.

The cabbie lost control descending a steep hill in fading light. 'God save us, save us,' he shouted like an evangelist. 'Runaway! Runaway!' The girl in Chabrier's arms did not wake; Chabrier giggled inanely. The cab lurched, the horse whinnied and then, the world turned upside down, the ground was where the sky had been and all was still. The girl cried. Chabrier was nowhere to be seen. The horse snorted. César struggled, crawled, pushed, to find himself in the road beside the overturned cab. 'Get help, Monsieur Franck,' the driver said nursing a twisted leg and bleeding from a cut above his mouth. 'The fat man's out cold.'

There was a large building near, an old inn but it looked deserted. Even then, César remembered, he was filled with expectation. A part of him knew that Chabrier and the driver, perhaps the girl, too, were in need of assistance: another force in him thanked God that Augusta loved him, wanted to bask in her adoration. But the expectation, a mad excitement, arose from a certainty stronger than anything else that he could sit at his table and tap out whatever sounds the madness of the day might have produced. But there were no sounds, only a buzzing in his ears, and the horse snorting.

He stumbled forward, finding an archway through which he passed and came into a small courtyard open to the sky. It was dark and terrifying. He called, 'Hello! Hello! Anyone about?' His agitation rising, he stumbled forward and was alerted by movement in the shadows. A light flared.

'Hello!' César said, 'who's there?'

In the darkness, shapes, bundles moved. César went towards the light, the naked flame of a guttering candle, and saw a half-dozen human forms huddled together, peering at him. The stench of alcohol was strong, and he could dimly see the derelict faces.

At that moment, outside the building, from the road, the driver called, 'Monsieur Franck! Monsieur Franck?' and César, confused, turned to go but one of the wretches suddenly and fiercely grabbed hold of his ankle in a grip of steel. 'César-Auguste?' he said, 'I thought I recognised you.'

César looked down into a face half-eaten away by disease and drink, an open sore on the man's forehead suppurating. 'Let go of me!' César cried.

'Yes, yes, it's you all right,' the man said without loosening his grip, but crawling forward away from his fellows with César trying to pull free.

'Monsieur Franck!' the driver called again, 'Monsieur Franck, where are you?'

'Let go of me,' César pleaded, and then shouting, 'I'm here, in the courtyard, I need help!'

'You don't remember me,' the man said as though the disappointment brought him near to tears.

César, struggling to get his leg free, said, 'I've never seen you before, go away!' and shouting again, 'Here, here, in the courtyard!'

'Never seen me before? Do you hear that?' the man said with a look towards his fellows: one of them, a woman, laughed. 'We were friends, César-Auguste, you and me, we were friends and you don't remember.'

'I've never laid eyes on you. Now, let go of me, I beg you.'

'Liar!' the man hissed. 'You know me all right.'

César cried, 'Help! Help! I'm in the courtyard!'

Suddenly, the man scrambled to his feet and took hold of César by the wrists. The smell was appalling, and César shied away; he could hardly breathe with disgust and fear. 'Franck, Franck, César-Auguste Franck playing the piano all day and night. And you don't remember your old friend Josquin?'

César cried out, a strangled, choking sound, 'Josquin,' he repeated.

'Ah yes, you remember to be sure –'

'Monsieur Franck! Monsieur Franck!'

'Give me some money, César-Auguste, I've fallen on bad times, please César-Auguste, give me some money.'

'Monsieur Franck! Monsieur Franck!'

'Only ten sous, that's all, César-Auguste. And I don't want charity, I'll give service in return. I know where there are women, César-Auguste, you were always one for the women –'

'No! Not me, not me –'

'Monsieur Franck!'

'Yes, *you*, don't come that, César-Auguste, you in the cave, you were no different from me, don't come the high and mighty with me, begged for it, you did –'

'No –'

'Oh yes you did!' Tighter his grip. 'You were always a stuck-up little bastard, thought you were a cut above me with your piano-playing all day and all night, but given the chance you were just the same. *Why didn't you invite me into your house?* Come on, César-Auguste, we've so much to talk about, so much to remember, old pals like us, come on, give poor old Josquin a sou for services rendered, César-Auguste, give me a bed to lie on –'

'Let go of me –'

Josquin punched him, fist raised like a hammer, hard on the side of his head. He remembered no more. When he came to himself, he was in his own bed in the boulevard Saint-Michel; his head was bandaged. Georges was saying he'd been robbed and beaten.

238

César slowly recalled the words written in sand; the runaway horse; Josquin. Augusta loves C. C loves C. C loves Augusta.

He asked about Chabrier and was told he had recovered; casually, he enquired after Augusta. Vincent said she had brought shame on them all and they had asked her not to attend classes again. And although his own response puzzled him, César was not unnecessarily alarmed. He thought: when I am well I will put all to rights. To Félicité's incessant questions about Fontainebleau, he remained silent.

'Tomorrow you may get up for a little,' the doctor said.

Five o'clock and the early dawn light, hopeful and auspicious, slid beneath the curtains, spilled liquid on the carpet. Thank you O Lord for giving me life this day. He was fifty-seven years old, he thought, he must hurry. He threw off the bedclothes, reached out to light the candle, floundered for slippers and gown and in the act of rising, the swinging movements of his legs, feeling the floor beneath his feet, sitting upright, the sound came then: a violin descending, a sound that rose from deep within him, stirring his senses, triumphant, sensuous, so unlike any sound he had ever heard or imagined, as if seeing for the first time the pale autumn sun beneath his bedroom curtains; and no recession, no diminuendo, but a gathering storm of music, pure, perfect, his to record.

Nothing intruded: he was oblivious to the unreality of creaking floorboards, the taste of coffee, water on his face, a clock chiming, discordant bells; he sat at his table, concentrated on the lined paper before him, heard what was in his head, knew it was already composed, complete and perfect, and that his task was to write it down. He dipped pen in ink and began. *Quintette, Fa mineur, C. Franck, I, Molto moderato quasi lento – Allegro. Violon I, Violon II, Alto, Violoncelle, Piano*; wrote in the four flats for the key signature, four-four time, the instruction *ff dramatico* and gave the first violin the theme which burst the confines of his being.

For two hours he worked that day and succeeding days, thought of nothing else except the perfecting of what he recorded. Nothing else. Rarely did he work in heat. Creation was a cold process, requiring objectivity, ruthless decisions, cruel self-discipline. His mind, heart and understanding were constantly and powerfully involved, his to rely on, creatures to do his bidding. The absolute standards of good and bad with which he had informed himself, he obeyed; the mystical consensus of those human beings who are similarly informed created in him a wish for the work to be admitted to their pantheon. The labour was slow, careful, prone to error, subject to revision, but in the end what he wanted to say, what he had always wanted to say, he said.

He risked all: the music was no longer a shield to hide behind, not an avoidance of life, of conflict, of love sensual or spiritual. No. He took his life in his hands and placed it in hazard. He had no other language, his music was both his means of perception and what he perceived. To set down these sounds which expressed such violent, savage and glorious forces in him was both a declaration and the physical act of love, a total sacrifice as great as any hero might make, pleasurable as any sexual experience, painful, joyous, ecstatic: whatever other humans do in order to commune with love or those they love, he did now, writing his music to Augusta, sacrificing himself: naked, he stood, the savage Christ. He entered the darkness and there was light. He gave of himself.

Two isolated events disturbed his energy. The first, encouraged him; the second threw him into temporary confusion.

One evening, playing through on the piano for the first time the climax of the third movement, the rising surge of harmony which he believed was an epiphany of his own immortal soul and his love everlasting, Félicité burst into his room. Enraged, she demanded, 'What is that music you are playing? I emphatically dislike it.' He made no answer; she withdrew, slamming the door and his heart sang, believing that her dislike of what she heard was proof of its power.

Some days later, he received a letter from Augusta:

11 rue Mansart
Paris
Wednesday

I have postponed writing this letter for days and weeks. Whether or not you will believe the contents is a matter for you and you alone. Trust me – I write with sincerity. I cannot apologise enough for what happened – I regret any pain and discomfort you have been caused – I would not have you hurt for the world.

At first I regretted your decision to banish me from class – but perhaps it is for the best – the fault has been in me not in you or your methods – perhaps I can learn more by the *practice* of my art and whatever mistakes I make will be mine and mine alone and you will bear no responsibility – I apologise again – I crave your understanding and your blessing.

Augusta Holmès.

To which, after deliberating for a day, he replied:

95 boulevard Saint-Michel
Thursday

Dear Mademoiselle Holmès,

I have received and thank you for your letter which I understand in every particular. I thank you for using such discreet language. I shall endeavour to do the same.

Let me say at once I made no such decision to banish you. The decision was made by others while I was indisposed. I have let it stand for reasons that I hope will become apparent. Your letter was timely. I had been meaning to write but was awaiting the conclusion to certain work I have recently undertaken, and which is now complete.

You have nothing to apologise for. If there has been fault it has been mine not yours. My methods are secret and the results not always immediately apparent. You are not at fault. Nothing you have done is in error. You will, dare I say, soon be encouraged to *practise your art*. You have my understanding and my blessing.

If you will be at the Société's concert on 17th January all, I feel sure, will be made clear to you.

I pray *your* understanding,
and remain
C
(C. Franck)

P.S. The song you sang in the forest was extremely fine in many respects. Was it your own setting? If so, I congratulate you.

C.

8

C

C (C. Franck)

Augusta loves C. She wondered, had he seen what she had traced in the soft sand?

She laughed.

Enveloped in steam, sipping iced wine, she rested her head on the enamel rim of the bath, and laughed not as she had done those years ago in Hartmann's, but inward, warm, welcome laughter.

We do odd things, Camille had said. Nothing happens by accident.

Do we contrive our own destinies? she asked.

Augusta loves C.

While Julie oiled her body, Augusta read and re-read César's letter. How would he encourage her? How would he make all clear? She would be impatient to learn.

She thought back to the forest, remembered being alone in the sheltered glade, singing, her legs tucked beneath her, leaning on one hand, idly drawing in the earth, Augusta loves C. But she could not remember what had been in her mind. Was it not an attempt to recall a vanished time, a golden past? To begin again? She was filled with warmth as though she had received by chance a blessing. His letter comforted her. The thought of César comforted her. She dared hope she had won his approval for what she was. Blessed. César and Augusta, she thought: a mountain-top, a world defied, the protector and the protected, *pater optimus*. Augusta loves C.

Idly.

PART FOUR

'In its search for dramatic expression, the *Quintet* oversteps the legitimate bounds of chamber music.'

Franz Liszt

A new and wonderful excitement infected César's thoughts: the thrill of deception. For days he agonised over the dedication. He knew he dared not openly place the *Quintet* at Augusta's feet: he would bring the world down on his head. No. The music must speak for itself. She, he was certain, would understand the depth of his feeling. It would be, must be, a secret between them. Briefly, he contemplated presenting the piece to Félicité, but that he thought of as a betrayal; besides, he might place in jeopardy all hope of Augusta comprehending his meaning if he was fool enough to dedicate the work to his wife. He wanted some neutral figure, someone uninvolved. He settled on Camille. After all, Camille had brought Augusta into his life.

Deception brought danger. What if Félicité also understood the *Quintet*, realised César was declaring his love for Augusta? She had already expressed her dislike of the work.

'It is cyclic, too, I imagine,' she said.

'Oh yes.'

'Ugly and cyclic.' She shuddered.

'The form is cyclic, my dear,' the content, well, not quite.

A devious line of thought, of which he had not thought himself capable, began to undulate in his mind. Félicité must be thrown off the scent. The danger was great; thus he had felt running from his father's house to join Josquin in the hills. As he was shaving himself, the plan presented itself. His excitation was high, like a child who had narrowly escaped discovery of a mischief.

The ice on the boulevard dramatised the precariousness of his position. The sky was stuffed with low cloud. Snow flakes were beginning to fall almost invisibly until they settled on the pavements, on the plane trees, on his tall top hat. The great metropolis would soon be white. At this moment of setting off, becoming part of the immense awakening, seized with a feverish longing for motion, he joined the great tide of people stomping through the mounting snow. Girls giggled; a thin young man slipped causing an eruption of casual laughter; the shop-keepers swept their forecourts. Here was the city. He was the conqueror.

Opposite the Luxembourg Gardens a portly man with an imperial said, 'Don't you think, monsieur, you should put your umbrella up?'

César stopped and stared, blinking feverishly. The man was vaguely familiar, but there was something odd, something not quite right. 'I beg your pardon,' César said, 'but do I know you?' In the light of recent events he had become wary of strangers.

The man said, 'Now, you don't want to read your letters out here in the snow, do you?' and beamed.

César's face crumpled into smiles. 'Good God!' he said.

'Ah, now you remember me, do you, monsieur, your old postman? I used to have a little more of a beard –'

'Of course!'

'I run a restaurant in Arles now.'

'I remember,' César said. 'You look prosperous.'

'Well, I wouldn't say prosperous, but I'm doing all right.'

'Excellent.'

'And you, monsieur? Just the same, I see –'

'Oh yes, just the same.'

'I'm here in Paris to visit my son. My wife's looking after things in Arles. And this morning – I've been here a week – I thought to myself, I wonder how the old gentleman is. So I got up especially early – mind you, in the restaurant trade you get up for market earlier than you do for the post – and here I am. I thought it'd be nice to see you.'

'How very kind.'

'And do you still get your letters out here in the street?'

'Not always.'

'Oh?'

'The postman, he's a young fellow, you see, he gets later and later.'

'Ah, these youngsters don't know what work is. Any chance of you visiting Arles?'

'Well, who can say? I've no immediate plans –'

'If ever you do, be sure to look me up. I'd like you to try my soufflé Grand Marnier. Light as the wind, they say.'

'Oh, I should like that. I'm very partial to soufflés. And you, my friend, how long are you to be in Paris?'

'Until the end of January.'

César reached into his pocket. 'They're performing a new work of mine at the Salle Pleyel. A quintet. The great Saint-Saëns is to play the piano. Perhaps you'd like to take your son –' He handed over two tickets.

'That is very decent of you, monsieur. But I better warn you that I'm not very good at music. Nor is my son.'

'Nonsense. Everyone is good at music. I'll be looking out for you. Be sure to be there.'

'I will. And, monsieur –'

'What?'

'Do put your umbrella up. You look like a snowman.'

César trudged on. There was no Chabrier on the bridge – had he gone, after all, to Spain? – and instead of making directly for the Conservatoire he hurried along the boulevard de la Madeleine, coming to No. 17, the offices of Georges Hartmann, his publisher, and presently sat in the very room where he had first encountered Hermann Zenta and where, he reflected, he had probably first fallen in love with Augusta Holmès.

As is the way with publishers, Hartmann greeted César with the news of someone else's success. 'Camille's Violin Concerto is played and played,' he said, holding up an untidy stack of letters. 'Requests for copies from all over the world. Amazing, isn't it?'

'Amazing.'

'And he's working on a dozen other things at the moment –'

'Is he, indeed –'

'Oh yes, I like a prolific composer,' Hartmann said, reaching out for his cedar-wood humidor to offer César a Calixto Lopez Alfred de Rothschild, saying, 'I wish I could tell you *Les Eolides* is doing well, but I'm not going to lie to you. We're pulping the remaining copies. Go on,' he thrust the humidor towards César, 'have one. They're a present from Camille.'

Pulp, thought César, *Les Eolides* pulp. 'No, thank you,' he said primly, and Hartmann, who loved Havana cigars, and smoked six or seven a day, felt somehow rebuked by César's refusal and flicked shut the lid. 'I won't have one either,' he said with an uncomfortable smile which then turned genial. 'Now, what can I do for you?'

César said, 'I have a favour to ask.' He tried to appear business-like.

Hartmann thought César wanted a loan, an advance; he put a limit on 200 francs. 'Ask,' he said.

'I don't quite know how to begin,' César said losing confidence.

'If it's money,' Hartmann said gently, 'I could let you have a hundred, a hundred and fifty francs.'

'No, no, no, no, no, no,' César said, 'oh no, thank you, no. I – I have my salary from the Conservatoire, my pupils' fees, no, I manage very comfortably. Of course, I can't rely on my music –'

'No, I know –'

'I teach composition in order that I may compose my own music. I've had a very small income from my pieces. One has had to do all manner of things. And, of course, I know nothing but music. I have no other training, no other skill, no other interest really. The world doesn't rate musical composition very highly so therefore one has to find other things to do. People like Camille are very fortunate. He is so greatly gifted –' but even as he paid the compliment, César thought, yes, but where is the man in the music? the gift is all that is apparent: where is the engagement, the greater involvement? what is the look of Camille's Christ? A handsome, groomed, elegant, urbane cosmopolitan, and oh, so clever, so very, very clever – and music simply pours out of him. He is capable of such variety. And I, well, I am everything he is not, and he is everything I am not.

From how many composers, Hartmann wondered, had he heard these disguised self-assertions? Always with the implication that their labours were the important ones and those of the successful trivial and superficial. 'Still, not only the public seem to like his music, but also serious musicians,' Hartmann said, wanting to defend Camille and the monetary return from which he himself benefited.

'Ah,' César said. 'I always suspect anything that is popular: it usually means it is available without effort. One has to make an effort. I mean, both composer and listener. I do not believe, for example, that you can listen just once to J. S. Bach's Saint Matthew Passion and pretend to feel or understand it. Oh yes, we all have to make an effort.'

Hartmann smiled inwardly. He knew all the techniques the unsuccessful musician used in order to bolster confidence, and César had just demonstrated the most frequent: the sly introduction of a giant – J. S. Bach in this case – so that it left the impression they were somehow linked in musical circles. Another favourite gambit, Hartmann had noted, was the assertion – he wished he had a sou for every time he had heard it – that success, fame and money were of no interest; only the music was important. I'd be a rich man, he thought. I am a rich man, he remembered.

'You see, it's the music which matters, nothing else,' César said because he believed it to be true.

Hartmann said, 'Now what's this favour you want of me?'

'Ah yes, I'm taking up your time, forgive me. Well, now, where to begin? I've – I've written a new work.'

'Good!' He tried to sound pleased, but thought of the piles of yellowing paper that would lie for months unwanted in the store room. 'An opera? A cycle of songs? Piano duets?'

'No, I'm afraid not. A piano quintet.'

'A quintet,' Hartmann repeated, guessing that the piano part would break the fingers of amateurs in the first four bars.

'For piano, two violins, viola and 'cello.'

'Splendid,' Hartmann said, and reached out involuntarily for a cigar.

'It will be performed in the second week of January.'

'I shall be there, rely on it.'

'I hope so –'

'May I have a sight of the score?'

'I'd rather not, if you don't mind. It's being copied at the moment and I'd like you to judge it without any preconceptions.'

'Of course –' Hartmann nipped the cigar with his thumb, put the end in his mouth and moistened it. 'But I don't see that's much of a favour to ask –'

'No, there's something else. It's – it's about the dedication. I've dedicated the *Quintet* to Camille.'

'Oh very nice –' Hartmann said, lighting a match and beginning

249

to puff deeply; clouds of heavy smoke lay between them like incense.

'Yes, I feel it's proper. Where would we all be if he hadn't put his energies into the Société? I want to pay him a tribute, but –' César halted mid-sentence, watching the smoke curl purposefully towards the ceiling.

'Go on,' Hartmann said, leaning back in his chair, contentedly examining the cigar.

'Well, it's my wife,' César said at last.

'What is?'

'You see, she doesn't like the *Quintet* or, at any rate, the little she's heard of it.'

'Well, wives aren't expected to understand great music, are they?' He tried to keep any trace of irony out of his voice.

'Oh, Madame Franck understands all right. She's a capable musician. Oh yes, she understands, but she doesn't like the cyclic form.'

'No, I expect not.'

'She begged me not to continue with the work –'

'But you took no notice?'

'I had no choice. One writes what one has to write.'

'Quite so,' But why couldn't one write operettas? piano duets? songs?

'That's why I have this favour to ask,' César said, reaching into his overcoat pocket and pulling out some well folded sheets of music which he placed on the desk. 'You see, years ago, when she and I first met, I wrote this song for her, *The Angel and the Child*. It's never been published.' He held out the copy, Claire's copy, to Hartmann.

'A song?' Hartmann said, glancing quickly at the words, an angel hovering, a child asleep, hands in prayer, nice, naïve, sweet.

'The favour is this: Would you consider publishing it? I would be so grateful. She would feel, I think, a little less excluded, so to speak.'

'Excluded?'

'I meant to say,' César hurried on, 'that since she doesn't like the *Quintet*, the song from our youth may be a – a –'

'A sop?' Hartmann said lightly.

'No. A little gift, that's all. A dear memory revived. Our abiding affection for each other reaffirmed.'

Hartmann smiled a lopsided, sentimental smile, swivelled in his chair so that he could reach the key-board of the piano and picked out the melody with one finger. 'Pleasant,' he said. 'Now, you see, that's what you ought to be writing. Songs. Arias. *Tunes.* Opera's where the money is.'

'That's what Madame Franck says. Well, will you?'

'Will I what?'

'Publish the song.'

Hartmann swivelled back to César. 'Of course,' he said expansively. 'I'd be delighted and honoured. Don't expect a big advance, that's all I ask –'

'Oh, I don't want any advance at all,' César said. 'I just want it published. If it sells, well, that'd be all the more pleasurable.'

'Done,' Hartmann said too quickly.

'One other thing. Could it, do you think, be published at once? There's not much time before the concert.'

Hartmann nodded good-naturedly. 'You drive a hard bargain,' he said.

César smiled. He took back the manuscript, dipped Hartmann's pen in ink, crossed out Claire's name and wrote on the title page, 'To Madame César Franck, in pleasant memories.'

Hartmann said, 'You're sure you won't have a cigar?'

Time passed in step to a slow march. The *Quintet* lay in suspended animation until Augusta heard it; the deception was set in motion. Each minute of each hour processed behind a cortege of unbearable expectation. On Saint Nicholas Day he presented Félicité with the printed edition of *The Angel and the Child.*

'I thought you had lost all the copies,' she said, twitching with suspicion.

'No, no, no, no, no, no –'

'You told me you had.'

'I was mistaken. I found it on the shelves.'

She glanced at the copy, saw the dedication. 'A Saint Nicholas Day gift,' he said, backing out of the boudoir as though leaving the presence of royalty.

Alone, reading the music, the tune sharply recalled youthful unhappiness which had grown into the unhappiness of age. Why does he publish it now, she wondered? Why now? Movement beyond the snow-tipped poplars caught her eye: a tramp pushing a pram filled with old rags took shelter under the tiled portico of the corner house beyond. Tears trickled down Félicité's cheeks. From the music room she heard César playing on the piano the vile descending melody from his new work. No change, she thought, no change, and later, when the tears had dried, she asked again, why now?

2

On the day of the concert, César saw or heard Augusta everywhere: in the street and crossing the Pont Saint-Michel; in Sainte-Clothilde, where he prayed before setting off for the Salle Pleyel, he thought Sainte Cécile looking heavenwards bore an uncanny resemblance to the object of his love. Collecting the corrected copies of the *Quintet* from Monsieur Pils, César heard Augusta laugh in the next room. On the omnibus two women conversing with each other were both Augusta's image. He arrived for the afternoon rehearsal at the concert hall, in the rue Rochechouart expecting Augusta to materialise miraculously. The place was deserted. He was an hour early.

The Salle Pleyel was mirrored from front to rear, from top to bottom. An intimate room in which plush and gilt and the crystal chandelier were doubled and redoubled. And César, too: he sat at the back surveying the room, the rows of empty seats, the platform arranged with piano, four chairs and music stands, and his own reflection from every angle multiplied to infinity. He had the impression of standing on an eternal threshold, as though all the images of himself were awaiting a signal to become one and indivisible.

Duparc and Vincent, joint secretaries of the Société, were the first to arrive. César asked, 'When do I make the presentation?'

'The presentation?' Vincent queried.

'The dedication copy to Camille. Before or after the concert?'

'Oh, after, Pater seraphicus. Let them take two or three bows, then come down to the platform and place the copy in Camille's hands.'

'But if the audience shouldn't like the work, won't that be embarrassing for me?'

'But they will like the work, maître,' Duparc said reassuringly.

'We mustn't break tradition,' Vincent said. 'We always make the presentation at the end.'

Fot the first time since the work had been completed, César glimpsed terror. Reality was beginning to impinge: soon, the hall would be filled; soon, Augusta would be there; soon, the music would be heard. He felt suddenly like running away, hiding, going to live abroad –

Martin Marsick, whose string quartet was to play, arrived next; followed shortly by the others: Rémy, the second violinist, Van Waefelghem, viola, and Loys, the 'cellist. But no Camille. Vincent twice left the hall to stand outside on the pavement as though to make Camille appear; but he did not. Duparc smiled sheepishly seeming to imply that the fault was his. The quartet tuned and retuned, glanced at their parts. Van Waefelghem yawned noisily. Marsick said, 'So damned insulting,' and beat his bow irritably on his violin.

'He's a wonderful sight-reader,' Duparc said.

Loys asked, 'Perhaps we ought to run through without him? You could play the piano for us, couldn't you, maître?'

Reluctantly, César agreed. Jumping from string section to string section, omitting any solo piano passages, the *Quintet* was rehearsed. Afterwards Rémy said to Marsick, 'Sounds like a piece of shit to me.'

3

Vincent was obliged to ask César to stop pacing in the foyer.

'Father,' he said, 'please come and sit in the artists' room. You can be quiet there. It does not do for the composer of a new work to be so animated while the audience is coming in.'

'Thank you, Vincent, but I must remain where I am. However, I shall try to keep still.'

253

'Do, Father, please.'

'Is Camille here yet?'

'Not yet.'

He scanned the faces of each new arrival, barely heard the many wishes for success heaped upon him: he waited in anguish for Augusta, but was greeted instead by Félicité. 'What a night!' she cried. 'The snow's turned to rain.'

'I will show you to your seat, my dear,' César said.

The seating arrangements he had planned with care, or rather he had chosen the seat Augusta would occupy with care, on or near the aisle in the third row. From a special position at the back of the hall, César would be able to observe the reflection of her face throughout the concert. It followed, therefore, that Félicité must be seated as far away from Augusta as possible.

'Here we are, my dear, I think this will do very nicely.'

'How did the rehearsal go?' Félicité asked.

'Quite quickly,' César said and returning to the foyer met Romain with Camille's mother on his arm.

'Ah!' César said, 'has Camille arrived with you?'

'No,' Romain said suspiciously. 'We thought he was here rehearsing.'

'No,' César said, 'he's had no rehearsal. He didn't attend, I'm afraid.'

Maman dismissed César's implied reproach with a wave of her bony, freckled hand. 'He's the best sight-reader in the world.'

He heard Augusta's voice but could not see her.

Maman said, 'And what may we expect from you tonight? Something uplifting, I trust?'

'I hope so,' César said, looking over the old woman's head. 'Do excuse me –'

Augusta was surrounded by a bevy of admirers, the *castrati* mostly, from Tortoni's, and like a Queen Bee attended by drones she processed into the hall. She did not look César's way, but he heard her voice –

'– refusing commissions left right and centre – so much to do – never been so busy – things have taken a turn for the better –' and her laugh, rich and enjoyable. César watched her every step of the way and only when she took her seat did he realise she

254

had an escort, an old man, much older than César, with flamboyant sideburns. 'Who's that with Mademoiselle Holmès?' César asked Vincent.

'Klosé. Captain Klosé. He used to teach clarinet at the Conservatoire.'

'Ah yes. Klosé.' César was suddenly jealous of Captain Klosé, remembering his bald pate glowing in the darkened stairwell.

Two or three minutes before the concert was due to begin Duparc rushed into the foyer with the news that Camille had arrived.

Vincent asked, 'Has he apologised?'

'Oh no,' Duparc said sadly.

Vincent gave a snort of annoyance as if the apology was more important than Camille's presence.

Duparc said, 'Come on maître, we'd better be getting in.'

César took his place. He watched Augusta waving to friends, talking animatedly to Klosé, dropping her cloak to reveal her shoulders and more, much more. If she would but look a little to her right, César thought, she will see me. Please God, let her look.

Applause greeted the Marsick Quartet; thunder greeted Camille. He was accompanied on to the platform by a handsome youth who was to turn the pages for him. Camille sat at the piano, beaming at the audience; he narrowed his eyes on seeing Augusta, and César saw her smile tenderly, head a little to one side; Camille smiled, too. The quartet was tuning.

César was aware of his heart thumping, of a sick feeling in the pit of his stomach, of cramp in his foot which he had to bang on the floor for relief. Now, now, César thought, another birth: Camille raised his hands. No, no, César wanted to scream, you don't come in for five bars, what are you doing? At that moment there was a flurry at one of the entrances and César recognised his former postman with a girl half his age and dyed yellow hair scampering late to their seats. Camille from the platform watched them beadily. Odd, César reflected; he remembered the man had said something about bringing his son –

Augusta caught César's eye. He tried to nod but his neck was rigid. She did not smile at him as she had smiled at Camille; her gaze was impassive, level, serious, dare he hope, tender?

'*Ars Gallica*,' Vincent said standing at the front of the
auditorium, his back to the platform. Cheers.

Camille waited for silence to descend. A cough. The rustle of
paper. A dying laugh. Silence. He nodded to Marsick. Marsick
raised his bow nodded and played the A flat to begin the descending
theme which signalled the start of the first movement, *ff dramatico*.
And Camille, a moment later, made his entry, gentle, *espressivo*.

César wanted to vomit. He could not stand to listen. Suddenly,
as though the work were new to him, too, he heard the music
with the ears of a stranger, the postman, Klosé, heard the imper-
fections, the eccentricity, the abject failure. He could not bear it.
Quietly but speedily he slipped out of the back door, into the empty
foyer, out into the wet street. Through the slush he tramped, head
bare, dashed by the rain. Close by a church clock struck the half:
in forty minutes, he thought, it will be over; he would return then,
not a moment before, he would return to failure.

Fool, o fool! he cried, how could he have ever imagined she
would understand? How could any sense be made of such inadequacy? He should never have let the work be performed. He knew
with terrible certainty that she, they, would hear inferior music,
would never, never perceive his life, his existence expressed in
every note. Would she hear the descent, the coming down? Would
she know that he loved in her all that he could not love in himself?
What he had seen as pus and corruption he had transformed in
his music into honey and fertile fields. Every note compounded
love, gratitude, pleasure at having been allowed to know her, at
being in her company, at making himself part of her now and
forever more.

Would that be understood? No. They would fuss – he could
hear them – over the inexplicable key basis, F minor, B minor,
F sharp minor, and F major; they would, he was certain,
misunderstand his passion, his longing for her. They will not hear
in the piano his yearning to have met her before she was born,
to have been loved by her before he was born. Will she hear
also his rage, such fury at allowing himself a partial rebirth,
an incomplete incarnation? The descent, descent, the peasant
woman singing, the slime-covered caves, the streams and Josquin
alive and wonderful. He walked and walked.

O fool, fool! What madness! Will they sleep and yawn and fidget? By now they will be beginning the slow movement, *Lento, con molto sentimento*, twelve-eight *dolce*, and in the piano *pp*. What will they make of it, the gentleness, the peace? Such peace which he may expect in his declining years from loving one so young and vital. They will nod off, bored, bored by being told he felt no pain, no misery, only the pleasure, profound and continuing, which love itself bestows. Regret, of course, but not despair. Regret for the passage of time, the shortness of life. And Camille, he knew, would take the tempo too fast.

He stood still in the cold rain. Time dissolved. Passers-by hurried past, giving him wide berth, an old lunatic, motionless, standing unsheltered, soaking wet, staring at street-lamps. Timeless. The hour chimed. He inclined his head to listen, turned, began to find his way back, putting a hand to his cheeks, unable to tell the difference between tears and rain.

Allegro non troppo, ma con fuoco, three-four, to the second violin *pp*, a flurry of alarm, because, of course, there is fear, the fear of loss although in the measured chords he wanted to tell her of his triumph and his hope – for what, he did not know, but perhaps for a sort of well-being, imperfect and contrary. He knew that death was more terrible in life than in eternity. They'd be looking at their watches now, shifting position, crossing, uncrossing legs, not long to go, they'll whisper. Oh Christ, let them just hear again the descent, the ascension, cyclic, again and again his ecstatic fall. The music, Augusta, *is* my love, physical, earthly, glorious, not some romantic, ethereal absurdity but love, passion, oneness, the orgasm itself. And he wanted her to believe that when he was dead his love, his music, this music, would live and she would still be loved by him. He wanted her to think of him, so late in life, dancing, singing, seeing the colour of the sky and the flowers too brightly, hearing the calls of birds and laughter, tears, anguish, joy more loudly than he had ever heard them, smelling the air, made dizzy by the elixir. God, he had only one way of expressing himself, and that was in his music, calling up the savage Christ, so late refound, for her, for life itself. Fool! O –

'Pater seraphicus! Quickly! It's over! Where have you been? Oh heavens, you're wet through, what do you look like? Here, quick,

257

the presentation copy, quickly, quickly. Go down to the platform and present it to Camille –'

He stumbled into the hall. Were the cheers reflected by the mirrors? The audience was standing, stamping, clapping, shouting 'Bravo! Bravo!' so that the chandeliers tinkled. His first thought was that they would not be applauding so wildly had they understood the work properly. Oh God, he thought, they like it, a failure, he knew it: dripping wet, leaving a trail of sludge, he trotted towards the platform, clutching the copy of the *Quintet* he was to present to Camille. But only the string quartet bowed to the acclaim.

'Where's Camille?' César hissed.

Marsick knelt on one knee. 'He's left,' he shouted.

'Left?'

'Walked out. Gone. The moment we were finished. He stormed off the platform, put on his coat and out into the night –'

Bravo! Bravo!

Confused, César placed the score on the platform turned to a crescendo of cheering. He looked to where Augusta sat. Her seat was empty. Klosé was there, applauding politely, but not Augusta: where was she? had she heard the piece? had she left before the end? where was she? Bowing, he glanced towards Félicité. Her seat was empty, too.

Where had everyone gone? Augusta, Camille, Félicité? Where? Why? What happened? Bemused, he continued to bow to the applause, to the renewed cheers, and was engulfed by the members of the Société, their friends and companions converging upon him.

'Beautiful –'

'Glowing –'

'Extraordinary –'

'So passionate –'

'Disturbing –'

But what he remembered was:

'Odd key-basis,' from Vincent.

Alkan gripped César by the shoulder. 'Well, my old friend, who'd have thought it? You've changed French music. I hope you realise that! Pure delight!'

Romain said, 'Oh, maître!' which could have meant anything.

Maman said, 'Take me home, Romain. I'm worried about Camille.'

The ex-postman, the restaurateur from Arles, hurried out of the hall. 'I'm sorry, my dear,' he said to his companion, 'I'd no idea it would be *so* boring. Still, only an hour of our lives wasted. I'm famished. Come, let's hurry –'

César, pummelled and shoved, slapped and embraced, tried to push a way through to Klosé, but Klosé was surrounded by the *castrati* –

'Such passion –'

'Such drama –'

'What happened to Augusta?'

'She couldn't bear it –'

'Not her style –'

'Oh, such passion –'

'So sensual –'

'So sexual –'

'Such drama –'

Klose snorted. He never understood words like sensual and passion ascribed to music. Music was music, good or bad, and what he'd heard – well, he'd reserve judgment.

A critic said loudly, 'Thank God we won't have to listen to that again. I can safely predict that we were present at a final performance.'

Duparc wiped away his tears. Vincent puzzled over the changes of key. César hailed a cab and sped across Paris to the boulevard Saint-Michel. And in the deserted Salle Pleyel, one of Monsieur Pleyel's sons found on the platform the copy of the *Quintet* inscribed to Camille and put it on the shelf in the store room thick with dust, cobwebs and the bodies of dead moths.

4

Nursery ritual of a man in his forty-fifth year: Camille on his knees, head buried in his mother's lap, weeping, the night-light burning.

'Hush, Camille. Don't cry so.'

'Oh maman, I'm so unhappy.'

'There are plenty more fish in the sea.'

'I thought it was *me* she loved.'

'And perhaps she does.'

'No, maman –'

'You may be mistaken, Camille –'

'No.'

He knew because he knew Augusta. No man would dare declare himself so publicly unless she had encouraged him. The moment the strings had played the theme, the downward thrust, and he had come in with the piano, tender and passionate, he suspected her betrayal. César and Augusta: laughable, ridiculous. What could she possibly see in him? Yet, the old man had declared his love for her clearly, blatantly, unequivocally, and she had sat as one struck dumb, Galatea.

Augusta loves C.

Ironic.

Catulle, Camille, César.

He had worried about Mendès, believing he was the chief rival, never thinking –

'You shouldn't have walked off the platform. You should have preserved your dignity.'

But he'd been so angry, dreadfully angry, and dreadfully jealous. Jealous of César Franck, for God's sake! He hated the *Quintet*, despised such sexuality in music. He never wanted to hear or play music like that again. Music must be abstract, develop out of tradition, cannot be free or fevered. He hated César, hated them all. He was finished with them. He would never go near the Société again. The music was bad, bad, bad.

'Hush, Camille.'

Oh God, he loved Augusta.

'You have such good friends, Camille. Treasure them. Romain –'

He would always love Augusta.

'Hush, Camille. Don't cry.'

Afterwards, standing on the ledge from which his son had fallen to his death, Camille gazed through his telescope at the stars, and returning indoors, sat at his desk to compose a sonnet to Augusta, beginning: Hate is the greatest praise. Be proud you have deserved it.

5

César heard Félicité crying the moment he shut the front door.

'Franck?'

'Yes, my dear?'

Slowly he walked the length of the passage, opened her boudoir door. She stood facing him, her back to the window, eyes swollen, but ablaze. Calmly she said, 'Adulterer.'

—

'Do you know what you've done? I'll tell you. You have committed adultery in public, Franck. You've brought disgrace on us with that obscene, depraved work. You have made me a laughing-stock, held me up to ridicule, your own wife, the mother of your children. I've sacrificed everything for you and this is how you repay me. Adultery, in public, with that vulgar exhibitionist, that filthy harlot.'

—

'I've no doubt she thought it amusing to be made love to in public like that. I suppose she connived at – at – this *display*! Have you been with her now? Is that where you ran off to after the performance? To be with your paramour? I hope you're more use to her than you are to me! You're vile, Franck, a hypocrite, a deceiver and what's more, *untalented*!'

—

'I am leaving Paris tomorrow. And so are you. I'm not going to stay around to be the object of pitying looks, of sneers, of gossip. You will accompany me tomorrow morning first thing. You've humiliated me as no woman, no wife, no mother, has ever before been humiliated. And I'm not going to remain in the city a moment longer than is necessary. And if you think I'm leaving you here to cavort with your Irish strumpet, you're very much mistaken. You disgust me!'

—

'We leave at ten o'clock for Marnes-la-Coquette. Now get out of my sight!'

He hurried to his music room, lit a candle turned up the lamp, sat on his piano stool. He ran a hand through his hair. He cried out with relief. He smiled. Oh God, he thought, perhaps after all the *Quintet* has been a success. The work had been understood. He laughed out loud. Never had he known such elation from his music, never been so praised, never experienced such a heightening of his perceptions. Adulterer, Félicité had said. Was it that clear? And Camille had stormed in anger off the platform. Had he understood, too? César prayed God it was so, for surely Augusta must now know of his love for her. How would she react? What would she say? Would they laugh again together? If only he could learn that she, too, understood the music, his triumph and joy would be complete.

He stared at the candle flame, watched it quiver in the draught, watched a moth attracted to the unsteady light and thought that if it escaped burning its wings, the cycle would continue. He would go away tomorrow with Félicité. Too much external conflict now would be destructive, he felt instinctively. He must bide his time. A strong sense of the future held him captive. He would compose. He would hear sound, tap the lately discovered source deep within. Such strength was new to him, such certainty. And, some time later, when his mind was absent of finite thought, when concern for Augusta had receded and his spirit was enriched with the profound conviction of his own destiny, he was drawn towards the window and heard or believed he heard Augusta's voice.

6

She changed into the clothes of Hermann Zenta. It was safest if she was to cross the city at night.

'Where are you going?' Julie asked anxiously.

Augusta silenced her with a look. She wanted to hear no sound other than the sound in her head, a fusion of sound, as though the entire *Quintet* had been reduced to a single, indistinct harmony which continued to fill her ears. She dressed hurriedly, in a sort of fever, not fully aware of what she was doing. She had one objective in mind: to see César. Wrapped in her cloak, the floppy hat pulled low over her eyes, she summoned a cab in the

Place Pigalle, proceeded to Tortoni's where she ordered the cab-driver to dismount and to enquire if César Franck was in the café. When she learned he was not, she continued across the river, alighting at the Observatory in the boulevard Saint-Michel. From there, it was no distance to No. 95.

She waited for a pair of gendarmes to pass before pushing open the creaking iron gates and slipping into the gravelled forecourt. Keeping to the shadows, she made her way to the rear of the apartment house, taking shelter in the tiled portico of the building beyond the tall, bare poplars. Snow was again beginning to fall; the wind had dropped perceptibly and the flakes descended as though weightless. From her hiding-place Augusta observed the sleeping house.

The ground floor, César's floor, was in darkness; the building had an impregnable, unassailable look. With the snow settling on window ledges and lintels, on the poplars and the front steps, it took on the air of a forbidden, benighted fortress. Should she take her courage in her hands and hammer on the front door, demanding to see him? No, he would never forgive her for that. What could she do? Write a note? But the written word, the wait for a reply, would not satisfy the urgent nature of her needs. She had to see him now. She paced up and down, blowing into her white-gloved hands for warmth, stamping her feet. Heavier now the snow.

In the narrow, sloping alleyway running down the side of the house, she saw a light, faint, flickering. At first she thought her imagination was playing her tricks, but the glow remained, a solitary and fragile proof of life in the place. Augusta stepped out from the portico; holding her cloak tight she walked slowly, carefully towards the dim, yellowish light.

César's music room, the window ajar, the lace curtains rippling, heavier curtains open a crack, enough to see the amorphous hue of candle-light. Standing on tip-toe she tried to reach up to tap on the window but the ground sloped too steeply and she was not tall enough. She picked up a handful of small stones and new snow, tossed them gently at the panes – pa, pa-pa-pa, pa, pa – stepped back and waited.

The candle-light rose, hovered uncertainly, drew nearer the window; a slow deliberate movement of the curtains, and then she saw César, his face, barely illuminated, looking this way and that out into the night at the pendant snow.

'I'm here,' she whispered, raising her hand, hoping he would see the white glove.

He started, raised the candle higher, narrowed his eyes, saw her, was still.

She came a step closer. 'Let me in,' she pleaded. 'Please let me in.'

He turned away, only a little, but enough not to have to look directly at her.

She said, 'I want to be with you. Alone.'

Stillness.

'I couldn't face you afterwards, not with people there.'

He gave no sign of having heard. They stood, she in the snow facing him, he at the window turned away; both motionless. Again she held up her hand, reaching out for him this time, but there was no response. 'I need you,' she said. And then: 'I want you.' And: 'I love you.'

He turned to her. Was he trembling or was it the wind threatening the flame?

'Let me in,' she said.

After a long while, he said, 'Tomorrow. Come tomorrow. At noon,' and retreated quickly into the room, drawing close the curtains, obliterating the light.

On the morrow she came again. The maid, a scarecrow, said, 'But they've gone away, mademoiselle. They've left Paris. I don't know when they'll be back. They didn't say.'

7

Marnes-la-Coquette, Seine-et-Oise: the river turbulent, the land-scape barren, the wind cutting. He walked the lanes oblivious to his surroundings. Fiercely he strode the fields, blackthorn in hand, cape flowing behind. Drenched by incessant rain, he marched the three miles to the bend in the river and back to the house where the Actress waited.

In the small front porch he removed his wet things.

'Franck!'

'Yes, my dear?'

'Come at once. I believe I have it.'

Books spread out across the dining-room table: Greek legends, the Bible, volumes of poetry. She did not look up – she had hardly looked at him for a week – but continued to write furiously.

He waited.

She broke the silence.

'Rebecca,' she said.

'Rebecca?'

'Genesis, Chapter 24.'

'Ah.'

'A perfect subject for an opera.'

'Ah.'

'A perfect vehicle for a public apology.'

'Yes, my dear.'

'Yes, my dear,' she repeated, but with scorn. 'You will write me an apology, a plea for forgiveness.'

'Yes, my dear.'

'Yes, my dear. You will write a work of noble religious sentiment. Rebecca, chosen to be the wife of Isaac by Abraham's servant, Eleazar who meets her at the well. There is a chorus of camel-drivers, and great possibilities for colourful, oriental music.'

'Yes, my dear.'

'Yes, my dear. Everyone will know that the *Quintet* was a dreadful aberration.'

'Yes, my dear.'

For three days he walked again out of doors in all weathers along the banks of the swollen river; he walked across the fields and watched the cows milked at evening. Another birth was to be endured. On the fourth day, he informed Félicité that Rebecca could not be an opera, but an oratorio in five sections.

'Very well. So long as it is religious.'

There were letters for him that morning from all manner of people congratulating him. From Hartmann unusually enthusiastic. From Duparc informing him that two more performances of the *Quintet* were to be given immediately, the first with Madame Poitevin at the piano. He enclosed a cutting from the *Guide Musical*:

The *Quintet* completely enthralled the audience, restraining them in silence at the end of each movement, not only from applause, but also from any kind of vocal acclamation, while at times it had drawn tears from the eyes of many among them.

Was this then success? He sat at the upright piano in the spare room. The mechanic in him of old began to work, but the savage Christ watched and was amused, waiting in readiness to be called when needed. And César marvelled at His ruthlessness, but the mechanic was impatient and worked at speed. Already an idea was forming, a musical sound suggesting – well, it would keep. He knew it would keep now. And Augusta?

Augusta.

How would he explain? He had said what he had to say in his music. What more could he add? gratitude? regret? He believed he had loved her. How was he to know that the love would be so speedily transformed? She, the object, was an instrument, a tool, a divining rod which had prised open a spring which must not be allowed to dry. She had freed a stoppage; the sound flowed freely. How was he to know?

Now, each morning when he swung his legs off the bed, having thanked God for giving him life, the moment his feet touched the floor there was sound: ear-splitting. To the sound he swore everlasting fidelity. Not to Augusta. The words, I love you, were a fond, warming memory, nothing more. He no longer hid his dreams from his waking self. If he tried he could not suppress the longings and appetites which she unwittingly nursed from one consciousness to the other. Creation was the pleasure, not the love. To survive was all. He felt somehow whole. He regretted, but only in passing, the pain he would cause. His music came first. To absolve himself, he thought of it as a sacrifice.

Augusta.

She had divined the spring. She had served her purpose.

Alas.

PART FIVE

'The first sight of her – a convalescent arrayed in a red flannel dressing gown – was rather a shock ... she was short and fat, her red hair powdered white – who shall say why? – and her white face helped out with black, red, and white, vigorously and wildly applied ... In fact, the general appearance was that of a barmaid of sixty.'

Dame Ethel Smyth

Reluctantly, Camille agreed to hold one of the pall-ribbons. He stood by the open grave, exuding ill-will; he had little love for the dead man; he had little love for anyone. Chabrier, fatter and at last distinguished, came forward to deliver the obsequies. Camille steeled himself, kept his eyes fixed firmly on the coffin. He hoped the eulogy would be brief; he did not care to hear another's genius extolled. He could, he supposed, be grateful that Vincent d'Indy was not giving the address; fortunately, he was detained in Valence. At least Chabrier, Camille had always been told, was the only one to treat the deceased as a human being; and he was jolly.

'Adieu, maître!' Chabrier began, hand raised, voice thick with emotion, tears streaming down his cheeks. 'In you we salute one of the greatest artists of the century, and also the incomparable teacher whose wonderful work has produced a whole generation of forceful musicians, believers and thinkers, armed at all points for hard and prolonged conflicts. We salute also the upright and just man, so humane, so distinguished, whose counsels were sure, as his words were kind.'

Jolly? Not a laugh anywhere, Camille thought. But, of course, there was an ironic laugh, Camille reflected: the dead man, written off, ignored, mocked, had taken them all by surprise. His works were played all over Europe, even in England: those hearty *Symphonic Variations*, the *Quartet* – well, the first movement wasn't bad – and that dreadful *Symphony in D*. Yes, a good, ironic joke.

Camille stared at the coffin, thinking, I am alive and you are dead. He tried to imagine the corpse: would they have dressed him in his best suit, the trousers too short, the coat too long? And would there be dandruff on his shoulders?

November, and bitter cold. Chabrier had finished. Camille looked up to see him comforted by Messager. Monsignor Gardey began to recite the final prayers. Camille scanned the faces of the mourners: Félicité, upright, unmoved; her son, Georges, solemn and pensive. The whole musical hierarchy, heads bowed, prayed for the departed and asked God to grant him eternal life.

A face: well back from the circle around the grave; a woman, rouged, bloated, smiling inanely. Something familiar about her. Camille reached into his pocket and surreptitiously fixed his pince-nez. The face came into sharp focus. He felt a familiar quickening, but also shock. A hag. For the first time that day, he was moved.

Augusta.

She was holding someone's arm. Camille moved a step back and saw a boy, eighteen years old no more, Spanish or Italian, hair greased, olive-skinned, a café gigolo.

Oh, Augusta.

The priest uttered the last amen. The sexton began to shovel earth on to the grave. Félicité laid a wreath and Georges led her away to their carriage. Camille only took his eyes off Augusta once, to stand head bowed by the grave, impatiently paying his respects to the dead. When he looked up she was gone. He pushed his way through the knot of mourners, barely greeting those he knew, and, emerging from the cemetery of Montrouge, saw the boy help Augusta aboard an omnibus which he boarded, too, bound for the city. Camille hurried to his carriage, ordered his driver to follow, and even while they pursued the omnibus he regretted his impulsiveness, but was somehow compelled to continue.

The couple disembarked near the Gare Saint-Lazare; they walked, the carriage a little way behind, to a crumbling house off the rue de Londres. But no sooner had they passed the concierge's lodge then they reappeared. Augusta head back, laughing, crossed the street and entered a bar opposite.

Camille sat back in his carriage. 'Take me home,' he said. A terrible depression swept over him, and awful black regret for the passage and cruelty of time. Slowly he climbed the steps to his apartment in the rue Monsieur le Prince. Quietly he let himself in.

'Camille?'

Romain was in bed with a severe cold. Camille trudged into the bedroom which was cluttered with suitcases and travelling trunks in readiness for a journey he was to make to Egypt. He sank heavily into a chair and stared into the fire.

Romain said, 'Well? What was it like? Did the sun pierce the clouds? Did the angels sing? No, don't tell me, I know: the old boy rose from the grave.'

Camille was silent. At last he said, 'Terribly lonely,' but more to himself than to his friend.

'Depressing, was it? I'm glad I'm ill and wasn't able to attend.'

Suddenly Camille looked up. 'I've been thinking, Romain. When we die we must both be buried in the family tomb. With Maman and the boys.'

'Oh Camille, for heaven's sake, don't be morbid.'

'No. I shall put that in my will. It's important to be with the people one loves.'

He did not mention Augusta to Romain, and so did not confide his reason for visiting Félicité, ostensibly to offer formally his condolences.

'Such a good man,' she said. 'Franck was such a good man.'

Camille tried to catch Georges' eye, but Félicité insisted on re-counting in detail how her husband had died, as though to recall the dismal events brought her comfort. 'He had an accident some months ago,' she said, 'on the Pont Royal – you may have heard. The carriage pole of a passing omnibus hit the cab in which Franck was travelling and struck him on his right side. He seemed to recover but in the end pleurisy set in, complicated by – by – what was it complicated by, Georges?'

'Pericarditis, maman.'

'Just so. He knew he was dying. Gardey gave him the Last Rites. But he was in great agony. A fugue, it seems, began to develop in his brain and he was compelled to follow all its ramifications. He begged the doctors to deliver him from this – this obsession. Before long, he lost the power of speech, except he was able to say over and over again, "My children, my poor children".' She nodded repeatedly. 'His opera, *Hulda*, was his finest work.'

Hulda, Camille thought, may have been the worst opera to have been written this century.

Félicité said, 'And he was very kind to you, maître.'

'To me?'

'We told him that *Samson and Delila* was at last to receive a

271

performance in Paris. He said, on his deathbed mind, he said, "It is very beautiful. Very beautiful!"'

Well, Camille thought wryly, perhaps *Hulda* wasn't so bad after all. He rose, kissed her hand, offered his sympathy. He turned to Georges and with the slightest inclination of his head, indicated he would like to see him privately. Puzzled, Georges accompanied Camille into the hall.

'I wonder if I could have a word with you,' Camille said.

'Of course.' Georges ushered him into the dead man's music room.

Camille explained he had an odd request to make. Years ago, so many years ago, Georges' father had done him the honour of dedicating a work to him, the *Piano Quintet*. Camille had never received the presentation copy. Did Georges by any chance have one, preferably signed?

Georges promised to look. He said, 'The *Quintet* was the turning point.'

Camille agreed.

'Odd business.'

'Odd?'

'Music, art, I mean. No accounting for inspiration.'

'No.'

'Well, if I find a signed copy, I'll send it round to you, maître.'

'Thank you. I'm leaving for Egypt in three days, I should like to have it before I depart.'

'I'll do my best.'

The following morning a signed copy of the *Quintet* was delivered to Camille and in the late afternoon he set off for the crumbling house near the rue de Londres.

2

He knocked on the door for a third time before he heard her voice. 'Who is it?' she called as though he had woken her from sleep.

'Camille.'

'Camille?' A pause. 'Go away.'

'Let me in, Augusta.'

'What d'you want?'

'To see you.'

'Why?'

'Let me in, Augusta.'

'I don't want to see you. I saw you at the funeral. You've got very ugly and fat.'

Now, another voice, the boy's, he guessed. 'What go on?'

'There's an ugly man at the door and I don't want to see him. Tell him to go away.'

A rat scuttled over Camille's shoes. Somewhere in the house the sound of breaking glass. The door opened. The boy, hair tousled, bare to the waist, wearing loose baggy trousers, said, 'You want trouble?'

Camille looked steadily at him, took out his wallet, removed two notes and offered them. 'I'm an old friend,' he said.

The boy grinned. 'Come in,' he said. 'Hey!' to Augusta, 'an old friend.' He pocketed the money so that she did not see.

Augusta, made up like a waxwork clown, wearing a red flannel dressing-gown, covered her face. 'I don't want him here, I don't want anyone here.'

Camille, with a look, dismissed the boy who went through a curtained arch. Camille caught a glimpse of an unmade bed beyond. Augusta continued to hide her face, but she could not hide her body: she had run to fat, her breasts hung low, her ankles were swollen. He turned his attention to the small room, devoid of chairs. The walls were smothered in tarnished trophies, in gigantic laurel wreaths of incredible age tied with faded ribbons. There were framed photographs inscribed with passionate messages; there were locks of hair flattened out behind glass and similarly dedicated; there was a satin shoe, a floppy velvet hat – Camille smiled fondly – and a dusty flute. One wall was given over to a full length nude portrait of her, a figure darting across a pitch-dark room, one slender finger outstretched, transfixing a brilliantly lit note, the rest of the keyboard plunged in gloom.

'Do you like it?' she asked. She was watching him now.

'Very effective.'

'Another Rembrandt, don't you think? I forget the artist's name.'

273

Camille made a delicate gesture of his hands, as if to say the matter was of no importance.

She said, 'You used to bring presents. Times have changed. You don't want anything from me anymore. You come empty-handed.' Her manner was aggressive, resentful.

'Not quite empty-handed,' he said.

'You're so famous you don't have to bring presents. I hear they're naming a street after you. The world's gone mad.'

The boy reappeared dressed.

'Where are you going?' she demanded.

'Out,' he said, and winked at Camille behind her back.

'Out where?' her eyes narrowed with suspicion and danger.

'Just out. I leave you alone with your old friend.' And he was gone.

'Carlos!' she called, but then waved at the closed door a mocking farewell.

'He'll be back,' Camille said.

'He plays the guitar divinely. I'm writing him a little concerto for guitar. An Apollo, don't you think? And so strong. Well, if you're going to stay, you may as well have a drink. What'll it be? Brandy or brandy?' She smiled but her eyes remained vacant.

'Neither, thank you.'

'Well, I'm having brandy.' She poured herself a large measure into a chipped tumbler. 'What are you doing here anyway?' She swayed as she drank.

Camille could not now think of a way to begin. He said, 'I'm leaving for Egypt tomorrow –'

'Egypt? What for? Are they going to mummify you?' She laughed.

'Quite likely. I wanted to visit you before I left. I don't know how long I'm going to be away, and when I caught sight of you at the funeral –'

'Oh, don't, don't. I shall cry again.' She sat heavily on the bare floor, legs spread before her. She loosened her red flannel gown as though she were suddenly suffused by heat; she dabbed at her powdered hair. 'I hate funerals, hate them. And why did they have that awful common little man, Chabrier, to speak? So pompous. Success spoils people. He used to be such fun.'

274

'The old boy liked him.'

'They should've had someone more distinguished. I could've told them a thing or two.'

Amused, Camille said, 'D'Indy was away.'

'Ugh! Prig! Self-satisfied ass. They were better off with Chabrier. Have you heard the latest? The last piece Franck ever wrote before his death, the last piece, for organ, he dedicated to me. To *me*!' She hammered her chest. 'Now I'm told d'Indy wants to alter it, wants it given to someone else. He says the old boy wasn't in his right mind when he died. But he was, he was – wasn't he, Camille?'

'Of course he was in his right mind.'

'You see? You see?' She tried to stop herself from crying, took too large a swallow of her drink, spluttered and coughed, ran a hand across her face, smudged her make-up so that she looked even more defeated. 'Oh, go away, Camille, for God's sake! Haven't I suffered enough without you having to remind me?'

Camille said, 'I didn't mean to upset you. On the contrary. I – I've brought you a gift. A copy of the *Quintet*. Autographed.' He handed her the score; the effect was startling. Her crying stopped abruptly. She stared long and hard at the title page, at the dedication, at the signature, C. Franck. She was unaware of Camille, of the room, of the fading light.

Camille took a step towards the door. 'I really must be going –' he said.

With terrible vehemence she cried, 'He betrayed me!'

'Oh, Augusta, don't –' Camille said as though he were in pain.

'Betrayed me, and deserted me! This –' she shook the music in her hands – 'this was my doing. He would never have written the *Quintet* if not for me. It was his way of making love to me, Camille. And I understood. I understood. But he didn't care. Cruel, ruthless old bastard. All he wanted was his music. Not me. Oh yes, he betrayed me all right, led me up the garden path, discarded me like a glove. I went to see him the very night of the concert and we were going to run away together, live somewhere on a mountain-top, defy the world, just he and I and to hell with everyone else. And what did he do? Went back to writing his religious rubbish. *Rébecca!* I saw him several times after that. And

275

you'd have thought we were strangers. He just smiled his stupid smile. He'd used me. Spat me out. And I was a child at the time, fatherless.'

'It's a long time ago,' Camille said soothingly.

'What's time got to do with it?' she snarled. 'What about me? Oh, don't go, I've no one to talk to, please stay with me. Have a drink. Just let's talk. I tell you this, he taught me everything except what music to write. He taught me how, not what. Thank God for Ireland. Did you ever hear my Home Rule songs, Camille? Masterpieces, little masterpieces, but the idiot French never understood their real worth. Didn't care that my people were trampled under foot, that I was trampled under foot. And my symphonic study, *Irelande*? Did you hear it, Camille? No? My songs? My operas?'

'You are the most distinguished woman composer in Europe, Augusta,' Camille said.

'Woman! Woman!' she said screwing up her face in disgust. But her mood plummeted; sadly she added, 'You don't know how difficult it is for a woman.'

Camille had reached the door, hand on the knob, waiting for an opportunity to leave. He wanted to say that it was difficult for everyone, man or woman.

Augusta said, 'Yes, he discarded me all right. Used and misused me. I sometimes think God's misused me, too. I was an instrument, a pawn, misused. Now I am finished. Alone. Unloved. The *Quintet* – my quintet –' she cradled the score as though it were her child – 'the *Quintet* was his first triumph. After that, he wrote wonderful things when he wasn't being religious. His opera – *Hulda*, is it called, *Hulda*? what a dreadful title – his opera is awful. But there were other things, all mine, all from the vein of gold I struck. And was he grateful? Bastard. Oh, Camille, don't go, please don't go. I hate this hour when it gets dark. I hate being alone now. You see, I hadn't counted on his ruthlessness. He was only interested in himself. Self. Self. Self-preservation. I'll tell you something, Camille, and I know what I'm talking about, self-preservation in my experience is what politicians, master-criminals and artists have in common.'

She wept freely. Camille stood stiff and uncomfortable,

regretting he had ever come, aching to be gone.

'You see, Camille, I wasn't ruthless enough. I was never prepared to sacrifice anyone except myself. That's because I'm a woman. Men don't give a damn. Must you go? Must you? It's difficult for a woman.'

She did not notice Camille leave. She searched for the brandy and drank from the bottle. 'Oh, where is Carlos? Why doesn't he come home? Difficult, yes, a woman has to prove so much *more*. Why did you remind me? I never want to hear that vile *Quintet* again.'

The light was almost gone. She peered at herself in her looking-glass, and wrote with her finger, Augusta loves C, in the dust. 'Carlos? Carlos?' she called. She remained at her dressing-table, staring, lost, the copy of the music tucked under her arm. The minutes passed as the years had passed. She rummaged among her things until she found matches. She lit a candle, held the score to the light. She could not bring César's face to mind, but she heard his music. Her music. Long after darkness had fallen and she had put aside the score, she heard in her head the passionate outpouring of sound, and was again loved.